THESE LOST

&

BROKEN THINGS

Helen Fields

Wailing Banshee

By the same author

Perfect Remains

Perfect Prey

Perfect Death

Perfect Silence

Perfect Crime

Perfect Kill

Writing as HS Chandler

Degrees of Guilt

Copyright

Published by Wailing Banshee Ltd
www.wailingbanshee.co.uk

A Paperback Original 2020
Copyright © Helen Fields 2020

Helen Fields asserts the moral right to be identified as the
author of this work

ISBN-13: 978-0-9571246-5-3

For Andrea Gibson & Ruth Arlow

The women who keep me sane.

Acknowledgements

The bulk of the thanks for making this book a reality goes to my husband, David Baumber. Not only did he encourage me throughout the writing and editing process, and listen to hours of plotting and research detail, he also made sure my vision for the book made it into the physical world.

Andrea Gibson was both my first reader and my proof reader. I owe her a debt of gratitude and never ending drinks. Responsibility for mistakes lies entirely with me.

Too many friends to mention encouraged me, tolerated me and got me to this point. Thanks to each and every one of you. And to Gabriel, Solomon and Evangeline.

Chapter One
Childhood 1891

The Dead Queen's Head was a blur of lights in the distance. Sofia tramped towards it through the fields, knowing she shouldn't be going there, excitement buzzing in her stomach. She jumped a ditch, missing her footing in the dark and slipped in the mud. It wasn't the way she'd wanted the night to start. She couldn't go in there looking like a child. She was twelve now, nearly grown up and as tall as her mother. What would they think if she walked in dirty and out of breath?

Sofia slowed down. Was she going to make a fool of herself? No, she'd planned this for months, had waited for just such an opportunity. It might be months again before she found another game close enough to their camp to be able to walk there at night. Getting away unnoticed by her parents hadn't been easy. It was tonight or never. She felt a flash of guilt, thinking about how she'd waited until her father was snoring, bundling clothes into her bed to form her shape and size, then sneaking away from their caravan like a thief. She told herself that what they didn't know wouldn't hurt them. If they gave her a bit more freedom she would have asked their permission to go, so it wasn't all her fault.

She understood why they didn't like her going out but it wasn't as if she couldn't take care of herself. It was the same reason they had men on watch at the edge of their camp, guns loaded and dogs ready. The locals didn't like it when they turned up with their travelling fair. The townsfolk would come and stare at the sideshows, so eager to believe the made-up horrors they displayed, to watch the girls dancing with snakes, to take their sweethearts on the rides and buy cheap liquor. Afterwards, they would go home and say what a nuisance the Romani were, how they tricked the money from their pockets and corrupted the youngsters. If they got stirred up enough, they sometimes came in gangs carrying torches, tried to call the men out for fights, threatened the women if they didn't move on. Once, they had set fire to some of the caravans. Her daddy and the other men had got blood on their hands that night. They'd

1

moved on before dawn and before the police dared come and investigate. Hypocrites, her Pa called them. Sofia rolled the word around her mouth.

The inn was closer now and she picked out a path in the moonlight that would take her to its back door. She'd heard that the game was to be in a back room, not the main bar. She crossed her fingers, hoping the men she'd heard talking at her father's stall last night had their facts straight. I can beat them, she told herself. I beat them almost every time when I play for Pa and this'll be no different. I'm as good a player as any man and better than most. For months she'd saved up the pennies she'd skimmed from her father's takings. It wasn't stealing, just taking what she was owed, was how she justified it. Without her, there would be no profit. At three she'd known the number and suit of each card. At four she understood the rules of all the card games her father ran, and by six she could add and subtract as well as any adult. Her brother used to call her a freak but she loved it, sitting behind her father on a little stool, no one suspecting the child as she patted his shoulder, watching the men gambling and predicting what cards were coming. She couldn't remember a time when she didn't have a pack in her pocket.

This was it, she thought. She was at the door of the inn and her first game away from her father's controlling eye. She had enough money in her pocket for them to want her to join. For a second she thought about turning around but if she did that she could never move on. All she would ever know was tiny stakes and groups of three of four men betting pennies a time. That would never make her enough money for the life she wanted. She dreamed of growing up to own a cottage by the sea: picnics, a beach, a tiny garden with a cherry tree. It wasn't such a big thing to wish for, she thought. A place to live without moving on every fortnight, without being scared of what was around the next bend. There had to be a better life outside the fair, somewhere safer, something permanent. This was the first step to finding it. I can do this, she breathed. I must. Putting one hand on the full purse in her pocket, Sofia went in.

There was no sudden silence when she went through the door because the room was already hushed. She saw that the game was well underway. Five men sat around a table watched by a dozen or so others at the edge of the room who were passing the time drinking and smoking, a couple already asleep or passed out. Sofia put her chin up and walked to the table.

The man dealing ignored her while they finished a round, then poured himself a drink and finally spoke to her. 'Lookin' for your daddy are you? Try in the bar.'

'I'm here to play,' Sofia said. For a second she thought they wouldn't laugh but they did. The dealer started it, the men at the sides following suit.

'Go away child,' he said when he was done. 'You've no idea where you are.'

Sofia threw her money onto the table. She didn't speak, wishing it was because she was tough, knowing it was because she couldn't trust her voice not to sound too high or to croak.

The dealer picked up the purse, tossing it from one hand to the other, looking Sofia in the eye for the first time. 'Not at my table,' he said. 'Too easy.' He threw the money back to Sofia.

'Let her play,' said a voice from the other side of the table. 'She came here for a reason and she has the means. I don't know why she shouldn't get her chance.' Sofia looked at the man talking. He had a foreign accent, and was blonde haired and blue eyed like the circus performers who sometimes travelled with her parents a while as they caught up with their own troupe.

Once he had spoken up, the others around the table joined in. They want the money, she thought. They think it'll be simple for them. She remained silent until the dealer had had enough.

'All right,' he said. 'If she's that daft and you lot don't care if you're taking her pocket money away, then I can't stop you.' He kicked a spare chair out towards her.

'Have a drink?' one of the players offered. She shook her head. Only idiots drank and gambled at the same time. She held her cards to her chest, kept her money where she could see it and glanced around. For the first few rounds she bet low, getting a feel for the table, waiting for her nerves to die down. Not long after, one of the other players declared himself out and disappeared into the front bar. That left five of them and the stakes went up. Four hands later and the man who had offered her the wine folded, picked up his remaining coins and went out into the night. At least, she thought, he had left the door open for a few seconds, the mixture of fumes from liquor, pipes and unwashed bodies starting to make her head ache.

When she won the next several hands, the players began to grumble. No one was laughing any more. The dealer was staring at her. Let him look, thought Sofia. This is what I came for. She pushed the stakes up with each hand, forgetting her audience, concentrating on the cards. She had taken a good packet of money already, more than enough to be proud of but there was still plenty to be won. Sofia considered briefly calling it a day going home, being grateful for her lot, but what would be the point? Coming all this way only to double her money, having to do this all again, when she could stay just a few rounds more and really win money worth having. And they had laughed at her. She should teach them not to do that again, at least.

Finally realising their luck had turned, the others quit the table so that only Sofia and the blonde man were left. Her remaining opponent had over-bet his hand a few times. She'd twice noticed him flexing his left wrist before putting down a sure winner. He knew what he was doing, there was no doubt about it, but she was a fair match for him, she decided. They played on, each winning and losing a few hands, until the pile of money before each of them was roughly equal. Just a couple more hands and then I must go, she thought. But one more large bet first, to make it worth while. She increased her stake as he wavered about whether or not to fold, all signs of his earlier confidence gone. When he matched her bet and laid his cards down she knew she'd been hustled. His flush beat her three of a kind and her money was gone.

Sofia felt heartsick. Digging her nails into her palms, she swept what few pennies remained into a pocket, leaving red blotches on her

4

shift where she'd drawn blood from her hands. As she rose to leave, the man pulled her down to whisper in her ear.

'One more round,' he said.

'I haven't enough money. There's nothing to play for,' Sofia mumbled.

'Don't look so unhappy, it doesn't suit you.' He slid a hand over her cheek and smoothed her long, dark hair. 'Such a pretty girl shouldn't frown. A last bet. If you win the hand, every coin on the table will be yours.'

Sofia stared at the mountain of money. There was at least ten pounds. Sofia thought she could go a decade without seeing so much in one place again. More than that, she wanted to win so badly that it was like a fever inside her. She didn't want the dealer to have been right to warn her away. She didn't want to have wasted months of saving and planning. She didn't want to go home feeling foolish and worthless. This wasn't how it was supposed to end, she thought.

'And if I lose?'

He smiled. 'If I win, we spend the night together and make love. You are still a maid, yes?' Sofia's deep blush was confirmation. 'Just one night. I will not hurt you, I promise. It's not such a terrible thought, is it?'

Sofia blinked slowly. I should run, she thought, get out of here and back to the camp as fast as I can. But the money was shining at her in the lamplight. She was good at this. Really, really good at it. This one thing was hers. She wouldn't fail again. She knew it.

'My name is Bergen. Yours?' He shuffled the pack, the cards clacking softly.

'Sofia,' she whispered, staring as he passed the cards fluidly from hand to hand.

'Sit down, Sofia. Let the cards decide.' She found herself sitting before she knew that she had. She looked at the gleaming coins and felt the cards warm from his touch.

'One more,' she said.

He didn't reply, glancing at his hand as if it was the least interesting thing in the world but he was breathing faster, Sofia thought, instantly terrified and overwhelmed by the enormity of the bet she'd made.

She had five clubs, a flush. It was a good hand. Not unbeatable, but close. She willed her eyes downwards. Her opponent was taking his time, giving away nothing. Finally, she laid out what she had on the table, sliding her fingers over the cards and looked up to see Bergen's reaction. He exhaled heavily. Sofia's smile broadened with relief and her arms were outstretched for the money when he threw his cards down over hers. She didn't bother to look, convinced she'd won.

'Don't be frightened, I shall be gentle with you,' he said. Sofia snatched her hands back. He had three tens and two fours.

'Full house,' she said. It came out as no more than a whisper.

'Luck has no favourites,' he replied, tilting his head as if he felt sorry for her. He took her hand and raised it to his mouth, kissing her fingers as if they might break. 'But a bet is a bet. My lodgings are upstairs. Come.' The men who had been watching from the sides were already standing up, finishing their drinks and crushing cigarettes beneath their boots. Not one of them would meet Sofia's eyes.

She began to panic. 'I can't,' she said. 'I'm only twelve years old. Forgive me, I shouldn't have made the bet. I don't know what made me do it. I shouldn't even be here. I'll find some other way to repay you, I promise. What'll my ma say?'

'What you tell or don't is a matter for you, but I will not be persuaded out of my winnings, so you can come willingly or unhappily, as you choose. You considered yourself old enough to come to a game in the middle of the night, with men you did not know, and were content to take money from the others when they lost. Surely you won't be a bad loser now that the tables have turned?'

Sofia looked to those left in the room with her but they were hurrying out, backs turned, as if nothing was happening. Surely someone would stop this, she thought. One of them would rescue her. She looked for the dealer but his head was down as he closed the door after himself on the way into the bar. Sofia held on to the table as Bergen began pulling her to the wooden stairs 'You don't want me to follow you home and tell your father of the bet you made, do you? He will not want to pay the equivalent price in coin.'

Tears streamed down Sofia's face but she stepped slowly towards him, head bowed, knowing she'd been beaten by her own pride as much as by Bergen. She was ruined and there was no one to blame but herself. Her family could never find out. There was no going back.

Chapter Two

September 1905

Sofia burst from the house, feet pounding the pavement, clutching the heavy skirt that slowed her. She could hardly see, eyes blurred with tears and the street shrouded in London's early morning smog. Tripping on the legs of a drunk sleeping off last night's excesses in the gutter she crashed onto her knees, shredding her palms on broken glass, but the terror of what lay behind forced her up and onwards, cursing the stench of sweat and vomit left on her clothes.

She raced around a corner and ploughed headlong into half a dozen brewery workmen loading barrels of ale high onto a cart.

'Slow down, lovely, you'll do yourself no end of harm like that,' said one as he slipped an arm round her waist.

'You in trouble are you? We can take care of that.' A huge, blubbery man pulled her into his chest and the others roared with laughter, surrounding her and enjoying the sport.

'Let me go, there's no time, please,' Sofia panted, slapping at their hands.

'In a hurry, is it? That's all right, we can be quick as you like, can't we boys?'

'Yeah, shouldn't take too long with a piece like you!' said another and a hand, grimy and stinking of fermenting hops, snaked up to her breast, pinching her nipple roughly. Sofia jammed her knee hard into the groin of the man in front of her, reducing him to a groaning pile on the ground as she thrashed her way out. He spat at her as she elbowed and clawed through his mates. 'Slum whore,' he yelled but she was sprinting up the street.

Gray's Inn Road was already busy with the early market traffic, forcing her to either slow down on the pavement or to take her chances running in the road. She dashed from the path of oncoming horses straight into a motor car which swerved, sending grit flying into her face. Barrow boys were delivering goods and children on errands were flitting around her legs. On any other day she would have enjoyed watching the chaos, but not this morning. Today, every flower seller seemed deliberately placed to trip her. In spite of the pain in her chest she continued to run. She ignored the protests of those she barged. The disapproving glares as she hitched up her skirt to run were immaterial.

By the time she reached Doughty Street she was near retching. She took an alleyway to the back of the house, wiping sweat from her forehead and tugging her dishevelled clothes into place. Muttering a prayer beneath her breath, she knocked the kitchen door. There was no reply. Under any other circumstances she'd have waited patiently but this morning she balled her fists and hammered.

'Mrs Hasselbrook, please! We need help.' When it finally opened she stumbled forwards into the housekeeper's arms.

'What in God's name are you doing? Mr Vinsant's already in a foul temper and you'll wake the mistress.'

Sofia recovered her breath as she dashed tears from muddy cheeks. 'It's Tom, he's sick, he needs a doctor. The hospital turned us away last night saying they were full. You have to let me see Mr Vinsant.'

'Tom was well enough when he left here yesterday. What can have taken him ill so fast?' Mrs Hasselbrook put an arm around Sofia's waist and led her into the kitchen. The maids stopped work and stared before the housekeeper waved an arm at them.

'Nettie, fetch a glass of water. And Ana, if you haven't finished polishing the master's boots in the next two minutes you can go up and explain yourself to him.' The girls sprang back into life. 'Drink this,' she said, handing the water from Nettie to Sofia. 'I can't let you up to see Mr Vinsant like that, he'll have you thrown out first and me straight after.'

Sofia put the glass down untouched. 'Either you let me up to see him or I shall scream until he comes down. Your choice,' she said.

There was a pause while Mrs Hasselbrook stood still, hands on ample hips. 'On your head be it, but you'd better have good reason. Wait here.' The housekeeper ripped off her dirty apron, replaced it with a clean one for above stairs and left the kitchen by another door. Blood rushed noisily in Sofia's ears as the maids tried to get on with their tasks around her. She stared into a mirror and barely recognised her own face, so pale that even her lips were ashen. Sofia smoothed down her long brown hair, not having had a moment to pin it up as she should have. Her skin was marked with dirty streaks that she rubbed with her sleeve. She looked like a street urchin, thin and grubby, irises so dark they appeared almost black, clothes askew. It didn't matter. Nothing mattered except getting help.

'Well, he'll see you,' said Mrs Hasselbrook reappearing. 'But he's running late and put out at having to find another man to replace your Tom today. Make it quick and don't get his back up. This way.' She led Sofia through the house, boots echoing on the polished floorboards, the newly fitted electric lights harsh against the pristine white walls and ceilings. Sofia felt as if she'd walked into a palace. Portly but fit, the housekeeper took the stairs briskly, muttering as she went although when she turned to make sure Sofia was ready behind her, the expression on her face was all kindness and concern.

Mrs Hasselbrook opened the study door but left Sofia to face her husband's employer alone. Emmett Vinsant was at his desk slicing into correspondence with a silver letter opener. Sofia guessed it was worth more than fifty doctors' fees. He was a huge man. At six feet and four inches he was a whole foot taller than Sofia, but it was his bulk that made him so intimidating. He was broad and well muscled. Sofia had seen him only a few times before and on each occasion had been struck by how overwhelming he was, with his dark hair, beard and grey-blue eyes. He slipped on his frock coat before motioning for her to step forwards.

'Come in, Mrs Logan. I gather you can explain why your husband is not at his post today.'

'Sorry to trouble you, Sir, but Tom needs a doctor. I know we've no right to ask but we don't have the money to pay ourselves and I'm so scared. I didn't know where else to come.'

'And you want me to pay for the doctor, is that it?' Sofia nodded, glancing downwards. 'As much as I would like to, that's something I just cannot do. I am not in a position to take responsibility for every one of my employees' medical bills. It's not just the staff here, I have to consider the men at my factories and the offices. You'll no doubt come to some arrangement with the doctor and I can recommend one if that would help. I shall, of course, overlook Tom's failure to attend work today and hope that he is back in the morning. Now, Mrs Hasselbrook will see you out. I'm sure it's not as serious as you think.'

Sofia didn't wait, convinced she was running out of time and knowing that pleading would only jeopardise her husband's employment. Vinsant had already turned his attention back to his desk as she let herself out of the study. Passing through the kitchen to the back door, the staff stood aside silently. She felt the floor begin to tip queerly beneath her feet and reached out to find a strong hand circling her wrist. Mrs Hasselbrook was ready to catch her.

'Ana, bring a cold cloth. Nettie, take the master his boots and open the door on his way out to the carriage.' Nettie stood gawping. 'Go on, would you, I can hear him coming down the stairs.' Sofia couldn't wait a second longer. She would have to beg at the doctor's door, knowing it was a fool's errand and that she would almost certainly be reduced to using the rogue physician who attended the slums. He, at least, would accept alternative arrangements for payment, although she'd heard that he occasionally asked for something other than money from the woman of the household when he could get away with it. She'd do it too, if it came to that. She couldn't lose Tom, he was her whole world. Without him she would fall apart. Mumbling her thanks to Mrs Hasselbrook she staggered out of the back door and down the narrow side alley to the street.

By the time she reached the road, Emmett Vinsant was climbing into his carriage. Sofia stood on the street figuring out which way to go. She knew of a doctor with offices on Southampton Row, close enough to Doughty Street not to waste any more time. Gathering her skirt, she stepped out just as the carriage set off. From the corner of her eye she saw a puppy run into the road, catching one leg beneath the wheel. It yelped then howled like an injured child. She should walk past, she thought. There was no time to spare for this. The dog couldn't be left the way it was though. The carriage halted and Vinsant looked from his window.

'What the hell is it now, Silverman?' he shouted at the driver.

'A dog, Sir, caught in the wheel,' Silverman replied, although he wasn't making any move to deal with the animal.

'Well, finish the bloody thing off and get me on my way,' said Vinsant. The driver looked at Sofia, pale faced. He hasn't the guts for it, she thought. Vinsant was already stepping down from the carriage and she knew the driver's reticence to kill the animal was apt to lose him his job. Worse than that, if he tried to destroy the animal halfheartedly, he was likely to cause it a lot more suffering than was necessary.

Sofia knelt down, stroking the puppy's head with one hand while she reached over its neck, fixing her arm around it hard. Vinsant was watching but she was past caring what he made of her behaviour. Pushing a knee beneath the pup to hold it still, she wrenched its neck up and round in a single move. There was a wet crackle as the dog's spine was severed, then Sofia wiped her hands and glanced at the driver. He nodded gratefully. Sofia acknowledged him and started to move away. Silverman would have to deal with the dead animal without her help. She got no more than a few steps before a voice called after her.

'Mrs Logan?' Emmett Vinsant approached. He came close, staring. Sofia could hear sand slipping through the hourglass inside her head. 'I was too hasty earlier. I value your husband's service a great deal.

Step into the carriage. Silverman will take you to our physician's offices and on to your home. You and Tom can arrange to repay the fee when he is well enough to return to work.' Sofia didn't move, half expecting the offer to be withdrawn again just as quickly. 'Off you go, I shall work from home today instead.' He studied her a few seconds longer, his face unreadable. Sofia had no idea what had changed his mind.

'Miss?' the driver called.

Sofia climbed into the carriage, unable to find the words to thank Vinsant, ridiculously concerned that her clothes would dirty the upholstery. She watched him stride back into his house as the horses began to trot. The brown-brick property was mid-terraced but had six bedrooms, Tom had told her. They had a country house, too. Beatrice and Emmett Vinsant would never have to worry about affording a doctor. Not that they would ever feel what she was feeling now. Tom said their marriage had been arranged. They were from different worlds. Emmett had provided the money and she the class. It was so different from the way Sofia had fallen in love with Tom. Once they'd set eyes on one another nothing could keep them apart and their lack of security and wealth had made no difference. Until now, when they'd found that there were some things only money could buy. Apparently, a good physician was one.

Fortunately, it was only a couple of minutes to the doctor. He came immediately when informed those were Emmett Vinsant's instructions and was kind to Sofia. She didn't dare ask about his fee. The thought of repaying it was too much of a burden. Tom earned twenty-five pounds a year. It was a good job and he was lucky to have it, but a doctor could charge as much as three or four pounds for a visit. It would take months to scrape that together once they'd paid for rent, food and fuel. She looked out at the jarring combination of money and poverty as they passed through The Strand's slums and realised how life for her, and for so many people in London, was balanced on a knife's edge. Sofia thought it had never seemed so precarious until now.

By the time they pulled up outside their home in Brewhouse Yard, Sofia's seven-year-old son, Isaac, was standing on the street, biting his nails and struggling to hold back tears. The doctor alighted first, holding out his hand to Sofia. It was a courteous touch, she thought, and felt sure that if anyone would look after Tom properly it was this gentle man.

'Mother, hurry,' Isaac said. She ran to the bedroom at the back of the house, throwing herself on her knees at Tom's side, feeling his temperature before the doctor had even entered.

'Tom, sweetheart, it's me. I've brought the doctor, Mr Vinsant sorted it all out. You'll be all right now.' His skin was grey and shimmered with sweat. His breathing sounded laboured and, although he had opened his eyes to look at Sofia, he couldn't speak.

'Excuse me, Mrs Logan, you must let me examine him,' said the physician at her side. 'Mr Logan, my name is Doctor Bader. I need to feel your stomach and you will have to release your hands from it. Can you do that?' There was no response from Tom who only moaned slightly when the doctor pulled his hands away and straightened him out on the bed. In the corner, a neighbour, Nora, sat on a stool with Isaac's little sister Sadie cuddled up on her lap. Isaac went to stand with them and Sofia turned to Nora as the doctor conducted his examination.

'Has he said anything since I left? Did he ask for me?'

'Not a word, pet. He's been asleep mostly, groaning a bit and I couldn't get him to take any water.' Sofia's face fell and the elderly woman put an arm round Isaac. 'These two have been good as gold for me though, haven't you, my dears?' Nora was timeless. Sofia had never asked her age, but she was a surrogate grandmother to all the children in the road and confidante to many of their mothers. She'd lived in Brewhouse Yard for more years than Sofia had been alive.

Sofia forced a smile. 'Thank you, Nora. You don't need to wait. We'll be fine now.'

'Let me stay a bit longer, why don't you? I can look after the little ones while you talk with the doctor.' Sofia nodded. Doctor Bader was pressing Tom's stomach firmly. There was no reaction until he let go when Tom doubled up and let out an earsplitting scream. Isaac put his head in his hands and his sister began wailing. Nora rocked her, whispering soothing words in her ear. The doctor motioned for Sofia to follow him into the front room

'Do you know what it is? Can you help him?' she rushed.

The doctor wiped his hands on a rag. 'I can't be entirely sure but the rebound tenderness in his abdomen suggests some internal inflammation, possibly an infection or a blockage. I'm afraid it would be too dangerous to operate even if we could find a hospital to take him, and that's unlikely given the number of cases they're turning away at present. His temperature is high but not dangerously so. All we can do is wait and hope he improves over the next day. I shall send some laudanum for the pain. Give one spoon every four hours and try to get him to drink hot water. If he has a blockage, it's important to flush his system through. I shall return tonight.'

'Is there any risk that our children might catch it?' Sofia asked.

'I don't believe so, but to be safe ensure that they eat and drink in a different room.' Sofia nodded and the doctor patted her on the arm. 'I'll be back around seven.'

'Thank you,' she said. As he left, the children ran to her and Sofia did her best to look unconcerned.

'Come along now, neither of you has eaten anything. Let's make some porridge and then you must go to school. I shall write your teacher a note to explain why you're late.' She kissed each child on the forehead and put the clinging Sadie back on Nora's lap. If she just carried on as normal, she told herself, then Tom would improve. She could hear his harsh breathing as she warmed oats in hot water and tried to concentrate on Nora's tale about the exploits of King Edward. Half an hour later, the children were walking up the hill to the schoolhouse and Sofia stole a few minutes to wash her face and tidy her hair.

In the bedroom Tom's body seemed to have relaxed out of the terrible knot it had been in all morning. Sofia fetched water and a clean cloth, cooling his head, trying not to disturb him. She recalled their wedding day, eight years ago on a cold March morning. There had been frost on the grass and it was threatening rain, but in her memory the day was

15

filled with light as she walked into the chapel. She'd been just eighteen years old and relieved more than anything that her mother had lived to see her wed, even if she was wasted with consumption. From the moment she met him, Sofia had known that Tom would be true to her and care for her well. He worked so hard at everything he did, it was ingrained in him. Not that they didn't argue, she could be fiery and he could be stubborn, but disagreements were always short-lived. When the children came along they had enjoyed every moment. Tom was as proud as a father could be and the children adored him. He was never happier than when huddled in bed, one in the crook of each arm, for a bedtime story.

A hand slipped over Sofia's, barely able to grasp it, but Tom's eyes were open and shining.

'You'd have made a wonderful nurse,' he whispered.

'Silly you,' Sofia replied smiling and kissing his cheek. 'Be quiet and get better.'

'I'll be back at work tomorrow, you'll see.' He fell back to sleep. Sofia let out a long breath and thanked God that her man was on the mend. His skin felt cooler and his muscles were relaxed. Sofia looked at the time. She had two hours before the children came home, so she laid down next to Tom, wrapping her body around his. Running one hand through his curly hair and kissing his neck as she had a thousand times before, she slept.

She stayed like that until the voices of the children roused her. Nora had fetched them for her. Sofia smiled and stretched, excited to see them and hear their tales of school. When the bedroom door swung open the children charged in excitedly but all she could see was Nora's face, wide-eyed and open mouthed.

At once she was aware of the chill of Tom's flesh against hers and she reached an arm out to pull the covers over him.

'Children, come with me,' Nora said in a hushed voice as she ushered them back out. Sofia kissed Tom, trying to wake him to see the children, but his lips were turning from cool to cold. His head flopped to one side when she touched it and Sofia frowned, her earlier panic returning. The door opened again and Nora came in. She knelt by Tom's side and pulled the blankets over his face.

'What do you think you're doing?' shouted Sofia. 'He won't be able to breathe like that!' She grabbed the blankets out of Nora's hand and the neighbour put a palm to Sofia's face.

'Sofia, love, you have to let him go. He's passed.'

'Get off me, you don't know what you're talking about. Tom's getting better. He just needs to rest.'

'He's not breathing child, it's his time.' Nora was quiet but insistent.

'No, he spoke to me. He was improving or I wouldn't have let myself sleep. He can't be dead Nora, he must be unconscious. We have to get the doctor. Send one of Jenny's boys. Quickly, we're losing time!' Sofia was screaming now, infuriated by the calm resignation on Nora's face.

'There's nothing you could have done. It's often the way when people are taken. They seem better, the pain goes, the body has a way of protecting you from the worst of it. Asleep or awake, he'd have slipped away. Perhaps it was the comfort of you there that made it bearable for him to let go,' Nora whispered.

'No!' Sofia was shaking her head, gripping Tom as if she could will his soul back into his body. 'No, it can't be. Tom? Tom? No, no, no, no...' her denial trailed off into sobs and finally she laid her head on her dead husband's chest and rocked against him. Nora stayed with her, stroking her hair and keeping the silence for an hour, then slipped outside and called to another neighbour, Jenny, who'd been caring for the children.

When she re-entered the house Sofia was sitting up, one hand still holding Tom's although his fingers wouldn't bend around hers in return.

'The undertakers have been called and I sent a message to that kind doctor who came earlier. Should I fetch the children inside to say their goodbyes?' asked Nora.

'I can't live without him, there's no point. And how will I feed the children and pay the rent? Why did this happen?'

'You have to steel yourself. You need to pay your proper respects to your husband and worry about the rest later. You'll find a way, people always do. I'll bring the children in.' Sofia nodded, numb.

Sadie and Isaac didn't understand the permanence of the situation, not really, but they cried in their mother's arms and kissed their father's cheek. Sofia tried her best to comfort them but she couldn't stop staring at Tom, feeling certain that at any moment he'd get up, ready to tell the children their story and settle them for the night. He looked perfect. There was no sign of the pain that had plagued him. It was cruel. Somehow it would have been easier if his face reflected what he'd suffered.

After an hour a carriage pulled up outside and Sofia opened her front door. A small group of neighbours had gathered in an uncomfortable silence. The doctor nodded at her then went into the bedroom. She watched him feel Tom's wrist for a pulse, hold a mirror in front of his mouth for signs of breath and lift each eyelid.

'What did this?' Sofia asked.

'It seems likely that his intestine ruptured. He wouldn't have survived surgery in his condition. How old was your husband?'

'Thirty-one.'

'He was peaceful at the end,' Doctor Bader told her. 'I am truly sorry there was nothing more I could do. I shall let Mr Vinsant know.' The undertakers came in as he was leaving, sombre men in long black coats, quiet and businesslike. A process took over that Sofia found starkly impersonal. By the time Tom's body was taken from their home, the neighbours had put on the black arm bands of mourning. Sadie ran up and grabbed her mother's hand.

'Where are they taking Daddy?' she asked.

'To the funeral parlour, darling. They'll look after him there,' Sofia replied.

'But he'll be lonely without us. Shouldn't we go with him 'til he wakes up?' Sofia couldn't answer her. A gulf widened inside her as she watched her beloved man leave the street where they'd lived happily for years and she knew that part of her was going with him.

'Come to me, love,' soothed Nora, picking up Sadie and patting her back. 'Leave your mammy be for a while, there's a good girl.'

Sofia remembered little after that. The children were cared for by others. She retreated into the house and put on her only black dress, tying a scarf over her head. She'd have to find mourning clothes for the children although she had no idea how she'd pay for them, then there were the funeral costs. She sat by the fire, although the flames had long since died out, and let the hours slip by.

Chapter Three

Sofia endured five long days and nights before Tom's funeral. She wrote to his remaining family but they were scattered across the north of England. Unable to afford the proper paper, she had drawn the thick black border that signified a death. Friends lent mourning clothes for the children and any neighbour who could spare it delivered food. That was just as well, the little money they had saved and hidden under a floorboard was soon going to be spent. Sofia passed hours each day in the rocking chair staring at their wedding photograph, clutching it to her chest and craving sleep because each time she awoke, for one blissful moment, she forgot he was dead. Sleep became her escape and the children learned not to disturb her because when she slept, she wasn't crying. She accepted visitors with a blank grace. What good could their words do? Their condolences wouldn't bring Tom back or feed her children. Leave me alone, she thought to every knock at her door. Just leave me alone.

Dreading the funeral, at times she wondered if she too hadn't died and been left in a world where she no longer belonged. She could see, hear and touch the children but they felt alien. She knew they needed her and had their own grief to bear, but the burden was too heavy. She wanted her mother, someone to take care of her, to put her life back in order. That was the worst of it, the chaos.

The burial was a small affair. They had to travel a way outside the city to the cemetery, London having long since run out of the space required to lay its populace to rest. There was no fuss. Tom wouldn't have wanted a great drama. The children were well-behaved, the finality of their father's departure leaving them in a dazed silence as they watched the coffin lowered into the grave. Sofia looked into the distance, unwilling to bid him such a gruesome farewell. She was vaguely aware that Mrs Hasselbrook was behind her and that, at the other side of the grave, Emmett Vinsant and a handful of men in his employ had come to pay their respects. She hadn't expected them, it was a poor man's funeral. She shuddered as she let the handful of earth fall onto his coffin, the hollow sound giving the awful impression that it was empty, that she had dreamt it all. It would be cold and dark in there, she thought, hardly a fitting way for such a warm man to spend eternity.

As the gathering drifted apart - for there were no means by which she could afford a wake even if she had the will to organise one - she realised the undertaker would be waiting to speak with her. She hadn't enough money to pay what she owed and was pinning her hopes on him accepting half the payment now and the balance when she found work. If she had to hand over another pound, then this month's rent would be spent and the landlord unmoved by her plight. It was too common a situation these days and grief alone wouldn't stop him throwing them out on the street.

She took Isaac and Sadie by the hand, threw one last look into the hole in the ground and began the long walk home. At the gates of the cemetery Emmett Vinsant was talking to the undertaker but when he saw Sofia he shooed the man away and removed his hat, inclining his head towards her.

'Mrs Logan, I'm sorry for your loss. My household will miss your husband. He was a hard worker and a good man. Please, allow me to escort you home.'

'Mr Vinsant, you've been very kind and it would have meant a great deal to Tom that you came today but I can't ask any more of you, Sir. Please excuse me, I have to see the undertaker and I don't want to keep the children out in the cold longer than necessary.'

'Your business with the undertaker has been taken care of, it was the least I could do, and the children will be warmer in the carriage. Go ahead, children, climb in.' Before she could stop them, they were off, the sombreness of the day replaced already by the excitement of a ride in a gentleman's carriage. Sofia couldn't refuse, it was such a blessing to see smiles on their faces. Vinsant held her arm as she stepped up and sat with his back to the driver as she perched nervously between the children who babbled and yelled when they set off.

'Children, quiet please, remember your manners,' Sofia said firmly.

'Let them shout, they've had enough quiet this week, I suspect. Would you like something to eat, children?' At this they both managed a shy nod, Sadie glancing at her brother to follow his lead. 'Your father spoke of you a great deal. Tell me, what school do you attend?'

'The Clerkenwell Mission School, Sir,' Isaac responded quietly.

'And do you enjoy it there?' Vinsant asked.

'I do, Sir, especially learning my numbers. Father always said I was good with mathematics like Mummy.'

Vinsant laughed good-naturedly. 'Is that right?' He turned his attention to Sofia. 'We'll take a detour by Doughty Street if you have no objection. My wife would like to add her condolences and Mrs Hasselbrook can make herself feel better by feeding the little ones. Do you have family staying with you?'

'No, Sir. My mother passed away some years ago and my father left us long before that.'

'No sisters or brothers?'

'I had a sister, but she died as a baby, and my brother is a few years older than me. He's in America. We've had no word from him for months.' Sofia couldn't meet Vinsant's eyes. He made her nervous. Tom had told her that Emmett Vinsant, born into a working class family, had made a small fortune when the railways became popular and the enormous, modern stations had sprung up around London. His factories made parts for the railways. Vinsant had been accepted into society because he'd married well, although Tom was more guarded when he talked about Mrs Vinsant. Emmett's wife Beatrice had rarely interfered with Tom's work and Sofia had formed the impression that she was slightly odd.

'Here we are,' Vinsant said. 'Come along children, Mrs Hasselbrook will have been back before us and I believe she was baking this morning.'

Inside the house, Sofia had expected to remain in the kitchen with the staff, so when she was taken through to the parlour, she was filled with an absolute terror that the children would break or spill something. She sat on the edge of her chair, trying to stop her hands from shaking. Even Isaac and Sadie were awed into silence. Staring at the two of them confined in the stately room, they appeared smaller, worryingly fragile. Sofia sighed. Without warning, the door opened again, and a stern faced woman entered.

'You must be Mrs Logan. I'm Beatrice Vinsant. I am so sorry about Tom. I hope you'll forgive my not attending his funeral, I had pressing business to attend to.' Sofia bobbed a curtsy that Mrs Vinsant ignored, extending her hand to be shaken instead.

'Thank you, Ma'am. Everyone has been so kind. Say hello, please, children.' There was a long silence. 'Forgive them, they aren't used to being in such a lovely house.' Sofia swallowed hard, expecting to be asked to leave at any moment.

'Don't apologise, please. The poor things have more than etiquette on their minds. This young man is the image of his father,' she said, putting a hand on Isaac's shoulder. Sofia smiled her agreement. Isaac's curly hair and gold brown eyes reminded her so much of Tom that sometimes the resemblance was painful. 'And you must be Sadie,' she said. Sofia watched as her daughter stared up at Mrs Vinsant. The woman was as thin and willowy as her husband was sturdy. Sofia was reminded of a school teacher, practical and no-nonsense.

Emmett Vinsant appeared behind his wife and coughed. Beatrice did not acknowledge him but it was clear that their conversation was finished. 'It was a pleasure to meet you, Mrs Logan. Goodbye, children.' As she left the room, Mrs Hasselbrook appeared in the hallway beyond.

'Isaac, Sadie, I believe there are some treats prepared which you might enjoy more in the kitchen. Your mother will be with you shortly.'

Their faces lit up and they raced behind the housekeeper to the back of the house. Sofia was relieved they wouldn't be eating in the flawless room.

'Thank you, Sir, for your kindness. I don't know how I shall repay you.'

'That was what I wanted to discuss with you,' he said, closing the door. 'Please, sit.'

Sofia felt like a fool. Of course, he wanted to arrange repayment of the debt for the physician and the undertaker. She was unprepared, unable to offer anything more than a promise to do her best to settle matters soon.

The window shades were fully drawn as was proper when a household was in mourning. Vinsant lit a gas lamp on a side table, turning off the electric lighting. The result was to throw the room into near darkness save for the small pool of light extending just around him on the sofa and her on the chair.

'Electric lighting is an extraordinary modern convenience but I'm afraid I still find it rather harsh. This is much more to my taste.' Vinsant said. Sofia felt claustrophobic. It was ridiculous, of course. She could leave at any time and yet she felt unable to move.

'I realise I owe you a great deal of money. All I can say, Sir, is that you have my word I'll get it for you just as soon as I can find work and put a few shillings by.'

'Mrs Logan, please stop. You have given me your word that you'll repay the fee for the doctor and, as concerns the undertaker, that was freely given and no repayment is necessary.' He crossed the parlour and lit a cigar, standing by the chimney for the smoke to leave the room. The end of the cigar flashed red in the gloom, briefly lighting Vinsant's face and filling the air with its woody scent.

'Tom told me a lot about you, Sofia.' His use of her first name made her uneasy, the surroundings and atmosphere more intimate than was fitting. Now that she was a widow she shouldn't be alone like this with a man. 'You're still just twenty-six years old, young enough to rebuild your life and you're resourceful, I gather you had to be. I know what that's like. I, too, was born without the benefit of a silver spoon in my mouth. I understand how you think and what you need. I can help you, if you'll let me.' He threw the cigar into the fireplace where it lay smouldering. Before realising he'd moved, Sofia found Vinsant standing in front of her, his tone hushed and without hint of a threat but more imposing than ever as she remained seated. She found herself shrinking backwards into the seat.

'You're beautiful and bright. A woman like you can be a very valuable commodity.' He ran one finger along the line of her jaw and Sofia hid a shudder. 'It would be no difficulty at all to find you employment.'

The cigar smoke and darkness combined to disorient her. She felt her head swim and knew she had to leave. He was too close, the room too warm. She thrust herself to her feet, swaying against him briefly. He made no effort to move out of her way.

'That's kind of you, Sir, and I appreciate the offer of help and I'll get you what I owe, but I'd rather make my own way.' Her voice wavered as she spoke but she kept her head high. 'And now I'd best find my children if you'll let me pass.'

Emmett Vinsant leaned to one side and extinguished the light from the gas lamp. Sofia froze, imagining his hands reaching for her through the darkness, knowing she couldn't scream, couldn't accuse him, that no one would believe her. When the electric lighting flicked on, she found him looking at her quizzically.

'My dear Mrs Logan, you seem overwrought, understandably. I only wanted you to know that I am here should you need me. Finding a job is not easy. Come back to me when you have exhausted your other options.' He had a half smile on his face. Sofia felt idiotic and confused. 'I'll remember that. Thank you,' Sofia stuttered.

'Good,' he said as he opened the door. 'Mrs Hasselbrook?' The housekeeper came bustling from the door at the end of the corridor. 'Take Mrs Logan to the kitchen, please, and be sure to see that she has a proper meal before she leaves.' He walked off up the stairs without a farewell. Sofia took a deep breath. The cigar smoke had been overpowering and even now she wasn't sure she hadn't just imagined the whole conversation. As she entered the kitchen, Nettie nodded her head at Sofia.

'Sorry about Tom, he was always real sweet,' the girl said.

'Shush now, Mrs Logan's had enough of that today. Let her eat in peace,' said the housekeeper and Sofia was glad. She'd run out of replies to the constant offers of sympathy. Sitting with the children at a slim wooden table she picked at a plate of ham, bread and pickles before making her excuses.

Back home, she set a fire in the range to heat water, made cocoa and put the children to bed, singing them to sleep as she mended a pair of Isaac's trousers. Each time she tried to reconstruct the scene with Vinsant in her mind she was torn between remonstrating with herself for her stupidity and feeling that he had stolen something from her. How could he not have realised how uncomfortable his proximity in such a dark and private space would seem? But he'd asked for nothing from her, offered nothing except help. Was her mind so twisted by grief that she was creating false demons? Tom had respected him, worked for him without complaint for years. And yet the thought of asking him for help, of being so close to him again, left her cold.

Rocking herself calm by the fire, Sofia opened the top few buttons of her dress and pulled out a heavy silver locket. Inside was a picture of her mother, mahogany hair tumbling over her shoulders and exotic almond-shaped eyes that betrayed her migrant origins. Sofia had inherited her mother's features and in turn passed them on to Sadie. In time, the locket would belong to her daughter and she would have a way of remembering her Romani roots. But it was her mother's smile that Sofia thought was the essence of her loveliness, dimples forming at each corner of her mouth, concealing an inner tenacity. Sofia let her tears fall untouched. Her mother always said that tears were sent to wash away pain, one drop at a time. It would take more of them than she thought she could ever cry to heal the pain of losing Tom. Putting another log on the fire, she tucked the locket away and determined to clean the floor and make broth before allowing herself to sleep.

'Mama, when is Daddy coming home?' asked a yawning Sadie, appearing from the bedroom.

'He's with us right now,' whispered Sofia, picking her up and stroking her hair. 'Watching us and listening to our prayers from heaven. Do you understand, sweetheart?'

'Yes, Mama,' she replied, but Sofia knew she didn't and that it would be a long time before her daughter could grasp the nature of their loss.

Chapter Four

Two weeks, Sofia thought. How could she have lost two whole weeks? It was a blur of Nora coming in and out, sending the children to school to keep some routine for them. Two weeks of wanting to get out of bed because it felt so empty, then wanting to get straight back in when she was up because it all felt so hard. Too hard. Sometimes she forgot what had happened and would call Tom's name to tell him something. In those moments she felt as if she would never start to feel better. And she didn't, not yet. But she was beginning to understand that the world was still turning and that she had no choice but to move with it.

There was enough money for next month's rent but the landlord, Cramborne, collected at the start of the month and then their savings would be reduced to almost nothing. It was time to find work. Nora had said she would watch the children after school. The problem was her lack of skills. She could sew but not with the speed of a seamstress. Posts that required literacy or numeracy were the remit of men, unless you were a teacher, lady's maid or nanny and she hadn't the experience or references for such positions. Steeling herself and putting on her bravest face, she set off to tour the local factories and breweries.

From one to the next she went, forcing a spring into her step as she went through each door. The smog from the chimneys had not kept itself to the outer bricks. The internal offices were stained grey brown and the air was heavy. Still she smiled, asked for work, stressed her ability to read and write and her willingness to work whatever hours, however many or few they could offer.

Some of the men she spoke to were polite, others brusque, a few laughed as soon as she began to speak. The worst of it by far were those who gave her pitying looks, as if she had no idea what she was asking.

'You don't want to work here, love,' one said. 'It's a distillery. Men around the stink of booze all day go a bit funny in the head. It's no place for a woman.'

'I can handle myself,' she said. 'And I'm sure they're all talk. I've known my share of men who like a drink.'

'Not like this, my darlin'. This is long hours with men who're tired and rough. They won't stop at a bit of name calling. Couldn't say as you'd be safe.'

'Please, I'll take anything. I can work nights, any shifts at all. Can you at least let me try for a week so I can show you.'

'It's not just you I'm thinkin' of. Girl like you in here, distractin' my men, it'd be bedlam in no time. You could try the laundry up on Skinner Street. My wife says they're always looking for girls. It don't pay well but you'd be out of trouble.'

'Thank you,' Sofia replied. He had, at least, tried to help.

That first day she went to a dozen breweries and distilleries, eight factories and several inns. It was the same tale everywhere. Either there were no vacancies or she wasn't suitable for the work. In a day of rejection there were two particular lows. The first was the landlord who said he would give her three shifts each week at his pub in exchange for taking whatever liberties he chose with her. The second was the only time she ventured into a shop. It was a tiny place, tucked away between a grocer and a butcher, selling material, buttons, thread and other sewing accessories. She was excited when she walked in. It was warm, properly lit, and it smelled like her mother's linen basket.

'Good afternoon,' she said to the lady behind the counter who was busy sorting hooks and eyes. 'Sorry to bother you but I was wondering if you might have any work available. I live quite close by and I'm a fast learner.'

The woman began to titter before she'd finished the sentence. Sofia laughed along, thinking there was some joke. When it didn't stop, Sofia's laughter trailed off.

'I'm...I'm sorry,' she said. 'I must have said something wrong. Let me start again.'

'No, please don't,' she sniggered. 'We only employ ladies here. Ones who bathe more often than once a month and whose clothes are not tatty and frayed. And before you embarrass yourself further you should know that there is a stain, from goodness knows what, on your skirt. Now I must ask you to leave before one of our customers comes in and sees you.' She lifted a lace handkerchief to her mouth as if to hide her continued laughter. Sofia wanted to reply. She wanted to say something cutting or lofty, or proud but no words would come. She stumbled from the shop, face burning, tears in her eyes and retreated home. For the four days that followed she did the same, avoiding the shops though and approaching only the industrial businesses. She told herself it was only a matter of time before she walked into the right place, somewhere with a vacant position or who would keep her name on their lists until work was available, but there was nothing. At some factories there were lines of men and women waiting to write their name down, each being told the same thing. Try somewhere else.

Sofia spent increasing amounts of time wondering how far she could stretch her savings, how small she could make their portions of food before the children became too weak. She thought of Vinsant's offer of work with each rejection but every time felt his touch on her face and determined to find work elsewhere.

She bought no meat now and the vegetables were past their best. She found that if she waited at the grocers until closing he would let her have what he was about to throw out for almost nothing. She tried to give them a little fish or cheese for strength once every few days but that was about to become no more than a memory. Cramborne's visit was looming and she had begun to dread the thought of handing over the last of her coins. It was money that Tom had earned, the last thing he had given her.

When she gave it away, she thought, she was giving away another piece of him. And the thought of paying the rent for the following month was keeping her awake at night.

'I'm hungry,' had become the children's constant cry. Isaac was visibly thinner and had lost his sparkle. Worse than that, Sadie had almost stopped complaining that there was so little to eat. Her stomach was full on just a few mouthfuls of bread and as hard as Sofia would coax, she couldn't stomach the boiled vegetables that had become their staple diet.

After ten days of searching Sofia found herself on Skinner Street, staring at the door to the laundry. She knew what such places were like. The women who worked there were like ghosts, working from eight in the morning until seven at night, pale from lack of sunlight, shrivelled from the heat, stinking from the foul water and harsh soaps. Those who managed to work there for more than a few months had a constant cough from the damp atmosphere. It won't hurt to look, she told herself. Just to be sure.

The steam hit her the moment she opened the door. A woman bustled up to her immediately.

'If it's work you're after, go through that door there, through the ironing room and into the far office. Be sure not to touch anything on your way.'

Sofia walked through rows of massive vats over which stood women in sodden white smocks, stirring and thumping, adding soap, keeping their heads back to avoid breathing in the vapour. Others were carting buckets of wet washing off to be wrung, and dumping yet more filthy linen into the water. Not one of them looked at her. No one spoke. It was, Sofia thought, like hell, except the fire had been replaced with water.

The next room she entered was completely different. Rows of women stood, each with an iron in their right hand, a pile of collars and shirts before them. Many had bits of linen wrapped around fingers, from the burns she supposed. Here the atmosphere was drier but no happier.

31

They would do this work, ironing item after item, standing up so that they could press down properly, for more than nine hours each day. Through the last door Sofia came to a woman at a desk who waved at the empty chair before her without looking up.

'Name?' she snapped.

'Sofia,' she replied.

'Surname. We do not use given names here.'

'Yes, sorry. Logan,' Sofia said.

'Experience?'

'I've kept home for several years, I'm recently widowed and I have two children.'

'No laundry experience?' the woman asked, finally raising her head.

'I was wondering if there were any positions in the ironing room, actually.'

'You start in the laundry room unless you have references. Do you?' Sofia shook her head. 'Forty-five minutes break for luncheon and thirty minutes for tea. You will provide your own shoes, we will give you a smock. I can give you four days work each week.'

'And the pay?' Sofia asked.

'Two shillings and six pence per day.'

'Eight shillings a week?' Sofia said. 'But I can't feed my family and pay the rent on that.'

'There are plenty of people wanting work. Take it or leave it. Perhaps in a few months you might progress to ironing. That pays three shillings. Any questions.'

'No, thank you. I understand.'

'When do you want to start?' the woman asked pulling a form from her drawer.

'I'll think about it for a day, if you don't mind. I'll come back when I've decided.'

'Oh! When you've decided? How lovely to be such a fine lady you can pick and choose. Let me know in the next week or don't waste my time again. See yourself out.'

Sofia retraced her steps, head down, trying not to see the faces of the women and girls as they strained their necks and backs, and wished the hours away. She thrust open the outer door and drank in the fresh air. Was this place to be her life for the next few years, struggling to exist, breaking herself physically and mentally. And if not the laundry, what was the alternative? There were no jobs. She had no experience, no training, no skills.

Sofia felt in her pocket for the few pennies she had to buy supper for the children. Cramborne would be by for his rent tomorrow. They couldn't exist on bread, water and boiled cabbage any longer. She had one last place to go for work. Swallowing her pride she set off for Doughty Street.

Vinsant wouldn't see her immediately, and Sofia worried that she'd missed her chance, keeping him waiting too long before asking for help. Mrs Hasselbrook delivered the message that he would meet with her that evening. He was sending his driver to fetch her at ten o'clock. It was awfully late to be going out. She would have to ask Nora to watch the children. A factory then, the night shift? At least she hoped it was factory work. Any other type of employment for women during the hours of darkness didn't bear thinking about.

With Isaac and Sadie tucked up in bed and Nora dozing by the fire, Sofia set off, staring at the nighttime streets from Vinsant's carriage as if she'd never set foot in the city before. It was transformed. Ladies and gentleman in their finery were taking unhurried walks between supper rooms and elegant hotels, no doubt indulging in pleasures available only to the privileged few. There was no sense of danger, no men ambling out of pubs drunk, no prostitutes waiting for custom in dark doorways. Sofia felt as if she'd been let in on a closely guarded secret. She realised she'd never been into the centre of London at night.

Soon enough Silverman, the driver, announced their arrival at St James' Street in Westminster. He helped Sofia from the carriage and showed her to a dark door set into the side of a lofty pale-fronted building, balconied at its upper windows, but otherwise quite understated. He knocked twice and the door seemed to glide open. Sofia was met by an impeccably dressed man, nose in the air, who managed to sound both bored and irritated at once.

'Your business?' he asked, eyeing Sofia up and down. A strong accent transformed his English into something much more exotic and formidable.

'Mrs Logan for Mr Vinsant. He gave instructions to fetch him the minute she arrived,' the driver spoke across her and the door opened wider.

'Come with me.' Stick thin, with immaculately shaped eyebrows, a black oiled moustache and half-moon spectacles, Sofia thought he was about as warm as the Thames in December. 'Do not speak directly to any of our guests unless you are asked a question or Mr Vinsant tells you that you should. You may call me Monsieur Lefevre, or just Monsieur, if that is easier for you. Do you speak French?'

'No, Sir, I'm afraid I don't and I'm not quite sure what I'm doing here, I thought I was going to one of Mr Vinsant's factories. There must've been some mistake.'

'No mistake at all, Mrs Logan,' said Emmett Vinsant entering the lobby. Sofia went to curtsy but he took her by the arm. 'In here, whilst I appreciate the gesture, our clientele expects to deal with staff who are less subservient. You should be polite, bow your head and mind how you address guests but you will not be considered from below stairs.'

'Forgive my ignorance, Sir, but I don't understand where I am.'

'Then Tom was even more discreet than I gave him credit for. This is one of three private members clubs that I own.' He spread his hands wide. It was a pompous gesture but Sofia understood why. The place was beautiful. Thick, crimson carpet ran throughout, with subtle lighting and not a clock in sight. She guessed the intention was for guests to forget the passage of time. Exquisitely carved tables with leather arm-chairs were spread spaciously about, ensuring privacy for whispered conversations and matters of business. Drinks and cigarettes on silver trays were being served to couples idling away their time and, from a room at the top of a wide staircase, Sofia could hear laughter and smell cigar smoke. 'Shall we?' He motioned toward the voices and Sofia fol-lowed a step behind.

A footman opened the glass doors as they approached and Sofia took in the crystal chandeliers, darkly patterned walls, and velvet drapes covering every window. Daylight was never going to be allowed to in-vade this room, Sofia thought. It was as if time stopped when you stepped inside. The source of the raised voices and excitement was a carefully arranged selection of tables surrounded by small groups of men and women, drinking, showing off and throwing good money after bad. It was a vast gaming room. There were long tables with roulette wheels, smaller posts where individuals played twenty-one against dealers and other table games Sofia was unfamiliar with. The players were mostly male but there were a few women present, some watching over the shoulders of husbands or friends, but a few of the bolder ones were join-ing in. Sofia was staggered by the wealth. The stakes were higher than any amount of money she'd ever seen. Here and there, Sofia spotted a few people who didn't fit in with the crowd, more concerned with who was watching them than the card play itself and either too relaxed or too showy.

'Tell me what you see,' Vinsant said.

'Gentleman with the grey hair at the end of the table to our left and the two men on the black and red table pretending to compete against each other. They're not guests. You got bonnets working in here, Sir?'

'Quietly now, Mrs Logan, that is not a term we wish our members to become familiar with. Let's talk somewhere more private.' They left the gaming room, went through a hall where a buffet so luxuri-ous was laid out that Sofia couldn't name half the sorts of food she saw on the table. At the end they turned into a darkened corridor where a man stood protectively in front of a door.

'Good evening, Mr Vinsant,' he said, unlocking and opening it. Although well mannered, Sofia knew from the bulge under his jacket why he was there. In Vinsant's office three large metal safes were lined up along the right hand wall. The furnishings were plainer than in the public rooms and the space was dominated by the large walnut desk behind which Vinsant seated himself, pointing towards the chair opposite for Sofia.

'Will you take a drink with me?'

'I shouldn't, but thank you,' she said.

'You're worrying what Tom would think, of course, but your husband was nothing if not practical. I would imagine him proud to know you've found a means to support his children. Let's drink to him.' He put a glass of whisky in her hands in spite of her refusal and raised his own. 'To Tom Logan, a man who knew how to get things done.'

Sofia raised her glass in reply then swallowed a sip, shocked by the burn in her throat. After a moment of contemplative silence Vinsant was done with the pleasantries.

'Tom told me you had some familiarity with gambling, that your family ran a similar business. He also said that on his best day he couldn't come close to beating you at cards, such a head for mathematics do you possess.' Sofia wasn't sure how to respond nor whether she was being questioned or complimented.

'Mr Vinsant, what I did as a girl is hardly the same as this. It was just small stakes, a bit of fun really. And I haven't played for a long time, I'd be out of my depth.' She put the glass down.

'The men you saw, bonnets you called them, do a fair job encouraging the more timid players, charging the atmosphere, raising the stakes. They make sure the tables are busy when the first guests arrive, put on something of a show with the dealers, you know how it works. What I need now is someone who can spot the players who win too much, too often. In particular, I need someone who can warn me if anyone is using a system to calculate probability and lessen their chances of losing, notify me if I'm at risk of making too great a loss. You'll be paid properly for your services, enough to meet your household bills and pay for childcare at night, with a little to put away for your own recreation. In addition, I shall provide suitable clothing. I appreciate your hours will be unsociable so there will be a carriage to collect you and take you home afterwards. If anyone asks what you do for me, you should say that you are an administrative assistant. I own a number of businesses, not just the factories and the private clubs but also an investment company and a political lobbying service. No one needs to know in which of my establishments you work.'

'Mr Vinsant, I'm not sure I can do it. I can't pass myself off as a lady.'

'Many of the people who come here are not what one might consider to be ladies or gentlemen, but they all have one thing in common: they like to play and have the means to do so. I wouldn't offer you this job if I didn't think you capable of it.'

'Isn't there something else. All those businesses you own. Could I not find a different post, Sir? I can read and write to a good standard. I don't mind hard work, in one of your factories even. I'm just not sure I fit in here.'

'Mrs Logan, I chose the person to fit the position. This isn't charity. You have skills that I require. My factories are heavy industrial places, not fit for women and there are no alternative posts. This is all I can offer you.'

'Are you sure, Sir, because I'm a fast learner and I think you'll find...'

'Forgive me for interrupting. I am a busy man. This is all there is, Sofia. You'll let me know soon I trust. Silverman will take you home.'

He rapped hard on his desk twice and the door swung open. 'Do have another look around, Mrs Logan. Captain Thorne will find you and take you back to Lefevre shortly.' The man Vinsant had referred to by rank passed Sofia in the corridor. She saw by his bearing that the title was genuine. He had the stiff-backed stance of a soldier and the right side of his face bore a crude scar that could only have come from a blade cutting deep from ear to mouth. She guessed he'd been one of the lucky ones to have returned from the Boer War. Plenty of others had been less fortunate, even if the British Army had prevailed in the end. Given how bloody and brutal the stories of the conflict were, she wasn't surprised that he was content to stand in darkened corridors guarding Emmett Vinsant and his fortune.

Sofia wandered back into the lounge and considered what it would be like to work there. No expense had been spared and she guessed that Monsieur Lefevre would be able to procure almost any service requested by a paying guest. A shriek of laughter and a slammed door down a hallway made her curious about the other rooms and, as the Captain had still not come looking for her, she went to explore.

At the end of the hall she turned a corner into a dimmer section of the building, quite different from the central areas, with a number of rooms on either side. One door had been left slightly ajar and she edged up to it guiltily, knowing she shouldn't be spying but unable to resist. Inside were four men with an equal number of female companions. One of the males struck her immediately as the ringleader, fond of the sound of his own voice, with a strong Scottish accent and curly red hair, talking business to the others as he slapped the girls' buttocks playfully and tugged at their clothes. Two of the women still had their skirts on but the others were down to corsets and garters, hair unbraided, showing no sign of minding the hands that travelled appreciatively up and down their legs. Sofia was transfixed. They didn't look unwilling or unhappy, quite the opposite. How strange, she thought, that women could choose such a profession. She had always perceived prostitutes as sad, lonely creatures but the women in there seemed to be neither. She was watching the Scot pull a laughing brunette down onto a chaise longue, when a hand covered her mouth and hauled her backwards. Whirling round, Sofia saw Thorne signal silence. He let her go when she nodded, beckoning her out of the corridor and into the main lounge.

'I was just interested,' said Sofia. 'I hadn't meant to pry.'

'Our guests value their privacy. Those are not the sort of men we want to upset. If you have questions about what goes on here, ask Lefevre.' The Captain was well spoken but abrupt. On closer inspection Sofia saw that he had once been handsome. It must have been a cruel blow for his face to have been so painfully disfigured. She guessed he was in his early forties, his soldier's physique unsoftened by the more sedate life. He was hard, in fact, in every way. His grey eyes gave nothing away as she mumbled another apology. Thorne escorted her to the outside door without saying anything further and Sofia didn't attempt to continue the conversation, embarrassed enough at having been caught spying on the club's working girls.

'Ah, Captain Thorne, has Monsieur Vinsant finished with this young woman?' asked Lefevre as they approached. Sofia didn't enjoy being referred to, rather than spoken to directly, but she wasn't stupid enough to let her annoyance show.

'Indeed. She will remain here while I fetch the carriage.' The Captain stepped outside.

'So, how do you know Monsieur Vinsant? Are you to work here? Does your husband not mind you being out for the whole night?'

Sofia raised her eyebrows, startled at being asked such invasive questions by a stranger. 'My husband, Tom, was one of Mr Vinsant's footmen. He's...'

'That was clumsy of me, I apologise,' Lefevre cut in, putting a hand on Sofia's forearm. 'I had no idea you were Tom's widow. We knew him well here. Your husband was a charming man, I am sorry for your loss.'

'But Tom was just a footman. I knew he sometimes travelled with Mr Vinsant but I don't understand what he'd have been doing here.' Sofia was taken aback. She'd had no idea about the existence of this place or these people. Perhaps she hadn't asked the right questions, or shown enough interest in his work, but Tom had never spoken about the private clubs or any other businesses except the factories and warehouses.

'You will find that Mr Vinsant cares very little for labels. When you work for him you are expected to adapt. I suspect that some wives might find that difficult to comprehend.' Sofia knew she had just given away more than she'd intended about her ignorance of her late husband's affairs and moved the conversation swiftly on.

'And you, Monsieur, are you married?'

Lefevre laughed. 'No, you sweet girl, not me. Who would want this life? I get home at eight in the morning, fall asleep for the day, wake up at five which just gives me time to bathe, eat and dress before I come back. Sometimes I feel as if I haven't seen the sun for months. Besides, marriage was always too traditional a situation for me. I prefer life without limitations, you understand?'

There was a noise at the outer door and Lefevre stepped aside so that she could exit. The carriage was waiting and the Captain helped her up.

'Thank you,' Sofia said, but he'd already turned his back. They set off, travelling east towards Clerkenwell. Sofia sank into the leather. Working there would offer her the security she needed and the conditions were good. Tom had rarely complained of Vinsant as an employer and it would be wonderful to be around people who had known him, to keep his memory alive. She asked herself what Tom would have wanted her to do, but no divine answer came. It was tempting. She would finally be able to play cards again.

Immediately the thought came, Sofia knew she shouldn't even consider working at the club. Things had ended badly enough the last time. She'd sworn to her mother and to Tom that she would never gamble again. Working in the club was nothing less than a gilded pathway to ruin. Her mother had sent her away from the travelling fair against her father's wishes, the only time she'd known her mother to make a decision contrary to his, and she did it to save her from the cards. If she went to work for Mr Vinsant now it would be a betrayal of all her mother had done to protect her.

She'd had the briefest taste of a forbidden fruit, seeing the tables, hearing the click of the dice, studying the dealers, sharing the thrill of the players. And she had loved it. She could have got lost in there, she knew, watching and listening. The need to play was like maggots crawling in her gut. It was her poison. Vinsant would have to be disappointed. There had to be work out there somewhere that would pay enough to feed and house them. She could not and would not pick up the cards again.

Chapter Five

October 1905

Sofia wrote to Vinsant, her reply brief but courteous, expressing her sincere thanks for his kind offer of employment. She walked the note to Doughty Street herself early the next morning, knowing that if she didn't act swiftly and decisively the temptation she was trying to resist would sink its parasitic hooks in her. Leaving the note with Mrs Hasselbrook, she wandered home. There was no point rushing. It would be almost as cold inside as it was out. There was no money for coal and she had no logs left. The choice for the coming week was whether to buy food or fuel. She should go to one of the parks, she thought, and collect fallen branches. That would save a few pennies. What little money she had left was better spent on bread and potatoes. The children would have to wear extra layers and she should cover the windows with sack cloth to stop the drafts. Returning home with a new determination, she realised the shillings on offer for the work at the laundry might well be the best she could do. If it was that or the slums there really was no choice.

Isaac burst through the door as she was dicing a few shrivelled potatoes, for once too excited to complain at the prospect of another thin, tasteless soup.

'Mummy, we're to have a visitor at school tomorrow. Mrs Weston said he was from a different country half way around the world!'

'That's exciting,' said Sofia hanging up the children's coats. 'So where's he from?'

'Quebec,' Isaac answered proudly. Sofia bent down to hug him.

'Quebec? That's in a place called Canada, next to America where your uncle is.'

There was a crash behind them. Sofia turned just in time to see Sadie hitting the floor.

'Sadie!' she shouted, throwing herself to her daughter's side. 'Fetch Nora,' she told Isaac. 'Sadie, darling, Mummy's here. Please wake up.' She held her daughter's head tenderly on her lap, stroking her forehead and staring at the purple lump already swelling there. Sadie's eyelashes were fluttering but she wasn't regaining consciousness. Sofia could hear footsteps approaching at a pace. Isaac was shouting before he'd even opened the front door.

'Nora wasn't there but I found a policeman, Mummy.' Sofia didn't have time to look at the man coming through the door before he was on his knees at her side, telling Sofia to fetch a cold cloth and some water. He put the wet rag on Sadie's forehead, loosened her collar, held her wrist and spoke softly to her. She came round slowly, muttering a few incomprehensible words at first, tiny hands grabbing at the air, face as white as milk but otherwise unharmed.

'I'm sure she'll be all right,' he said. 'The bump will go down. She just looks a bit washed out.'

'Sorry, I just panicked,' Sofia said. 'I had no idea she was unwell. It was lucky you were there.'

When Sadie was well enough to be propped up in Sofia's arms, the policeman took off his helmet and laid it on the floor. Isaac crouched next to it and ran a finger over its surface.

'Isaac, don't touch,' Sofia said.

'That's all right, go ahead.' He lifted the helmet onto Isaac's head.

'It's so heavy!' Isaac gushed. 'Do you have to wear it all the time?'

'Most of the time,' the constable said, grinning back at the boy. 'You forget it's there after a while.'

'We should let you go. I'm sure you've places to be. Thank you so much for helping with Sadie.' Sofia stroked her daughter's hair.

'Glad I was here. And I'm just off duty. I've moved in a few doors down, that's why your boy saw me in the road. I'm Constable Danes. Charlie.'

'Sofia Logan. I hadn't realised you were a neighbour, sorry. Nora usually tells me everything going on around here. Can't believe she missed that bit of gossip.'

'The Irish lady next door? She hasn't spoken to me yet. I think she's trying to decide if having a police constable in the road is a good thing or not.' Sofia laughed.

'Mummy, I'm hungry,' Sadie said in a small voice. Sofia realised she had nothing to feed her until the soup was made.

'I'll put the pan on to boil,' Sofia told her, resting Sadie against the chair. She could see Charlie looking around as she threw the tiny potatoes into the pan and added some vegetable peelings to make the stock tastier.

'I'll be off then,' Charlie said, winking at Isaac as he took the helmet from him. 'You've things to do.' He shook Sofia's hand as she thanked him again. When he left Isaac was full of questions about him that Sofia couldn't answer.

'How old do you have to be to become a police constable, Mummy?'

'I don't know sweetheart,' Sofia replied.

'Well, how old is Charlie?'

'I've no idea, around twenty-eight or twenty-nine I'd guess.'

'He's very tall, isn't he? Do you have to be tall to be in the police?'

'You should ask Police Constable Danes next time you see him.' A knock at the door had Sofia rolling her eyes and drying her hands in her apron. She didn't need visitors now. When she opened it she found Charlie holding bread.

'I didn't think you'd want to wait until you'd finished cooking and this is more than I need, living alone. Please take it.' Sofia's first instinct was to turn it down, hating to think this stranger thought she needed charity but when she looked back at Sadie, so dreadfully thin, she swallowed her pride.

'Thank you, Charlie. That's very kind. I'll repay you, of course.'

'No rush,' he said. 'It's enough to have made a friend here,' he said, smiling as he walked away.

His brief time inside their house had been enough to show him that Sadie had fainted from hunger. They couldn't carry on like this. The children would grow ill and Sofia hadn't an inch of spare flesh on her. If she didn't find work soon matters would become desperate.

Sofia broke the bread into pieces, put some on a plate for Isaac and fed Sadie tiny mouthfuls. It was fresh and smelled wonderful. Charlie must have just bought it. She felt guilty at having taken it but pleased that he was there. With his gentle dark eyes and soft voice he seemed an unlikely candidate for police work, but beneath that Sofia suspected there was a steadfastness that might prove unshakeable.

'Mummy,' Isaac said. 'Can we not buy our own bread anymore?'

'Things will get better,' was all Sofia could say. 'I'll find work and we'll have more food. Don't worry, my darling.'

Sofia attended the Skinner Street laundry the next morning to be told the manager was not in and to try again that evening. She was disappointed but determined to see it though. There was cheaper housing around and, although they would all have to live and sleep in a single room, at least she could be sure the money from the laundry would cover the rent. She would still be short for food and fuel but she would just have to keep looking for other work to cover those costs.

It was mid afternoon before Sadie ran in alone, crying so bitterly she was unable to tell Sofia what was wrong.

'Sadie, you shouldn't have run away from Isaac,' Sofia chided gently. 'It's not safe on your own.' She picked her up and walked to the door, looking out for Isaac.

'He's not coming,' Sadie sobbed into her shoulder. 'They've taken him.'

'Sadie, calm down. What are you talking about? Who's taken him?'

'They said he stole Mrs Weston's purse. It was in Isaac's bag. Policemen came and took him away.'

Sofia's head was swimming. Grabbing her keys she dashed to Nora's, left Sadie and began a desperate sprint to the school. It was inconceivable that Isaac would have done such a terrible thing. He was a good boy and an honest child. Yesterday though, for the first time, he'd really grasped their circumstances, seeing his sister faint, feeling hunger he'd never had to endure before. It was enough to make any child behave out of character. But stealing? It had to be be a mistake. Her son would never do such a thing.

Her thoughts were black and buzzing as she reached the Clerkenwell Mission School. Sofia was frantic. She flew inside to find Mrs Weston at her desk, calmly marking papers.

'Where's Isaac?' Sofia shouted before she was half way across the classroom.

'Your son is in the custody of the police, Mrs Logan, as he should be. He stole my purse, thinking himself alone in the classroom during break. Sadly for him we had a visitor here today who witnessed the theft with his own eyes. I had expected better from your family. Perhaps with the passing of his father standards have slipped.'

'You sly-mouthed old bitch!' Sofia yelled. 'How dare you make this about my husband's death. Don't expect Sadie back here tomorrow.'

Sofia smashed through the tiny rows of single wooden desks and straight backed chairs as she ran out. It couldn't be true. Isaac had never stolen a thing in his life. She didn't even know where he'd been taken. She thought how terrified he'd be, with no idea what was going to happen. Her mind was full of images of him being dragged off, crying and calling her name. How could she have let this happen? Was he so hungry that he was stealing to buy food?

Sofia walked home, trying desperately to figure out which police station to try first. As she was about to knock Nora's door, she thought of Charlie. It seemed wrong, asking for help from someone she barely knew and what would he think? Still, he was her best hope. It didn't matter if he judged her. She had to find Isaac. Sofia gritted her teeth and knocked.

'Mrs Logan, Sadie's better today I hope,' Charlie said.

'Isaac's been arrested,' she blurted. 'I'm sorry, I've got no right to ask but I don't know what to do.' He looked at his pocket watch.

'Where's Sadie?' he asked.

'Nora's,' she said.

'Tell her we'll be a couple of hours. I need two minutes. You can explain what happened on the way.'

Sofia had no idea where they were going. Asking questions meant wasting time. She ran into Nora's house and gave her the briefest details. By the time she was back at Charlie's door he was in his uniform, waiting. They made their way to Islington Police Station as she told Charlie what she knew and admitted her worst fear - that Isaac had done exactly what he was accused of because of Sadie fainting the day before. Charlie listened without talking until they reached the station.

'It's still early enough for them to take him before the Magistrate today. If they've a statement from a witness it'll be dealt with promptly.'

Sofia sobbed. 'Then what? He won't survive in prison Charlie. Isaac's never had a night away from me in his life.'

'I know the Magistrate and he's a fair man. I'm going to speak with him on Isaac's behalf. Let me see what I can do.'

She nodded, trembling and he led her to a bench then disappeared into the building. The hour that followed felt like the longest of her life. Police officers came and went, some escorting prisoners, others joking with colleagues. It was a different world, one she had no idea how to navigate. The courts were no more sympathetic to children than to adults. Poverty was regarded as a plague in the city, stealing a grave crime. Her story was no different from thousands of others. Isaac's fate was out of her hands.

Charlie returned alone, looking troubled.

'Tell me,' Sofia said, clutching his hands.

'I explained everything to the Magistrate that you told me on the way here. He was kind and understanding but,' he hesitated, 'Isaac wouldn't admit what he'd done. I think if he had, then I'd have better news for you.'

'So where is he?'

'The Magistrate was understanding and agreed he needn't face trial but he's been sent to Clerkenwell Workhouse with orders that he shouldn't be released until he's accepted what he's done. It was the more lenient course than prison.'

Sofia held her hands to her face, hopeless and wearied.

'No,' she sobbed. 'You know what those places are like. Please Charlie, you have to do something. He won't make it through the night.'

Charlie put his arms around her and held her head to his shoulder. 'I'm so sorry. I've done all I can. The Magistrate can't be seen to be lenient. He won't back down any further. Come on.'

He led her, weeping, home. Nora stayed with her that night through grim, dark hours. It was too much to bear, the thought that she had let her boy down so badly. Charlie had quietly delivered another loaf of bread and some cheese and Sofia didn't hesitate to accept it. She wouldn't let Sadie down for the sake of her pride as she had Isaac. She knew she should have taken the job at the laundry the second it was offered. It was only that she'd been so sure she would find other work and desperate not to be separated from the children so many hours each day. Now the opportunity was gone. The manager wouldn't bother with her after she'd missed another appointment.

Sofia was at the workhouse gates before seven the next morning. It was vast, four storeys high with barred windows. She knew that inside there were separate wings for men, women, boys and girls less than fourteen years old. Children were only allowed to stay with their mothers until they were two, then separated. These days there were so many lying hungry in the slums that you had to apply to be allowed in.

There was a hush surrounding the building, the only sound the occasional cry from the hospital wing where they housed the insane along with the sick and dying. Perhaps prison would have been the better option. This was a cruel way to show leniency.

She rang a bell until a hunched man shuffled out.

'I need to speak with someone about my son. He was brought here yesterday on the Magistrate's instructions,' she said. He let her in and she followed him to a door. Inside she was led up a staircase and along a dim corridor into a large room with a table at one end and a chair a good distance from it where she was told to sit. A few moments later a puffed-up man smoking a pipe entered and sat behind the table.

'Mrs Logan, I am the Master here,' he said. 'Your son's causing us a deal of trouble. He shouldn't be here, by rights, it's only as a favour to the Magistrate. He's done nothing but cry and moan since he got here.'

'Can I see him?' she asked quietly.

'No, Madam, you cannot. Your son is a criminal. He will still not admit his crime and is on low rations and work duty until he does. Furthermore, he was uncooperative overnight. He wouldn't be quiet when the other boys were sleeping. He was taken aside and dealt with. You may write to him and I urge you to instruct him to reconsider his story. I gather you've found yourself in some personal difficulty. I am willing to consider an application for you and your other child to be housed here. You'll have to work, of course, laziness is the disease of poverty, but we provide three meals a day and a bed.'

'I'm not bringing my daughter to this place,' she replied, horrified. 'This is no place for children. See you keep my son safe. If he is hurt in your care, I'll...'

'You'll what, Mrs Logan? Do you think you're the first to tell me what you think of the Workhouse? You've no job, no husband, two children and no means of keeping them. You might be glad of this place one day and we'll see how you speak to me then.' He stood abruptly and left, leaving Sofia shaking. For all her hatred of this place and the man who ran it, here at least her boy was being fed. It was a terrible thought, that they could provide better care in this grey, soulless place than she could at home. She felt utterly broken. She could do nothing more for Isaac. Even Charlie could do nothing else to help. There was only one thing left to do.

Emmett Vinsant was not in. Sofia was reduced to pleading with Captain Thorne who promised to pass her message along. Exhausted, she retreated home. For hours Nora comforted her and told stories of her childhood in Ireland. Sofia did her best to play with Sadie but part of her was still in the workhouse, smelling the sloppy gruel that would be breakfast cooking in the kitchens, listening to the silent pain of the poor who had ended up voluntary prisoners within, wondering what the Master meant when he'd told her Isaac had to be dealt with. When his shift was over, Charlie appeared with milk and turnips. He made Sadie a toy boat from an old newspaper while Nora chopped the vegetables. Sofia rocked herself in the chair, sometimes hearing the conversation around her, mostly not. She wondered if Thorne had even passed on her message then decided he wouldn't dare not to. Why had she turned down Vinsant's offer of work? If her mother could see her now, her family separated by those iron gates, she wouldn't hesitate to tell Sofia she'd done the right thing.

When she heard knocking at the door, she barely had the energy to look up. Charlie opened it to find Emmett Vinsant himself standing there with an arm around Isaac's shoulders. Sofia was across the room to grab him before a single word was spoken, clutching him to her chest. Isaac said nothing at all, just clung silently to her.

Charlie and Nora let themselves out. When Sofia could speak, she turned to Vinsant.

'How did you do it?' was all she could say.

'The Magistrate and I have several mutual friends. When he realised your husband used to work for me it didn't take much persuading to release the boy. The workhouse had only to be paid compensation for housing him overnight and they were happy to remain discreet about the matter. I was glad to help.'

'I've been so foolish. Every time I think I'm doing the right thing, I make matters worse. I'd like to take the job, if it's still mine to ask for, Sir.'

He smiled kindly and she was ashamed to remember how badly she'd thought of him after Tom's funeral. What can have been going through her mind to have believed him so low, she wondered. He had saved Isaac, and in doing so had saved her too.

'Very well, but you must make sure the children are properly cared for while you're working. We don't want any more incidents like this one, do we son?' Isaac didn't respond, only burying his head on his mother's shoulder.

'Isaac, answer Mr Vinsant right now. I want your word there'll be no more stealing,' Sofia said, more sharply than she'd meant. He jumped out of her arms and ran for the bedroom before she could catch him.

'Leave him,' Vinsant said. 'He's still scared but you can be sure he's learned his lesson. What boy didn't make a mistake or two growing up? The driver has a basket of food from Mrs Hasselbrook. I'll leave you to your children,' he said.

'Mr Vinsant, thank you. I don't know what I'd have done if you hadn't stepped in. I owe you everything. I'll do whatever I can to make it up to you,' Sofia said. Vinsant tapped her on the shoulder sweetly and returned to his carriage.

The basket that Silverman brought in was packed full of meat, cheese, bread, biscuits and even a bottle of wine. It was incredibly generous after everything Mr Vinsant had already done. She had been so wrong, she thought, letting her past demons control her. She wasn't a child any more. Whatever she'd done then, however scared her mother had been for her, those years were long since gone. This was her chance to make everything right and Mr Vinsant would see that no harm came to her. It was a fresh start.

She carried Sadie to the bedroom where she found Isaac already tucked up.

'You haven't taken off your clothes,' she said. 'Let me help you.'

'No,' he said rolling over and staring at the ceiling.

'Isaac, don't be silly. Take your clothes off now.' He looked blank for a moment then complied slowly.

Sofia froze. His back was woven with welts, sore and burning red. She reached out to touch his skin but he flinched.

'Who did that to you?' she asked hoarsely.

'They used the cane when I couldn't stop crying last night.' Sofia couldn't breathe. It was unthinkable that anyone could be so violent to a child. 'They said they would teach me to lie. But I wasn't lying, Mummy, I didn't steal that money.'

'Isaac, hush, let me bathe your back,' she said choking back tears. Fetching a bowl of warm salt water, she dabbed at the flayed skin.

'It wasn't me,' he said. 'Someone put that in my bag. I wouldn't take Mrs Weston's purse. The man said he saw me but he can't have done.'

Sofia put a shirt over his back to keep the wounds clean. 'Darling, why would he lie? I know you were upset about Sadie fainting but you shouldn't have done it.'

'But I didn't, I told you, it wasn't me!'

'Isaac, that's enough. I can't cope with this now. You're back, that's all that matters. I'm just grateful you didn't end up in the gaol. No more talk of it, do you understand? I can't bear to think how close I came to losing you. You need a few days to heal then I'll find you a new school. You should write a letter to thank Mr Vinsant. Now you need some sleep.' She kissed him on his cheeks and forehead before closing the bedroom door and returning to the chair by the fire.

Every time she closed her eyes she saw the marks on his back and imagined the pain of each blow. The blame for his crime lay with her. She should have been the one left scarred and fearful. She had to create a better life for them. The workhouse Master would be burning in hell before she or either one of her children stepped through those gates again. She would do whatever it took. As for working at the club, she was strong enough not to start gambling again. She would be there to work, to earn money, not to get sucked into the thrill of throwing a dice. Vinsant knew all he needed to know about her. The rest of her past she could keep hidden. Needs must, Sofia chanted to herself as she finally fell asleep. Needs must.

Chapter Six

December 1905

It had been more seamless than she'd anticipated, the transition into a working woman. In spite of all Isaac and she had endured to reach this point, she was proud of herself, supporting the family from her own earnings. It was liberating. Tom had always earned the money while she kept house and she'd loved every second of it, waiting for him to come through the door no matter how late, house clean and dinner waiting. He'd been gone three months and there still wasn't a day she didn't wake up and reach out for him, but with every passing morning the shock was slightly less when her hand found only cold sheets and empty space. Daytime was hardest, once the children had taken their arguments and laughter off to school, but her working hours meant she needed to sleep then. The children had barely noticed the change. Although she might be tired, she was always there to cook tea, read with them and tuck them into bed.

When she'd accepted the job, Vinsant had sent her the details of a dressmaker. As a result she had three beautiful gowns, tight waisted with flowing satin skirts and light billowing sleeves, she would never have been able to afford from her own purse. Her first night at the club had been disconcerting. She had felt out of her depth and outclassed, but the other bonnets and dealers had been kind, welcomed her and explained any unfamiliar games. Soon, she was able to lose herself in the excitement, given money at the start of the night, knowing Captain Thorne would ensure it was all accounted for at the end of her shift. She gambled, chatted and encouraged the real players until five each morning. Lefevre was there to answer her questions and tell her how she was doing. He always insisted on making tea for them both during their short breaks. It became their ritual, those few minutes together. He would ask about the children, even Nora, and what Sofia had done during the day. As the days multiplied into weeks she looked forward to her conversations with him as much as she did the whirl and bustle of the tables. She found out that he was from Paris, although he laughed about it as if embarrassed that he was something of a cliché. Sofia loved to hear his tales of Monaco where he had trained as a dealer, with gambling clubs mysteriously burning down and being rebuilt grander than ever, the numerous attempted robberies and one jealous wife who had shot her husband dead as he sat at a roulette wheel with his mistress. Lefevre was never lacking a scandalous story.

Sometimes, in a more serious mood or when Sofia seemed down, he would recount a snippet of conversation with Tom or an amusing moment they'd shared. When Sofia probed more deeply into what work Tom had done for Vinsant at the club, Lefevre would retreat into Frenchness, raising shoulders and eyebrows in an exaggerated shrug and muttering that he had no idea. He was protecting her, she thought, but no amount of questioning would change his resolute vagueness. Lefevre was the only person at the club with whom she felt she could be herself. The other staff were friendly enough but it was superficial. Everyone was out for themselves and why shouldn't they be? Lefevre, in spite of his aloof facade, was the heart and soul of the place.

They were long nights and Sofia's back took the brunt of the punishment but she never complained. It was a small price to pay for regular work. By the time she arrived home in the mornings, Nora would be tidying and ready to go. It was the perfect arrangement in so many ways that Sofia couldn't believe how lucky she was. She'd kept her promise to Vinsant and told Nora that she was an administrative assistant. Nora had stared at the fine dress she was wearing with a disbelieving expression but said nothing. The lie felt pointless and grubby. Sofia didn't really understand why her friend shouldn't know the truth but a deal was a deal. Mr Vinsant was being sufficiently generous that he was entitled to set his own terms.

The only excitement so far was Sofia's discovery that one guest had been successfully using a card counting scheme. He'd been winning hands of twenty-one so regularly that his luck took him well out of the bounds of probability. Sofia checked her theory by distracting him with talk, loud laughter and her hand upon his arm. Sure enough, he lost the next several rounds miserably. Mr Vinsant was so pleased with her that he agreed to write off Doctor Bader's outstanding fee in thanks. Sofia was delighted. She felt valued, important and was in her element drifting from table to table, receiving admiring glances and offers from the single men, and occasionally from the married ones too when their wives were absent. Turning them down with a friendly word was easy. Sofia had no interest in them other than to help them part with their money. It was never dull. She moved between Mr Vinsant's three clubs so that the guests didn't see her too often at any one venue but was always most at home in St James'. When she remembered how hard the decision to take the job had been, she felt foolish. She loved to play the tables with the other guests but she could leave it there. The cards didn't entice her as they used to. Her mother could rest easy.

As the carriage took her home that morning, the shop windows were decorated with the reds and greens that heralded the coming of Christmas. She called for the driver to stop so that she could look in a store window at the most beautiful clockwork toys she had ever seen. Peering through the glass, it was like a fantasy world. A train sat on tracks surrounded by sparkling snow. Tiny houses were finished in minute detail, laughing model children smiled with joy at piles of presents left by Saint Nicholas and the scene was finished with a black velvet curtain upon which glimmered golden stars. Sofia reached out a delicate hand and made believe that Tom was standing next to her, making secret plans as they had always done at this time of year.

'Would Isaac like the train, do you think, my love?' she asked in a low voice. The imaginary man next to her reassured her that their son would love nothing more. 'And Sadie? What about the clockwork rabbit? I'll wrap it in pink ribbon.' Tom, in Sofia's vision, kissed her, and told her that Sadie would be the happiest girl in the world on Christmas Day. 'I'll make up for all they've suffered. You'll see. I shall give them the best surprise they've ever had. You'll be proud.' She let her hand drop back to her side, a lump rising in her throat.

At home, Nora was making the children breakfast.

'You're late. Everything all right?'

'Nora, spend Christmas with us. I'll do the cooking, you won't have to lift a finger. Please say yes.' Sofia took the bread from her and began cutting chunks off.

'What's brought this on?' Nora put plates on the table. 'It's a few weeks off yet.'

'I know, it's just that I don't want them to spend Christmas thinking about their father,' Sofia replied softly so that the children wouldn't hear. 'Having someone else here to play games and distract them would help, that's all. It shouldn't be a sad day. They deserve better than that. And I want to thank you for all you've done. What do you think?'

'Of course I will, silly girl. Have to turn down all the other invitations I've had though.' Nora stuck her nose in the air and sniffed. 'Going to be some very disappointed people out there.' They laughed and Sofia slipped an arm around Nora's waist, kissing her on the cheek as she picked up the butter.

By the time Sofia arrived at work that evening her good mood had been dampened by the price tags on the toys she wanted for the children. Lefevre was his usual astute self, prying insistently until she told him what was wrong.

'It's nothing, Monsieur, just money, the same problem we all have.'

'But you are paid well, are you not? Surely it's more than enough for you and the children.' 'I just wanted to make Christmas special, to make up for all they've been through. I don't have the sort of money I need for that.' Sofia was tidying her hair before facing the guests when Lefevre peered over her shoulder into the mirror.

'Why don't you join the game? The other bonnets and dealers sometimes play together after the club has shut. Mr. Vinsant doesn't mind. He says it keeps them sharp. You're a better player than any of them.' He was tucking a strand of hair behind her ear when Captain Thorne entered.

'Monsieur Lefevre. I think Mrs Logan is ready for work now, don't you?' He held the door open for Sofia. She expected him to stay and talk with Lefevre but he followed her to the tables.

'The closed games aren't for you,' he said. 'The men like to unwind on their own. Lefevre shouldn't have mentioned it.'

'Thank you, Captain, but I don't need your advice.' She looked at his hard face and wondered if there was any tenderness left inside.

'It wasn't advice.' He walked away as the dealers filed into the room. Sofia stared after him. The games would be authorised by Emmett Vinsant himself. Nothing happened here without his say so. One good win would be enough to get her the extra she needed for Christmas. After that she wouldn't play again.

The night dragged as she waited to talk to Vinsant. She caught Thorne checking on her a couple of times at the Hazard table although there was nothing the guests could do to influence the dice. The only scam was to estimate probability in their heads and few could do that at speed, especially given how much alcohol most of them consumed. It was the ones who made one drink last an hour or more who needed watching. They were concentrating, here not just to play but to win. Sofia had learned that watching the cards was futile. The story was in their faces. The stress, the concentration and the tics and twitches that revealed all.

At last it was five in the morning and the stragglers were being gently ushered to the exit. Vinsant was in his office talking to Thorne when Sofia knocked. The Captain had a hand on his gun before he'd even turned his head. He was a man who would shoot first and worry about consequences second, thought Sofia. She supposed that was why Vinsant kept him so close.

'Mr Vinsant, might I speak with you?' she asked.

He nodded for her to enter but Thorne kept his seat as she took hers.

'That's quite all right, Captain. Perhaps you would go and see that the maids have begun cleaning.' He waited until his man had exited then smiled at Sofia.

'I've been meaning to speak with you. You've settled in well, I hope, Mrs Logan.' He could be charming, she thought. When he smiled it was generous and unguarded. He had given her so much already. She hoped it wasn't tempting fate to ask a further favour.

'I'm very happy and I wanted to thank you for all you've done,' she said. Vinsant bowed his head and allowed her to continue. 'I hope you don't mind my asking but I was told there were other games, after hours, and I thought you might give me permission to play.'

'Sofia, may I call you that? Forgive me for sounding paternalistic, but do you not think your children need you once your work is over for the night?'

'But I only want to play a single game and it's my children I'm thinking of, Sir. I'd like to do more for them this Christmas, especially Isaac after, well, you know what he suffered,' she said.

'Indeed and I was only glad to have played a part in returning him to you. You're a gifted player, my dear, but your colleagues take no prisoners when they play for their own money. I have only your best interests at heart. I really couldn't give this my blessing if I thought it would end badly.'

Sofia balked at the thought that he considered she was at risk of losing. Having spent the last two months proving that she was a match for anyone, guest or staff, she felt the sting of a slight and it made her all the more determined.

'I wouldn't ask unless I was sure I could cope. I give you my word that I won't let it affect my work. I know my limits.'

59

'You're sure there's nothing I can say to dissuade you?' he asked. Sofia shook her head. 'Very well, then you have my permission. Be sure to come to me if you have any concerns.' Sofia excused herself, proud that she hadn't allowed herself to be put off. Lefevre told her there was a game arranged for the next night and she went home contemplating what colour box each child would like best for their gift.

By the time she finished work the following night she knew her colleagues had been told to expect her for the game and they seemed unvexed in spite of Thorne's warning. The game of choice was Quadrille with a pack of forty cards and complex rules. Sofia had her fair share of trump cards and won enough rounds not to be down on her money by the end but she hadn't made any substantial profit. The other bonnets were lively and brash during the game and it made Sofia feel oddly at home. It was like being back where she'd learned to play, with raucous laughter and cursing accompanying the waves of victories and losses. The game had been good for her. It was innocent fun, moderate stakes, low pressure. Next week they'd be playing twenty-one and she couldn't bear to miss it. She was determined she would win what she needed then and that would be the end of it. She kissed an unusually sullen Lefevre goodnight and all but skipped through the door of the club to the carriage.

Seven days closer to Christmas and Sofia was more desperate than ever to spoil Isaac and Sadie. The city's shops were bursting with holly, ivy and candles. Guests at the club were served mulled wine generously laced with the best brandy and Sofia could smell cloves before the front door was even opened. She was to have three days holiday starting on Christmas Eve and was practically counting down the hours until she could lie in bed cuddling her excited children, later enjoying the small feast she'd already prepared a hundred times in her head.

That night, she and the other bonnets agreed to pay a dealer to stay late so that none of them had to sit out to deal. Sofia knew there was no strategy that could fool the others, they'd all been at the tables long enough to spot patterns of play. She would be counting cards of course, it was second nature, but she had to be careful to hide it, able to chat and laugh as she had the previous week. The first few hands she won and lost randomly. Then Sofia put a larger bet on than she had in all the previous hands together and the dealer stole a glance at Lefevre who'd come in to observe. He gave a discreet nod and the dealer accepted the bet. Drawing a pair of eights she cursed her bad luck, staring at the pile of money she'd so confidently staked. She split the hand and told the dealer to add another card to each. The first addition was a four. Sofia had no choice but to go again and a queen appeared. The dealer turned the dead hand over and waited for Sofia to tell him what to do with the second.

I can't lose this, she told herself. It's too much money. I bet too much again. Why did I do that? She kept her face placid but inside she was burning. Losing the sort of money she'd put on the table would not only mean no presents, it would leave the most meagre of Christmases.

She nodded at the dealer and he turned her a ten. The hand was good enough that she could stick and hope the dealer couldn't match her score or she could gamble, really gamble, in a way that probability demanded she shouldn't.

'Another card,' she said and the noise around her faded as he revealed it. She saw the flash of red before the number and it took a few seconds before she realised a three had made twenty one. The dealer went bust.

Sofia went home with an extra four pounds and five shillings, amounting to nearly eight weeks' wages. She had stopped straight after her win, not fool enough to tempt fate. It was all she wanted and more. The next day she planned her trip to the toy shop and the butcher to order the goose. Back home she hugged Nora as if she hadn't seen her for weeks then watched over her babies until they woke.

She had earned it, she thought. She'd been brave and gambled at the right time. It wasn't recklessness but the benefit of experience. Worrying about how close she'd come to losing was pointless. Surely she should be able to enjoy the victory a little? Sofia counted and recounted her winnings until the sharp fear of losing she'd felt during the game slipped away.

Chapter Seven

January 1906

The club was too quiet, Sofia thought. It made the hours drag. When there weren't enough people on the tables it was impossible to get big games going. After the lavishness of the festivities, everyone seemed to be staying at home. The regulars still attended but spent more time relaxing in the lounges. The serious gamblers came in late and played for an hour or two but the atmosphere was lacklustre. When there was nothing else to do, Sofia would lose herself in memories of the children's faces on Christmas morning.

Sofia had made the children wait until Nora had arrived before opening their presents, but she'd been in the house only seconds before they were shouting to be allowed to open their boxes. Isaac couldn't speak, spellbound by the beautiful toy until he threw himself into his mother's arms, thanking and hugging her. Sadie cried and refused to take her toy out of its box for a whole hour in case she broke it. Sofia gave Nora a bottle of French brandy, obtained by Lefevre at a very reasonable price, and new winter gloves. It was only a token given the help she'd been and Sofia was thrilled to see the joy on her friend's face. For herself, Sofia had bought a hat and scarf that she could wear to play outside with the children when the snow came, and for travelling. Even in the carriage it was awfully cold in the small hours and she needed the extra warmth. The goose was succulent and there was enough left over for a few more meals. They played games all afternoon, read books by the fire and imagined what Tom would have made of it all.

'Mummy, if I give my rabbit back, can I have Daddy home instead?' asked Sadie, clutching the newly named Mrs Bun to her chest. Sofia fought back tears and knelt on the floor with her daughter.

'Darling, nothing can bring Daddy back but he knows how much you love him if you're willing to give up your present. I'll leave a plate of food for Daddy when you've gone to sleep tonight so that when it's quiet he can come and share our meal. What do you think of that?'

Sadie nodded, satisfied, her attention back on the rabbit. Isaac said nothing, staring into the fire. It had been much harder on her boy who missed his pa every day but rarely spoke of him. Sofia kissed his head tenderly.

'We'll be all right, sweetheart. It might not be exactly the way it was before but this is a new start. I miss him, too.' Isaac said nothing, adding another log to the fire for something to occupy his hands. Apart from that brief touch of sadness, it was wonderful. It hadn't been hard to provide such a memorable day and she still had a few shillings left over. When Nora asked where the money had come from, Sofia had invented a generous Christmas bonus. Nora didn't need to know the truth. The information would be met with either a lecture or quiet disapproval. It would be the last lie, Sofia promised herself. After all, there would be no need for any more.

In the boredom of a quiet evening, one of the other bonnets sidled up to Sofia and whispered in her ear.

'Playing tonight? Mr Vinsant said we can have the room for an hour after closing.'

'Sorry, William, but I'm out.'

'Oh, come on,' he badgered. 'You took all that cash off us, least you can do is give us a chance to catch up!' She smiled but shook her head and was pleased to be rescued by guests approaching the table. 'Think about it,' was William's parting shot.

The prospect of joining another game had been playing on her mind. It wasn't just a treat to have fed the children so well over the holidays, it was a relief. Knowing that she could provide a good cut of meat, the freshest vegetables and fruit, felt like an insurance policy against the oncoming influenza season. Extra money could be put away in case the doctor was needed again. She continued to justify it as the evening progressed, ignoring the excitement she felt at the chance to pit her wits and luck against the others. She didn't acknowledge how good it would feel to win a hand, nor the exhilaration when the cards were waiting to be picked up. She couldn't admit that she simply wanted to stay. So when William caught her eye later she gave him the tiniest nod, carefree and confident of what she was doing.

Lefevre was already pouring tea when she went for her break. He too was in a duller mood than usual. Sofia struck up conversation to fill the quiet.

'You know, Monsieur, you never told me why you came to England. Monaco and Paris seem so glamorous. Why did you leave?'

Lefevre handed her a china teacup and saucer, and mopped up stray tea leaves. He seemed a million miles away, as if he hadn't heard her question, but as he sat down he began to speak.

'In 1895 I found a position in one of Paris' most exciting and notorious clubs. I was working as assistant to the Maitre d' and it was heavenly. Every other person who came through the door was a writer, a painter or an actor and it was an adventure, you know? Then I fell in love. His name was Bertrand and he was like a god, tall and dusky skinned. For a few months it was everything I'd ever dreamed but the more I wanted him the more he grew bored. I should have known it would not last. He was always too good for me. When he took up with a new lover I couldn't bear to see him but still he came to the club. It was too much. I wanted to be as far from there as I could, so I came to London. Wet and grey perhaps but better than the Paris I left.' He seemed so melancholy that Sofia didn't know what to say. She reached out a hand instead and slid her fingers over his. He jumped at her touch. 'You must not feel sorry for me,' he said. 'It took me some time to recover but I found love again. It is very precious. I feel terrible for the loss you have suffered.'

'It's getting better,' Sofia replied. 'Of course I have bad days. But Christmas was wonderful, being able to spoil Isaac and Sadie. And tonight, thanks to your suggestion, I have a chance to win a little more and treat them again.' Lefevre pulled his hand from beneath hers, standing abruptly and collecting the china.

'You should go,' he said. 'Thorne will be studying his pocket watch.'

Sofia was surprised when she found out that the game that night was to be Baccarat. Had she known in advance, she might not have joined. There was no part of it that the player could control. Everyone was dealt two cards, their value was calculated according to the rules and the player with the highest score would win. Sofia had always thought it a game for children or fools. The dealer controlled the pack and luck controlled the cards. Many clubs had refused to allow the game to be played since the Royal scandal a decade and a half ago and Sofia was pleased. She couldn't make a fuss, though, and appear unsporting.

The game that night was short-lived. Sofia lost the second hand and the third and was down several shillings by the time Lefevre walked in. 'Mr Vinsant would like to show a private guest around. He requests that you end your game early tonight. You have ten minutes to ensure everything is in place.' Sofia stared at him, aghast.

'But we've only been playing twenty minutes.' Lefevre shrugged his shoulders and walked away. Sofia went after him.

'Monsieur, I am out of pocket this evening. If we leave now I'll have no chance to win it back. Can't we use a different room?' Her voice was more shrill than she'd realised and Lefevre gave one of his disapproving frowns.

'Mr Vinsant has said that everyone is to leave. There will be another game later this week, I guarantee. You should go home, Sofia, you look out of sorts.' He left her alone in the hallway, fuming both at her stupidity and at how desperate she'd sounded.

By the time she got back to Brewhouse Yard Sofia's mood was turbulent. She had lost money. Enough that it wouldn't affect the household payments but she hated to lose. Her frustration evolved into anger, mild at first but as she tried to sleep the heat inside her grew. It was the fault of the other bonnets. They had deliberately chosen a game with no skill required. That was no game at all, in her opinion. They had as good as stolen her money. Well, she would win it back. The plain facts were that she was the superior player and a woman, and they resented her for it. Next time she would choose the game and not for the pathetic stakes lost tonight. Her money would be back in her pocket within a week, ten fold.

The next night no one wanted to stay late after work. Perhaps, she thought, she had been too forward, too obvious. The games were for fun, a chance for the bonnets to relax. She rethought her strategy and knew she should wait until invited. It irked her but she knew she must be friendly and appear disinterested. Secretly she studied the bonnets, watching for the unique mannerisms that showed their strengths and weaknesses. Three more days to wait and it felt like torture. The joy was gone from it now. She had to play. She had to win.

The game of choice was twenty-one. Lefevre had offered to act as dealer and it started well. Sofia made back the lost shillings and the cards seemed to favour her. William soon threw in his hand, declaring Sofia's talents unnatural and, although he laughed as he spoke, his words stung. It marred her confidence and during the next hand she became muddled, lost count and couldn't predict the cards effectively. Then she over-bet and went bust, leaving the dealer an easy victory and her back down to the same money she'd started with.

Hands came and went but Sofia couldn't get into her stride. The others were talking to her constantly, asking about the children, about Tom and her future plans. Finally she gave in. She'd lost enough for it to hurt tonight. After a large glass of brandy she knew she shouldn't have had, she gathered her things and watched Lefevre slipping into Vinsant's office. She had thought her employer gone for the night. Perhaps he was avoiding his wife. In the few months she'd been in his employ Sofia had never seen the couple together.

It felt like a long journey home. She could pretend that it wasn't her fault, that the losses didn't matter, but she knew better. She hadn't been able to stop when she should have. Occasional bad luck was unavoidable, losing was part and parcel of playing, but continuing when the tables had turned was stupid. Half a month's wages gone. The past felt all too close, as if the intervening fourteen years hadn't happened. It had always been the same when she was beaten. There was the humiliation, self-loathing, the sensation that she had been wronged, followed by the sure knowledge that next time she would win. Sofia knew it would result in an obsessive day of shuffling, dealing, counting, testing the odds. It had been the same every time. Except with Bergen. The last time she had over-bet and lost like this, she'd believed with her whole heart that would be the end of it. When she lost then, of course, there was so much more than just money at stake.

Chapter Eight

Childhood 1891

Someone will stop him, Sofia thought as Bergen dragged her up the stairs. One of these doors will open and they'll see what's happening. But in spite of her sobbing, ignorant of her noisy pleas, not one door moved. Too quickly they reached the German's room and he pulled her inside. She felt bile rise in her throat and clutched her stomach. Bergen handed her a bowl before she could foul his room. As she was sick, he poured a glass of water.

'Rinse your mouth out,' he said. She realised that nothing, no tears, no amount of sickness, would soften him. He tossed the key on top of a battered wardrobe in the corner and drew the sackcloth curtains.

'If you scream,' he said, 'I will gag you. It does not bother me either way but it will be easier for you if you are not bound.' Silent tears ran down Sofia's face. She wouldn't scream. She didn't want anyone to see her with him, knowing he would tell them she had bet her virginity with a stranger more than twice her age. 'Come here.' He sat on the bed and motioned for her to stand before him. She shuffled her feet and he didn't rush her. He was enjoying it, she knew. It was all part of what he'd bet on. She wanted to take it back, to be in her caravan, in her own bed. She would never go out again. If it would all just stop, she would never, ever go out again. Sofia was shivering so hard her jaw chattered. He made no comment but turned her face slightly so that the lamplight caught it more fully.

'You are beautiful. It must feel good knowing that men look at you and want you. Powerful, yes? You knew I wanted you. You knew and still you made the bet. Take off your dress.'

'Please don't hurt me. You seem kind and this really isn't what I want. I'm so sorry, I'll get you double your money. Just let me go.' He said nothing. 'Please, I want to go home.' As she began to sob again Bergen smiled broadly and Sofia knew, as certainly as she knew it was still hours until dawn, that it was exactly what he had been waiting for.

'You know what I don't like, Sofia? I don't like women who tease. You gambled like a whore and now I'm going to teach you how it feels to be one. I told you to take off your dress.' She wished the world would swallow her up, to be anywhere but there. 'Do it!' he yelled and even as she cried out, she began fumbling with her buttons. She thought he would lose his patience but he didn't. With every second that her terror grew, she saw him become more relaxed. Her head was spinning and she fought to stay on her feet. He was inspecting her as if she were a circus freak. Sofia put a hand out to steady herself, certain she would lose consciousness but still his face loomed before hers as he licked his lips. Finally she was in her vest and drawers, shoulders hunched, arms wrapped around herself, for what pathetic shelter they gave.

'Now remove my clothes,' he said and rested back on the bed, leaning on his elbows to watch. Sofia tried to reach his shirt buttons without needing to touch the bed but he had moved too far back and she had no choice but to put one knee up along side him. Her hands were shaking so badly that each button became a jigsaw puzzle. His eyes crawled over her body and with the repulsion she felt came the fire of adrenaline. She gritted her teeth.

The slap came from nowhere. It was brutally hard and delivered with a chilling vehemence. Her cheek burned as if her face had been shoved in a fire. Her nose was dripping blood but she stayed completely still with the realisation that this man could, and quite possibly would, kill her if she angered him further.

'Look at me like that again and I will fuck you first with my prick and follow it up with my knife.' He reached under his bed and grabbed a long, sheathed knife. Sofia glanced at it but was more captivated by Bergen's face. She knew what a knife was. The creature in front of her, though, was something different than he had been earlier. His face was a twisted sneer, his teeth bared in a way that was more animal than human.

'All right. I'm sorry. Don't hurt me,' she whispered. He nodded.

'Get on with it,' he muttered as he threw the knife back under the bed and lay down. Sofia was quiet, even the shake scared from her fingers. This wasn't about sex any more. It was about surviving the night. She undid the buttons of his trousers, trying not let her fingers brush the insistent upward pressing of his penis, staring at the ceiling.

'Watch,' he said. 'Look away again and you'll be sorry.' Sofia did as he said. She began to count slowly in her head, telling herself that time was just numbers and that if she counted high enough then morning would come. He could control her and what happened here, but not the passage of time. She tried not to see his grimy underclothes or breathe in the stench of his unclean flesh.

Bergen pulled her by the arms so that she sat astride him. He was panting now and Sofia knew the little control he had left wouldn't last much longer. She tried to lift herself off his body but he pushed her down so that she could feel his penis digging through her drawers. He slid his hands up her arms slowly to the vest straps and then began inching her top down. She tried to force herself to let him just carry on but her instincts were too strong and she dashed his hands away. It was futile and she knew it but the feel of his fingers on her, squeezing, pinching, the sound of him gasping as he thrust at her was too much.

'You can fight me if it makes you feel better to pretend you don't want it, but you won't stop it happening. I like it when you struggle, you little bitch.' He had her vest off now and Sofia was sobbing again, shaking her head from side to side as he reached down to remove his underpants. When he wrapped her hand around his penis she began to plead, over and over, to him, to God, to anyone who might hear her terrified and alone in the dark. She promised she would never gamble again, she promised she would be good forever, she said she was sorry, she asked for help and she cried for him to stop. No one heard. He ripped at her drawers as she struggled.

'That's enough playing, get on your back,' he growled and threw her down so that she lay beneath him, shoving his knee roughly between her legs. Saliva dripped from his open mouth onto her face and she turned her head away but he grabbed her by the hair and wrenched it back round. 'No, you don't. I want to see your face.' With his other knee Bergen forced her legs wide apart and positioned himself so that he was ready to take her. He lowered his quivering body down and she could feel the awful pressure as he fought her muscles.

He gripped her throat and lowered his face to hers. 'Just stay still while I fuck you, you cunt!' he snarled. Sofia was ready to give in.

When the door smashed open Bergen was half senseless. The man was upon him before he could speak, his meaty arm around Bergen's neck, wrenching it back hard, the tip of a knife pressed into a throbbing vein.

'Get off my daughter before I slit you open,' said the voice. It took Sofia another half minute to come to her senses, overwhelmed by relief and equally ashamed that her father should see her naked, legs apart, beneath a man.

'Pa, I'm sorry,' she said. 'I didn't know what would happen.'

'Did he have you?' he asked.

'No,' she said. 'I'm all right.'

'Then get dressed,' her father replied. 'We're not finished yet.'

Chapter Nine

A tap on her shoulder had Sofia whipping round ready to defend herself. The man behind her stepped backwards, hands in the air.

'Mrs Logan, I startled you, I apologise. I just wanted to make sure everything was all right, with you getting home so much later than usual.' Sofia said nothing. She'd been so consumed with anger after losing the game that she had no idea how long she'd been standing in the street.

'Constable Danes, thank you, I just...' but the explanation wouldn't come. She was tired and tearful.

'Has something happened?' She shook her head. 'Shall I unlock your door for you?'

'I don't want anyone to see me like this,' she whispered. He looked around in the early morning gloom but no one else had ventured out into the freezing morning yet. Satisfied that they were not being watched, he took Sofia gently by the arm and escorted her a few yards up the road where he opened a door and stepped back for her to enter. She paused momentarily and he took his hand off her.

'You're welcome to come in until you feel better but if you'd rather not...' She stepped forward numbly, certain only that she couldn't bear the children to see her so upset. He removed his own coat but didn't try to take hers, then lit the fire, waited until it was properly alight and pulled up a battered but comfortable chair for Sofia. 'I'll make some cocoa unless you'd prefer a glass of wine. It's not particularly good I'm afraid.'

She very much wanted the wine but it was bad enough to be in a man's house in the early hours. God only knew what he'd think of her if she started drinking alcohol.

'Just cocoa, thank you,' she said and he boiled water and washed cups. Minutes later he handed Sofia a hot mug that she clutched to her chest. Charlie sat on a stool and poked the fire.

'It's cold, even for January. Dreadful being out on duty in this weather, takes me a good hour to thaw out after a shift.' When Sofia didn't answer he carried on, talking about things requiring no response as she sipped her drink and the colour came back to her face. Finally, Sofia realised he had gone quiet and looked up.

'Thank you,' she said. 'I'm not normally like this.' He met her wan smile with a concerned expression.

'You don't have to explain but if I can help then I'd like to. If someone has hurt you...'

'No. I did something foolish and now I have to put it right. It was my own fault but thank you.'

'I'm sure you're being too hard on yourself, Miss,' Charlie replied quietly.

'Sofia,' she said.

'Sofia then. It suits you.'

'Could I wash my face before I go? I shouldn't like Nora to see me in this state, it'll be next Christmas before I hear the last of it.'

'Of course, let me warm some water for you, won't take a moment.' Whilst he did so, Sofia glanced around. The house was of the same size and design as hers although it felt much larger with only one person inhabiting the space. Every item in view was neatly folded, stacked or hung on a variety of shelves and hooks, fireplace recently swept and not a trace of dirty crockery, cutlery or clothing in sight. It was neatly kept for a bachelor, she thought, and might have been almost too orderly if it wasn't for the multitude of pencil sketches adorning the walls. She looked more closely at the beautiful landscapes, intense portraits and still life studies.

73

'Where did you get these?' she asked.

'Oh, it's just a hobby, a way to fill my time when I'm not working. Silly really.'

'I don't think they're silly,' she said. 'You're very talented.' He said nothing, but smiled shyly. When she'd tidied herself up, he walked her the few steps home.

'Thank you. Again,' Sofia said.

'You know where I am,' he replied with a nod.

That day, sleep delivered not rest but dreams of gaming tables stretching endlessly into the distance taunting and tempting her until she snapped awake. She turned to the comfort of the whisky bottle increasingly often until it was easier to leave it beneath her bed than traipse through to the living room. The nightmare was the first of many and soon they came so often that Sofia sometimes wondered if she was asleep or awake. The children looked at her warily, although she couldn't see it through the tiredness. Nora was sometimes distant and watchful but Sofia told herself that she was paying the woman to look after the children and needn't feel guilty about the hours she was keeping. At the club too often until dawn, she lost money more than she won and had stopped keeping a tally of her remaining savings. As time sped by, Sofia realised she hadn't visited Tom's grave for a month, too tired after work to even contemplate the journey.

At work she became paranoid that her fellow staff were talking behind her back. Captain Thorne, hardly friendly before, was openly cold to her, rarely even uttering a greeting. Monsieur Lefevre was optimistic, telling her she would make up her losses, encouraging her to be positive. And if she was drinking more than before, it was only after the games, seldom during and who wouldn't want to drown their sorrows when life was treating them so unfairly? She was on a bad run, that was all. Everyone had them. She couldn't stop when she was so far out of pocket. All she needed was one good game to repair the damage to her finances then she could quit. This time, she convinced herself, it really would be for good. Emmett Vinsant was often absent. She knew that nothing happened at the club without his knowledge and didn't doubt that Thorne reported her every failure to him but if it bothered Vinsant, he did not send word. He, at least, was willing to let her make her own decisions without treating her like a child.

On the last day of the month, there was a knock at the door when she was trying, and failing, to sleep and sipping whisky to ease the process. She ignored it the first and second times, shouted at the caller to go away the third and wrenched open the door ready to be blunt on the fourth. Before her was Mr Cramborne, the landlord.

'Last day of the month, Mrs Logan. Rent's due,' he said. He was a squat man with purple mottled cheeks and hair so greasy it brought the rancid taste of cod liver oil to Sofia's mouth. Today, she swallowed her dislike and put on her sweetest voice.

'Mr Cramborne, sorry, if I'd known it was you I'd have opened the door straight away. It's not a good time right now. I'm just home from work and exhausted. Could you come back tomorrow?'

Cramborne scowled. 'Rent's due today. Tomorrow's for idiots, might never happen. I'll take my money now, thanks.'

'I'm just not feeling very well, you see,' Sofia tried but Cramborne was unmovable.

'Best hurry up then so I can leave you in peace.' Sofia scowled, thinking there were some things just as sure as death and taxes and the persistent nature of her landlord was one of them.

'Very well, give me a moment.' She closed the door although he didn't move back an inch as she did so. There was no money left in her purse. All that had gone into the club's coffers last night. Her last pay envelope was empty, too. She cursed as she pulled back the rug and dug a knife into the groove of the floor boards to take money from the hidey-hole. When she opened the tin inside, she saw only her reflection in the bottom. The notes and coins once secreted there were gone. At some time, the precise details of when and how blurred by liquor, she had squandered her safety net. Sofia opened her door again to Cramborne as he picked at a scab on his neck.

'I don't have it today. I forgot that I left my purse at work. I'll get it to you tomorrow morning, though.'

'You didn't forget to buy whisky, did you, love, judgin' by the smell of you?' Sofia couldn't argue and it wouldn't have helped. 'If I don't get all I'm owed when I knock on your door next, I'll have that house empty in less than an hour and you and your brats can see how warm these streets are at night.' She knew it was no idle threat. He walked off without a second look, Sofia's distress precisely the insurance policy he'd wanted. She watched until he was out of sight then slammed the door hard. Kicking the loose floorboard into the fireplace, she flung her arm across a chest of drawers, sending ornaments, mugs and clothes flying, pummelling the wall and finally falling to her knees. It wasn't until she gashed her arm on broken crockery that she stopped.

How had it happened? Everything she'd worked for, the pride she'd taken in having a job, her promises to the children that they would be secure. All destroyed. It was beyond comprehension. Sofia watched uncaring as blood dripped from her arm, making no attempt to stem its flow, even in that moment thinking only of playing one more hand to win back what she had lost.

Chapter Ten

February 1906

Sofia wondered how she'd made it to work. Nora had come in and cleaned up the mess without a word. Somehow that was worse than the disapproval she'd had been expecting. The children had stuck by Nora's side and Sofia didn't even try to prise them away from her for hugs at bedtime. Nora had bandaged her arm but the cut was too low to be entirely hidden by the sleeves of her evening dress. Sofia noticed Lefevre eyeing the injury and was relieved when he didn't comment. Only Captain Thorne questioned it, blocking Sofia's way in the corridor. She should have expected such ungentlemanly behaviour from him, she thought.

'What happened?' he asked.

'I slipped, smashed a mirror and cut my arm. It's barely a scratch,' she said.

'Perhaps if you spent more time at home, you'd be less tired and less prone to accidents,' he replied quietly. 'You should keep that out of Mr Vinsant's sight.'

'And you should keep your opinions to yourself,' Sofia snapped, regretting it immediately. She needed Thorne today. 'Sorry, you're right, I am tired. Could you ask Mr Vinsant if I could see him tonight, please? It's important.'

'Maybe it's something I can sort out,' Thorne said.

'I hardly think so and I don't want to share my business with just anybody. If you're too busy with your other duties I'll send a message through Monsieur Lefevre.'

She didn't see him again until nearly two in the morning.

'Well?' she snapped.

'In his office, now. Keep it brief. He only has a few minutes before his carriage is due.' Sofia wanted to sprint through the corridors but forced herself to follow Thorne sedately and hide her desperation.

At the door Vinsant ordered them to wait a moment. The moment turned into a minute, and expanded into five but to Sofia it could have been hours. She gnawed her nails and shifted from foot to foot.

'If you're that nervous, then maybe you shouldn't be going in there,' Thorne said, but before Sofia could retort the door swung open.

'Mrs Logan, what a pleasure. Come in. Do join us, Captain.'

'I believe Mrs Logan wanted to see you about a private matter, Sir. Perhaps I should check on Monsieur Lefevre?'

'Not at all, Mrs Logan knows how much I rely on you. Bring us both a drink, won't you?' Thorne did as he was told although Sofia thought he seemed uncharacteristically uncomfortable. Certainly it wasn't out of sympathy for her. More likely he found women an annoyance. She hadn't wanted to talk in front of anyone other than Vinsant but there was no way of getting rid of Thorne now.

'Thank you for seeing me,' she began.

'Of course. What's troubling you?' She was reassured by the friendly tone. Mr Vinsant wouldn't let them be thrown out onto the street. Her earlier panic seemed ridiculous now.

'I've got myself into a bit of difficulty, Sir. My landlord is threatening to evict us. I have to pay him in the morning and was hoping you'd lend me the money. You could take it from my wages over the next few months.'

'Mrs Logan, as a rule of thumb I do not lend money to my employees, you know that. I recognise that I've bent the rules for you previously but I do not appreciate being asked to continue doing so.'

'I know that, Mr Vinsant, but there's no one else I can ask.'

'One moment,' Vinsant cut in, opening a heavy ledger. He flicked through a few pages, settled on one then ran his finger down a column. 'Here we are. You've had your wage for this month, so that's gone I take it?' Sofia nodded. 'According to Lefevre's accounts, you've called forward a large proportion of next month's earnings also.' She flushed, remembering she'd insisted Lefevre write a tab against her income, confident that her luck would improve. Unfortunately, fate had been less inclined to help than Lefevre. 'So, the reality of the situation is that you would also be unable to meet next month's rent. Were you planning to ask for that as well?' His voice was harder now.

'I'll have put everything back to rights by then, Sir.' Sofia rushed.

'By gambling even more? You may be good, but you're not so masterful as to be able to beat the odds every time. It eats away at you, doesn't it, the need to win? I've seen it before and it only gets uglier. Well, not at my expense and not in my employ. If you can't handle yourself in a few friendly games then you've no business being here. I was obviously wrong when I selected you for this position.'

He was going to sack her. How could that have happened? Sofia felt dizzy. This wasn't how it was supposed to go.

'But I, I don't...' Sofia stuttered.

'It's quite simple, Mrs Logan,' VInsant said. 'I would feel concerned with you continuing to work the tables. If you cannot look after your own money then I have no faith in you being responsible for mine. Tom had notified me of your gambling addiction, of course, but I'd assumed maturity would have rectified the affliction.'

'Tom told you that?' Sofia gasped. 'I was just a child.' Sofia leant over the table towards Vinsant and Thorne grasped her arm. She tried to shake him off but the grip was solid.

'Your husband understood that there should be no secrets between a man and his servant. He recognised that I owned not only him but each of you whom I supported.'

'You don't own me!' Sofia spat. Thorne started to pull her towards the door but Vinsant held one hand up so that he loosened his grip just short of releasing her.

'Sit down, Mrs Logan, we're not done. There's still the matter of the debt you owe me.'

'Go to hell,' she cried. 'This time tomorrow I'll have nowhere to live. Why should I be worried about what I owe you?'

'Because your children still need a mother and I don't like bad debts.'

'Is that a threat?' Sofia asked.

'It is a very simple statement of fact. Did you think you would get special treatment? You are in a perilous situation, Mrs Logan, so I urge you to listen carefully.'

'What exactly is it you expect?' She sat back down.

Vinsant refreshed his brandy and took a sip. 'I want you to handle a dispute for me. Sometimes women are better able to act un-noticed. There is a man who owes me a great deal of money but he shows willingness to repay his debts. Unlike you, he can but chooses not to. He has simply moved his custom to other clubs where he will incur similar debts before moving on again. A man like that, unchecked, is bad for business and for my reputation. I have to be taken seriously so that other debtors know better then to expect leniency. He needs to be dealt with.'

'I don't understand,' said Sofia. 'What is it you think I can do that the courts or Captain Thorne can't?'

'So far as the courts are concerned, there would be questions about why I lent so much and the amount of interest incurred. Further-more, this gentleman and I have been involved in numerous contractual dealings over the years and I shouldn't like him disclosing the details for his own advantage. As for the Captain, he is too recognisable and too closely linked to me for this particular task. You, however, can disguise yourself and will just be another face in a place where men only bother to look at women's bodies.'

'I still don't see how I can get your money back.'

'I don't want the money, not any more. It's past the point where that would be good enough. What I want is for the man in question to suffer the consequences of ignoring my warnings. You are going to kill him for me.' Vinsant lit a cigar and she watched the smoke drift towards her as his words sunk in.

'You're a madman,' said Sofia, staring at Vinsant through the haze.

'I can assure you I am not. I believe passionately in paying my own debts and in having what is owed to me repaid. My business can be unpleasant but everyone who comes here understands that. I'm sure your own father taught you no differently.'

'I know how it works,' Sofia said softly. 'I meant that you must be mad if you think I can or would do that. I don't care what he owes you, I could never kill anyone.' She walked to the door.

'You did it before,' Vinsant replied.

Sofia stopped dead. 'What did you say?'

'You heard me.' Vinsant moved so that there was nothing between them. 'You killed a man. Your husband told me everything, Sofia, so can we drop the innocent act?' Sofia drew one hand back ready to slap Vinsant but Thorne was ready for her, sticking out his leg and tipping her over it so that she crashed down, smashing her cheek on the chair arm. She cried out, trying to get up in spite of the pain and the blood that was gushing down her face. Only Thorne's boot grinding her hand into the floor prevented her. 'I'm giving you a chance to keep your children safe in their home after their miserable mother gambled her income away. Think about it. It was you who asked me for help, after all. And I've called in favours to bail your son out of the workhouse once already. Would you be the cause of his return?'

'I won't do it and nothing you say can change my mind.'

'That may be so, but I make it my business to know where my associates' bodies are buried and yours, my dear, is a German fellow lying at the bottom of a chalk pit with a viciously inflicted wound to his head. Let her go,' he told Thorne. Sofia got up, holding her face with her good right hand and nursing the other under her arm. 'Sleep on it, there's a good girl. You'll see sense.'

'I'd rather cut my own throat,' she said as she backed away from Vinsant.

'It looks as if you already tried that with your arm. Didn't work, did it?' Sofia jolted at the memory. Vinsant was right, she'd brought this on herself.

She fled without even grabbing her coat, leaving Lefevre staring speechless from the doorway. No one tried to stop her. They had all known, she thought, as she ran wildly through the streets. She felt sick as she imagined Lefevre reporting her growing debts to Vinsant. Why had no one tried to persuade her not to play?

Worse than the humiliation of her debts was Tom's betrayal. There could be no doubt about it. Tom had told Vinsant everything. She stopped, exhausted, bile rising in her mouth as she leaned in a dark corner, sobbing and hiding her face against the cold, rough bricks in shame. She'd been such a fool to think she could escape her past, more of a fool to have been so trusting.

Chapter Eleven

Childhood 1891

Sofia's father never left any mistake unpunished and she knew the night he stopped Bergen from raping her would be no exception. She should have known what was coming. Romani law meted out its own uncompromising form of justice. When her father told her to get dressed she had automatically obeyed but it was only whilst lacing her boots that she realised her father was making Bergen do the same. The German was quiet and watchful, knowing a beating was coming and not stupid enough to think he could dissuade an enraged father, but he'd be waiting for the chance to escape or retaliate. He didn't know her pa, though, Sofia thought. The man was granite, neither excessively tall nor overly muscled but what he lacked in build he made up for with sheer bloody-minded fearlessness. Sofia knew every one of the scars that marked his body from knives he had grabbed rather than avoid and blows he had refused to flinch from. Broken bones were the calendar by which he re-called past years and the men he had felled were less feathers in his cap than bookmarks in the story of his life. Sofia adored and was daunted by him in equal measure.

Hands tied behind his back and a gag in Bergen's mouth, her father pushed him out of the back door of the inn with Sofia scuttling behind. She knew better than to speak. In this mood, her father wouldn't hesitate to use his fists on her before starting on Bergen. They walked briskly away from the village but at the point Sofia expected to take the path through the woods to their camp, her father pushed Bergen in the opposite direction. They continued for a good twenty minutes over increasingly rough ground, until Sofia was shivering with cold and her feet were aching from treading the stoney path.

'How did you find me?' Sofia asked when the silence finally became intolerable

'One of the men watching the game owed me a fair packet of money from last week. He rightly thought I'd let him off the debt if he came and told me what he'd seen. You've got a lot of work to do to pay me back for this mess, girl.'

In the pale moonlight Sofia could just make out the upper edges of the chalk pit when they arrived. It was unnaturally quiet, a place which seemed entirely drained of life. She didn't like it, not that voicing her feelings was an option, she knew. Her pa obviously had a purpose in mind. With the gag removed, Bergen spat into the dirt and looked coolly at her father.

'Come on then,' he said. 'If you were any sort of man, you would take the bindings from my wrists and let me defend myself.'

'I'm not here to punish you,' Sofia's father replied. 'I'm not bothered about you.' He held the blade to Bergen's throat, turned him around and pushed him to the edge of the pit. 'It's my girl who needs teaching a lesson. You're just here to help. Pick that up,' her father said, motioning to the ground at Sofia's feet. She saw a large boulder, heavy enough that it would take both hands and a huge effort to lift. 'Now!' her father shouted, startling her as she scrabbled for it, breaking her nails on its rough surface. She wasn't going to argue with him. Things would only get worse if she did. She lifted the rock and offered it to her father, thinking that Bergen was about to get a much worse beating than she'd imagined but it wasn't until he shook his head that the reality of the situation set in.

'You did this. You fix it,' her father said.

'I can't. Please Pa, I don't want to,' she said, tears falling as she spoke, knowing argument was futile but unable to conceive how she could do what he wanted.

'It's him or you, you understand? If he lives, you'll be shamed forever. You brought this on yourself, going off on your own, taking money you hid from me like a thief.'

'That's what I told her,' Bergen said in a strangled voice, cockiness gone. 'I said she should not have made the bet but I won't tell anyone what she did. Just let me go. You're right, she does need to be punished, but you don't need to hurt me.'

Sofia stopped looking at her father and turned her attention to Bergen instead. Had he really just said she needed to be punished? After what he'd done to her, was he really trying to ingratiate himself with her father? She recalled Bergen trying to force himself inside her as she pleaded with him to stop. He babbled on, saying he had no idea she was so young, how he had children himself. Her father said nothing. Sofia took one step forward, then another and the weight of the rock seemed less the closer she got. As she raised her arms, the fear left her. Of course he had to die. There was no option, she understood that now, and it was liberating, the sensation of powerlessness. She could only do as she was told. As she took her final step and stood, feet apart to steady herself, she memorised the scene: Bergen trembling, her father watching her approach, the point of his blade shoved hard into the German's neck to still him, and the darkness of the sky almost a mirror of the pit below.

'You had it coming,' she whispered to Bergen, knowing he would turn his head just enough to see her smash the rock into his skull, wanting him to understand he was going to die at her hand, relishing the desperation in his final second of life and she felt the thrill of knowing she had won in the end. When stone collided with skull there was a crunching noise, deadened by soggy flesh and splintered bone. Sofia didn't shrink from the hot spray of blood that covered her. She licked her lips and tasted him as he fell to his knees. As she let the gore covered rock fall, she kicked Bergen's back lightly and that was all it took to send him over the edge of the pit. She heard his body thud against the side, rocks rolling with him a while until there was nothing but the sigh of the wind. Eventually her father tossed the stone that had been her weapon over the edge to follow.

'Let that be a lesson to you,' he said, although the anger had disappeared from his voice, replaced by something less knowing.

'It was,' replied Sofia plainly. One she would not forget.

She returned to the camp to find that orders had been given to pack up, and went straight to her caravan. Her mother asked no questions at all, handing her soap and pointing at a bowl of water. It took a long time to wash away the blood, and longer still to pick the tiny lumps of flesh from her clothes. How did the human body work so well when it could be so easily broken, she wondered, studying the remnants that had attached themselves to her.

As she undressed for the second time that night, Sofia found in her pocket a stray penny, the only one not lost. She tucked it into one of the long woollen stockings she'd worn that evening, tied a knot to keep the coin safe and hid it at the bottom of her clothes chest. Expecting nightmares, she felt only the noisy thrum of adrenaline-laced blood in her veins. For a few days everything was normal. Almost, Sofia thought, as if nothing had happened at all. Until her mother told her she was to be sent away.

Chapter Twelve

February 1906

Sofia had made her dreadful confession to Tom after several months of marriage, the telling issued in broken pieces, with him having to prompt and make assumptions. He hadn't judged her. In fact he'd called her brave and extraordinary, reassuring her that she'd only done what was necessary. Sofia had felt the burden of the crime lift and been able to close the chapter in her mind. She'd had no idea, then, that it would come back to haunt her so many years later.

When she'd cried herself dry, she began the walk home. London's usual nighttime dangers didn't trouble her. The streets were slippery with rain and muck from the thousands of carriages and horse drawn buses. Straw had been spread to soak up the foul rivers that the streets had become, but now the fodder was brown pulp, splashing her skirt, soaking her shoes and making her stagger as the debris clumped around her feet. Inevitably she fell and rose again plastered with the composting mixture. The few people who noticed her crossed the street and no one met her eyes. She looked feral: a disturbing combination of a beautiful filthy dress, bloodied face and wild expression. Sofia tried her best to stay in the present, to decide what she should do, several times losing her way through familiar roads, sometimes seeing the edge of the chalk pit so clearly she believed she might fall, holding her hands out to steady herself like an old drunk. When she wiped tears from her face and saw blood on her hands, she thought it was Bergen's until the sting of the cut on her cheek brought her back to reality. Tom would look after her, bathe her face and put her to bed. Then she remembered that he was dead. In her mind, time continued to slip as she walked.

By the time she got home, Nora was already awake.

'What in God's name happened?' she hissed. Sofia was just grateful the children were still sleeping and staggered to a chair. Nora took a cloth, dipped it in some freezing water and began dabbing Sofia's cheek. 'Have you been attacked? I should fetch that policeman. Your eye's half black. What'll the children think? And look at your hand. Talk to me girl! Who did this?' Nora was frantic.

'I did it all to myself,' Sofia replied.

'You're talking nonsense, that blow to your head has you confused. You must change your clothes before the little ones see you, you'll frighten them half to death in that state. Come on, let me help.' Nora began tugging at her dress but Sofia pushed her away, shrinking into the chair.

'Get off me, Tom' she said. After a few moments Nora took hold of Sofia's hand.

'It's me, Nora. Look at me, pet.' With an effort Sofia did as she was told. 'You're safe at home. Tom's gone, love, but he'd have hated to see you like this.'

'Tom did this to me!' Sofia shouted and the older woman recoiled backwards into a shelf of pans. 'Tom betrayed me and now I've lost everything. I'm glad he's dead! You don't understand what he's done. I'm going to lose the house. We'll be thrown onto the streets and I've lost my job, so don't tell me I'm safe. It's over, Nora! Me and the children, we're all as good as dead.'

'Mummy? What's happening?' Isaac was out of bed, shaking. He looked terrified. She held out her arms to him but he backed away and she remembered she was covered in blood from the gash on her face.

'Isaac, I'm sorry, everything's all right. Come here,' she said. Instead, Isaac ran back to the bed where Sadie's face was barely visible as she hid under the blanket.

'Mummy didn't mean it. Please don't be scared.'

'Let me,' Nora said. 'They woke up with a start, is all. You get cleaned up while I calm them down then we'll all have breakfast.' Sofia knew Nora was right. She let her friend fuss over the children and dry their tears while she washed and put on her black dress. She slipped fingerless gloves on to hide her blackening hand and kept her hair loose to cover the worst of the injury. As the children dressed, Nora laid the table and Sofia sliced bread. Nora chattered to keep Isaac and Sadie occupied and when everyone was ready, Sofia asked the children to sit up to the table. They looked nervous but did as they were told.

'I'm sorry I scared you,' Sofia said. 'I had an accident last night and it made me very confused this morning.'

'You said you were glad that Daddy was dead,' Isaac whispered, not touching the food on his plate and trying his hardest not to cry. 'I hate you.' He ran from the table to the far corner of the room where he threw himself onto the ground and wept. Nora put an arm around Sadie as Sofia went to her son. She didn't touch him, knowing she'd done too much harm to heal easily. Instead, she sat on the floor with her back against the wall and waited while he got the worst out of his system.

'I don't blame you for saying that,' she said. 'You're right to feel angry. The last few months have been very hard. Please forgive me Isaac, I love you. You and Sadie are all I have left.' When Isaac's sobs eased he sat up, no longer pulling away but still not ready to be close to her. She didn't blame him. There was no excuse for the way she'd behaved.

'You said we were going to lose the house. I don't understand why we have to leave. Where will we go?' Sofia stared at her son's face, so like his father's, trying to be a man but just a terribly scared little boy. She put an arm around him and this time he didn't fight her.

'I'll sort it out, I promise. There's nothing to worry about. Now go and eat your breakfast before your sister finishes it all off.' He didn't look convinced but he went, and Sofia busied herself washing the blood off her dress. As it was a Saturday morning there was no school so Nora put the children in front of the fire with their books and told them to study. When they were properly distracted she sidled up to Sofia.

'What'll you do?' Nora asked.

'I don't know,' Sofia replied.

'You know I'd have you to stay with me but I've only the one room and the landlord'll be on me like a shot if I have anyone else staying there.'

Sofia put down the soap and reached one hand out to hold Nora's. 'You can't help us now, although I know you would if you could. Sorry for shouting. I wasn't in my right mind. You've been so good to us.' The knock at the door was earlier than expected but not a surprise. Cramborne had always been impatient. Sofia dried her hands and took one last look around. She wouldn't have time to pack but it didn't matter, there was nowhere to take their belongings to and Cramborne would want to keep the furniture to sell in lieu of the outstanding rent. She opened the door.

Her landlord wasn't alone this time. The two men with him were obviously intended to ensure there was no resistance. Cramborne wasn't going to waste a minute getting a new tenant in.

'Good morning, Mrs Logan. What's it to be, then? Paying up or getting out?' Cramborne asked.

'I don't have your rent, Mr Cramborne, and I know we'll have to leave but I've been out all night trying to get the money together. I need three hours to pack our things. For my children's sake, would you allow that?' Sofia asked. Cramborne's thugs leered at her.

'I'm afraid I've got people ready to move in right now. My boys here can speed things up for you though.' One of his men took a step over the threshold and Isaac rushed forward to push him back out. Cramborne grabbed the boy by his collar and held Isaac at arm's length as he kicked.

'Now then lad, you let the grown ups do what needs to be done or you'll get a thick ear. You and your sister had best wait outside.' He pushed Isaac roughly away and Sofia reached out to catch him.

'Keep your hands off my children, Mr Cramborne,' said Sofia, trying to keep her temper and save the children additional upset.

'Or you'll what? In you go lads, I want this place empty in fifteen minutes.' Sofia could hear Sadie crying inside.

'Mummy, you said it would be all right. What are they doing?' Isaac asked. Sofia had no answer. He could never understand the position they were in. The boy ran from her arms and threw himself onto the back of the man ripping Tom's clothes from the drawers. 'Get out of our house. Those were my daddy's clothes. Don't touch them!'

'Isaac, no,' shouted Sofia. 'You have to stop, we can't fight these people.' She pulled him away but he thrashed in her arms.

Nora was soothing Sadie who was crying and asking for daddy. The place was in chaos with Sofia stood still at the centre of it all, not trying to pack, not even moving. All she could see were the gates of Clerkenwell Workhouse.

A voice from the doorway cut through the slamming, banging and wailing.

'Mrs Logan, a word,' Captain Thorne called. Sofia had half hoped for this and half dreaded it.

Nora stared. 'Who's that?' she asked.

'Look after the children,' was Sofia's reply. She and Thorne walked a few steps away from the threshold.

'Mr Vinsant's offer of financial assistance stands,' he said.

'Are his terms the same?' Sofia asked, although she knew the answer.

'They are,' Thorne replied.

Sofia watched the scene unfolding inside her house. Isaac had frozen, Nora was uncharacteristically silent and Sadie was terrified.

'He'll have to pay at least three months' rent,' Sofia said.

'That's agreed,' the Captain replied. 'But you'll still owe the gambling debts. Just so you understand.'

'Of course I understand,' she bit. He stared at her and Sofia thought he had more to say but after a moment he walked towards Cramborne.

'Here,' he said thrusting a purse at him. 'Take this and leave Mrs Logan alone. Don't come back here for three months and before you go, get those louts to put everything back in order.' For a moment Sofia thought Cramborne was going to refuse the money, but she saw the uncertainty on his face, the way he eyed the carriage in which Thorne had arrived and the scar on his face, and decided better.

'It'd best all be here,' said Cramborne in a sullen attempt to have the final word but Thorne had already returned to Sofia.

'Don't come back to the clubs or any of Mr Vinsant's premises. You're not to contact him. You'll be sent word when he wants you.' Sofia nodded. 'And don't be foolish enough to think you can change your mind.' Cramborne had called his men off but ignored Thorne's order to put the place back to its original state. Sofia didn't care, she just wanted them out. Given what she'd just agreed to do, she had more than broken furniture and scattered clothes to worry about now.

Chapter Thirteen

March 1906

Vinsant sent a messenger bearing a single bulky envelope. She left it on the mantlepiece untouched until the children had gone to bed, loath to open it and make the situation more real. When she did, the first thing she saw was that Vinsant had enclosed more money. With it was a letter.

'Dear Mrs Logan, I am glad you accepted my offer of help. The Captain tells me you understand our arrangement. The enclosed will pay for food and fuel while you get back on your feet. It can be repaid in time with the other outstanding amounts. In the meantime, my men will keep watch to ensure your continued security as your late husband would have wanted.'

Sofia realised she was foolish to have worried about the letter. There was no way Vinsant would have put his instructions in writing. The messenger had even returned the coat she'd left at the club. Just as well, she'd been wondering how she would afford a new one. Nora had asked about Thorne and Sofia had told her, honestly, that he was her former employer's man and explained that the money was a loan given out of respect for Tom. She visited every evening now, even though she wasn't needed and Sofia didn't mind. Another body in the house made the place warmer and the children adored her. Sofia, too, found that having Nora to chat with, to share the local gossip and the chores, kept her from fretting about what was to come. She needed to keep her neighbour close. If anything went wrong, she had no one else to take the children in. She pushed that thought away. She had no more room for doubt than for conscience.

Two weeks later Sofia was summoned to Hyde Park where Thorne met her by the sluice gate at the eastern end of Serpentine Lake. She saw the children to school then walked through the city, enjoying the first signs of spring, still cold, but with a blue sky that softened the grey of the buildings and lightened her journey. Thorne was waiting when she arrived and Sofia's hackles rose as she saw him looking impatiently at his pocket watch. It was almost laughable, meeting him in such a beautiful place, row boats out on the lake optimistic of sunshine, the long bridge with its lazy arches rising from the still water. The unbroken horizon of trees and shrubs was so richly green that the colour was close to overwhelming but the headiness of dewy grass and damp earth was heavenly. And here she was conspiring with a man who was the opposite of all things natural and beautiful, face hidden by hat and scarf like a robber.

'I'm not late,' she said as she approached.

'You're not early,' he quipped. She didn't prolong the exchange, just stared into the dark water, waiting for her orders. 'This Friday night, Whitechapel High Street. Find number one hundred and two then go through the archway beside it into the alley. There'll be a blue door on the right. Knock twice and say you've been sent specially for their usual gentleman guest. You'll be asked no questions, but shown to a room. Be there by eleven o'clock. He'll be shown in expecting to spend his customary three hours with a whore. Settle him down, put him at ease. He always asks for brandy. When he does, you're to put this in his drink.' Thorne handed Sofia a small vial from his pocket. It didn't look like there could be enough in it to harm a grown man but he warned her. 'Take care not to let a drop of it touch your lips. It'll begin working within minutes. You must stay until he's fully dead. Do not leave until then and be sure to keep him quiet. When it's over, clean him up, get him into bed, strip his clothes off and make it look as if he died during sex. With any luck, his family will be so ashamed that they'll want to bury him quickly and without an autopsy.'

Sofia, vial tucked safely in her coat, rubbed her hands together against the chill wind. 'And what if he wants more in the first few minutes than just chat and a warm welcome?'

'Use your imagination,' Thorne answered. 'It's not as if he'll ever be able to tell anyone what happened. Dress for the part and keep as well disguised as you can. You'll have to walk there and back, Mr Vinsant can't risk a carriage.' Sofia nodded. It was bad enough that Thorne knew her business. The last thing she wanted was Vinsant's driver involved as well.

'And when I've done it? What about my outstanding debts to Mr Vinsant?'

'Get the job done first, then we'll talk.'

'What if I get caught?' Sofia asked, quieter now.

'Don't get caught,' Thorne said and for the first time since she'd met him, she saw a half smile on his face. 'But if things go wrong, you're not to mention this arrangement. Talk and Mr Vinsant has people in places you cannot imagine who will see to it that you never reach trial. Remain silent and you have Mr Vinsant's promise that your children will be raised by a good family and supported into adulthood.' It was the most Sofia could hope for and she was in no position to bargain.

'I'll contact you a few days after it's done,' he said, walking off before he'd even finished the sentence. She stayed a while, enjoying the park in spite of the cold, watching the reflections of clouds playing on the water. Hyde Park was full of warmly wrapped nannies pushing prams. It seemed so long ago that her own children were that tiny. The years had flown past and yet they were no less vulnerable. They would survive without her, as she had without her parents, but it wouldn't be the same. No one else could love them the way she did.

At home, she looked for somewhere to keep the vial that prying fingers would not go. There was no way of identifying what foul liquid it contained but Isaac and Sadie wouldn't hesitate to uncork and taste it. She waited until they were asleep then hid the delicate glass below the floor boards, grimacing at the irony of such lethal cargo filling the space where she once kept her savings.

Friday morning, Sofia told Nora she had to visit an old friend of Tom's who had been taken ill, setting off at tea-time to visit him during the evening then staying with his family a while and returning in the small hours. A few pennies spent in a pawn shop had bought some clothing that seemed appropriate and a wig she'd boiled for hours. Some of the hair had been lost as a result but it was better than lice. She found cheap rouge that would do for both lips and cheeks. The vial of poison she'd stitched loosely into the lining of her bloomers so that whatever happened, she could get hold of it. She'd also slipped a kitchen knife into her bag. If it all went wrong, she might be left fighting her way out. She kissed Isaac and Sadie goodbye, thanked Nora and left home hoping she would be back there again the next morning. If not, her children would be subject to the Vinsants' charity and that thought did nothing to warm Sofia's heart.

Sofia wandered past Whitechapel's slaughter houses and meat markets thinking she could never get used to living with the smell. It made Brewhouse Yard seem blissful. The poverty stricken migrant workers, desperate for even the bloodiest of work, had no choice in the matter. It was a grim place. Tom had told her it was the easiest district of London to obtain opium, prostitutes or weapons and she had thought then how exciting it sounded. The reality was both chilling and depressing. Sofia would never willingly have gone there alone at night. She found a busy inn at the end of the High Street and nursed a cup of ale for somewhere to sit and something to do. Hours later, crouched in an alleyway beneath her coat, she removed the clothes she'd been wearing over the gaudy red corset and black bloomers. The wig was a mass of ugly red curls, but it did its job and made her unrecognisable. She painted on red cheeks and lips then peered in a scrap of mirror. She thought she looked like a fairy tale witch but the sad truth was that no one would give her a second glance on the nighttime streets of Whitechapel. Here, it was camouflage rather than costume.

Once Sofia had found the archway, she positioned herself across the street and watched for half an hour. Every now and then a man would wander through and sometimes a woman would walk out, lighting a cigarette or swigging from a bottle. Eventually, she had no more reason to delay so she waited until it was quiet then walked across and knocked twice.

It opened immediately and she spoke precisely the words Thorne had told her. A wizened old woman, so well wrapped in layers of shawls and blankets that her only visible features were her eyes and nose, let her in muttering something foreign then shuffled off up a creaking staircase motioning for Sofia to follow. At the very top, she threw open a door. In the centre of the room was a large bed covered in what must have once been a beautiful red velvet throw, now matted and stained. There were various bottles on a sideboard and Sofia scanned them to find the brandy. She stoked the fire and made sure the curtains were fully closed, noting that the outlook was directly into houses behind. She slipped off her coat and hid her bag in a chest of drawers where she found a disturbing array of whips and leather bindings. This was a room that catered for many different tastes. None of it, she hoped, would be requested tonight. Sofia slid the knife between the mattress and base of the bed. She was tempted to open the stitches where she'd secreted the poison but it would be worse if the vial fell out before she was ready to use it. A double knock at the door below hailed the man's entry. She wondered fleetingly if his wife knew what he did on a Friday night. Most likely the lady was just glad to have the house to herself, Sofia thought.

She didn't allow herself to hesitate in opening the door. The slightest thing that seemed off would put him on guard. He looked her up and down as if she were a horse he were about to bet on, apparently decided she was fit for his purposes and entered, slamming the door carelessly behind him. She let him speak first: he would know the way this usually went.

'Hang up my coat,' he said, passing it to her. She did as she was told, taking in the immaculate cut of his clothes and the silk lining of his overcoat. If he was in financial difficulty, he certainly showed no sign of it to the outside world. To her relief he was in his fifties, paunchy and out of shape. He might be a lot heavier than her but she'd be faster. When he sat on the bed and held his legs out for her to remove his boots she knelt at his feet, keeping her eyes down.

'Don't speak much, do you? I like that. Some of the other girls do nothing but jabber from the second I get through the door. What's your name?' He took her face in his hands and turned it left and right.

'Millie,' she said.

'You're not bad looking. Take off my trousers.' He leaned back on his elbows and watched as Sofia struggled with the button holes stretching too tightly over his belly.

'Wouldn't you like a drink first?' she said.

'I'll tell you when I want something,' he replied. She spent the next few minutes removing his clothing as he arranged himself on the bed. He didn't bother to cover himself with the throw, just lay there as if she would admire his body. She wondered what enjoyment he could get from it, knowing the woman servicing him wasn't there by choice. He was as far from appealing as she could imagine. 'Take off the corset.'

Sofia gave a nervous cough as she began to unlace the front. 'Do you mind if I pour myself some wine?' she asked.

He looked surprised. 'The girls here aren't usually supposed to drink anything. I thought you were new. Go on then, but not too much. You've got work to do.' Sofia cleaned a glass. 'Might as well get me a brandy while you're there,' he said. Sofia rolled her eyes upwards with a silently mouthed thank you.

'Of course,' she muttered, hoping he would leave her to it, but he sat up and watched her go through the bottles. The room wasn't dark enough to give her the cover she needed to get to the vial. Sofia moved a glass to the edge of the counter and knocked it with her elbow as she poured his brandy. It shattered as it hit the floor and she managed a surprised shriek.

'I'm sorry, Sir, I'm so clumsy.'

'Oh, for God's sake,' he moaned.

'I'm a bit nervous,' she twittered. 'You were right, I've not been doing this long. I'll have it cleared up in just a minute.' She lent down and noisily pushed the fragments of glass together on the floor as she ripped the stitches in the top of her bloomers with her free hand and pulled out the vial. She put the shards in a cloth on the chest of drawers, popping the cork and pouring the liquid into the brandy. There was a second when she could smell the acidity but it was quickly masked by the strong liquor. Making sure there was none on her fingers, she handed him the glass.

'Sit down,' he said, patting the bed.

She was torn. Just drink it, she thought, finish it so that I can get out of here. But at the same time her hand itched to knock the glass from his grip. She didn't know this man, had no idea if he deserved to die or not. Sofia gulped her wine. The decision was out of her hands. She was powerless. Powerless was as close to blameless as she could get. She held up the little liquid that remained in her glass to his.

'To the future,' she smiled. He laughed at that. For a man who spent every day running from past debts, she guessed the future was the only thing left to toast.

'The future,' he echoed as his glass hit hers and he took a swig of the brandy. Sofia had to look away. He ran a sweaty hand up Sofia's thigh. She tolerated the contact, knowing it wouldn't last long.

'Let me put your drink down for you,' she whispered.

'You're eager,' he said and finished the liquor in one more swallow. 'Come on then.' Sofia toyed with clearing away their glasses and put a few more coals on the fire. 'I'm paying for sex, not a domestic servant,' he said.

'Let me just make sure the door's locked,' Sofia said as sweetly as she could manage. Ensuring the key was fully turned, she looked back to see him rubbing his stomach before belching loudly.

'Bloody wife, I should never have let her order pheasant, she knows it disagrees with me.' The first beads of perspiration were appearing on his face.

'Would you like some water?' she asked, keeping her distance.

'No, I want you to get on the bed and spread your legs. I'll be fine in a couple of minutes.' He gasped as his belly cramped, his face paling even in the glow of the flames. She shoved the chamber pot beneath his mouth as he began to retch and when the contents of his belly hit the air she smelled the bitterness. His vomit was dark red, part bile, she thought, and part blood. The coppery odour told her he was bleeding internally already. He was on his knees, eyes filling with tears as his body rebelled against the poison. When his stomach was completely empty, he tried to get up, failed and held out a shaking hand to her.

'Help me,' he said hoarsely. Sofia backed against the door, saying nothing. 'You stupid damned whore, I have to get to a doctor. Get me dressed.' A trickle of blood ran from his nose to the corner of his mouth. He wiped it with the back of his hand and Sofia studied his growing panic. He was up on one knee and reaching for his trousers when Sofia kicked the clothes beyond his grasp.

'What are you doing? You'll get your money, but I have to see my physician,' he said. Sofia had to make sure he didn't open the door but she wasn't prepared to get into a fight, terrified that if he vomited on her she too would be affected by the poison. She dashed around him, over the top of the bed and thrust her hand beneath the mattress, grabbing her knife. It took a few moments for him to focus.

'So that's it. Who paid you? It doesn't matter. I can give you more, however much it was. Look in my wallet. There's enough to keep you satisfied and I can get you whatever else you want. Just get me a carriage and tell the driver to take me to the nearest hospital.' He seemed so certain she would do as he said. Sofia tossed his wallet onto the bed unopened.

'I'm not allowed to help you,' she told him. He made it up onto both feet, swaying and lurching towards her. 'Just sit down, the worst of it will pass soon. I don't want to hurt you.' She was talking about the knife but the irony of it wasn't wasted on him.

'Don't want to hurt me?' he said. His whole body was drenched in sweat and flecks of white foam flew from his lips. Sofia backed as far away as she could. He saw her terror and tried a sudden dash for the door. Sofia launched herself at his knees. He hit the floor and curled into a ball, groaning. Sofia stood with her back against the door, barring any further attempt at escape. His was dribbling a yellowish liquid and she covered her nose and mouth against stench filling the room.

'I don't want to die,' he said. 'Don't let me die.' He held out a hand to her and Sofia made herself think of Bergen, years ago in another tiny bedroom. Bergen hadn't cared how badly he used her, just as this man wouldn't have cared if his evening had gone according to plan.

'It's not up to me,' she said, knowing she was only talking to fill the air with the sound of something other than his groaning. 'Mr Vinsant said you haven't paid what you owe. You must have known they'd come for you.' He was past responding.

Repulsed as she was by his reeking body and encrusted mouth, she stared at him. She'd missed the last few seconds of Tom's life. Gently, almost tenderly, she knelt down next to his twitching body and shifted his head to see more clearly. His eyes were circling wildly, perhaps in pain, more likely from sheer terror, fighting in spite of the sure knowledge that his time was up. When the last breath was expelled raggedly from his chest she peered closer to see what would happen but there was no mystical light, no revelation, no angels or demons appearing to collect him.

When she laid his head back down on the floor Sofia felt nothing. She waited for remorse and when none came she searched her mind for shame, but that too was elusive. What surfaced after that was hard to define. Sofia tried to be glad it was over but what she truly felt was glad she'd done it. There was a satisfaction, a completeness to it. Upon standing it was as if her legs had grown stronger and the room seemed smaller. The thrill of being alive and unharmed was intoxicating.

She couldn't think about it now, she told herself, she still had work to do and it was going to be unpleasant.

Pouring water into a bowl she washed him, getting the blood and vomit off his face and hands then scrubbing the inside of his mouth. When she'd regained control over her stomach she knew the worst was still to come and prepared by covering her mouth with a cloth as she turned his body over. As she suspected, he had soiled himself in his final minutes. She cleaned up as best she could and bagged the cloths she'd used. They had to be thrown away somewhere far from here. She hauled his body onto the bed wrapped in the throw, rearranging him under the sheets. His mouth was pulled into a grotesque gape and she put one hand on his chest as if he'd passed away grabbing at his heart.

She shoved his glass and the empty vial in her bag, making sure her wig was in place and, as an after thought, put the bottle of brandy on the bed next to him on its side, the contents sinking slowly into the bedding. Putting more coal on the fire to help burn out the stench and tidying the room to its former state, she turned her attention to his wallet. She wasn't a thief and hadn't come here to rob a corpse but she knew that no self-respecting whore would leave without payment. A full wallet would raise suspicions rather than lower them. She pulled out the notes but left the change in his pocket, checked that the knife was tucked into her waistband and made for the door. The feeling of the coins in her hand stirred a memory and she paused. She gripped the door handle, needing an anchor, pretending she didn't know what she was about to do. The door handle lost the battle. Sofia returned to the dead man's pocket where she rifled through the coins, finding the one she wanted by size and thickness, then pulled out the penny. It was a bad penny, a wormy voice chanted in her head, a bad penny. Cleaning it, pocketing it and ignoring the voice, Sofia made her way back down the stairs.

The old woman let her out without a word, Sofia's face covered sufficiently that she could never be recognised. If the stinking rags in her bag caused the woman any concern she didn't show it. Sofia was walking along Whitechapel High Street in less than a minute. She travelled for quarter of an hour before shoving most of the contents of her bag into a box of rubbish discarded in a side street, then slowly began to lose her costume. After a time, she took off the red corset beneath her coat and threw it into a bush as she walked past a tiny park. The vial she dropped down a drain and the brandy glass she smashed in the street outside a pub. As she left the physical traces behind, relief spread through her. She hadn't lost her nerve. It had been wretched and sickening but she'd been strong and brave. There was very little she couldn't do when she put her mind to it. Tom had always said he would protect her. That seemed like a sad joke now. She had never needed protecting at all. Sofia felt alive, fiercely alive, in control and powerful. Killing wasn't the way other people imagined it to be. It was deeply personal, an act that revealed the most basic, stripped down centre of yourself. A therapy, she thought. Sofia checked her racing pulse, feeling lightheaded. It had been a long day.

In Brewhouse Yard, she paused outside Charlie's door wondering if he was home or out on duty. Tomorrow, she decided, she would cook him a beef stew. She still owed him so much, more than she could ever repay.

At home, in her most secret place, a stocking lay in the bottom of an old chest of clothes, worn with age, the knot in it stuck so fast she had to work it gradually with her nails to open it up. Without inspecting the contents nestling within, she dropped in the coin.

Chapter Fourteen

March 1906

What in God's name does he think he's doing coming here this morning? Sofia wondered, stopping her scrubbing to stare through her window at Vinsant's carriage. It wasn't even twelve hours since she'd left the whorehouse. He expected a report, she knew that, but how could he be so reckless as to visit publicly? She opened her door, tidying frantically to the sound of approaching footsteps.

'Come straight in, I'm sure you don't want to be seen in my street,' she shouted.

'That's not the case at all,' a woman's voice answered. Beatrice Vinsant appeared through the doorway and Sofia flushed.

'Ma'am, I'm sorry, I thought...' she caught herself. Mrs Vinsant had no idea that Sofia had worked in her husband's clubs. From what Lefevre had said, the woman was heavily disapproving of some aspects of her husband's businesses. Sofia presumed her religious beliefs rendered gambling immoral.

'That's quite all right, Mrs Logan. I apologise for not warning you of my visit. My husband said he had heard nothing from you for some time and I was anxious to know how you were coping since Tom's death.' Sofia remembered her manners.

'Will you sit down, Mrs Vinsant? I have tea or hot chocolate.' Sofia felt flustered. She had no idea what she was supposed to say or do.

'That's kind, but I shan't stay long. Do sit with me,' she said. Beatrice asked about the children, the neighbourhood, Christmas, then seemed to run out of conversation. She got to her feet and began pulling gloves on, frowning as she did so. 'I'm involved in an organisation that helps women in your situation. We assist them in finding suitable positions and ensure that their children are brought up without threat of poverty. Would you allow me to refer you?'

'I'm doing quite well on my own, thank you, Mrs Vinsant. I was never one for taking charity,' Sofia said, doing her best not to let the irritation sound in her voice.

'It's not charity. We just try to protect widows from those who would take advantage,' Beatrice continued.

'I don't need lessons in caring for my children or finding work, thank you, but I am very busy doing both, so if you'll excuse me.' Sofia held the door open.

'Well, you know where I am if you need anything,' Beatrice said quietly.

'That's kind but it won't be necessary,' answered Sofia, shutting the door as her visitor exited. She was furious. It was beyond comprehension that Beatrice Vinsant should assume the lower classes were incapable of looking after themselves. The last thing she needed was more people meddling in her life. They wouldn't offer any real help, perhaps teach her to sew so that she could get a seamstress job working twelve hours a day for pennies, or to cook so that she could get up at five in the morning to make breakfast for those too grand to prepare their own meals. She wasn't going to be doing any of that. Little wonder Tom had so rarely spoken of Beatrice.

She busied herself making a stew for Charlie and delivered it immediately. He invited her in and she paused politely by the door as he gathered up scattered pencils and paper.

'I hadn't meant to interrupt you,' she said.

'You're not, I was drawing and I can't quite get it right so I'm grateful for the distraction.' He looked so cross with himself that Sofia was amused.

'Can I see?' she asked.

'No,' he replied. 'Sorry, I just don't show my drawings until they're finished. What can I do for you?' His manner seemed brusque and she thrust the pot towards him, eager to leave.

'Here, I made you this. It's nothing very exciting, just a beef and potato stew, to thank you for everything.' Charlie set it on his stove.

'You didn't need to, not that I'm complaining. I'm not much of a cook.' He smiled broadly and Sofia relaxed. 'I'll make us some tea,' he said and she sat down. There was a newspaper open which she flicked through but found no obituaries relating to the previous night before realising it would have been too late for the death to appear in today's papers.

'Not working today?' she asked.

'I'm on night duty at the moment. I get home at about six in the morning but I can never sleep then.' Sofia fiddled with the mug, wondering if asking more was bold, stupid or both.

'Much excitement round here, then? Must get a bit dull, dealing with drunkards and thieves,' she said.

'Oh, you'd be surprised,' he said. 'Everything comes alive at night. For some reason people seem to think they're invisible. Truth is, of course, the city never really sleeps. I should think you're happy to have stopped work. Better to be tucked up with your little ones after dark.'

'It is,' she agreed. 'Although I may still get the odd night's work if someone's ill. It'll pay me enough to keep going.' She felt self-conscious at the lie, getting up abruptly and knocking a pile of sketches across the floor. When she knelt down to pick them up he took her arm, insisting she shouldn't trouble herself. Sofia thanked him and left, trying her hardest not to look back at the papers. Each sketch had been of a woman smiling wistfully. Sofia tried to push the image away but couldn't. The more she recreated the woman's face in her mind, the more certain she became that it was her own. Sofia flew through her door. It explained why he'd been so uptight when she arrived. Her husband had not yet been dead six months, she thought. What sort of man pursues a widow in mourning? But he hadn't. He hadn't said or done anything ungentlemanly. She told herself that it was improper, but the truth was that she was quietly thrilled by the discovery. Sofia tried to concentrate on sweeping floors and changing beds but caught herself glancing into the mirror, trying to see what he saw. Charlie Danes was an unknown quantity and a dangerous friend to have after last night. The sensible course of action would be to keep her distance.

Soon enough the papers reported the unfortunate demise of Jonathan Fitzpatrick, aged fifty and married to Eleanor, complete with a photograph taken at Ascot the previous year. Horse racing had been his favourite hobby. The column said he'd been taken unexpectedly by ill health, presumed a heart attack. So the family had covered up the circumstances of his death as Vinsant had anticipated. After all, who in society would want the scandal of a death in a whorehouse?

On Friday, she was called to a north London factory to see Emmett Vinsant in a cramped makeshift office amidst sheds that smelled of damp and oil. Thorne was absent but Vinsant's driver stood outside the door. They kept their voices at a whisper and Sofia was mindful of her temper this time.

'You did well, Sofia, I knew you would. You should have had more faith in my judgment.' Sofia stayed quiet. It was extraordinary that even now he should congratulate himself more than her. He handed over an envelope and Sofia peered briefly at the contents. There was money in there, not a huge amount, but enough to keep her family for another month or two.

'What's this for?' she asked. 'I still owe you money from the games. I don't want any more debt.'

'And how will you survive? The task you performed has balanced out the loan relating to your rent but there is still the matter of the gambling debt. I may need your help again. Consider this an advance.' Sofia put the money on his desk.

'I thought it was over,' her voice shook. She had come to see Vinsant believing they were to settle terms for paying off the remainder of what she owed, but not this.

107

'My wife visited you,' he said. 'I understand that she offered assistance in finding work but you refused. She seemed to get the impression that you do not want employment. Is that correct, Sofia? If so, then I fail to comprehend how you can hope to repay me or improve your situation.'

'Mrs Vinsant was very kind,' she choked, 'but I don't want anyone interfering in my affairs. If I'd realised you'd sent her...'

'Oh, please don't be under any misconception about that,' Vinsant interrupted, laughing. 'My wife does nothing on my account. I'm sure she was simply trying to convert another woman to her ill-conceived cause.'

'Pity doesn't put food on the table,' Sofia said.

'Quite so,' he snapped. 'You're entitled to be mistress of your own destiny which is precisely what I am offering you. Have you had to work one single day since you left the club? Have you had to dirty your hands for a few paltry pennies? You have not. So please try to understand that I am being generous and expecting remarkably little in return.'

'Remarkably little?' Sofia spat, her voice low but colour rising in her cheeks. 'I took a man's life. Do you feel no regret over it at all?'

Vinsant leaned across the desk. 'And how many nights' sleep have you lost, madam?' Sofia cast her eyes to the floor. She'd suffered nothing by way of an uneasy conscience. 'Exactly,' Vinsant finished.

'And if I take the money? I want to be clear this time what your terms are. I won't be yours to command.'

'I'll let you know when I need your services again. Make no mistake, given the things I know about you, in this matter you are very much mine. Should my wife call on you again, pretend you've found seamstress work. As you assumed, it's better to avoid her particular type of charity. And that police constable friend of yours, the man I saw at your house when I rescued your son from the workhouse.'

'What about him?' she asked.

'He might be useful to us. Just as a way to check what the police do or don't suspect.'

'Can I go now?' Sofia asked. Vinsant took hold of her hand. She stood still, half way between repulsion and indignation that he should feel entitled to be so familiar.

'You have a gift, Sofia. Some people might not call it that but I recognise your value. You can act without consequence upon your conscience, take a life as if you were merely chopping meat for supper. You are a weapon. I long doubted the reliability of your husband's disclosure until I saw you snap the neck of that pup.' He raised his other hand and stroked her throat with his thumb. When she tried to pull her head away, hard fingers wrapped around the nape of her neck. 'You're a natural killer, Sofia. The time will come when you'll thank me for setting you free.'

Outraged, Sofia shoved his hand off her neck and dashed for the door, wrenching it open with such force that Vinsant's driver fell into the room. Sofia glared at him and Vinsant swore at the man as she ran. Sofia lost no time in getting away, not wanting to witness the treatment Silverman was about to get for listening in on a private meeting. As tempted as she'd been to throw the envelope back in Vinsant's face, he was right in believing she wouldn't. She was too far entrenched to think that refusing his money now would get her out of the mess she was in.

Sofia made sure that every waking moment was spent playing with the children when they were not at school. She repaid Nora's kindness by nursing her through a hacking cough and fever, reading her a newspaper when she could get one and cooking for her. Little happened save for the arrival of a letter from Tom's sister, Mary. She was living in York with her husband and enquiring about the children, offering to take them if necessary. Sofia had only met her once. Tom and his sister had never been close, she being several years older and not at all like her good-natured brother. Tom had blamed childlessness for her failure to soften over the years. She and her husband had tried unsuccessfully for a family, until Mary's age put it out of the question. Tom always thought it was why they hadn't visited, so jealous was his sister of the little ones running around causing chaos. Mary must have pounced on the idea of adopting Isaac and Sadie after Tom's death, Sofia thought, so much so that she doubted the woman had stopped for a second to grieve the loss of her brother. Determined not to allow it to upset her, Sofia threw the letter into the fire. Mary wouldn't be able to interfere from such a distance. If she were genuinely concerned, she could have sent a few pennies to help.

She kissed each angelically sleeping child and retired to bed, willing herself to imagine a better future. What came was an excitement, a sensual coil in her abdomen. She thought of the whorehouse and the sense of power having taking Fitzpatrick's life. For the first time since childhood, she had felt truly strong. Where there should have been terror, there was the knowledge that she could fight and win. Pride and remorse rose as one within her. What sort of deviant was she to recall such a thing and respond as if touched by a lover? Sofia got up and splashed her face with freezing water, hating her own body and hating the guilt she felt, trying not to look at her face in the mirror marked by swollen lips, dilated pupils and sweat soaked hair. She was spent.

Chapter Fifteen

Childhood 1891

It was bleak. That was Sofia's first thought upon seeing the farm she would call home for what remained of her childhood years. Bleak, miles away from anywhere, and grey. She hated the greyness. Winter had dug its heels in by the time Sofia arrived. She couldn't remember ever having been so cold. The wind seemed to have crept inside her body, leaving her numb. She spoke only when spoken to and buried the desperate sense of abandonment in the hard physical labour that filled her days. She wondered vaguely how much her parents had paid the farmer to take her in but never asked. What good would the answer do her? If they'd paid a lot it meant they wanted rid of her at any cost, too little meant she was worthless. Every few months her mother sent a letter reminding her that she was loved and missed, but it didn't change anything. They'd abandoned her.

Bill Marney and his wife Letty had no children of their own to work the land, and made up for it by collecting society's unwanted. Very much the head of the household, Bill was quicker to raise a hand and cuff a head than he ever was to open his mouth and speak, and that applied both to the farmhands and his wife. Letty, in turn, took out the harshness of her own life on those further down the farm's hierarchy. Sofia found herself on its lowest rung. The Marneys worked long hours, no strangers to hard graft and toilsome living, but their own experiences had not left them sympathetic to the plights of their charges. Quite the opposite. The most casual of complaints was apt to win you a blow and additional chores. Taking more food than your allotted share was a grave sin and Bill had been known to take off his belt as a reward, not that Sofia ever ate enough to rally his temper. Over the years, the farmer and his wife had come to resemble brother and sister, rough and ruddy skinned, hair fit to nest in, each missing more teeth than remained. Letty bathed rarely and Bill almost never, the usual means of getting clean being a tub of cold water in the yard. To Sofia, the constant sensation of grubbiness was not just unpleasant, it was intolerable. Even in the freezing cold, in the dark if necessary, she would run to the river half a mile from the farmhouse and bathe. She told herself that it meant she wasn't like them.

Amongst those waifs and strays dumped at the farm were Mac and Saul. Mac, half deaf but at eighteen already as strong as the proverbial ox, was the most valuable of them. He said little and ate much, which Bill tolerated as an acceptable price for his physique. Mac had not been blessed with the fastest of brains, but with his brutish body came a bullying personality. Sofia saw it from the very first, in the spluttered exaggerated laughter and mean sneer of his mouth. He was to be avoided where possible and put in his place quickly if she wanted any peace. Then there was Saul who, Sofia thought, could not have landed in any corner of the world less suited to his character. It was a sick joke. Tender and shy at fourteen, Sofia took comfort from the fact that she had found someone even more displaced than herself, a kindred spirit to cling to in those dark days. The Marneys worked them to the bone in return for bed and board, Sofia's parents sending money when they could, not that Sofia's life was ever easier for their contribution. The farmer was getting by far the better end of the deal but where else was there to go? Beyond the boundaries of the farm lay danger, cruel men who would only take advantage of her and the prospect of doing the vilest things to earn a living. Here, at least, the worst of her chores was mucking out the animals. Gruelling it may have been but Sofia knew it was still better than the alternatives.

She had a grudging liking for the farmhouse itself, it being a survivor which was the way Sofia had come to think of herself. An ancient, thick-walled structure, it had been built and rebuilt over countless years as it fell foul of weather and careless owners. The heart of it was the kitchen with a fireplace large enough to sit on brick-ledge seats at the chimney base. Here they would cook, eat, wash and dry clothes in winter, be dealt orders and reprimands, and pass the long, lifeless evenings from November to February. Sometimes in a fit of good cheer Letty would bring in fresh flowers from the field but then she would drop back into her usual moroseness and the blooms would be forgotten until brown, shrivelled and stinking with rot. That was how she would end up if she stayed too long at the farm, Sofia thought.

The men worked the Marneys' twenty acres, a fair sized holding except that the land was hard to farm, yielding crops only with constant attention. Sofia tended the cows, sheep and pigs but when the harvest was poor, even feeding the livestock was problematic. The barns needed mending, tools were old and blunt, and the thatched roof above Saul, Mac and Sofia's rooms was woefully thin. She quickly learned to rescue every scrap of blanket, leather and sack she could to sew together for extra warmth on draughty nights. Sofia thought it made life on the road in their rickety old caravans seem like one long holiday. She'd been with the Marneys a few weeks before mid-December arrived, a stark reminder of how different her life was now. Family Christmases had always been wild celebrations. There may not have been luxuries or gifts, but to Sofia there was always a feeling of belonging, sustained merry drunkenness for the adults, and good cheer that lasted well into the New Year.

The only concession to Yuletide that first year at the farm was the killing of a hog. Sofia was used to cooking and cleaning but she had never prepared meat from the carcass, let alone slaughtered it before. It would be a lesson in country ways, Bill had told her. No one had any business eating an animal unless they knew how to kill it. To that end, late one evening Mac took her into a shed where the stone floor had been scrubbed, and a chain and hook slung over a beam. Letty gave Sofia a thickly waxed apron to wear and Saul stood quietly in the background as the hog was brought.

'I don't want to do this,' Sofia muttered, but no one paid any attention. Bill held the hog still as Mac slipped a rope around its hind legs. Before she could protest, Mac swung a heavy log, cracking the pig between the ears so hard that the animal went down without a sound. In one smooth move, Bill lifted it by the rope and slung it onto the hook, hoisting it clear of the floor above the bucket he kicked into place.

Mac stepped forward and thrust a knife into Sofia's hands. She felt nauseous. Failure or refusal, though, would mean constant taunting, teasing, being given all the rotten jobs. She just had to be brave and get it over and done with. It was better than letting them think they had her beaten. She walked forward and grabbed the animal by one ear. It was stunned but alive. With the knife clutched hard so it wouldn't slip from her grasp, she stuck it in one side of the neck and wrenched the blade around in a clean line. The blood flow was immediate and intense with the animal's heart still beating. It twitched and spasmed but thankfully never regained consciousness. Sofia stood entranced by the dark waterfall filling the bucket below. She could smell it, metallic and musky, tiny droplets spraying the air and creating a hazy rainbow every shade of red. It took longer than she thought to drain, the final drops falling ten minutes after she'd slit the vein.

Saul dragged the full bucket of blood out of the way and replaced it with an empty one. Sofia eyed it with surprise but she was damned if she showed weakness now. It couldn't get any worse, she thought, cringing at Mac's closeness as he stood behind her, taking her right hand in his and holding the knife with two fingers cupped over the top of the blade. He held her hand up high to the furthest part of the pig's underbelly and pressed the tip of the blade firmly into its skin, motioning for her to pull down. Sofia gritted her teeth and cut downwards towards the hog's head in a single sweep. Sighing with relief that it was over, she looked back up at the carcass where the belly gaped as its contents ceded to gravity, enveloping her in a reeking, gelatinous mountain of organs and intestines. The pig's innards slid beneath the apron and onto her skin. She gagged, scratching furiously at her face, spitting the foulness from her mouth, trying to get her breath as she heard Mac braying with laughter. It was Saul who took her arm and pulled her out of the slither-

114

ing entrails. He wiped her face gently, with a blank look that told Sofia he had been where she was, that the joke was well worn. She was shaking with the shock of it, repulsed by her own shame but beneath that a more powerful emotion was being born, one that helped loosen the vice of humiliation and gave her a reason to stay where she was instead of running as fast as her legs would carry her. Sofia had her first taste of the desire for vengeance. It was warming, she thought, and heady.

The twenty-fifth day of December began like every other. Sofia rose at half past five and helped milk the cows. Two hours later she collected the eggs from the chicken coops, left them fresh grain then went for breakfast. The next hour was spent pulling parsnips from the field until Letty called her to the kitchen. After only the briefest of detours through the woodland at the back of the farmhouse, Sofia went in to chop vegetables and lay the table. It was by far the best meal since she had arrived. The portions were generous, the pig fat had dried into crackling, there were blood sausages and bacon to accompany the roast pork and piles of vegetables like Sofia had never seen before. Only Mac was treated to a little something extra, mixed into the stuffing just before she served him. She watched his face as he fleetingly registered the bitterness until the salt and herbs hid the taste. To Sofia's delight he filled himself until he was fit to burst.

It took another thirty minutes to work once they'd finished their meal. Mac had thrown himself before the fire, rubbing his swollen belly and reminding Sofia, appropriately, of the pig. She heard his stomach growl before he noticed it himself and then there was no stopping it. He paled and gave a long belch which had Letty yelling at him to get out before it was too late. In seconds he was dashing for the door and across the yard with the dogs chasing him for sport. Sofia glanced through the tiny window where she could just make out his figure doubled over in the line of trees as he vomited, dropping his trousers simultaneously to empty his bowels of the poison, and fighting the cramping pains that would make him wish he were dead but which, she knew, would not go so far as to give him such relief.

115

Mac spent the night in the barn with only an old blanket and the animals for warmth. Letty, disgusted, had told him he wasn't sleeping in the house. Bill had swiped him round the head for being so greedy he'd made himself sick and Saul had watched on, quiet as ever, with only a questioning raise of his eyebrows at Sofia. If he suspected what she'd done he never said a word. It had been Sofia's Christmas gift to herself, the coming-of-age knowledge that she could and would survive anything and that cutting the throat of a living animal or crushing ivy berries and feeding them to a man who had humiliated her, were all part and parcel of the life she was to lead.

Chapter Sixteen

May 1906

Sofia cherished the period of peace that followed. Nora recovered slowly. Sofia added to her wood pile when the older woman was unaware, inviting her to eat with them on the pretence of needing help with the children. She saw Charlie on the street a few times but didn't knock at his door again, feeling awkward, wanting to see him but unsure what to say. Her money was lasting well enough, not that there was any excess, but the basics were covered.

On the second Tuesday evening of the month, a single sharp knock at the door hailed a change. When Sofia opened it, heart heavy at the prospect of finding Captain Thorne, her stomach dropped like a stone.

'Invite me in then, Sofia, don't stand gawping. It's bad enough I've had to come to this god-forsaken end of the city.' Mary Flathers had her brother's colouring but none of his character. Sofia took her sister-in-law's hat and coat, clearing space as the children stirred and peered curiously round the bedroom door at the visitor.

'Children, come and say hello to your Auntie Mary,' Sofia said. It would be strange for them, seeing this woman who looked so like their daddy. Where Tom's hair had been curly hers seemed to frizz out of control. Their eyes were almost identical in shape and colour but his had shone with humour where hers were hooded giving her an untrusting look. Perhaps Sofia was seeing only what she chose to, given her ambiguous feelings about Mary. Neither of the children had ever met her in person although Sofia had mentioned her occasionally. It had seemed important to let Isaac and Sadie know they had family, albeit that she wouldn't have chosen to introduce them like this.

'Don't stand all the way over there then, come before the fire so I can see you properly,' Mary snapped. She regarded them from her full height without bending down. You could tell she hadn't had babies of her own, Sofia thought. Self-consciously, Isaac held out his hand.

'It's nice to meet you, Auntie,' he said.

'Ah, so you do have some manners. I should think so. Your father wouldn't have wanted you growing up like wild things.' Sofia watched Mary, tall and spindly, inspecting the children and it felt as if their home had been invaded by an enormous spider.

'Mr Flathers and I are staying at a boarding house a mile west of here. I was hoping we could see something of the children while we're in London.'

'And what brings you all the way from York? I know you felt it was too far to travel for Tom's funeral,' replied Sofia, unable to resist the barb.

Mary ignored it but couldn't stop the angry red blotches flaring on her cheeks. 'Mr Flathers has come to settle the affairs of an uncle who left him a substantial amount of money. We don't come down south unless we have to, as you know. I wonder at the way ladies behave here. We passed by Buckingham Palace in the cab only to see women chained to the gates. Their hats were on the ground and they were shouting like fishwives. I fail to understand why you would raise two youngsters in such a city. We tolerate no such behaviour up in York.'

Sofia was becoming more familiar with the suffragettes. The papers were full of the exploits of the Women's Social and Political Union. It seemed a world away from Sofia's worries and she inwardly cursed the protestors for providing Mary with material for complaint.

'It doesn't affect us round here. We keep ourselves to ourselves. The children are busy with school and I hardly ever go into the city.'

There was another knock at the door and Sofia wondered why she couldn't just be left alone. Nora shuffled in unaware of the disagreeable visitor.

'That sack of maggots Cramborne was sniffing around again today. Had the nerve to ask me if you was consorting with some gentleman to get him to pay your rent.'

'Nora!' Sofia broke in, desperate to stop her babbling. 'This is Tom's sister, Mary Flathers. She's visiting from York. Mary, this is my neighbour.'

'Sorry, my lovely, didn't know you had company. I help with the children on nights when Sofia's busy,' Nora added by way of introduction. Mary smiled back as if she'd been given a gift.

'And is that often?' she asked in a breathy voice.

Sofia intervened before Nora could do any more damage. 'It's getting rather late. I should probably be putting the children back to bed.' The clacking of hooves echoed up the street and Mary peered through the window, making a play of having to rub it to see through the dirt.

'Mr Flathers is waiting so I'll say goodbye for today and visit tomorrow afternoon when the children are home from school. They can show me their lessons. We have a lot to talk about, Sofia, and I should very much like to hear about this mysterious gentleman who's been paying your rent.' She turned and bared her teeth at the children, the strained efforts of a face unused to smiling. 'Goodnight children, make sure you say your prayers, now.'

Sofia counted to ten before shutting the door or she knew she'd slam it so hard she was likely to wake the whole street. 'Off to bed, my darlings,' she hustled Isaac and Sadie away as Nora settled herself before the fire. 'And Isaac,' she called him back for a moment. 'Please say nothing to your aunt and uncle about the workhouse. It would upset them terribly. Do you understand?'

'Yes, Mummy,' he whispered. She wished she hadn't reminded him of it. He never talked about it and Sofia understood his desire to simply forget rather than relive. She had spent many of her own childhood years doing just that. But Mary couldn't be told what had happened. She would wield it like a weapon.

'Not much like your Tom, is she?' she muttered as she poked Sofia's dying fire.

'Not at all,' Sofia replied lightly, but she felt nauseous. What could Mary want? Not just a friendly visit, that much was certain.

She wiped the window herself so that Mary left no mark on her home and became aware of a face on the other side. She shrieked, putting one hand to her mouth to stifle the noise. By the time she reached the door her nerves had given way to brittle laughter.

'Charlie, you gave me the devil of a fright. What were you doing there?'

'I was just coming home from a shift and saw you staring out of the window. I thought something might be wrong.'

That made Sofia laugh even harder. She knew she couldn't trust herself to speak. When she looked at his face, so serious in spite of her hysterics, the sound turned into a sob.

'Is Nora with the children?' he asked. Sofia nodded. Coherent speech was still some way off. 'Then come to my house.' He put his coat round her shoulders for the short walk and, once inside, pulled out a small bottle of whisky. 'Here, drink this,' he said, pushing a glass into her hand. He didn't speak again until she'd finished it all and the colour had returned to her cheeks. Even then he simply asked if she felt better and, satisfied with her response, stared into the fire.

'Did you never think of marrying, Charlie?' Sofia enquired, glad to think of something other than her own situation for a while.

He sipped his drink before replying. 'I've met nice girls who'd have made wonderful wives, women I could probably have been happy with, there was just never...' his voice trailed off and Sofia worried that she'd brought back a painful memory.

'I'm sorry, I shouldn't have asked,' she said.

'No, I don't mind, it's hard to explain.' He put his glass down on the flagstone floor. 'I never wanted to just be content. In the same way that I don't want to be your average constable who gets to work on time, leaves on time and shines his boots. I want to help people, make a difference, change things.' He stood, agitated and took a step towards the fire. 'Spending a lifetime with someone should be about more than getting to the right age and settling down. I wanted to find a woman who would make me lose myself in her. Is that the way it was between you and your husband? Because if I can't have someone I couldn't live without, then I honestly think it's better to have no one at all.'

Sofia was taken aback by the change in him. 'Tom made me feel safe and loved. I trusted him to protect me, to make me happy. He was wonderful and tender, and I thought I knew everything about him.'

'Thought you knew?' Charlie asked. 'What changed?'

'He did. There was someone else, apparently, more important to him than me.'

'He was unfaithful to you?'

Sofia smiled. 'In a way I suppose he was. Not with another woman. It's complicated. But you're talking about passion, Charlie, and that fades sooner or later.'

'I don't believe that,' he said. 'There's no single rule that governs every relationship. People get lazy, that's all. They settle for the sake of having an easy life. They won't wait and search and hold themselves back for that one special person.' He tensed with the force of his emotions. Tiny beads of sweat covered his face and veins stood out in his neck.

'Is that what you're doing?' She went to comfort him, placing a cool hand on his forearm. 'Waiting for the perfect partner? Because I'm not sure such a person truly exists.'

Charlie stared at her hand on his arm. 'I am.'

He was going to kiss her, she thought, seeing him lower his head to hers as if watching two strangers from a distance. The way he wound one arm around her waist and the other around her shoulders. How she seemed to be weightless and unresisting. She saw herself tip back her head and part her lips in anticipation of his. Too easy, Sofia thought, too willing. What will he think?

But Charlie didn't seem to be doing much thinking. He tasted of whisky and woodsmoke. Sofia jerked as adrenaline shot through her and she saw Jonathan Fitzpatrick dying in front of her again. It should have repulsed her, ruined the moment, but instead it spread a dark heat across her chest, hardening her nipples and dripping down into her abdomen, liquefying her. Charlie pulled her against him so hard she could barely breathe and still she didn't push him away. She felt alive, frenzied, drunk.

'Sofia, have I hurt you?' Charlie whispered hoarsely.

'Of course you haven't. What are you talking about?'

'You're crying,' he replied, wiping a tiny stream from her cheek. 'I'm so sorry, I shouldn't have taken advantage of you like that.' He stepped away from her, ashen faced.

Sofia absent-mindedly stroked her other cheek. He was right. She'd been crying but she had no idea why. He had already picked up his coat, ready to walk her home.

'Charlie, please don't feel bad. It wasn't you,' she reassured him, but what would any man think when the woman he kissed was reduced to tears?

'You're very kind,' he responded, opening his door. Staying would only prolong his discomfort so she left with no more words. He escorted her home then retreated, with Sofia resolving to visit him the next day and set matters right.

Everything was upside down. She was entering men's houses late at night, allowing herself to be kissed half way through her year of mourning. Tom's sister had appeared out of the blue and was unlikely to disappear until she'd got whatever it was she'd come for. It was all too complicated. Sofia had no idea why she'd cried as Charlie kissed her. It wasn't sadness for Tom, although that should have been at the forefront of her mind. What sort of woman was she? Perhaps not so different from those whores at the brothel. That was what she'd been thinking about when she'd started crying. Was it remorse? That wasn't how it had felt.

The memories fused, Charlie's hands on her, her hands on Fitzpatrick. Sofia shook her head. What she needed was sleep. Tomorrow she would be clear-headed enough to make sense of it all.

The new day was clear and sunny. The children awoke early, running around noisily, jumping in and out of the patches of sunlight streaming through the windows. Nora was already preparing breakfast by the time Sofia climbed out of bed. When a note appeared under the door Sofia felt a flash of joy, imagining that perhaps Mary had changed her mind and wouldn't be visiting today. Instead, there was an invitation from Monsieur Lefevre to meet him that afternoon at a tea shop on Gray's Inn Road with no return address. She was obviously expected to attend.

Mary arrived early, well before the children were home, with her diminutive husband Henry, the archetypal Yorkshireman, trailing behind. He spoke few words, nodded his agreement when necessary and looked around with constant disdain as if the mere existence of London was a matter for disapproval. Sofia wondered at their physical compatibility, she being taller than most men and he as round about the stomach as he was high. Still, Henry and Mary were a perfect, dour match for one another. Sofia marvelled that fate should hand out gifts like unexpected inheritances so freely to such grudging people. Still, she was Tom's sister. She welcomed them, had cleaned as best she could, and made sure there was food to offer. Mary ran a dust-seeking finger along a shelf as Sofia poured tea, ignoring her and concentrated on Henry instead.

'Will you be staying long in London?' Sofia asked.

'We'll be returning to Yorkshire as soon as,' he replied.

'It's too smoky down here for Mr Flathers,' Mary cut in, taking the proffered cup. 'We wouldn't have come at all if signatures weren't required. Of course, with such a significant amount of money it's best to do things properly.' Henry harrumphed and Sofia realised he was silencing his wife. Obviously matters of finance were not to be discussed so openly. 'When will the children be back?'

'Quite soon now,' said Sofia. 'Not that I don't appreciate your interest but you never came to see them when Tom was alive. Was there any particular purpose to your visit now?' They shot a quick look between themselves and Sofia suspected they hadn't anticipated her asking such a forthright question. It was Mary who answered.

'We believe we have a duty to ensure that my brother's offspring are being properly raised. You had such a troubled childhood yourself, what with travelling all over and your parents leaving you so young. It's not difficult to imagine you struggling with the two of them on your own. You've already been reduced to asking your neighbour for help.'

Sofia bit her tongue as she considered her response. Too sharp and she would make an enemy she didn't have time for. Too simpering and this would never end.

'I see,' she replied simply. 'More tea, Henry?' Sofia refilled his cup when he nodded. 'Well, it's kind of you to be concerned but there's no need. I've been letting Nora help with Isaac and Sadie because she needed the extra pennies and won't take charity. Myself, I've been doing some work for Tom's old employer, night shifts so I'm around during the day to care for the children. Tom always worked long hours and rarely saw the children except in the evening so my life has changed hardly at all, except of course, that I miss him terribly,' she added. 'What was it, exactly, that you thought you could do?'

There was another pause until Henry decided that blunt was best.

'They should come and live with us,' he said. Sofia could have pretended to be surprised, but she wasn't. 'This whole city is filthy and heaven only knows how things'll go with that Liberal in charge. Your so called new Prime Minister, Campbell-Bannerman, is about to bring the country to rack and ruin. You've got women chaining themselves to fence posts, shouting in Parliament, assaulting police constables. The conservative backbone of the country has been forced out. And just look at this place. It's barely big enough to call a shed. We can provide a good education, a proper home, fresh air, and a disciplined upbringing. You should be grateful we've come.' He stopped. Sofia looked at his stony face and guessed that was all she'd hear from him. He plainly expected her to agree and obey.

She did her best not to show the fury erupting inside her. It would do no good in the long run. People like the Flathers were best pacified so she adopted a tone she hoped was kind but firm.

'I appreciate that my home is not as grand as yours and that you don't approve of London but this is where my children belong. This is the place Tom and I chose for our family. I feel very sad that you've not been blessed with children yourselves but Tom's death changes nothing. Isaac and Sadie are mine and it's me who'll raise them. It's bad enough they've lost a father. No amount of money, fresh air or schooling can bring him back and they're not going to lose their mother as well. If that's why you came here, I'm afraid you've had a wasted visit.'

'Raise them?' Mary laughed bitterly. 'It's a wonder neither of them has followed the same fate as my poor brother, Lord only knows what you feed them. I was telling Mr Flathers that Isaac should be much taller at his age.' Sofia choked back a laugh at the irony of the very untall Henry being lectured by his wife on the horror of having an insufficiently grown nephew. 'And Sadie is skin and bones. I'd be amazed if she eats anything at all. Their clothes look like they've been patched up a dozen times. And what was that about a gentleman friend paying your rent? Our Tom must be turning in his grave.' Her face had taken on a vicious sneer. 'What sort of woman lets a man pay her rent? It's all got to be repaid at some time or have you reached a special agreement?' The implication wasn't veiled in the slightest and it was only the sudden entry of the children that saved Mary from Sofia's spiralling anger.

Isaac and Sadie said hello and answered questions politely enough but without any great interest in the couple. It was only when Sadie said she was hungry that Sofia looked at the clock. She was late for Lefevre. It would take her some time to walk to the tea rooms and she hadn't been able to ask Nora to watch the children.

She braced herself for the smugness that would ensue. 'As you're here, I wonder if perhaps you'd like to spend some time with the children while I go food shopping. Isaac can read to you and Sadie can show you her letters. Would you mind?'

'I think that's a splendid idea, especially if you're busy. I have a woman who delivers our food to the door. It's all much fresher that way. You go, Sofia.' Henry seemed less pleased. Sofia suspected the thought of spending time in a small space with children was terrifying to him but it was this or leave Lefevre waiting and she wasn't going to do that to one of Vinsant's most trusted employees.

'Thank you,' she did her best to sound gracious. 'I'll be back by five to give them their dinner.'

She half walked, half ran to Gray's Inn Road and was out of breath by the time she arrived. Millie May's tea house was set back from the main road, between a book shop and a gentlemen's outfitters that catered for the many barristers working in the vicinity. It was busy, almost every seat taken and a few people standing, the air thick with cigar smoke. Each table was covered in crisp white linen with a lace overlay and fresh flowers artfully arranged in a central silver vase. Plates of sandwiches and cakes were delivered then cleared, crumbs brushed rapidly from floors and tables by girls in long black dresses covered in spotless white smocks. It was so busy that Lefevre had to stand and wave before Sofia noticed him. He was his usual self, a lively, dry witted companion who had the good grace not once to refer to her overnight disappearance from the club. It was only when Sofia enquired what had prompted him to invite her to tea that he appeared perturbed.

'Mr Vinsant requested that I should,' Lefevre replied. 'Not that I hadn't wanted to see you, you understand, but I would not have contacted you without his authority. He is unforgiving with his employees as I'm afraid you found out. A few weeks ago he sacked his driver, no warning, without pay. The idiot turned up at the door of the club begging to see Vinsant. Captain Thorne was sent out to deal with him.' Lefevre raised his eyebrows at her knowingly and Sofia recalled the moment Vinsant's driver, Silverman, had fallen through the door. Hardly a surprise he'd been given his marching orders.

'Mr Vinsant told me to give you this. He said I should stay with you as you read it but that I was not to look at it.'

Sofia smiled. 'And have you?' she asked gently.

'No. I may gossip like an old woman, my dear, but I am not so curious about Mr Vinsant's business that I would risk an encounter with the Captain's boot. You read it, I shall drink my tea. He said you were to be handed it at ten to four precisely.' He gave her an envelope, blank on the outside with a single sheet of paper inside covered in neat script.

She peered at it through the smoky gas light, having to read the first few lines several times until she deciphered the writing.

'S. There is a man who comes in to take tea every weekday afternoon at four. He will be wearing an old fashioned cloak and using a cane. He has a slight limp affecting his left leg, white hair and is in his sixtieth year. When he enters, the serving girls will clear a table for him in the window irrespective of who is already there. He shouts his orders as he is rather deaf. This man seeks to have my interests in a land owner-ship dispute set aside. Our usual agreement, you understand. Mrs Hassel-brook has another letter for you with all the details which you should collect tomorrow along with a few items belonging to your late husband.' It was unsigned, of course. Sofia was too surprised to be angry. He even had Lefevre delivering orders to her now and she was left sitting in a public place waiting for a man she was supposed to kill. She studied her friend as he sipped his tea. Vinsant was devious. Here she was, visiting with a man who would never dare question the situation, providing her with company so that no one would approach her. When the bell above the door rang to signal a new entrant Sofia recognised him immediately from Vinsant's description.

More interesting than the man himself was the reaction his entry provoked from the serving girls. There was a visible tensing and eventu-ally one shoved another towards him. He was a few tables away and the room was humming with noise but still she heard his voice over the din.

He barked his order in a gruff, military style. The girl's hand trembled as she leaned forward to remove the newspaper that another customer had left on his table and he made no attempt to disguise his long stare inside her blouse, licking his lips. When she wobbled the table in her haste to move away he shouted an insult at her clumsiness.

'Mr Loftis would like tea with scones and cream, please,' Sofia heard her say to the women behind the counter who were preparing the orders. 'And best not keep him waiting. He's in one of his tempers again today.'

Mr Loftis was repulsive, was Sofia's first assessment of the man. Many other gentlemen walked past tipping their hats or bidding him a good afternoon, although he did not once respond. Given their proximity to Gray's Inn, Sofia took it that Loftis was a lawyer, smartly dressed with an over-bearing nature, careless from self-importance. He looked older than sixty years, his skin deeply marked about eyes and forehead as if he had frowned so much that his face had forgotten how to straighten itself out. He slurped his tea as he read some papers and tiny droplets clung to his chin, napkin unused on his lap. Her only regret about the prospect of ridding London of this particular man was that it would inevitably involve her getting closer to him than she would easily stomach. Sofia chatted amiably with Lefevre until she'd seen all she needed. Time was passing rapidly so she made her excuses, kissed her companion on each cheek in the French style as he'd taught her, and set off for home.

Nearing Brewhouse Yard later than intended, she broke into a run, desperate that her sister-in-law should have no reason to call her irresponsible. It was close on half past five when she burst through the front door ready to make her apologies but all was silent, the rooms empty, children's coats missing, the fire not set and kettle cold. They'd been gone a long time. Seconds later she was hammering on Nora's door.

'Oh yes,' breathed Nora. 'They went off in quite a fancy carriage, all of them together, the children wrapped up in their coats even in this nice sunshine.'

'Did they have any bags with them?' Sofia asked, her stomach a hard knot.

'I don't know. Possible, I s'pose. Children looked excited to be going out,' Nora replied.

'Damn that interfering bitch!' Nora began to ask what was wrong but Sofia was already sprinting to the end of the road, looking this way and that along the main street. She would have gone after them but hadn't asked where their boarding house was. How could she have been such a fool? She'd given Mary exactly the opportunity she'd been waiting for. After pacing back and forth in the living room for several minutes, she forced herself to sit. They wouldn't try to leave for York so late in the day. They'd be travelling in the dark. And they'd have packed up the children's clothes and toys. Unless Mary didn't want to keep any of their old things. What would she tell them? That their mother couldn't cope any more? That they were better off away from the den of vice that was London? Sofia grimaced in the growing dusk. It occurred to her that perhaps it was Vinsant's doing. Had he called Mary here, even provided the money for Henry, so that Sofia would have nothing to focus on except doing his dirty work?

She bit her nails as she sat rocking. Calling the police would do no good. They wouldn't trouble themselves with a tale of children out with their aunt. She picked up an old doll of Sadie's and stroked its hair, imagining her daughter in her arms. Perhaps this was better for the children after all. No, she couldn't think like that. Isaac and Sadie were happy, content, and they loved her. She contemplated what might happen to them if she got caught. They would be Mary's then anyway. Hers to kiss goodnight, tuck into bed, Henry's to discipline and teach to fish. She cried herself into a stupor and then to sleep.

'Mummy, Mummy!' came the excited shouts before the front door was even open. 'We went to the park and then to the fair and Auntie Mary let us go on the rides and Uncle Henry bought us candy-floss and liquorice!' Sofia couldn't respond. She was down on her knees crushing the children to her chest. Sadie was wearing a pretty new hat and Isaac

129

was clutching a wooden toy gun. Mary and Henry let themselves in and watched as Sofia composed herself.

'What an exciting evening you've had!' Sofia told the children. 'I hope you said thank you to your Aunt and Uncle. Now go and wash your hands and faces. It's past bed time.' They rushed into the back room, chattering noisily about their adventure. Sofia waited until they were out of earshot before addressing Mary.

'You didn't tell me you were going out,' she said.

'We thought we'd treat the children while we were visiting,' Mary answered without bothering to disguise the chill in her voice. 'And you were gone so long we wondered if you were coming back at all.'

'What a ridiculous thing to say,' Sofia hissed at her. 'As if I'd just go off and leave my children. I told you I was going out to buy food. It might have taken longer than I'd expected but you knew perfectly well where I was going.'

'Oh really?' Mary said, an unpleasant smile twisting her mouth. 'Where is it then?'

'What?' Sofia muttered.

'Your groceries, my dear. The ones you were out so long collecting. Because I can't see any sign of them, can you, Mr Flathers?'

'I, well, I...' Sofia was gasping for excuses but Mary was not an opponent given to relinquishing victory.

'We'll be off now. The children are quite safe and they've been fed, no thanks to you. We're going back to Yorkshire tomorrow but I shall expect regular accounts of how they're keeping otherwise perhaps we'd best leave it to the Magistrate to decide who they should live with. Mr Flathers can afford a good lawyer now.' They left.

Sofia had no idea if Mary's threat to take the children from her was even possible but she didn't doubt that if Mary could do it, she would. Isaac rushed through, pretending to shoot the gun, eyes glazed from sugar and tiredness. His sister followed, wrapping a thin arm around Sofia.

'I like Auntie Mary, Mummy. Can we see her again?'

'I don't know, sweetheart,' whispered Sofia, kissing her daughter's forehead and smoothing her hair. 'They live a long way away.'

'She bought me a new hat,' said the girl wistfully as Sofia carried her to bed.

'And very beautiful you look in it, too,' she told her, tucking in the bedclothes as Isaac joined her. 'Now get some sleep.' The children drifted off still beaming from their marvellous afternoon and, as Sofia watched them, she seethed.

Putting Mary and Henry out of her mind, she concentrated on Loftis and the job she had to do, imagining how good it would feel to unload her anger and frustration at the unfairness of the world. It helped.

Chapter Seventeen

Sofia was in Doughty Street by ten o'clock, retrieving two pairs of Tom's boots from Mrs Hasselbrook and pocketing the envelope Vinsant had left for her. She was a few yards away from the house when his carriage entered the road. Strange, she thought, that Vinsant should come home when she was due to visit, but it was Beatrice who climbed out. She looked tired and unkempt, odd so early in the day. Without warning a young woman ran up, shouting at Beatrice and waving her arms. For a moment Sofia thought she was going to attack, but when she got closer she threw her arms around the older woman, sobbing and smiling at the same time.

Sofia stepped into the shade of a tree to watch unseen. It was a strange show of emotion so publicly and the girl was obviously not of Beatrice's social class. Mrs Vinsant accepted the embrace for a few seconds before patting the girl's back and pushing her gently away. Sofia couldn't hear the exchange but Beatrice reached into her handbag and passed the girl a sheet of paper. Beatrice said her goodbyes, straightened her coat and glanced around self-consciously. Sofia concealed herself better. It wouldn't do to be found spying. As Beatrice stepped inside the house, the movement of a curtain in an upper window caught Sofia's eye. So Captain Thorne was watching Beatrice too, ever his master's beast, ensuring nothing happened that Vinsant didn't hear about. Sofia wondered what Beatrice could be doing to warrant such scrutiny.

Back home, she locked her door and emptied out the contents of the envelope, money, a key and a letter.

'Lefevre reported that he very much enjoyed your company yesterday. I hope you are happier now that you have accepted our arrangement. You will find sufficient money here to cover any expenses. Below is the gentleman's home address. The key is for the drawer in my desk at the small office where we last met. It will be left unlocked this evening. There you will find something to help should you need it. This matter must be dealt with before the end of the month when the case proceeds. You will be properly compensated if the conclusion is successful.'

It was more money than she'd expected and it occurred to her, unhappily, that the increase might be a reflection of the greater risk involved. She told herself it was more likely a reminder of how much Vinsant had at stake if she failed. She already had an idea of how to approach Loftis and, if she performed convincingly, she might kill two birds with one stone. Waiting seemed pointless so she burned the letter, put on a smart dress and headed for the Temple.

The door she sought was in Fleet Street, yards from the imposing gates of Middle Temple Lane. She stared at the entrance, hearing Tom's voice in her mind. He had brought the children here once, regaling them with the adventures of Sir Walter Raleigh, a member of Middle Temple before his journey to the Americas. Isaac and Sadie had looked in awe at the grand buildings and high windows. It must have seemed as foreign as the moon to them and yet they'd hung on every word their father had said. Tom had always been fascinated by history whilst Sofia was more intrigued by the world unfolding around her which was precisely how she had lost concentration and looked instead at the nameplate on the wall next to her, announcing the premises of Ambrose Friendly, Solicitor. It had struck a chord and the memory had never faded.

Sofia didn't allow herself time to become nervous, knocking and waiting only moments before being welcomed by a young man, cap on head and suspenders going awry as he transferred piles of heavy books from trolley to desk.

'Come in, Ma'am. Someone'll be out to see you,' he said, bowing his head but unable to take off his hat for the fullness of his arms.

'Thank you,' Sofia said smoothly, taking a chair in the cluttered reception area. Dusty pyramids of books covered every surface, interspersed here and there with slabs of papers wrapped like parcels in pink ribbon. A variety of impressive certificates hung on the walls but in the middle of them all was a painting of a man and his dog. Engraved on the frame was the name Wellington. It was a humble touch in an otherwise forbidding setting. Footsteps approached from behind an inner door and a more elderly version of the man in the painting appeared.

'Madam, forgive me, I had no idea you were waiting. In fact, I was unaware of any further appointments today. How may I help you?'

'The fault is mine.' Sofia adopted the accent and airs of the guests who had squandered so much money at the club. 'I am rather ashamed to say that I've not made an appointment. It's an urgent matter and you were recommended by a friend who wishes to remain nameless.'

'Of course, my dear. I have a few minutes to spare and should be delighted to assist. I am Ambrose Friendly,' he remembered to introduce himself. He was precisely as his name would have him: kind, well-mannered and grandfatherly. In spite of his average height, Mr Friendly held himself straight, and was smartly dressed but not showy. The glasses perched low on his nose seemed the signature of his profession. Sofia smiled. In spite of the circumstances and the charade, she felt delighted with her choice of lawyer.

'It's a pleasure to meet you. Veronica Probert.' She held out her hand confidently and they exchanged pleasantries for a minute. 'Is that your dog, Mr Friendly? He looks a fine animal.'

'Indeed he is, and as good a companion as one could wish. If only human beings were so loyal. But you didn't come here to listen to me philosophise. What can I do for you?'

'I would like you to approach a barrister to advise me in a troubling legal matter, Mr Friendly. His name is Loftis and I believe he is in chambers in Gray's Inn. Do you know him?'

'Of course, I've encountered him a number of times although I could introduce you to other members of the Bar who might prove more...' he floundered, '...sympathetic.'

'I appreciate that but I have had Mr Loftis recommended to me as I did yourself and I am pleased with the results so far.' The gentle compliment brought negotiations to an end. 'I should like to leave some money to settle both your account and Mr Loftis' in advance. I shall call back tomorrow afternoon to find out when and where I can meet with him. Relations at home are rather sensitive and I would prefer not to receive any communications there.' Sofia slid an envelope onto the table containing enough money to ensure that her wishes were seen to promptly. 'It's a family matter on which I seek counsel. I hope we can progress matters in the next week.'

That night she returned to the factory. The desk drawer took some jiggling where the wood had warped with damp. Sliding her hand in, she felt the icy cold of gunmetal on a velvet sack. It was a strange journey home with the weapon sitting heavy in her pocket. More than once, she found her hand snaking its way back inside her coat to stroke the satiny wooden handle and run her fingertips over the engraved metal barrel. Sofia had grown up with guns. Her Romani family kept one in every caravan to see off unwanted visitors. On the farm they were reserved for vermin, poachers and destroying animals. She had forgotten how alluring they could be. Sofia bundled Nora off home with bread, jam and thanks, telling the neighbour she was too tired to talk but wanting only to inspect her cargo more closely.

It was a Velo-dog, a short-barrelled handgun, common enough that she'd seen plenty before. She loved the little fold away trigger that fitted up under the barrel. Sofia pulled it down, checked it wasn't loaded and held the gun at eye level, one finger caressing the trigger. It was small enough to hide easily but powerful enough to kill if you were reasonably close to your target. Inside the velvet bag was a leather case and ammunition. She felt torn. As much as she disliked having a gun at home, part of her felt reassured by it. Wrapping the whole bundle in an old rag, she tucked it away at the back of the highest cupboard.

Five days later she met with Ambrose Friendly again and together they walked up Chancery Lane and east along High Holborn until reaching Gray's Inn and Loftis' chambers. The red brick structures were immaculate. The legal chambers were filled with a gravely hushed atmosphere so oppressive Sofia wondered why anyone would choose to work there. Burgundy, brown and dark blue books lined the corridors as if bright colours might disrupt the onerous professionalism. Mr Friendly had tried again en route to persuade her to find alternative counsel but she wouldn't be swayed.

A junior clerk showed them into Loftis' room and fetched coffee while they waited for counsel. Sofia thought the room exuded pomposity from the gleaming mahogany furniture to the dark velvet drapes and heavy wallpaper. It was a space that declared the value of the time one spent in it. She felt uncomfortable, as if the space were a rough woollen dress making her prickle and itch but she had come here for a purpose and the room, like its occupier, had to be tolerated until she was done. Now that Mr Friendly had played his part in facilitating the meeting, Sofia was anxious that he should leave. He was a decent man and she took no pleasure in deceiving him.

'You may go now, Mr Friendly. You've better things to do than listen to my woes.'

'But my dear Mrs Probert, sometimes barristers can be the most intimidating of fellows. You might find you would like some support. I would caution you against my leaving.'

She patted his arm. 'You are terribly kind, Mr Friendly, and you'll understand that there are some things it is easier to discuss with as few people as possible. You have my word that if Mr Loftis upsets me then I shall seek different counsel but I am well used to unsympathetic men.' He gave in and a few minutes later she was treated to an audience with the esteemed Mr Claude Loftis who wasted no time getting down to business.

'What is the nature of your problem, Mrs Probert, and how is it you think I can assist?' he lit a cigarette and gazed through his window to the square below.

'I am widowed, Mr Loftis, with young children. My husband's barren sister and her husband would raise my children themselves and have threatened to petition the Magistrate. I need to know what course this matter might take.'

'And do they have grounds? By which I mean, they must first assert that you cannot properly fulfil your role as mother before a judge would remove the children from your care. Why would they do such a thing?'

'They are childless and in a better financial position than I. My sister-in-law would have it that I am failing to bring them up as well as she could, something I deny of course.'

'There would have to be concern for the children's welfare, some evidence of your failings. Just because they believe themselves capable of better parenting is no reason for the law to intervene. Are you sure there is no other aspect to their claim?'

Sofia pulled out a handkerchief and pressed it to her mouth. 'I'm sorry, it's rather hard to say.'

'I've been in practice for more than three decades. I dare say there's nothing I could hear from you that I haven't heard a hundred times before.' He had begun perusing a document on his desk and tapping his fingers. Sofia looked around the room as she sniffled. Above the desk hung a large oil painting of Loftis in his grey horse-hair wig and black gown, but there were no pictures of anyone else in sight.

'Are you married, Mr Loftis?' she asked faintly.

'No. Too busy with the law. Why do you ask?'

'Because you might be better placed to understand how hard it is for a woman alone. You see, my sister-in-law's husband has sought to comfort me. A little too closely, if you take my meaning.'

Loftis put down the papers that he had found so fascinating. 'Are you sure you're not imagining this behaviour? It might simply be the actions of a concerned gentleman.'

'It goes beyond what one might term concerned,' she replied.

'Then I think you had best tell me the details. Leave nothing out, so that I can judge for myself.' He licked his lips as he had in the teashop, completely unaware of the habit. Sofia noticed though and knew exactly what he wanted to hear. He could have his pathetic thrill. She would make him regret his indecent enjoyment of her feigned abuses later.

'It started with the occasional hug which would last a few seconds longer than usual or he might hold me more tightly than was comfortable. Then there were the frequent touches, a hand on my arm each time I passed him or his fingers in the small of my back.' She paused, playing her reluctance to its hilt.

'Do carry on, Mrs Probert, this is no time to be coy.'

'His touching became more intimate. If we were seated at the dinner table I would find his hand on my thigh. Then in his library, whilst we were supposed to be discussing my financial affairs, he stood behind me and I can only say that he was rubbing himself against me. I could feel that his intentions were more than platonic, you understand?' Loftis was red-faced.

'And was there ever anything more than that?' he all but panted at her.

'There was one occasion. I feel so ashamed.'

'Unless I have all the information I cannot guarantee to help you.' Sofia was disinclined to give him any more pleasure but had to be sure she'd adequately baited the hook.

'Last week, I was signing a document at his house so he invited me to sit at his desk. He leaned over my shoulder as I was writing and slid his hand down into my dress. He did it so slowly that at first I thought he must not be realising what he was doing, then it carried on into the top of my corset. It didn't stop, Mr Loftis. He pushed his hand

138

down over my bare breast and began to...you can imagine the rest.'
Judging by the look on his face, he could.

'And you didn't stop him?' he asked.

'I didn't know what to say, I was speechless. I can't tell anyone.
They would either not understand or worse, not believe me. Tonight he
has invited me to his house to discuss the children's future. I know I must
go but my sister-in-law is in Canterbury visiting her mother. If I accuse
him he'll no doubt say I'm fit only for the asylum. Please help me, Sir.
What should I do if he continues to approach me so indecently?'

'You should come straight to me so that we can record the
details. In that way, he will not be able to allege that you have concocted
the matter.'

'But it will be at night, Mr Loftis, when your chambers are
closed. I cannot go home to my children and their nanny in such a state.
It would cause a scandal from which I should never recover.'

'Come to my home address but please tell no one I've offered to
help you in this way. It is irregular, if you take my meaning, but I cannot
bear the thought of a young lady being so distressed and having no way
of unburdening herself. Take this.' He wrote down his address which
Sofia accepted with a quick glance.

'I'll see myself out, Mr Loftis, please don't stand. Thank you for
your kindness. I sincerely hope that I shall not need to take up your offer
of sanctuary.' He nodded, serious to the last but he would lock his door
after she left, she thought, and let his imagination finish the story in
whatever twisted way he chose. And he would probably not emerge for
some time.

At home, Sofia settled the children and asked Nora if she
wouldn't mind sitting for them that evening on the pretence of visiting an
old friend. She wore a black skirt and white blouse, one she could bear to
lose, if she had to. Sofia pulled off the top three buttons, leaving the
threads hanging but putting the buttons carefully away to be sewn back
on later. She wore her most comfortable shoes for the long walk, knowing she could run in them if necessary, chose a hat that covered much of

her face and took down the gun. Huddled in a corner, Sofia loaded it and tucked two extra bullets deep into a pocket, waiting until after dark to leave home.

Loftis lived on Thanet Street, between Gray's Inn and the Euston Road. It took a good forty minutes to walk there but it was still too early to knock on the door. She needed to watch a while, which was less easy than she'd hoped without an inn or hotel to lose herself in. Sofia opted for the side of a house where she could shrink against the brickwork and try to avoid notice. Inside Loftis' relatively modest two-storey home lamps shone dimly although she was too far away to see any movement. It was as well that she waited. At ten o'clock, his front door opened and a woman exited whom Sofia presumed by her clothes to be a housekeeper. Even then, there was still too much traffic on the street to move unseen.

By the time she heard a nearby church chime eleven, Sofia was freezing and stiff. The days might be warm in May but the nights retained their damp chill. Checking up and down the road one final time, she wrenched apart her blouse, letting her nails scratch the delicate skin of her chest. At the last moment, she slapped her own face as brutally as instinct would allow. Still not sure she would be convincing enough she repeated the blow two, three times more. Her cheek was raw and stinging. She could do no better than that and crossed the road to her counsel's front door.

Ringing the door bell late at night in such a quiet street would cause nosy neighbours to pry, so Sofia leaned over the black wrought-iron railings and knocked on the front window. It took some time but eventually the curtains parted to reveal Loftis muttering miserably. When he realised the troubled Veronica Probert had taken up his offer, though, his face was quite the picture. He made his way to the front door fast, looking around as he opened it, making sure she hadn't attracted attention. Sofia wasted no time in beginning her sorry tale.

'Mr Loftis, forgive me. Your offer was so kindly given and yet I'm sure you hadn't believed I would need your help.' She did a convincing job of remembering her state of undress, pulling the tattered halves of her blouse together but not before Loftis could soak in the details.

'My dear girl, calm yourself. Come into my study.' He took hold of one hand to lead her and his touch made her shiver. 'You are frozen to the bone. Sit by the fire and tell me what happened.' Loftis was wearing a blue velvet house jacket, a few dribbles of gravy from a hastily consumed dinner marking its lapels. He smelled of red wine and meat with an underlying odour of mothballs and Sofia had no desire to touch him. He scared her, she didn't mind admitting it. Forcing the thought from her mind, she studied her surroundings. A miserly number of gas lamps had been lit for the evening, casting deep shadows at each end of the hallway and leaving the other doorways impenetrably dark. There was no way of knowing how to find the back door if she needed an escape route, so she simply had to ensure it didn't come to that.

Loftis showed her through to his cluttered study and pointed out a seat. Sofia removed her coat for unencumbered access to her skirt pocket as Loftis poured himself and her a large measure of brandy then pulled a chair up close to hers. Sofia had no trouble showing him how badly her hands were trembling, so cold she would have to wait a while before she could trust her limbs to move with sufficient strength or dexterity. She pretended to compose herself before speaking and spent those quiet moments evaluating what sort of opponent Loftis might prove. He used a cane and, judging by the purple mottling on his nose and cheeks, his limp might be the result of gout. He was of average height and wiry-framed. His hair had seen too many years to retain its pigment but there was no reason to doubt his acuity of mind. She mentally thanked Vinsant for the gun, unsure how else she might bring the man down.

'That's better. Finish your brandy before you try to speak.' He managed the semblance of a smile and Sofia made herself appear to relax, casually forgetting to hold her blouse so carefully shut. She drained her glass and put the heavy crystal down on the side table next to her.

'Thank you,' she said in a small voice. 'I'm so grateful. The world can be a cruel place.'

'Indeed it can. But it is my task to ensure that you are protected. Explain to me how your evening unfolded, omit no detail although I can see you've been assaulted about the face.'

As if she'd forgotten it, Sofia brought a hand to her cheek, flinching as she touched the newly bruised bone. 'That wasn't the worst of it. If all he did was beat me, I might be able to tolerate it.' Loftis nodded in a suitably sympathetic way, but his eyes were alight with an unsavoury anticipation. 'He was the perfect gentleman throughout dinner, conversation was normal, he didn't touch me at all, so when he asked me to his study afterwards I thought I'd be safe. He locked the door behind us and I knew then what he had planned. He told me he would persuade his wife not to take the children from me if I gave him what he wanted. I was so afraid. He pinned me against the wall and when I wouldn't kiss him, he ripped my blouse apart.' It gave Loftis an excuse to openly stare at Sofia's chest. She wanted to leave right then, to put her coat on, make an excuse and go. Loftis made her skin crawl.

'Yes, I see, do continue,' he muttered, his voice thick with an emotion Sofia didn't care to contemplate.

'Then he grabbed my arm and spun me round so I was facing the wall.' Sofia's eyes began to fill with tears. They came more easily than she'd anticipated. Her nerves were beginning to take over. 'He pushed himself against me and lifted my skirt,' she faltered. 'I'm sorry, I don't think I can go on.'

For a second frustration appeared unmasked on his face. 'But it is vital I know all, so that we can report the matter, if necessary.'

'I understand,' Sofia rubbed her forehead. 'Do you think that I might have a glass of water and a handkerchief?' He couldn't refuse but was reluctant to stand up. When he left the room, the reason for his reticence was all too obvious in the cut of his trousers. Sofia felt nauseated and transformed her disgust into anger. Here he was, playing the part of guardian, opening his home to her so that he could take perverse gratification from her assault. Anger exploded into hatred as she took out the gun and drew down its trigger.

She waited until he was back in his seat before revealing the gun. Sofia watched his expression turn from confusion to incredulity to fury. Squeezing the trigger, she braced her arm for the upward force that would follow and when it didn't, she found herself lifting her arm anyway, her muscles so convinced of what was coming. As she struggled to comprehend what had happened, Loftis attacked.

He hit the gun from her hand with vastly more force than she'd expected and her last conscious thought was that she'd drastically underestimated him. Loftis dealt an explosive blow to her ear. The pain was instantaneous and her head filled with a clamorous ringing, unbalancing and stunning her. She fell back in the chair trying to get her bearings as he whirled round, grabbing a cushion and thrusting it into her face. She saw it coming but he was fast and her arms hadn't the speed or strength to stop him. Head stuck between the chair behind and the cushion, flesh crushed against teeth, it was as if she were drowning. Blood from her split lips flowed down Sofia's throat which she sucked painfully into her windpipe as she gasped for air. She tried desperately to push the cushion away but he had his whole weight behind it. Loftis was knelt across her lap to pin her and she could hear his laughter in waves as black spots began to swim before her eyes.

She gave up trying to shift the cushion and went for his face with the nails of her right hand, until he grabbed her wrist and twisted it painfully. Her left hand had been flailing about and hitting nothing but air until, drained of energy, it dropped. When it hit something hard and cold, she grabbed instinctively. Registering the brandy glass, she smashed the edge against the wall and rammed it like a circle of knives into the side of Loftis's face. Instantly the cushion dropped away as he scrabbled to deal with the circular crevasse between ear, eye and cheek. Loftis jerked back off Sofia's lap, leaving her gasping for breath, vision dim and throat raw. She could only watch as he ripped out the glass, sending a bloody eruption from the jagged wounds that sprayed a gaudy pattern across the wall, carpet and Sofia. A horrible sucking noise drew Sofia's attention to the space between face and glass where ruby tendrils stretched like a tightrope. Stuck to the glass was a gelatinous blob. Sofia recognised the mass and stared at what remained of Loftis' face. When it dawned upon him that he'd pulled his own eye from its socket, Sofia knew she had no choice but to cut off the inevitable screams. Using what strength she had left, she kicked out a foot out and sent him flying, landing on his back. Sofia picked up Loftis' weapon of choice and shoved the cushion over his mouth. Had he not lost consciousness quickly, Sofia knew she would never have been able to overpower him. His body shook so fiercely that she struggled to stay on top, but she concentrated on balancing her body weight through the cushion, depriving him of oxygen. Minutes passed before she felt certain enough to climb off and she knew she would never forget the time and force it took to kill by suffocation. The human body could go remarkably long without air.

Sofia flopped into the chair exhausted, aching and battered. Worse, she was covered in blood and still had to get home unnoticed and deal with Nora. She had no idea if the fight had made enough noise to alert neighbours or passers by. Retracing her steps, picking up gun, coat, hat, and Loftis' handkerchief, she put the glasses in the kitchen where she washed and dried the intact one and wrapped what fragments she could locate for removal. At Loftis' desk she pulled out every document, removing what money was there and creating as much mess as possible, to make it appear a burglary. With that, she went to the back door of the house which she unlocked and left standing open. It was the best she could do.

No more than half way home the sensation of drunkenness hit. Sofia staggered to one side wondering if it was the brandy or the head injury affecting her balance, and recovered against a tree. Ground spinning, she pressed a hand against her lips to contain a burst of laughter. The world lurched again and she grabbed the tree trunk. It was a blessing that the streets were deserted because the longer she stood there, contemplating the enormity of what she'd done, the more aware she became of the adrenaline still coursing through her body. One arm around the tree, nails scraping bark, Sofia fought to quell the excitement. It was unwanted, obscene. Loftis raised his brutalised face in her mind and, where there should have been revulsion, a steady thrumming rose inside. Her hands twitched remembering the power with which she'd stifled his breath and she cried out, torn between self-loathing and satisfaction. Her depravity was unspeakable. She jerked away from the tree trunk in disgust at her body's betrayal. Sofia restrained herself until she'd lurched to the junction, navigating the corner and vomiting violently in the gutter. Was it not enough to be capable of performing such atrocities that she should find pleasure in them as well? She wouldn't accept that. Her reaction could not be a response to the kill, but the relief of surviving the encounter. That must be the explanation. It was a simple chemical reaction.

A plodding walk home helped steady her nerves. Nora, blissfully asleep and unaware, heard and saw nothing as Sofia entered and washed, shoving the white-now-red blouse beneath her bed for later disposal. In her skirt pocket she found a penny that hadn't been there before, one from a pile of coins on Loftis' desk. She'd seen them on entering the study, the coins orderly amongst the other debris of his life, as if he had been sitting counting his coppers on her arrival. She just hadn't been aware that she had taken it. Sofia found her stocking and dropped it in, where it clinked at the bottom cheerfully, in good company. Four pennies she could never spend.

The gun was returned to its hiding place at the top of the cupboard and for the first time she questioned why it had failed to fire. Vinsant would answer for it, she decided. Her life had been put in the balance. Nonetheless, a valuable lesson had been learned. Rely on no one, trust no one, weapons must be tested, plans rehearsed. The next time, she thought, if there had to be a next time, she would be better prepared.

Chapter Eighteen

Sofia told Mrs Hasselbrook she was visiting to repay her debt for the physician who had treated Tom. She felt a twinge of guilt at misleading her but it was a necessary lie. Vinsant maintained the pretence of being pleased to receive her until Mrs Hasselbrook left the room.

'Explain yourself,' he hissed. Her answer was a gun pointed at his chest. He took a casual step back, smiling.

'What is it you think you're going to achieve? You can't shoot me here.'

'You're damned right I can't. I couldn't shoot anything with this!' Sofia slammed it on the desk.

'I see,' said Vinsant. 'That's the reason for this impromptu visit, is it? You think I knew.'

'Are you denying it?' she spat. 'Because last night felt very much like I was being sent to my death.'

'A fate which plainly did not come to pass. I had no idea the gun would fail to fire. Think about it. If you'd been killed or captured at Loftis' house it would only have been a matter of time before someone linked you to me. That gun has been in my cabinet for years. The truth is I never had cause to use it. I take it the gentleman came off worse.'

'He won't be conducting any more cases,' she said.

'Good. Here's half your payment.' He handed her an envelope but Sofia didn't bother to count the notes. The only reliable thing about Vinsant so far had been his money. 'The remainder will be set against your gambling debt. I have another task for you. Joseph Carlisle, the Member of Parliament. The details are in the envelope.'

'But it was just yesterday,' Sofia gasped. 'You can't ask me again so soon!'

Vinsant ignored the complaint. 'House visits to me are forbidden. Get control of your paranoia, Mrs Logan. You are far more valuable to me alive than dead and if I preferred you in the latter state it would not be left to chance.'

It was a dismissal. She considered a retort but decided against it, closing the door harder than she'd intended, only to come face to face with Mrs Vinsant.

'Are you quite all right, Mrs Logan?' Beatrice asked, her voice low, her eyes on her husband's study door.

'Thank you, yes. I was visiting to settle a debt I owed Mr Vinsant.'

Beatrice stared at her cheek. 'That looks painful,' she said. 'What happened?'

'The children were playing bat and ball. Serves me right for getting in the way,' Sofia murmured. 'I should be on my way.'

Thorne's scarred face appeared from the stairwell. He nodded stiffly at Beatrice as he passed then entered Vinsant's study.

'Come to the parlour with me a moment,' Beatrice said, leaving Sofia no choice but to follow her obediently down the stairs. Mrs Vinsant sat down on a two-seat sofa, patting the cushion next to her.

'I hope my husband's not bullying you, Mrs Logan. We can do without repayment of any money you might have been loaned. You could have come to see me about it.'

'With respect Ma'am, it was your husband who helped me when I needed it. It hardly seems right to go behind his back. I pay my debts and I don't like to be beholden to anyone.' Sofia was thrown. Obviously Vinsant and his wife weren't close but she hadn't expected this. She wondered if she was being tested and if Beatrice might not report the whole thing to him later.

'I appreciate that, but you can talk to me in confidence if you feel as if you are being put under pressure.' She was hard to read. Her face was the picture of concern yet Beatrice was not the kind of woman one would naturally turn to for sympathy. Whatever the position, Sofia wasn't foolhardy enough to think she could betray Emmett Vinsant and survive.

'Mrs Vinsant, you know nothing of the pressure I am under trying to keep myself and two small children. Your husband has done nothing but assist,' Sofia said.

'He keeps a closer eye on you than I would find comfortable in your circumstances, I know that,' said Beatrice, frankly.

Sofia had had enough. The conversation could only lead to trouble. 'As he does you, I've noticed, if only through Captain Thorne. Perhaps you should be less worried about me and more worried for yourself.'

Beatrice sat back, putting a little distance between them and regarding Sofia with a new caution. 'John Thorne is my husband's man, Mrs Logan. We have nothing to do with one another. He certainly does not spy on me if that's what you think. He was taken on by my husband when he returned from the Boer war. His record as a soldier was impeccable and, as far as I know, he is a good man.'

'Then you don't know him very well,' Sofia replied.

'Very well,' said Beatrice, getting up. 'I was wrong to interfere and I apologise for having kept you. I shall send Mrs Hasselbrook to see you out,' and without further discussion she left, as strange and changeable as Tom had described her.

From Doughty Street, Sofia walked to the Houses of Parliament to trace a route from there to Joseph Carlisle's home. She had gleaned from the papers that he was a fiercely religious man who opposed gambling in all its forms as inherently evil. He evangelised regularly and publicly on the point and was trying to raise enough support to have Parliament outlaw gambling completely. Carlisle was holding an open debate in a church hall in Kensington that Friday and Sofia had decided to go along and see the man for herself.

The venue was unlike any church hall she had ever visited. They had been small, dark places, with leaky roofs and patched windows. This one was well funded by the local great and good: Kensington did not tolerate the appearance of poverty. The hall was light and airy, recently painted in cream and hung with samplers quoting scripture. Every gas lamp was lit and rows of wooden chairs were set out in anticipation of a large crowd. Joseph Carlisle was not going to be disappointed. By eight o'clock the place was packed with only standing room at the back. There was a fair mixture of men and women, some with placards in support of the very vocal Member of Parliament, one large group of women interested only in rallying support for the banning of alcohol and others who had come solely for the spectacle.

Carlisle was introduced in lofty terms by the local vicar. The just-so Mrs Carlisle, whose hand her husband had kissed sweetly as he took to the stage, watched him with a smile that would make angels weep. Sofia was left cold. Godly men professing the evils of gambling were nothing new to her. She had grown up with such men decrying her Romani family as corrupt and tainted. He submitted no arguments she hadn't heard a hundred times before, albeit that he delivered his submissions with a breathtaking passion. Little wonder he'd been elected to public office. Carlisle made passing reference to the ladies pursuing alcohol temperance, committing to nothing but pleasing them sufficiently to ensure their continued support. He was undoubtedly a skilled politician, more than capable of understanding that there were some arguments you could win and some that would simply lose you votes. The illegality of alcohol was just such a subject.

It wasn't until a young woman with a northern accent asked a question that the evening took a more interesting turn.

'Mr Carlisle, the Women's Social and Political Union are canvassing Members of Parliament to show their support for women being granted the right to vote. Will you pledge your support for us, Sir?'

Carlisle took a long sip of water pretending a parched throat, but it was a poorly masked play for time.

149

'We have not gathered here tonight to debate the issue of votes for women. It is a wide reaching issue and best revisited at another meeting.' There was a long and pregnant silence until a voice was heard, quietly but clearly, to say "shame" and others in the group echoed the sentiment. The young woman was attending in organised company, thought Sofia. She looked at the questioner and saw the unmistakable profile of Beatrice Vinsant leaning to whisper in the young woman's ear.

'Will you not state your position, Mr Carlisle. It's simple enough: Do you support us or not?' the woman insisted.

The gentlemen of the press had their pens poised for his response and Joseph Carlisle's face was the picture of pious irritation. 'One first has to consider what guidance the Bible provides for us. The good Lord designated leadership to men, to provide for wives and daughters in all things, including making the choices that will best benefit them. If gentlemen abandon that precious duty and pass on the decision making burden to their wives, then we fail to do that which our Lord has instructed.'

'What of women who have no husband? Who should speak on their behalf if not themselves?' a new voice asked, not impolitely but with an air of genuine confusion.

'In such a case it is incumbent on the gentlemen in society to come together and ensure that the decisions we take are for the good of all. No lady is beyond the scope of our collective religious and political conscience.' He was flushed with self-satisfaction but had underestimated the women and, far from being quieted by his response, another took up the cause.

'Did God not create women with brains and hearts just as he did men? Is it not time we were given a chance to properly use the faculties with which we were blessed?'

'But it is also a matter of education,' Carlisle countered. 'Of worldliness and familiarity with the political arena. I should not dream of making decisions in my home regarding what food to serve at a dinner party or which linen to purchase. My wife is better equipped to decide upon such matters in the same way that I am better equipped to deal with finance and governance.'

Sofia felt sorry for his wife. A growing noise was issuing from the group of women who were conferring before giving their response.

'So women cannot comprehend or judge such matters, is that where you stand, Mr Carlisle?'

'The Bible tells us it is a man's place to lead, to set an example to his wife, and a wife in gratitude should be obedient and accept her husband's greater capacity to understand the more complex aspects of life.'

'Did you just say, "A wife, in gratitude, should be obedient," Mr Carlisle?' Beatrice stood up, making no effort to disguise her outrage. 'For what is it that you think we should be grateful? For our husbands controlling our finances, our comings and goings and even, as you would have it, our opinions? Shame on you, Sir. Do not refer to the Bible to excuse such misogyny and bigotry. If you must hold such low views of the capabilities of women at least have the courage to acknowledge them as your own.'

Her intervention was a show-stopper. The women around her began to clap, rising to their feet and looking delighted with Carlisle's lack of response. It was the vicar who retaliated with the first boo. More men's voices joined his then, very deliberately, Mrs Carlisle joined them. Several other women immediately closed ranks with the Carlisles and soon Beatrice's group was outnumbered by an angry mob. One of the men at the back had slipped out earlier and reappeared flanked by four police constables. They barged their way through to the women who, by then, were being jostled and harangued. Sofia heard no polite request for the group to leave, only a hasty scramble to pull them out, and a shouted direction to arrest them for disturbing the peace.

Sofia made sure her face was not visible and shrank to the back of the hall, half-intrigued and half-terrified that the unusual events would lead to someone paying her more attention than she wanted. More police arrived to assist and Sofia followed them out watching Beatrice's back, at any moment expecting to find that it wasn't her at all. She was ready to swear that she must have been confused or mistaken until a man appeared from a side alley, taking Beatrice by the hand and yanking her out of the group of women. A single police constable noticed but when he saw the scarred and furious face over Beatrice's shoulder, he plainly thought she was in far more trouble with him than she would be at the police station, and moved on. Captain Thorne had been sent to deal with Vinsant's troublesome wife. Perhaps now the naive Mrs Vinsant would believe what Sofia had told her about him.

Carlisle was an awfully public target and Sofia was in no doubt about the amount of attention his death would attract. Fortunately, such an outspoken figure would have as many enemies as he did supporters, and his death might benefit any number of people. His house was continuously staffed and his work place was one of the most closely guarded buildings in the country which left the journey between the two.

Sofia had to call on Nora more often than she liked, the older woman becoming frailer by the month and the children more demanding. For three consecutive evenings, Sofia was at the doors of Parliament as he left, each time dressed differently, standing in a new place, blending in with the crowds. By the fourth day she knew what she had to do and approached the task with military precision.

She wore Tom's old clothes beneath her coat, pinned up her hair inside a workman's cap and put her own larger hat on top. Away from the house under cover of dark, Sofia shed the outer garments and left them under a crate round the back of one of the breweries. She was so slim that no one could have told her from a lad in the breeches and baggy shirt. She rubbed soot from a factory window over her face as she went across the city to Westminster where she waited for Carlisle. She knew the route he would take, he'd not deviated from it in the last few nights. He lived in Romney Street which meant he would follow the river south then go west along Great Peter Street, down Gayfere until he reached Smith Square. That was where Sofia would have her best chance to attack.

St. John's, in the centre of Smith Square, was an imposing white church, more like a small cathedral, the edges of which were not well lit at night and surrounded by enough trees and shrubs to give cover. The area was quiet and stately, with no local inns ousting troublesome drunks onto the street or attracting travellers. The sort of people who could afford to live here did all their nighttime travelling by horse drawn carriage or even in flamboyant but unreliable motorcars. Carlisle, different from his peers in this one regard, always walked home, his habitual late return not owing solely to long working hours but also to his enjoyment of a few glasses of wine or liquor of an evening. She had watched him swaying as he walked, talking to himself or humming, his reticence to denounce alcohol apparently arising from more than the simple desire to maintain the popular vote.

Sofia had none of the anger that she'd felt approaching Loftis and surprisingly little of the fear when waiting in the brothel. What she had this time was a cool head and the desire not to get caught. She'd been left detached by his display in Kensington. Carlisle was nothing to her except part of the larger picture, necessary to pay her debts and keep her children from the workhouse. If she experienced any uncertainty, those simple thoughts banished doubt from her mind.

When he came into view, she prepared to move then noticed a woman crossing the street. Sofia crept around the edge of the building following Carlisle's progress, keeping her back to the brickwork, crouching low in the shadows and undergrowth. When certain he was alone, she ran out of the bushes behind him, drew a metal-tipped cosh from her trousers and smashed the weapon down on the back of his skull. A noise like the crushing of a nut shell was followed by a dull thud and the tinkle of coins hitting pavement as the contents of his pockets hit the floor. He had neither seen nor heard her coming and, because he fell forwards, she never even glimpsed his face. He was undoubtedly dead. Enough grisly lumps of flesh were stuck to the end of the cosh to assure her of that. Sofia was transfixed. She'd expected something different. It had been too easy and now here she was, standing over a lifeless body face down in the road.

Distant voices shocked her into action. She grabbed Carlisle's feet and dragged him into the bushes. There was no point inviting discovery until she was away. She wiped the end of the cosh in the grass, shoved it back in her trousers, paused momentarily in the road to pick up a coin, this time aware of her need to acquire one, and set off at a fast walk towards the Thames. At the water's edge Sofia quietly lowered the cosh in, feeling a tug of regret. It had been Tom's, kept at home in case of burglars, and had stood in their wardrobe for many years. She chased the thought away, not liking the idea of Tom looking down and seeing what she'd become. Sofia went as quickly as she dared without drawing attention, until Clerkenwell's familiar roads greeted her.

Back in Brewhouse Yard she found herself reaching for her front door before realising she was still dressed as a man. She made her way back to where she'd hidden her clothing and shed the disguise, shivering as the night air found her naked skin. The wildness surged through her like a spray of boiling water. Sofia reached for the wall, leaning both hands on the brickwork and gasping for breath. Grimacing with effort, she dressed in her usual clothes, hid the disguise in a coal shoot, wiped her face clean and returned to the street.

She told herself she could walk past Charlie's door, that it was best to forget he was even there, but from the second her body had registered its mutinous excitement she'd known she would end up there. Charlie was still hauling on trousers when he opened the door, frowning at the state of her and pulling her inside.

'What happened?' She could see the panic in his eyes, thinking her either unwell or upset. Charlie stepped closer, putting a gentle hand on each shoulder. His expression changed. Her pupils were dilated, lips swollen and darkly red, a light sheen of sweat on her forehead, chest rising and falling so fast she might have just run a mile. 'Sofia?' he whispered.

She brought his head down to hers, knowing she couldn't answer his questions. Charlie didn't hesitate in responding, fastening his arms around her, his body taut with desire. They kissed for only a minute before he carried her through to his bed, shedding his shirt then unbuttoning her dress. She was not coy, intent on enjoying his reaction to her nakedness as he stroked her breasts.

'You're so beautiful,' he said.

'You sound surprised,' she teased as he lay down.

'I thought I'd scared you away,' Charlie kissed her neck.

'Just the opposite,' Sofia replied, running her hand down his chest and stomach to silence him. Charlie was pushing down his trousers as she hitched up her skirt, kicking off her drawers and folding one leg around his back. He resisted the invitation a few moments more, running his tongue between her breasts past her bellybutton until she was half-crazed, spine arched off the bed, biting her lower lip as she came. Charlie buried his face in Sofia's neck and she held him, Carlisle finally fading from her thoughts as she lay exhausted.

Kissing her forehead, Charlie pushed the stray hairs from her face and pulled a blanket over them both. 'Can you stay?' he asked.

'For a while,' Sofia said. 'Nora's with the children.' He'd want to know what had prompted her visit, she thought. With a wistful smile she turned her back, drawing his arm around her and nestling her head under his chin, hopeful that Charlie wouldn't risk spoiling the moment with an interrogation. Sofia was convinced she wouldn't sleep, but it took only the steady rhythm of Charlie's breathing to lull her into dreamless rest. Four hours later their perfect bubble of warmth was shattered by an insistent knocking at the door. Sofia started, terrified that something had happened to Isaac or Sadie.

'Stay there,' Charlie said quietly. 'Don't let anyone see you.' He said it for her sake, not his, she knew. The gossip would ruin her. He ran his hands through his hair and splashed water in his face before opening up.

'You're wanted, Constable Danes. A body's been found. It's a Member of Parliament apparently, so it's all hands on deck. You're to report to Bow Street straight away.' The messenger left immediately, no doubt on his way to rouse other unsuspecting constables enjoying their day off. Sofia's stomach shrivelled to a knot. As Charlie returned she leaned back against the pillow and formed the false likeness of a smile with her lips.

'I've got to go,' he said.

'I heard. Give me a minute. I'll get dressed and follow you out. You'll have to make sure no one's around.'

He sat on the bed. 'I wish the morning hadn't started like this. I'd give anything for another hour with you.' She giggled at how rueful he sounded, like a love-struck lad. 'Are you all right?' he asked. 'You look pale.'

'Don't worry about me. Get dressed, you can't turn up for work like that!' He slid an arm around her waist, kissing her hard before standing and stretching.

'What made you come here last night? Not that I'm complaining, of course,' he laughed.

'I didn't realise you'd want an explanation,' Sofia replied, smiling and climbing into the clothes that had been left strewn across the floor.

'I was just thinking that if I knew what had made you come, I could make sure it happens again.' Sofia flushed at the memory of arriving at Charlie's door. He took the blush as embarrassment. 'I'm sorry, you're right, we don't need to talk about it. Just tell me this isn't all there is. I don't want to leave wondering if it's the last time I'll see you.'

'Of course it isn't,' she said. 'Now, get me out of here before Nora sends a search party.' She made it to her own house with no audience at all, watching Charlie set off up the road to find out who had been murdered and why. Sofia made breakfast and wondered how many times a person could kill before they made a mistake and got caught. More than three, she prayed. Hopefully, the answer was many more than three.

Chapter Nineteen

June 1906

The sudden ferocity of summer was overwhelming. The children played outside from dawn 'til dusk, fruit stands appeared on every street corner and Sofia lazed in the shade watching Isaac and Sadie play as if she hadn't a care in the world.

She attended Joseph Carlisle's funeral, knowing it was stupidity but unable to keep away. In the event, the cemetery was filled with hundreds of onlookers, the crowds drawn as much by the manner of his death as his status and Sofia was in no danger of standing out. His untimely demise had been much examined in the newspapers with prominent church leaders bemoaning the loss of such a good man.

There were suggestions that he had been the subject of a robbery although Sofia, in the heat of the moment, had forgotten to check his pockets. One newspaper had speculated that a political opponent had ordered his assassination and another that his outspoken criticism of certain sections of society had caused such offence that the killing was retributive.

Carlisle's wife seemed much more at peace with her husband's passing than Sofia had expected, greeting those around her with sombre thanks for their kind wishes. She looked utterly unfazed by her promotion to centre stage and was in no hurry to disappear after the service. If Sofia didn't know better she would say the woman was enjoying the attention. It made her wonder what the late Mr Carlisle had been like in the privacy of his own home.

The Vinsants didn't put in an appearance at the funeral, and little wonder after Beatrice's ejection from her last encounter with Carlisle. Sofia had considered the irony of that evening many times since leaving Kensington Church Hall. If it was a coincidence then it was a strange one. That Beatrice and Emmett Vinsant should unknowingly have an enemy in common was almost comical. A poster appearing across the city that week had announced that the Women's Social and Political Union, led by the increasingly familiar figure of Emmeline Pankhurst, was expanding from its Manchester office and setting up shop in London. That would explain the northern accent of the woman who'd asked the first question. Sofia found it hard to understand how they could be so obsessed with the right to vote when most women were struggling to put bread on the table and keep their children safe from illness and exploitation. Although curious, she had concluded that these were women with too much time on their hands and not enough else to worry about. Public support for the rebellious suffragettes was low and Sofia believed it would take more than a few well timed questions and leaflets to make the world listen.

That month, Charlie spent an increasing amount of time with Sofia, entertaining the children and doing odd chores. He repaired a pane of glass that Isaac had accidentally cracked with a stone and mended a collapsing chest of drawers, showing Nora the same attention, often fetching and carrying for her. The long hot days were a gift, saving money on wood and coal, eating cold cuts of meat instead of boiling up casseroles. Sofia's natural pallor was replaced by a healthy glow and she laughed more than she had for a very long time.

Isaac's eighth birthday crept up on her, the month had passed so quickly. As it fell on a Sunday she decided they would take a picnic to Hyde Park. She had bought him a kite and some marbles and the park was the perfect place for him to try out his new toys. Sofia invited Nora but the walk was too far. Instead, Charlie offered to carry the picnic. After ten minutes, it was Sadie who needed carrying so Sofia took the basket and Charlie hoisted a delighted girl onto his shoulders with Isaac running alongside as they sang a marching song. Sofia marvelled at how life could give so generously with one hand and take so cruelly with the other. Charlie Danes kept her sane. He gave her a hand to hold when no one was watching, a strong pair of arms when she needed help and the extra attention that the children missed so much. Sometimes he visited at night, when the children were soundly asleep and they could sit and whisper together about her life and his work. A couple of times Nora had fallen asleep at Sofia's after dinner and she'd been able to slip to his house for a few hours. They didn't talk then, holding one another tightly in Charlie's small bed and making love. They were always careful not to be seen. There would be no tolerance for a widow bedding a man while her children slept a few doors away.

Through it all, Sofia learned to separate the two halves of herself. She killed once in June and then again in July. The first was a debtor, a regular at the tables in the club. She'd followed him home one night, so drunk that she didn't even need to break into his house as he'd neglected to lock the door. The man had passed out on his bed. All she'd had to do was cover his head with a leather sack, and lean her body weight on it. He barely struggled. The second was one of Vinsant's employees who had long been suspected of stealing from the factory. It was the first chance she'd had to use the Velo-dog after getting its blocked barrel cleaned at a gun shop south of the river. She felt worse for him than any of the others. The man had children and was providing for them but Vinsant had insisted that it would send out a message to others who might be tempted to try the same. Whenever she killed, Vinsant was out in public, where no one could forget his presence and Captain Thorne, the man to whom suspicion would immediately fall in an investigation, was always at his side.

As each man lost his life to Vinsant's unlikely assassin, Sofia became sweeter and gentler at home. Nora sung her praises so often, calling Sofia the daughter she wished she'd had, that the children had begun to tease her for it. Isaac and Sadie flourished and there was enough money to buy healthy, wholesome food and a penny each for a bag of sweets on Saturdays. Sofia loved telling them stories at night, always Tom's privilege in the past, but now she found herself filling his shoes in ways she never thought she would and they seemed to be recovering from the loss of their father, asking for or about him less. She was more confident, in every part of her life.

If the police were suspicious that any of the deaths were related, they didn't declare it through the newspapers. She probed Charlie for details every now and then. He rarely shared any details and she was pleased to know that none of the deaths seemed to have been linked. It was only his conclusions about Carlisle's death that caused her any concern.

'That murder, the Member of Parliament, did they ever get who did it?' she asked one afternoon as they watched the children play with a hoop in the road.

'Not yet. But I think we will. There was a witness, gave a good description and she saw which way the attacker took off.'

Sofia steadied herself against the dizziness that threatened her.

'That's progress for you then,' she murmured. 'Would she recognise the murderer, do you think?'

'You interested in becoming a detective now, are you?' Charlie teased.

'I just don't like the thought of such people running around the streets, that's all.'

'You and me both. Isaac, mind your sister!' he shouted to the children.

'So would she, do you think?' she persisted, pressing harder than she was comfortable with but unable to stop herself.

'I think there's a good chance she would, yes although she said something strange. Apparently the murderer was dressed like a man but the witness seemed sure it was a woman. Just from the way they moved and ran. It's an interesting one. Don't you worry. We'll solve it.'

Sofia smiled as convincingly as she could before making her excuses and retreating inside. She couldn't ask Charlie anymore, certainly not the details of the description. Breathing slowly, doubled up on the bed she waited until she could think straight. They could never prove it was her that night. Surely dressed as man she was safe from recognition. And yet she'd been foolish enough to turn up at Charlie's door without explanation. If he thought about it hard enough...no. She was being paranoid. There was no reason for Charlie to suspect her. Even so, she had been careless. If she got so carried away each time, sooner or later Charlie would start asking questions. There could be no more mistakes.

Sofia thought through what loose ends she might have left. It was a point of pride that she was never unnecessarily torturous. There was no point attracting additional attention. All she ever wanted was for the police to be hunting a burglar, an opportunistic passer-by or a jilted lover. Signs of blood lust would trigger a manhunt. The lure of it crept up on her occasionally, triggered by the slightest and strangest things. The scent of copper as she walked past a factory, a trickle of berry juice on the greengrocer's hand, and the first moment of silence in complete darkness. It was nothing as precise as a desire to kill, more a dull ache when she recalled how liberating it had felt. She told herself it was all about Bergen and the fear with which he had poisoned her. All of it sprang from him. If she felt the same thing each time she took a life now, who could blame her?

In the last week of July she was summoned to meet Thorne at a tavern in Southwark. He was there before her, looking unusually carefree and casually dressed, a pint of ale on the table before him. He pulled a chair out for her and ordered Sofia lemonade. Sofia took a sip before speaking, parched after the long walk.

'So Captain, what is it this time?'

'You may as well call me John,' he said. 'It seems we're destined to continue working together.'

Sofia couldn't help but laugh. 'We hardly work together, do we? Deliver the message and get it over with, would you?'

'We're supposed to be meeting for a pleasant drink in a pub like old friends or new lovers. Mr Vinsant's enemies are not beyond having him or me followed so act the part. Sit back and pretend you're enjoying my company. It won't kill you.' As little desire as she had to spend time in his company he was right, so she unbuttoned her coat and relaxed.

'All right then. Seeing as we've got to play this game, tell me something. How can you bear to be servant to a man like him or has he got something over you too?' Sofia asked. Thorne took out a cigarette case, puffing volumes of smoke into the air before answering.

'It's a job and I'm grateful for it. Many households would be too ashamed to have someone with my disfigurement appearing before their friends or guests. Mr Vinsant is not so fainthearted.' He took a draught of ale. 'Your husband worked for Vinsant many more years than I. Shouldn't that concern you more?'

Of course it should, Sofia thought. It wasn't hard to see what Vinsant was when you got close to him and it was impossible to believe that Tom had been naive to his ways of operating.

'How did you come to work for him?' she asked less abrasively.

'My family served Mrs Vinsant's family before she was married. I came back from the Transvaal four years ago. It took another two years to repair the wound to my face and recover. It proved impossible to get work until I approached Emmett. He likes having a man who can handle a gun and, better than that, I have no wife or children to distract me.'

'Did you never want a family?'

'A machete relieved me of having to consider it an option.' He rubbed the scar absent-mindedly and Sofia wished, in spite of her dislike, that she hadn't made him so self-conscious.

'What was the war like? I've heard such horrible stories of Africa and the barbarians.'

'The truth is they're no more barbarians than you or I. For the most part they live simple lives, hunting and farming. Like most wars, it was bloody and brutal and pointless.' He finished his pint and waved at the landlord for another.

162

'You don't sound much like a soldier,' Sofia said. 'Weren't you fighting for your country? Tom used to say it was our duty to lead the world, to show what it is to be educated and live in a decent society.'

'We burned the natives' farms, put them in prison camps to stop them assisting the Boer army and left them there to starve and rot. Your husband spoke in idealistic terms because he never had to pick up a weapon and kill someone in their own country, in their own home. The more people I killed and friends I watched die, the less sense it made, especially when the real reason we were there, was to control the region's gold mines. It never seemed a good enough cause to justify killing.' Sofia knew better than most the cost of taking a life on someone else's orders. They reached an uncomfortable silence until Thorne's drink was brought to their table.

'What was it you needed to see me about?' Sofia asked, grateful to change the subject.

'Next Sunday night there'll be a man on a train, returning home after a weekend at a country house belonging to a friend of Mr Vinsant. It'll be the last train of the night back to London and it's usually empty. He needs to be dealt with.'

'Why?' Sofia asked before she could stop herself.

'You still need justification, do you? That's probably a good thing. He's been taking bribes to lobby Members of Parliament which isn't unusual, but then he approaches whoever has a conflicting interest and asks for even more money to back off, without returning the original bribe. He's supposed to have been assisting our employer for some time now without results and was given the choice to make things right or give the money back. A lot of money. The gentleman in question has ignored the very clear messages he's been sent and now his time has run out. The details are in here.' He handed Sofia a heavy, brown paper bag.

'That looks like more than a sheet of paper,' Sofia commented.

'Strawberries and some of Mrs Hasselbrook's scones. She thought the children might enjoy them.' Sofia peered inside the bag, breathing in the smell of fresh baking and noting the slip of paper.

'There's also money for your train fare and something you might need. Be careful, it might prove rather sharp.'

She folded the top over and pushed the bag to the side of the table. 'And what of Mr Vinsant's businesses? Are things better now that some of his obstacles have been removed?' It seemed ridiculous talking in riddles, but she didn't dare speak any names aloud. If Thorne was concerned about being watched, perhaps she should be, too.

'There seems to be less public opposition to gambling and Vinsant has plans to build a new club. Speaking of which, Lefevre is no longer working. He's unwell. The doctor hasn't identified the cause but he's weak and his muscles are wasting.'

The news was a blow. It had only been two months since she'd seen him. 'Can I visit him?' Sofia asked, hearing her voice wobble. She liked Lefevre. He was so outgoing and vibrant, it was appalling to think of him fading.

Thorne thought about it. Sofia knew Vinsant didn't like his staff socialising, presumably so that they had less opportunity to compare notes about their employer.

'I don't see how it could do any harm,' he said, taking out a pencil and scribbling an address on the bag. A nearby clock chimed the hour and Sofia realised she ought to be on her way home. Still, she had one more question while Thorne was in a talkative mood.

'And what about Mrs Vinsant? I'm surprised a lady like her is mixing in such troublesome company.'

The Captain stared at her blankly for a moment until understanding dawned on his face. So she was not supposed to know about Beatrice's suffragist alliances. Vinsant was trying to keep it quiet. Thorne leaned forward so there was no way anyone could possibly overhear.

'You stay away from Mrs Vinsant, Sofia. It will land you in the worst kind of trouble. Mr Vinsant doesn't want anyone talking about it.' She backed away from his angry, agitated face, and put on her coat.

'I'll remember that. Do thank Mrs Hasselbrook for the scones and I'll see to it that this,' she held the up bag, 'gets sorted.'

164

The walk home was improved by the setting sun casting reds, oranges and pinks across the river. She had plenty to think about, not least Lefevre, but when she arrived home to Charlie reading Sadie and Isaac a book, Nora frying up cured bacon and eggs for tea and a vase of fresh flowers on the table, she put her troubles aside. This was what it was all about, she thought, the reason she was doing what Vinsant wanted.

It was the last day of July before she was able to visit Lefevre. He lived in rented rooms above a hat shop in Holborn. After knocking for some time on his door she assumed he was out, perhaps visiting the doctor or even recovered and returned to work. She was about to leave when she heard a slow shuffling.

'Who is there?' a thin voice asked.

'It's Sofia, Monsieur Lefevre. Captain Thorne gave me your address, I hope you don't mind.' The door opened and a hand beckoned her in although he kept his body hidden from view until it was shut. When she saw why, it was impossible to hide her shock. 'God in heaven, what's happened to you? When I saw you at the tea shop you looked fine. How can you have lost so much weight so fast?'

He trudged up a flight of stairs to his rooms where every curtain was closed. It looked as if he hadn't been out for weeks. It looked as if Lefevre had been sleeping on the sofa. The detritus of sickness was scattered around, bowls, cloths, glasses of water and bottles containing a variety of liquids and powders. There was a rank smell, deep seated though Sofia did her best not to acknowledge it. She could see through the back window that accessing the privy meant Lefevre tackling rickety wooden steps from the kitchen to the yard, certainly not safe in his condition. He'd obviously been reduced to using a chamber pot and emptying it whenever he had the strength to make the journey outside. It was dismaying that he should be alone in such a state. Lefevre collapsed onto the sofa and pulled a grubby blanket across his legs.

'Something has been strange for a few months. At the start I just lost my appetite. I thought it was influenza or a stomach complaint.

When I last saw you I was starting to feel weak and sometimes faint but I was still able to work although I required more breaks. It wasn't until my clothes no longer fit that I knew it was more serious. Now here I am, a shadow of my former self, quite literally.' He attempted to joke but it was too real to be funny. Sofia tucked the blanket around him, noting the sharpness of his bones, ribs sticking out as if every inch of meat had been stripped away. He was more skeleton than man.

'Can the doctor do nothing?' she asked.

'I've had leeches regularly but he is unsure of the precise cause. I have been passing some blood,' he stopped himself. 'I apologise for talking of such things, a lady should not hear this.'

'Don't be silly, Lefevre, I'm neither a lady nor capable of being shocked by anything you say. What else did the doctor suggest?'

'He left some medicine and recommends that I eat as much fatty food as I can. He says I should have plenty of sugar, potatoes and bread but when I do my stomach hurts. I don't seem to have the energy to eat these days.'

'You must try,' Sofia said. 'Are there groceries here?'

'Yes,' Lefevre sighed, the effort of the stairs and conversing taking their toll. 'My friend who owns the shop downstairs brings me food each day.' Sofia plumped a pillow and slid it behind his head.

'Get some sleep, I have a couple of hours free. I'll make you some soup. You must keep up your strength.'

He didn't argue and Sofia knew that the proud, feisty man she'd first met must be terribly ill to allow her to invade his kitchen. For the next two hours she chopped, boiled and prepared soups that she stored in pots and pans. She took one warm bowl through to him before leaving, stroking his arm until he opened his eyes.

'Try to eat this while it's fresh. I've left more in your larder.' He lifted a shaky spoon to feed himself but he was drained. She knew that if she left he would give up and slip back to sleep. 'Let me.' She took the spoon from his hand and, in spite of his initial protest, he gave in after tasting the broth. It took a long time to finish and all the while she spoke of the children's summer, the increasingly militant suffragettes, how they had taken to protesting at Westminster, and of her new friend, Charlie. She wiped his mouth respectfully, as patient and loving as she would have been with Sadie or Isaac, and when she laid down the spoon he put one hand over hers.

'You are a good person, Sofia. I knew it from the first moment I saw you. And a wonderful cook. If I'd taken you home to my mother, she would have told me to marry you. Sadly she was always going to be disappointed as far as marriage goes. I don't think she'd have enjoyed me bringing home my gentleman lovers quite so much.' He managed a croaky laugh and Sofia was pleased to see a little colour in his cheeks.

'Get some rest. I'll come again in a couple of days. Until then, promise me you'll eat at least one bowl of soup each day.' She kissed his temple. 'I'll see myself out.'

Sofia felt cold, shivering in spite of the sunshine, and twice she took a wrong turn in spite of how well she knew the roads. Whatever was wrong with Lefevre, it wouldn't be cured with soup. She would have invited him to stay with her, but there wasn't the room and the children wouldn't be able to bear it so soon after losing their father. What she wanted more than anything else was Charlie, his strong arms around her and the distraction of his sweet smile. Instead of heading east for home, she went west across the city to Bow Street Police Station. Charlie was due to finish his shift in half an hour which would give her enough time to get there and meet him. They could walk home together and enjoy the breeze that was blowing away the increasingly stale odour from the Thames.

Bow Street Police Station was an imposing building, high fronted and severe, with grand architecture and fortress-like lines. Sofia wondered idly what it was like in the cells, with only a tiny slit for a window and nothing but a wooden bunk and tin bucket. When Charlie appeared through the doors she skipped across the road, dolefulness gone, and slipped her arm through his, delighted by the surprise and pleasure on his face.

167

'Mrs Logan,' he said. 'I hadn't expected to bump into you so far from home.'

Sofia played along. 'Well, Constable Danes, I was visiting a friend and thought it might be nice to walk home together. Do you mind?'

'Mind?' he echoed. 'I must be the luckiest man in Bow Street.' Sofia grinned as they began to walk.

'Mrs Probert?' A voice called from behind. Sofia heard it but failed to make the connection until it was repeated. 'Mrs Probert? Do excuse me,' she heard a man say, obviously pushing past someone to catch up with her. She kept her eyes forward, quickened her step and pulled Charlie along slightly. Once she felt the hand on her elbow, it only took the time for her to stop, turn and face Ambrose Friendly before she had played out the whole scenario in her head. Charlie would become suspicious, she would be found out, tried, sentenced and hanged.

'Go on ahead,' she told Charlie but it was too late. He was already stepping protectively forward.

'Mr Friendly,' Sofia said, before Charlie could say he was mistaken. 'How are you?'

'I'm very well, Ma'am and most glad to have seen you. I've wanted to speak with you for some weeks now but I had neglected to write down your address. You always picked up your correspondence from my office.'

'I don't understand,' Charlie started, forcing Sofia to interrupt.

'Forgive my rudeness,' she said. 'Police Constable Charlie Danes, this is my solicitor, Mr Ambrose Friendly.' Charlie shook the lawyer's hand but he was looking at Sofia.

'Pleased to make your acquaintance, Constable. I was on my way to advise a gentleman who is being questioned at your place of work. Some of my clients are rather more agreeable than others,' Ambrose said. Charlie managed a polite smile but not a reply.

'Mr Friendly, perhaps I could visit you tomorrow with regard to any outstanding matters?' Sofia asked.

'Oh, I shouldn't like to put you out with the children to care for but I'm afraid your counsel, Mr Loftis, has passed away.'

'Goodness,' said Sofia, pressing a hand to her mouth. 'I'm so sorry to hear that. How is Mrs Loftis coping?'

'Small mercy perhaps that there was no Mrs Loftis, for he was killed in his own home.' He waited as Sofia reacted with precisely the right amount of horror before continuing. 'I only wanted to return the money you left for his services as he did not put in a bill for the time you were with him, unless you'd like me to instruct different counsel to take up the litigation.'

'That won't be necessary, thank you, the matter is settled.'

'Then I can reimburse you now.' He pushed several notes from his pocket into Sofia's hand which she thrust into her bag before Charlie could calculate how much was there. 'Please don't hesitate to call should you need anything else.'

'Thank you,' she murmured, already moving away.

'My pleasure, Mrs Probert,' he replied.

There was a long period of silence during which Sofia was torn between rushing in with an explanation and keeping quiet to avoid appearing guilty. Before she could decide, Charlie found his voice.

'Sofia, I don't like to ask you to explain yourself but I can't stop from wondering what's going on. Who was that man and who does he think you are?' He looked more concerned than irritated and Sofia knew that the manner in which she answered would mean more than the substance of what she said. She stopped still on the pavement and stared Charlie straight in the eyes.

'I should've said something but things were so new between us that I didn't want to burden you. Tom's sister, Mary, visited unannounced and was threatening to take the children. I needed legal advice but was scared of the process. I know it wasn't rational but I decided that if they thought I was a proper lady, I'd be taken more seriously. I'm sorry that you got involved in my lies and I'll understand if you can't forgive me.' She cast her gaze to the ground while he considered his response.

'If you'd told me what was going on, I'd have gone with you,' he said.

'And how would that have looked? Me, newly widowed, being accompanied by a gentleman friend. They'd have judged me before I'd even got through the door.' Charlie couldn't disagree with that.

'Let's get going,' he said. 'Isaac'll be running rings round Nora by now. She'll need rescuing.'

Sofia slipped her hand back through the loop of his arm and changed the subject before he could think any harder about it.

'You should have had children,' she said. 'You're wonderful with my two.'

'Maybe it's not too late,' he answered. 'It's difficult with my job though. I work all hours, get called out in the middle of the night, sometimes I don't see daylight properly for a month and I'm hoping to train as a detective.'

'Isn't that what you already do?'

'Not exactly, it's a lot more detailed,' he said. 'Science is changing how we do police work all the time. Last year the Fingerprint Branch at Scotland Yard solved a double murder with one print. You'd be amazed what we can tell about criminals from what they leave behind.'

'Sounds scary,' Sofia replied, trying to be interested when she would rather have talked about anything else in the world. She didn't allow herself to think about what the police did after the bodies were found, and the idea that they might have her fingerprints was the stuff of nightmares.

'The only scary thing would be to leave such devils out there unchecked. It must be awful to think that your own counsel has fallen victim to a murderer. He of all people should have been wary of robbers.'

Sofia didn't want to talk to Charlie about Loftis. Thinking about how badly wrong that evening had gone still unnerved her. 'It's dreadful but I barely knew him. He offered a few minutes of advice and I never saw him again. How much do you know about it?'

'I didn't go to the scene but I heard from someone who did. They believe the murderer was after information or revenge even though they tried to make it look like a burglary. Let's not talk about it. I don't want to make you afraid to walk out of your door at night.'

'No, please go on. I'd like to know what happened after he advised me so kindly. Why did it not seem to be a burglary?'

'Because the attacker failed to take anything from any room other than the study. In my experience, when a burglar has gone to the trouble of breaking into a house they steal from more than just one room. They hadn't even gone up the stairs. Nothing was taken except from the room where they found his body.'

'Could it not be that the attacker was disturbed?' she asked.

'His bed was still made, the housekeeper had just changed the sheets for him. That means he was probably still downstairs when the murderer entered the property. If they'd come through the kitchen door he'd have heard, gone to see what was happening. It makes no sense that he was killed in the study. Something doesn't add up. Unless he knew the person who killed him, of course.'

Sofia felt the blood draining from her cheeks and knew she couldn't continue the conversation, whatever Vinsant wanted from her. She was suddenly convinced that Charlie could see the guilt written across her face.

'You're right, I'm sorry. It's harder than I thought to talk about such things. I think I'll go home and rest a while if you don't mind.'

'Of course,' he said, looking concerned. 'Will you be all right?'

Sofia nodded and reassured him, but it was a lie. How long before the police got more information, started extending their enquiries? And now Charlie knew that Loftis had been her counsel. If they found out that Loftis had been at odds with Vinsant, then Charlie could hardly avoid wondering about the coincidence.

They parted company for a while. He went to his home and she to hers, relieved to be away from him, worried that at any second she might say a wrong word. At the same time she longed to put her arms

171

around him and let him chase the shadows away, to make her feel safe and happy and normal. She inwardly cursed her father for making her take the German's life. If he'd never shown her that she could kill, she wouldn't have ended up so perilously close to death at the end of a swinging rope. Still she couldn't forget the feeling of power, the surge of something like immortality when she wielded a weapon and changed the shape of the world around her.

The children were a blessed distraction, wanting food, baths, stories and games. She gave Nora dinner as payment for her help, with more brandy than usual, not that her friend was going to complain about such generosity. At ten o'clock, when the last rays of summer sun had finally melted away, Sofia went to Charlie, unable to stay away even if she was tempting fate.

He opened the door all smiles, the anxiety of the afternoon set aside. They drank hot chocolate and talked about the children and Nora. Only once midnight had rung the capital's bells did Charlie draw her onto his lap, kissing her lips and unbuckling her skirt. They made love without words but in the dreamy half-sleep that followed, Charlie asked the question Sofia had been dreading.

'I was just wondering - the money. It seemed to be a lot. I can't understand how you're managing to pay your rent and food, often Nora too and now lawyers' fees as well.' Sofia sighed. Simplicity and honesty were the ghosts that would haunt her.

Chapter Twenty

Childhood 1893

Finally, the day Sofia had been waiting for arrived. Bill and Letty Marney had gone to a cousin's wedding and would be gone twenty-four hours. Sofia had been planning what she would do for a month. She woke Saul at four, an hour before first light, although she had lain awake a while before that. The two of them fed the animals early then Saul mucked out the cart horses while Sofia saw to her chores inside the house, careful not to wake Mac. At last, they let the cattle out into the field to graze and the day was their own, a picnic of cheese, pickles and freshly baked bread tied into a table cloth and the world waiting for them. That's the way it seemed as they sprinted across the fields and into the distant woods.

On and on they ran until neither of them recognised the lay of the land, joyfully lost, exactly as they had both wanted. Finding a river, they stripped off their outer clothes and raced in, splashing and screaming. It was paradise, Sofia thought. Almost as if she had stolen time from someone else's life. They were climbing the river bank, shivering and laughing, before she noticed the patchwork of scars on Saul's back. Without thinking she ran her fingers over the raised, red skin. Saul froze. He didn't turn or say a word. Sofia dropped her hand. Saul grabbed his shirt and pulled it over his shoulders, throwing Sofia her top without looking her in the eyes.

'You want to know what happened,' he said. It wasn't a question.

Sofia didn't know what to say. She spent so much time thinking about her own misery, the mother she missed so much and how she hated the monotony of life at the farm, that it hadn't occurred to her that Saul could have been through equally terrible things himself.

No, she thought. She didn't want to know. She wanted her image of beautiful, sweet, Saul to remain intact. There was enough sadness inside her already.

'Yes,' she said.

Saul pulled the food roughly from the tablecloth and threw an apple at Sofia. He tore off a chunk of bread and chewed it thoughtfully, staring at the water. Sofia watched him, thinking how his green eyes seemed even greener in the bright light, worried that his skin would have burned already in the sun, and wished she could touch him again, hold him, tell him the scars didn't matter.

'My parents are religious. They're not bad people, really, they just live by strict rules and I wasn't what they'd expected,' he smiled.

They were bad people, Sofia thought, but she knew better than to say it. Saul could remember them any way he wanted. It wasn't her place to make it harder for him. But if they weren't bad people, he wouldn't be here.

'I couldn't conform to their standards. I tried, and I wanted to, but I couldn't change. By thirteen they'd tried every way of making me better, praying for me, punishing me, nothing worked. That's why they sent me here. It was easier for everyone that way.' He tossed what remained of his bread to the birds and lay on his back, one arm over his eyes as if shielding them from the noon sun. Sofia thought he just didn't want her to see the tears at the corners of his eyes.

She didn't understand. What could any parent find in him that was such a disappointment? He was gentle, respectful, the only one of the farmhands who didn't stare at her behind or down her shirt at any opportunity. He always said please and thank you, filled his evenings reading books, and Sofia hadn't once heard him raise his voice. In her eyes he was perfect. At the farm, he was all she had. For the last two years, their free hours had been spent together, perched on a branch or in a corner of the barn, leaning against one another for warmth or comfort, confiding their dreams. She couldn't imagine life without him.

Throwing her apple core into the tree, Sofia walked over and sat down next to Saul, curling a lock of his sandy hair in her fingers as she gazed at him. He opened his eyes.

'What?' he whispered, smiling.

As she leant forward to kiss him, she saw his lips part slightly and closed her eyes. There was a second when it was all anticipation, breathless, floating silence. Then a soft hand on her shoulder stopped her. He said nothing, cheeks reddening.

'Is something wrong?' Sofia asked but he didn't reply. There was only an embarrassed silence and the knowledge that the perfect day was over. 'I'm sorry,' Sofia mumbled, stumbling away.

'Sofia, please, it's not you,' he said, getting to his feet.

'I don't want to talk about it,' she shouted. 'I thought you liked me and now I've ruined everything.'

'You haven't, it's just...there's something wrong with me,' Saul blurted out. Sofia turned. 'My parents said I was an aberration.' He was shaking, trying to control it, but failing. She put her humiliation aside and went back, put her arms around him, not in the way she had wanted to before, but as close as she could remember to the way her mother used to hold her.

'Don't say that,' she replied. 'Your parents were wrong. You saved me. I couldn't have made it through this alone. You're my only friend and I love you.' She rocked him until he stopped shaking, thinking how fragile he seemed, how breakable, and wondering why that made her feel stronger. Even if he didn't love her the way she loved him, perhaps that feeling would be enough to survive on. For a while, at least.

Chapter Twenty-one

August 1906

Sofia rose from Charlie's bed and walked to the small back window where the first August moon, full and yellow, shone light into the alleyway behind. She thought of what Emmett Vinsant would do if he found out she'd told anyone about her relationship with him but he was no threat if she was already convicted of murder. She needed to protect herself first and that meant telling Charlie enough truth to convince him. Perching on the sliver of window sill, Charlie's shirt around her shoulders, Sofia stared outside.

'I love August,' she began. 'Hot days and heavy nights. When I was little we could make enough money on an evening like this to get us through the winter. The heat does something queer to people, makes them loose with their wallets, men show off in front of women. My mother used to call August the month of fools and lovers. I guess she was right, there were more babies born in May and June than at any other time of year. The sun makes people wanton.' Charlie didn't interrupt but he pulled up a chair and lit a cigarette.

'I gamble, Charlie. I bet money on card games. Sometimes I win and sometimes I lose. One of my earliest memories is of sitting on my pa's knee with him handing me a card and making me say its number and suit. I could do sums long before I learned the alphabet. At seven, I could add and subtract faster than the adults. By then I was sitting in on the games at every fair, watching the play, giving signals by tapping my father's back when the cards didn't add up right and I thought someone was cheating. Many men got a beating on their way home courtesy of those little signals. It was my way of life and I took pride in it.' Uncharacteristically Sofia plucked the cigarette from his fingers and inhaled. It tasted bitter and hurt her throat, the discomfort oddly grounding and re-assuring.

'I don't think my mother ever liked it but each of us had to pay our way. I was luckier than some of the girls. Those with fuller figures were chosen to lure the men in. The uglier ones were made up, glued with hair and set in false chains like freaks. The men worked long hours lugging heavy machinery, protecting the camp from attacks, making spirits from fruit or vegetables, and were sent out to steal when times got really hard. Nearly every one of them spent time in prison. Life was tough and never taken for granted.'

'Did you never think about running away?' Charlie asked. Sofia forgave him for thinking it was a terrible way to grow up. It must have seemed completely alien to anyone who hadn't been part of the huge rambling beast of a family. For her, it had been home in spite of the hardships.

'No. I did wish we could stay in one place. I had this stupid dream of living by the sea, tending a vegetable patch and fishing. I wanted to be like the other children I saw as we travelled, who went to school and who seemed to belong somewhere. I never felt that but I loved my mother and I had real value, not just to my family but to everyone in the camp. In some ways I was a bit like one of the freaks they dressed up and stuck bits on to entertain the gullible, but my abnormality was invisible. By eleven I could count cards better than any punter who'd ever tried their hand with us. I was sent away because it got out of hand. My mother didn't want me living that life anymore and I understood her reasoning but the desire, the need, to play never died.' Sofia fetched a glass of water, her throat dry after the cigarette, considering how much to say and what to hold back. 'After Tom died I needed money, so I got involved in gambling again. I've had some wins and some losses but, to cut a long story short, that's where the money came from. I don't know how much longer it'll last but for now I can pay my way.'

'Is that why Tom's sister wants to take the children?' Charlie asked.

'Yes,' she lied, returning to her window sill perch.

'I see,' said Charlie thoughtfully. 'There are some dangerous people involved in gambling. I've seen enough retribution to know how they do business. Whoever runs your games isn't going to be sympathetic if your luck changes.'

'It's all right,' she said. 'It's Emmett Vinsant. He was Tom's employer and he knows about the children. He wouldn't let me come to any harm. You don't need to worry.' She knew she shouldn't have given the name but wanted to reassure him and it would explain why she'd been given credit in the first place.

'All the same, promise you'll take care. You don't know what these types are capable of.'

He was preaching to the converted although he had no idea how ironic his cautioning was. A sudden movement outside made her jump back from the glass and Charlie raced to catch her before she could crash to the floor. She laughed at her own clumsiness, standing up to look out of the window.

'There's no one there,' Charlie said. 'Let's go to bed. I'll wake you before light. Don't leave now.' He seemed satisfied and Sofia felt better for telling some of her story. She climbed into bed and laid her head on his chest.

On the morning of Sunday 5 August, Sofia took the Peterborough train from Kings Cross station. She'd bought a newspaper to pass the time and to hide her face, if necessary. She would go all the way to the end of the line, needing to get lost in a big town for the day. In a bag, she'd packed sandwiches and fruit for lunch and had money to treat herself to tea and cakes in the afternoon. Most important was to look like any other day-tripper, enjoying the weather and shops. Spending the whole day was vital. It was too much of a risk to be seen travelling one way then back again immediately.

Peterborough's streets were wide and the air so much fresher than London that Sofia marvelled at how the place even tasted different. After an hour wandering around the vast Cathedral, Sofia took a slow walk along the banks of the River Nene where she ate lunch, throwing morsels to the increasing circle of ducks at her feet. By the time she'd retraced her steps, she was thirsty and found a tea room at the edge of the beautiful park where she passed the remaining hours until returning to the station. It was late by then and she was flagging. When her train was finally boarding she was terrified that she'd fall asleep.

Perhaps she did doze, alone in the carriage, so dark she could see virtually nothing of the passing countryside. It wasn't until the train began to brake in readiness for its entry to Knebworth village station that she realised how late it was. For a few seconds, Sofia wished herself anywhere but there, until she spotted the man and curiosity overwhelmed her. He was the only person waiting to board. As described to her, he wore a brown top hat, overcoat and a paisley silk scarf. The scarf was his touch of flamboyance and would be useful for her later. He stepped aboard the train with a sneer crinkling the bridge of his nose as if disdainful of public transport, and the expression made her feel better about her task. It was twenty minutes before the next stop. The emptiness of the carriage was essential but it would make the sound of her footsteps conspicuous. She didn't want him to look at her and she certainly hoped he wouldn't smile, although he didn't seem the friendly sort.

The conductor entered unannounced and Sofia dipped her head pretending shyness. He was kind and looked away, stamping her ticket with nothing more than a muttered 'Ma'am'. When the man in the silk scarf handed the conductor his ticket he didn't bother to say a word. He could have given her pause by making good-natured small talk, but she was spared the touch of humility that might have made her feel regret later on.

The train lurched unexpectedly and she clutched her bag to her stomach. She must remember to pay Nora for looking after the children today. And then there was Charlie. He had stopped asking difficult questions, waiting patiently until she chose to talk, without hint of judgment. Sofia had let him draw her last night, sitting motionless for hours while the children slept, giggling at his serious expressions and bursts of self-admonition when he felt he wasn't doing her justice. Around Charlie, she could almost pretend she was normal.

Recognising the outskirts of the oncoming town Sofia knew she'd been daydreaming again. It wouldn't do. Sooner or later she would make a mistake. She felt the familiar shiver down her spine as she timed her approach and told herself it was just nerves making her breathe faster. She walked casually towards the seat backing on to his and knelt lightly, positioned as if to pray, but it was much too late for that. With one hand she reached over the seat and sliced the immaculately sharp blade from left to right across the front of his neck, the other holding back his forehead to keep the windpipe tense as she severed it. Like playing a cello, she thought. The gurgling of air through blood was almost inaudible as she leaned over to whisper in his ear.

'We all of us have to pay our dues. It's a hard lesson but the man in charge said you had to be taught it.' His eyes rolled upwards in their sockets and she saw the panic in them, fingers fluttering uselessly at his split neck. He had it coming, she reassured herself. Thorne had said he'd been given fair warning.

Sofia stopped to memorise the deed, retracing the knife's journey through his throat with her fingers, feeling the soft, warm, wetness of flesh and fluid punctuated by ragged cartilage, like exploring a willing mouth, and had to wrench herself away. She pulled his perfect paisley scarf over the wound, buttoned his coat to the top, pushed the hat over his face and allowed the body to slump as if he were taking a leisurely nap while the train carried him home to London, one penny poorer.

As she pulled on her gloves and prepared to disembark, an internal voice nagged her. Stepping off the train at Wood Green Alexandra Park station she embraced the discourse within, and contemplated whether she was simply doing what Vinsant required or if there wasn't a darker truth. That this way of repaying her debts was a gift. Didn't it provide a vital, self-excusing obligation to kill? She tried to remember if she'd ever felt remorse or guilt after taking a life. She was a victim of circumstance, Sofia concentrated on that. She was fighting to survive against the odds and had no choice in the matter, but even she felt the truth of that slipping away like scree beneath her feet.

Outside the station she turned right and walked to the corner of the road. Seconds later a carriage pulled up and a man hollered for her attention. She didn't recognise the driver, huddled in a long, dark coat and huge hat but Thorne had said she'd be met so she trusted fate. It took another half hour to reach Clerkenwell but before entering Brewhouse Yard, the carriage stopped and the driver climbed inside with her. Sofia felt fleeting fear until Thorne revealed his face. She smiled with relief until an impossibly strong hand grabbed her by the hair.

'You're going to get yourself and everyone around you lynched. What were thinking taking the police constable for a lover?' He pushed Sofia away and she flew back against the seat, shocked by the pain of her bruised scalp and the realisation of how much trouble she was in with Vinsant.

'I don't know what you're talking about,' she stuttered but he had surprised her too much for the lie to be convincing. The slap came from nowhere and, although not dealt hard, it brought tears to her eyes. Sofia felt the shame of it more than the pain, the humiliation of knowing she'd done something so stupid and the crawling disgust that she'd been watched doing it.

'It has to stop, do you hear me? You tell Constable Danes it's over, that you're bored of him, that there's someone else. How long did you think you could keep it a secret?' Thorne was furious and Sofia saw that he was also afraid.

'I was lonely,' she said in a tiny voice.

'You were an idiot,' he spat. 'Mrs Vinsant's already been arrested twice and now this. How much more scrutiny do you think it'll take before someone gets in real trouble? Your instructions are to end it, straight away. No amount of information we might get from him can make up for the risk you've taken.' He threw open the door, covering his face with his hat before following her down.

She trudged home, the absence of the usual rush of adrenaline all the more notable for the sense of impending grief. She stopped outside Charlie's door, knowing she couldn't knock it, wishing he would sense her there and open up but he didn't. Of course she couldn't have him, not the way her life was now. It had been too good to be true. Her life just didn't work out that way.

At home, she scraped congealing blood from beneath her nails and bit her tongue to stop from sobbing out loud. Isaac called out in his sleep and she kissed his forehead. Emmett Vinsant was right that Charlie was an unwarranted risk and yet she longed for someone to hold her at night and chase away her demons. Perhaps his loss was her punishment, balancing out whatever invisible scales controlled her fate and maybe, if she gave him up, she and the children could stay safe.

The following day, Sofia walked the children to school then took Nora a little money and food. They had a cup of hot chocolate made with fresh milk as a treat and Sofia fetched some logs when she saw Nora feeling the cold even in the dwindling summer heat.

'Been spending a bit of time with Charlie then, love?' Sofia reddened at his name as if her neighbour had read her thoughts. 'I'm not judging. You deserve a bit of company, especially a decent man like him. You shouldn't let time pass you by, you're only young once.'

Sofia didn't feel young that morning. 'I hope Isaac and Sadie behaved well yesterday,' she changed the subject but Nora wasn't so easily put off.

'They were fine. Growing up fast, mind, and Isaac needs a man to guide him. Charlie's good with him, you could do a lot worse.'

'Nora, I'm still in mourning and the children need my full attention right now. Charlie's lovely but he's just a friend.'

Nora choked on the sweet, powdery chocolate and coughed hard into her handkerchief. Sofia watched, worried that the children had worn her out and fetched water as the coughing abated. She'd been planning to ask Nora to help out again that night while she went to talk to Charlie but decided against it.

There was nothing left but to invite Charlie to dinner that night, even with the children there. She baked potatoes, serving them with smoked ham and buttered carrots, even managing to pick up a chocolate cake for pudding. The children reacted as if it was Christmas and Charlie turned up with a pocket full of sweets and made paper aeroplanes from an old newspaper. The children ate more than either Sofia or Charlie, his appetite uncharacteristically reduced. As she washed up, he read to the children by the fire, making them laugh before they bemoaned their bed-time. Sadie gave Charlie a shy goodnight kiss and Sofia cursed herself for making the evening a celebration when it should have been anything but.

With the children asleep, Sofia couldn't delay the conversation any longer. She held her hands out to the flames in spite of the perfectly warm room.

'It was a wonderful meal, thank you,' Charlie said, sipping his tea and smiling shyly. 'I'm glad you're not worried about people seeing me here anymore. Isaac's asked me to teach him how to set up my fish-ing rod next weekend. I think he's hinting that he wants me to take him to the river for a day.' He looked pleased at the prospect, as if he'd passed a test.

'He shouldn't ask,' Sofia replied. 'He knows how busy you are with your work.'

'He's just a boy,' Charlie grinned. 'They don't think like that. And he knows I don't mind.'

'He isn't used to having a man around,' Sofia said. 'Even when Tom was alive, he was out from dawn 'til dark. He said he was lucky having a job where they accepted he couldn't live in but it meant long days.' She was putting it off, trying to find the right way to tell him it was over. Charlie got out of the rocking chair to put another log on the fire, sitting by her feet and staying there.

'It's not been easy,' he said. 'I know that. And it's still early days but I adore the children. Little Sadie breaks my heart every time she smiles at me. I love you, Sofia. You and them. I keep telling myself not to rush you.' He picked up one of her hands and kissed her palm tenderly. She looked away from him into the fire. The words she needed to say wouldn't come. 'But I want to help, to make you happy. I can provide a steady income. You wouldn't need to work or, well, do anything else to get money.'

'Charlie, don't,' she whispered, furious that she hadn't had the courage to say what was needed before he'd begun to speak.

'Let me finish. I've thought about nothing but this for days and I want to get it out before I lose my nerve. Sofia, I know you're still in mourning but I want to marry you. I'll wait until you're ready, and until the children can understand it properly, but I want you to take this and keep it safe. It's my promise to you.'

With shaking hands he thrust a small, leather-covered box into her hands. She knew she shouldn't open it, that the right thing to do was pass it back with a sorrowful smile and a quiet refusal but her hands betrayed her, lifting the lid and staring inside as the firelight played around the edges of the ruby shining proudly against gold.

Was she cursed, she wondered, to love and lose, and love and lose for as long as she lived? Charlie took the ring from the box and slipped it on Sofia's finger. When he looked into her eyes, she couldn't help but smile. His face was alight with hope, happiness and tears. She brushed them away.

'Charlie, it's beautiful. You're beautiful. But I can't accept it now, you know I can't make that promise while I'm still in mourning.'

'I know you can't wear it. Just keep it somewhere safe until you can. It's yours,' he said and she knew she couldn't tell him they should part. He deserved one perfect night of happiness. It would cost her nothing to wait a day before returning the ring with a credible excuse.

Charlie stayed another two hours as they basked in the warmth of the fire and each other. Sofia hid her self-loathing so well her own mother couldn't have spotted it. When she told him she loved him she couldn't have been more sincere, even though she knew with absolute certainty that she was a creature far worse than the devils from which Charlie had promised to protect her.

Chapter Twenty-two

What little time was left for sleep, brought nightmares. She knew she was dreaming but couldn't force herself to wake, suffocating under the imagined weight of being watched and judged. Faces flashed and faded in her mind, Charlie, Tom, Captain Thorne, Mary Flathers, her mother. Sofia awoke with a slowly growing anger in the pit of her stomach and the knowledge that she was running out of time to change her fate. It was no good waiting for orders and threats from Vinsant, hoping that everything would miraculously come good. It was time to take control of her destiny.

She saw the children off to school, telling them she loved them and that if she wasn't home when they got back, they should go to either Nora or Charlie's. With that, she sat outside her front door in the sunshine, pen and paper on her lap and wrote two long letters. The first was to Mary. She explained how well the children were doing at school, talked about their many friends, and how fit and healthy they were. In conclusion, she said how nice it was that the children had finally met their Aunt but that, given the Flathers' failure to maintain a relationship with Tom or the children for the preceding several years, she did not think it appropriate for them to visit again. The letter was courteous but direct and she felt some pride when she'd finished it, grateful that her mother had insisted she learn to read and write. Many of the other children in their camp hadn't been taught. Her mother had struggled with it herself and Sofia was more teacher than pupil by the age of ten. Without such skills now she would have no prospects at all and she would be need all her options open very soon.

The second letter was to her brother in America. Sofia wrote everything and nothing, on losing Tom, tales of Isaac and Sadie, London, the marvels of electricity and the new telephone booths appearing in the city. She told him about the Liberal government and how England was changed since his departure. Finally she said that she longed to see him again. She never believed he would read it and yet she sat for the best part of an hour, vaguely aware of the comings and goings of the street, and wrote every word as beautifully as she'd been schooled.

She put each letter into an envelope, sealed them and marked the addresses on, with the envelopes turned into her chest so that no one else could read the destinations. After that, she put some coins in her pocket, made sure the house was tidy, and left.

There was a telephone booth on Clerkenwell Road, a wooden structure already rickety with damage from drunks and youths, and she entered it nervously, never having used one before. Pennies at the ready, Sofia dialled the exchange. Finally, Mrs Hasselbrook announced that she was on the line to the Vinsant's residence.

'It's Sofia Logan here,' she said with more confidence than she felt, disconcerted by the crackling line and slight echo of her own voice. 'Would you pass a message to Mr Vinsant for me please? Tell him thank you very much and I would be pleased to come and speak with him in St James' at four o'clock today.'

'Very well,' came the stilted, too loud reply. Mrs Hasselbrook was no more comfortable with the technology than she, thought Sofia. Outside the telephone booth she adjusted her already perfect hat, making sure she was in plain sight then wandered slowly to the post office where she bought stamps but declined the offer from the post master to leave the letters with him, choosing instead to walk outside to the pillar box. When she'd made sure the correspondence was clear of the slot and beyond retrieval, she walked through the city towards her rendezvous with Emmett Vinsant. She forced herself to look confident and unafraid, stopping at a tearoom for lunch where she made a point of sitting in the window and taking her time with the sandwiches she ordered. It was half past three when she left and she peered in shop windows to fill the remaining thirty minutes before knocking on the door of the club.

Thorne hauled her in, glaring until there was another knock and a man she didn't know entered.

'Mr Vinsant's waiting in his office,' Thorne said curtly. Sofia saw the bulge inside his jacket. She'd anticipated he would be armed and prayed for sufficient time to say what she needed before they did anything drastic. Vinsant didn't bother to look up when she entered, the mysterious third man left in the corridor, as Thorne shut the door.

Emmett Vinsant was wearing tails. He obviously had plans for the evening and she knew he'd be incensed by her summoning him. It was either a bold or foolish move and she'd made it knowing he had to believe she was the one holding all the cards. Thorne checked her coat and skirt pockets before Vinsant addressed her. For a long time he said nothing at all and Sofia sensed he was waiting for her to explain herself, apologise, so she kept her mouth firmly closed leaving him no choice but to speak first.

'Mrs Logan, I'm not sure you understand the position you're in. I thought I'd made myself clear when you turned up unannounced at my home but apparently you don't have the intelligence I'd credited you with.' Still she didn't rise to the bait. 'As is happens, a meeting was always going to be necessary so I'll forgive your stupidity.' Sofia let the smallest of smiles touch the edge of her lips and inclined her head as if giving him leave to continue. She noted the flare of annoyance darken his cheeks and maintained her silence until he showed his hand. 'You were warned two days ago to cease your relationship with Constable Danes.'

'That's right,' she acknowledged sweetly, as if they were making small talk at a garden party. The veins on his neck began to stand out.

'Yet last night you invited him into your home, where he spent the evening with you, Isaac and little Sadie.' Mentioning the children was low, but if he intended it to shake her, it had quite the opposite effect.

'He's a neighbour,' she said, head tipped slightly to the side as if she were talking to someone of limited understanding. Vinsant slammed his fist onto his desk. Thorne took a step closer to her chair and for the first time Sofia felt panic blossoming in her chest.

'Did you think I wouldn't have you watched? It is beyond comprehension that you should be so idiotic and bloody minded. You were warned that there would be consequences if you failed to obey. You were supposed to befriend him, use him to gather information as to the progress of the police investigations. Instead I find that you're sleeping with him, whispering God knows what as he beds you!' he yelled, leaning over his desk and raising his voice so loud Sofia found it improbable that the entire square wouldn't hear. 'What have you told him?'

'He knows nothing,' she said. 'Did you seriously think, after all I've done to repay my debts and keep my children safe, that I'd let him be party to our business? It'll be my neck before yours, Mr Vinsant, don't think I don't know it.'

'You're to stop seeing him immediately. You and the children will move elsewhere in the city and you'll have no contact with him again,' he said, composing himself.

'No,' she said and this time he laughed.

'Think very carefully about what you say to me. I'm a tolerant man but I have my limits.'

'I don't intend to call things off with Constable Danes, nor will I be moving house and you won't need to be tolerant any more, Mr Vinsant, because I'm no longer yours to order.' She heard Thorne's sigh behind her and knew she'd reached the point of no return. Time to make her point was running out. 'I don't work for you. Specifically I am not going to kill anyone else on your behalf. I've more than settled my debts. We're even and I'm finished.' She stood up, knowing things would get worse before they got better and bracing herself for it. Vinsant nodded and Thorne circled an arm around her neck.

Vinsant stood no more than three inches from her face, his breath reeking of stale cigar smoke and whisky, the heat of rage pouring from him. 'You don't tell me we're finished. I own you.' He jabbed his finger into Sofia's shoulder rhythmically as he spoke but she didn't allow herself to flinch. 'You still owe me plenty. The debts you accrued have interest running that'll take you years to repay and let's not forget the money you've been living on these past few months. It seems you need a reminder of the fact that I'm in charge. Captain?' Sofia knew that if she didn't play her hand now she'd be beaten to a pulp.

'I didn't come here to argue,' she said. 'I sent two letters to my lawyer today, with instructions on the envelope to open one immediately and the other only if anything should happen to me. If I die, or am beaten so badly that I'm left as good as dead, he will open the second letter. Everything I've done is in there, each detail, your instructions as well as an explanation of what you had to gain from each death. The letter says you threatened to kill Isaac and Sadie if I didn't do as you ordered. By the time that correspondence is opened, I'll be beyond caring and you'll be breakfast for the crows.'

Vinsant was absolutely still, like a bull before charging, sizing her up.

'Ask Peters,' he growled at Thorne who disappeared through the door and had a whispered conversation in the hallway.

When he returned, Thorne kept his eyes lowered as he spoke. 'Peters says she sat for a couple of hours this morning writing lengthy letters which he saw her seal in envelopes and post. He says she spent the rest of the day shopping and having lunch.'

Thank God Peters wasn't slacking on the job, thought Sofia, who had been counting on the fact that she was being watched and that it wasn't just a symptom of her paranoia. Vinsant roared and smashed a decanter from his desk across the room.

'You whore's cunt!' he exploded at her. 'Your children can spend a lifetime in the poorhouse and see what it's like being gnawed by rats in their beds.'

'That's not going to happen, Mr Vinsant. If I end up in the workhouse I shall stop eating. You'll have given me nothing to lose if my children aren't by my side. I'll starve myself until I die and then those letters will be opened anyway.'

Vinsant sent what items were left flying against the wall as he cursed and yelled.

'I'm not asking you for anything else. I shall look for work and stay out of trouble. Our paths need never cross again. Stand aside please, Captain Thorne.'

Sofia willed herself to show no desperation to get away. It was only when she stepped through the front door into bright sunshine that she allowed herself to believe she might make it out unhurt. It was several minutes later, when she had put some distance between herself and the club, that the first semblance of a smile appeared on her face but not until Brewhouse Yard that she thought she might have succeeded in putting her life back in order. Only when the children were in her arms, did she let herself believe it had worked.

She bought steak pies for supper, thrusting a note under Charlie's door for when he got home from his shift, and made an apple crumble with custard for pudding. The evening was filled with silliness, the children clambering back time and again to their mother for hugs as if she'd been away for months. In many ways she supposed she had. If her eyes wandered to the door or window every few minutes then no one seemed to notice. Nora filled up with well-deserved food and wine then disappeared home, with only the slightest wink at Sofia on her way out. The children took their time falling asleep, full of sugar and frivolity. Tom seemed hardly to be a shadow in Sofia's thoughts any more. It was time to move on.

When the children were both snoring Charlie took Sofia by the hand. 'What changed today?' he asked.

Sofia couldn't help but smile at his nervous expression. 'Me,' she said. 'I changed. And yes.'

It was several seconds before Charlie seemed to understand what she was saying and then several more before her feet touched the ground again. He swung her round in his arms until she was dizzy and out of breath, laughing so much she couldn't tell him to stop. Two small faces peered round the doorway in wonder at their mother's helpless giggling and it took another fifteen minutes to settle them back to sleep. When they were finally quiet, Charlie drew her into his arms and kissed her.

'I had the horrible feeling today that something was wrong,' he said. 'I'd convinced myself that you were going to say no. What happened?'

'Nothing,' she said. 'I just decided the time had come to let myself be happy again. Thanks to you,' she held his hand to her cheek. 'Don't ever let me go, will you, Charlie?' she asked.

'I promise I will never, ever let you go.'

Later that night Sofia spent a while looking at old photos of Tom and her, and thought he would have liked Charlie. She made plans for the first time in months, not of weapons and alibis but of outings and celebrations.

The last three weeks of August came and went in a haze of walks in the park, picnics, one trip to the fair and another to the circus. Sofia was careful with money but not afraid to enjoy life and she had begun to search for work. Just the fact that she was contemplating a job made her feel better. The children were growing up fast. Isaac was rebelling a little, which Sofia secretly enjoyed, and Sadie was no longer fragile.

She and Charlie had to maintain their facade as neighbours, but spent increasing time at one another's houses and worried less about moving between them after dark. Sofia thought less about Emmett Vinsant but found herself wondering about Beatrice whenever she saw posters demanding "Votes for Women". Sofia still couldn't apply the Women's Social and Political Union's rhetoric to her own situation but she had the growing impression that she may have judged Beatrice too harshly. At least she didn't spend her day organising dinner parties or obsessing over how best to please her husband. Quite the opposite. It must have taken a substantial amount of courage, Sofia thought, to accept the social stigma that came with protesting in public.

Sofia had a short reply from her sister-in-law stating how disappointed she and Mr Flathers were that Sofia wouldn't see reason and that she hoped the children would be allowed, at least, to holiday with them. There was no repeat of the threat of legal action and Sofia decided it was best not to respond. She doubted it would improve matters between them to continue the correspondence.

Charlie celebrated his twenty-ninth birthday on August 31 and his fellow constables took him out for the evening. He desperately wanted Sofia to join them but she refused, telling him their relationship had to be kept secret a while longer, but the truth was that socialising with Charlie's police colleagues felt like too great a risk. Instead, she and Charlie took a day trip to Hastings where she wore her engagement ring, taking off her gloves on the train and gesturing wildly at everything until Charlie noticed. She was taken aback by his tears. His hand scarcely left hers for a minute that day and she sat on his lap at the seafront as he sketched boats skipping on distant waves, and new mothers parading their prams proudly up and down the promenade. Sofia stared at nurses pushing consumption patients, taking in the healing qualities of the sea air, wrapped in blankets and bundled in wheelchairs.

They reminded her of Lefevre. Sofia had been to see him many times and no amount of food seemed to slow the weight loss. He had good days and bad, times where he was his old, witty self and others when he couldn't make it to the door to let her in. She had her own key now which was just as well, he wasn't safe taking the stairs alone. His doctor had begun to prescribe only pain relief rather than anything to reverse the illness, saying there was nothing more medicine could do and that he should pray for a natural recovery. Lefevre didn't believe he would get better and, in spite of her protestations to the contrary, neither did she. All Sofia could do was be a good friend and visit often. She knew it wouldn't be enough.

September's opening days gripped London in a heatwave that the papers declared had topped ninety-five degrees Fahrenheit. Beaches were flooded with sun-worshippers, parks were besieged by picnickers and shade was at a premium. Charlie had taken a few days of perfectly timed leave following his birthday and transformed the road outside Sofia's house with a makeshift awning, blankets on the floor and an old tin bath filled with cold water for the children to splash in. To Sadie's delight he had also magically produced a sack of sand he spread about in a mass of trays, pots and pans where he and the children played on a make-believe desert island. For three long, hot, noisy days the sun brought happiness and not once, not for one fleeting second, did Sofia think about the things she had done and resolved to do no more. After that the temperature settled although it remained pleasantly balmy. Charlie went back to work, Isaac and Sadie to school, leaving Sofia to attend a matter long overdue.

Visiting Tom's grave was, she found, more calming than distressing. Laying a bunch of carnations she shed a few tears, apologised for her absence then tugged moss from the grassy patch.

'The children are fine,' she said. 'Isaac is less than a head shorter than me now and growing cheekier by the day. Sadie is full of fun and never more than an arm's reach from her brother. She adores him. I think even more so now that you're not with us.' She regarded the plain headstone solemnly as if expecting an answer. 'Your sister came. She wanted to take the children. Maybe it was your passing that brought it home to her, how little time we all have and how important it is to have people to love and who'll love you back. At least, I'm going to give her the benefit of the doubt and believe that. Perhaps her childlessness finally became too much for her to bear. Anyway, she's gone again and I think she's moved on. That's what I'm doing as well, Tom.'

Sofia leaned back on her elbows and watched birds swoop across the sky, hungry for insects and playing on the breeze. 'I don't know why you told Mr Vinsant about what I'd done. It's cost me dearly but I came to say I forgive you. I'm going to look to the future and I think Charlie can help me do that. You'd like him, the way he is with our little ones. So that's what I came to tell you.' She picked up the mound of moss weeded from the grave and brushed dirt from the inscription of her husband's name. 'I miss you. I wish it had been different. If you hadn't left I would never have done any of it. I'll come back soon, with the children next time. Goodbye Tom.' Sofia kissed her fingertips and ran them across the top of the headstone as she left.

Charlie was working nights that week, giving her the time she needed to clear her head and her cupboards, packing Tom's remaining things so that the children could have them later, clothes she could recut for Isaac, putting aside tools she might get a few pennies for. It proved cathartic. There was more space in the house when she'd finished and more room in her heart for Charlie. She found it hard to comprehend that you could love someone so much and move on so quickly, but her life had not stood still and she understood better now that she could not afford to do so either.

Nora handed her a package the following afternoon, left by Charlie. Sofia opened it to reveal two framed pictures, a pencil sketch of each child that Charlie must have done the previous week. Sadie was sat in the tin tub so that only the upper half of her body was visible, straw sun hat flopping around her ears, a bucket in one hand, face alight with a smile as she splashed, tiny white teeth gleaming and eyes sparkling. Isaac's picture was a closer study of his face, head in his hands as he lay on his stomach reading a book, a tiny frown, his features showing the handsome young man he would become, sun picking out the highlights in his hair and freckles on his nose. It was extraordinary how Charlie had found details that she didn't notice, seeing the children every day, the way Sadie's nose crinkled to one side when she laughed, and how Isaac raised one eyebrow fractionally higher then the other when he was concentrating. Each sheet of paper had been set in a slim wooden and glass frame that would preserve the moments Charlie had captured so elegantly. He must have worked on them every spare moment.

'Bless his heart, he's good, isn't he?' whistled Nora.

'In many ways,' Sofia replied, clearing space on the mantelpiece for the new treasures. 'Maybe too good for me.'

'That's nonsense, that is. Don't you start talking like that, my girl. He's lucky to have you. Now come on, you promised to help me fold my washing then you can walk with me to the greengrocer. I swear potatoes are getting heavier as I get older.' Sofia laughed and allowed the subject to be changed but the malignant growth of the idea that she was undeserving would not be appeased as conveniently as Nora.

September's progression saw the summer slowly waning, taking with it the long, light evenings. Isaac and Sadie had begun to complain about being brought inside so early, the street having become their playground until much later than Sofia would normally have allowed but for the Indian summer. Whilst Sadie was still easy to pacify, Isaac needed more careful attention and Sofia had to entertain him constantly with games, books and activities. Most of the time it was fun and brought them closer but there were times when it was as if he wanted to see how far she would go to keep him occupied. Natural, she supposed, to be challenging her authority with his father gone and Charlie couldn't step in too heavily for fear of upsetting the order of their family. Sometimes, though, after a long day of cooking, cleaning, and caring Sofia ran out of energy and patience. That was when Isaac seemed to be at his worst.

'Children, wash your hands for supper, please,' Sofia called.

'Yes, Mama,' Sadie replied coming into the kitchen. There was no sign of Isaac so Sofia left it another minute before reminding him, although he still did not comply.

'Isaac, come along please,' she called again, her voice a little louder and firmer.

'Not hungry,' the boy shouted from the bedroom.

'Supper will be on the table in a moment and I don't want it to go to waste so come through please.' Her tone was short and clear. She put Sadie on a chair and gave her a plate of food then went to fetch her brother. He was lying on his stomach on the bed, folding an old newspaper and making a point of refusing to look at his mother.

'Isaac, coming along sweetheart, you'll be hungry when you're trying to get to sleep.'

'I don't want to go to sleep so early. I'm not little any more. I want to go back outside.'

Sofia sat on his bed and stroked a lock of hair back from his forehead. He jerked away.

'It's getting late and you've school tomorrow. Now come along, the food getting's cold.'

'You're not listening to me,' Isaac shouted, red faced, hands clenched into fists.

'Last chance, Isaac, and don't raise your voice to me,' Sofia said, beyond negotiating.

'I'm not eating stupid supper!' he yelled, stamping a foot and crumpling the newspaper into a ball before throwing it into a corner.

'Fine,' Sofia said. 'But you'll stay in here for the evening. We'll talk about this in the morning when you've calmed down.' She closed the bedroom door quietly and joined a subdued Sadie at the table, expecting at any moment to hear the door creak open and her son to emerge apologetic and ready for food. When he didn't come after a minute she was surprised and ten minutes later she considered going back to him but knew it would be an admission of defeat. Instead, she finished her meal, cleared the plates and read to Sadie in front of the fire assuming he'd sulked himself to sleep. Sadie was nodding tiredly by the time Sofia finished the book so Sofia picked her up and carried her through to join Isaac in the bedroom.

The scene was chaos. Isaac was in the middle of the bed, surrounded by half the contents of her wardrobe and drawers. Every photo, item of jewellery, shells collected from beaches, even Tom's old razor was scattered across the blankets and in the middle of it all a girl's stocking, untied, as Isaac counted the pennies he'd shaken from it. Isaac's face, rebellious for a half moment as he looked up, transformed into a picture fear and upset when he saw the look in his mother's eyes.

'I'm sorry.' His voice was thick with the tears that were already on their way.

'Put it down,' Sofia hissed. Isaac scrabbled to pick up the pennies and shove them back into the stocking. 'No, don't touch them, I don't want your hands on them!' With each word her voice rose until it was nearly a shriek, Sadie adding to the wailing as she awoke abruptly when Sofia landed her ungently on the bed.

Isaac was sobbing now, defiance evaporated, just a small child reaching his arms out for his mummy. Sofia picked up each penny carefully, rubbed them free of fingerprints then dropped them one by one back into the stocking. It wasn't until the stocking was tied in its original state that she registered the children's distress.

'Help me put everything back,' she told Isaac who rushed to return the contents to their places in the wardrobe, clumsy in his haste. 'Be more careful,' Sofia snapped.

'Yes, Mama, sorry,' he retreated into his baby name for her. Minutes later the room was as it had been before and Sadie's tears had stopped.

Sofia put them both to bed, a brief kiss on each forehead and nothing more was said. It was only when she reached for the kettle that she saw the stocking still clutched in her left hand. It had to be hidden somewhere more secure. She knew she should dispose of it, spend the pennies and throw the stocking away. Untying it once more, intending only to add the few coins to her purse, she recalled the face of each victim as if imprinted on each of the eight coins. Only one brought her to tears. With reluctant hands she put her prizes away and hid the stocking on the top of a kitchen cupboard where it would never be accidentally found.

It was harder to put the memories somewhere so inaccessible but she was determined not to slip. She wouldn't punish Isaac. He was just a boy with a boy's natural curiosity. She should do more with him, spend more time, be all he needed. September had enough warm days remaining that they could walk and visit and explore in the evenings and at weekends. Perhaps the children didn't need to go to bed so early after all.

Chapter Twenty-three

October 1906

The leaves hadn't yet begun to turn the first time Sofia experienced a wave of melancholy. At first she felt only as if she'd forgotten something but couldn't put her finger on what. Missing Tom, she thought, but she knew that wasn't really it. The house, maybe, which felt smaller than ever, even in Tom's absence, now that the children were growing bigger and increasingly physical. So she cleaned, moved furniture around, changed what little she could but it didn't make any difference to her mood. Some days later it had evolved into something closer to longing. As hard as Sofia tried to pinpoint the cause, she found nothing. The children were happy, Isaac's ordeal in Clerkenwell Workhouse all but forgotten, Charlie was happy, she was happy. She dismissed it, smiled brighter than ever and carried on.

Charlie occasionally asked if everything was all right and Sofia would look at him with her eyes large and questioning, at a loss to understand why he was worried. As the days went by, though, she wondered if he wasn't right. There was a hollow place inside her. She needed a job but employment was still hard to find, and if it was administrative or mathematical work then the preference was always for a man, no matter how impressive her skills. She knew that employers considered men more consistent, less given to illness or problems with children and, of course, less emotional. It would be easier to find work as a nurse maid or seamstress but she had no experience of either and there were plenty of women desperate for those positions. She had thought it would be simpler than this but her lack of references made progress impossible. Charlie had applied to join the detective division and was either working or studying, anxious not to let the opportunity go to waste. Sofia was thrilled for him. She wished she had something other than the children to occupy her.

Each day seemed to bring more routine and less spontaneity. She pondered life in her kitchen, thinking she'd never felt the hours drag so badly before. It was daydreaming that made her snap the paring knife blade as she prepared turnips for a stew. She cursed the breakage, the knife had been her sharpest, but it was plain the metal had separated irreparably from the wooden handle. She tried two others from her drawer but they weren't strong enough. It was only then that she thought of Vinsant's knife, hidden in her winter boots at the very back of the wardrobe, and it seemed almost to call out to her. She dismissed the idea. She couldn't chop vegetables with the same blade she'd used to sever a neck. She struggled on with a poor replacement, twice slicing her hand and becoming more frustrated with every cut.

Sofia cursed the clumsiness of her hands and the bluntness of the knife but a memory was slithering its way into her subconscious and, as hard as she looked at the turnip and the useless blade, the less she saw them. Her mind told her she was cutting vegetables but in the recesses of her imagination the shapes were more akin to head and scalpel. With one more slip and sorely grazed knuckles she stormed to her wardrobe, dragging out the boot and shaking the knife free of its wrapping. It lay, gleaming. There could be no harm in using it. She could clean it in boiling water first and who would know the difference? It was an object, a tool. It had no consciousness. It wasn't an omen or a talisman. But still, in her hand the metal rang. She felt safer just holding it, she thought, then reconsidered. Not safer, she had no cause to feel unsafe. She was a stronger version of herself. Empowered. Emboldened. She strengthened her grip on the knife and began to work on the turnip, relishing the speed and dexterity with which she could butcher it. When dinner was made she considered returning the knife to the boot but it seemed a waste. Into the back of the kitchen drawer it went. It would save her buying a new one and it was ridiculous, she convinced herself, to hide it.

Sofia was in a better mood that evening than she had been for several days. She roused Charlie from his forensic science papers and law books, entertaining him by recounting the local gossip and teasing him about his studying. He stayed with her that night, the door between them and the children locked, as they made love in front of the fire. Sofia looked at his face and tried to stay in the moment but other images vied for her attention. As she bit into Charlie's shoulder, Loftis died once more beneath her and a man on a train ceased his thrashing and slumbered forever.

'My darling,' Charlie whispered. 'My sweet Sofia.'

Reliving the killings in her imagination became habitual and dispelled the domestic monotony. In the beginning that was enough. The memories did not remain faithful to her though, and day by day they weakened, leaving herself less fulfilled, craving a greater sense of self-worth, a more vital experience.

Sofia handled the knife often and when that grew bland, she brought out the gun, cleaning it, admiring its simple design and lethal capabilities. She wished she hadn't dropped the cosh into the Thames. Charlie had slipped into the habit of coming to her house for supper, giving money but expecting her to cook, or that was how it seemed. The children were irksome too, making too much noise in the confined space when Sofia wanted to be left quietly. They made constant demands on her to play, to read, to feed them. Sofia craved the dark. Night time, when she could find a reason for Charlie not to stay, was her mind's playground.

At night she could remember the dark things she had done and imagine what more she was capable of doing. She dreamed of terrorising men who stumbled through the streets drunk, pissing in the gutters and fouling the air. In her head she was immortal, untouchable, a beautiful terror. It's only pretending, she told herself. Pretending is all right. It's not the same as planning to hurt anyone. And if it kept her sane, then surely what she was doing was actually a good thing.

With every passing week, she resented more and more being reigned in by the conventions of motherhood and domestic house-keeping. It wasn't that she didn't love the children but they were so needy. She took to walking long distances after they left for school, relishing finding new streets and seeing foreign faces, all food for her rapacious imagination. Just walking back into the house felt like drowning. She had begun to lose track of time as she walked, forgetting to eat or drink during the day, undaunted by rain or cold.

'Mummy!' Isaac shouted as she turned back into Brewhouse Yard after a hike that had taken her miles south of the river and back. He ran to meet her.

'What's happened?' she snapped. 'Why aren't you at school?' He looked sheepishly at his sister who eyed the ground. 'Don't look at her, answer my question!'

'School finished an hour ago,' Isaac responded in an unsure voice. 'We've been waiting for you. I was worried.'

Sofia found a sarcastic reply waiting to leap out and bit her tongue. She struggled to think what she should do, how she ought to behave, then reached out a hand for Isaac. He shied away and she felt an intense irritation. Why did they have to be so pathetic? She hid her hateful expression too late and Sadie began to cry, doing her best not to let her mother see, but her thin shoulders juddered with the effort of containing it. Sofia unlocked the door, picked Sadie up and carried her inside, rocking her in the chair with Isaac standing uncertainly a foot away. She stretched out a patient hand, waited for him to take it and drew him towards her.

'I'm so sorry,' she said. 'I didn't mean to forget the time. Please don't cry,' she whispered as Isaac too gave in to tears in the crook of her arm. 'I don't know what's happening to me. Forgive me. I'll make it better, I promise.' She cried with them a while and prayed that it would be enough to want so desperately to change.

It shocked sufficiently to slow the downward spiral but not halt it. She put on a happy face, and engaged with the children in the hours between the end of school and bedtime. They often asked for Charlie at night, wanting him to read them stories or talk about their day. Sofia knew they craved his reassuring, earthy presence.

'I'm sorry if I've been a bit...' Sofia scrabbled for the right word as Charlie washed the dishes.

'That's all right,' he said. 'I didn't like to say anything.'

'But you should've done,' she replied. 'I don't want you treading on egg shells around me.' She was at odds with her temper again, irritated by the slightest comment.

'I just meant that I don't want to pressure you. I wasn't sure if you weren't regretting your promise to me so I thought I'd leave you alone to figure it out.'

'Oh,' was all she could get out. 'Thank you.' He put an arm around her waist, and kissed her, running his other hand up towards her breast.

'Actually, I'm as tired as a cart horse tonight. Could we leave this 'til tomorrow?' She picked up a dishtowel and returned to the sink.

'Sure,' he replied, not pressing the matter but putting on his shoes. 'See you then.' He didn't kiss her as he left and his words were spoken softly but she knew he was hurt, and within Sofia a knot of pain released itself at sharing some of her misery.

She shut the windows, drew every curtain, locked the door and sat by the fire to daydream, damned if she did, hopeless if she didn't.

The next morning Sofia couldn't get out of bed. When the children pleaded for breakfast she told them to call for Nora who came obligingly and fed them, after fretting over Sofia so long that she'd had to pretend to fall asleep. It was true that she was exhausted, barely sleeping, entranced by her own creativity. This morning, though, she was filled with a yearning that she knew wouldn't be satisfied by exercise or imagination. She needed to stimulate herself, to fill the hole that had grown so vast it was threatening to swallow her. She got dressed, tucked the gun into the waist band of her skirt hidden by a loose blouse, took plenty of money and set off for Whitechapel.

She knew where all the games were held and who ran them. The other bonnets had talked about it non-stop: where to go for the highest stakes, who not to trust, what name to drop to get in. At the back door of a pub just starting to fill with shift workers finishing the early, she knocked five times and waited for the door to open. An elderly man blinked at her.

'What d'yer want?' he slurred, showing teeth so brown from ale and pipe smoke Sofia thought they may not have been cleaned for years.

'The game,' she said. 'William Browning said you'd let me in.'

'Argh,' he growled, but stood aside and she averted her head as she passed him. Up a brown corridor the same unpleasant colour as the man's teeth she went, then down a few steps into the cellar. If her fellow bonnet, William, hadn't described this to her in detail she'd have been sure she was being led into a trap but, sure enough, through another door was a room with four tables. At each one sat a circle of men. No women were present. It was easy to see that these were serious players. Even with the strangeness of a female entering, they were still not curious enough to look up from their cards.

Seasoned gamblers they may have been, but many were drinking and some were obviously running on the sort of credit that ended up being repaid in broken bones. One of the tables was populated by a more concentrated group, cards well guarded, stakes high but not excessively so and no small talk. Sofia stood behind an empty chair and waited until the dealer nodded at her. No one welcomed her as she sat down except with appraising glances, anticipating what she might bring to the table in terms of cash and risk. Sofia was transported back to the games her father used to run. These might be the very same men.

They were playing tricks for a central pot, and the bidding started low. She knew that if she lost the first few hands and then began winning she'd be branded a hustler, so she won the first and the second, then lost three, won another and lost one for an hour or so, coming out roughly even. The stakes rose then and she knew they'd been working out what she was worth and how she played. Counting cards on a five man table playing tricks was possible, not without an element of luck, but she maintained a relaxed appearance as if she weren't paying too much attention.

Sofia waited for the excitement to hit her. There was a substantial amount of money on the table, not the least of which had come from beneath her floorboards. She had brought more out than she'd intended, knowing this attempt to renew her interest in life wouldn't be worth her time unless she had a lot to gain. Or to lose. She won, as she'd known she would, and had enough cash to leave satisfied but that wasn't the point. She wanted to play again but the others were drifting away.

'Twenty-one?' she asked the dealer. He nodded his agreement and Sofia put her money on the table.

After eight rounds she'd won three and lost five. Then her luck changed. She kept her bets even until she'd lost four in a row then feigned frustration and shoved all her remaining money down. The dealer looked towards another man who'd done nothing but sit in a corner, silently studying each table without a word. Eventually he picked up a mug and drank. It was the sign for the dealer to begin shuffling the cards.

Sofia's heart was thumping. She was playing a dangerous game. Counting was all well and good but mathematical probability and luck were often opposed. It turned out that luck wasn't required today. She hit twenty-one on the nail, the banker wasn't even close. As she put her hands forward to draw her money and wait for the banker to deliver his share, the man from the stool slammed a riding crop onto the table a hair's breadth from her fingers.

'You're a cheat, missy, and you'll take not a penny out of my room today.' Sofia should have felt vulnerable but there was an unshakable calm inside that she found annoying. She finished stuffing her cash into the pocket of her coat without speaking. 'Did you not hear what I said you poxy bitch? That money's mine.'

Sofia shook her head. 'No, it's mine. You can't make the cards give you an ace and a queen and that's the hand I won with. My sleeves are rolled up and my hands never left the table. You lost fair and square.'

'You were counting when you were playing tricks. Do you think I'm green? I was watching you like a bloody hawk.'

'If that's right, and I say you're mistaken, then you were happy enough to let the banker take his share and let the rest of your customers get robbed by me. If you thought I was cheating why did you let me place the last bet?'

He wasn't going to be drawn into a debate he couldn't win and responded in a more predictable way. The end of the horse whip flew up to strike her cheek so that the tip rested just below her eye. The pain, like a bee sting, brought tears to her eyes but no emotion at all. Sofia felt numb. She sighed, thinking how boring it all was and wondering how she could have spent so many years believing this to be the centre of her universe. Now it seemed dull and petty. She put one hand in the air and slowly slid the other into her pocket. It came back out full of metal rather than cash and she extended her arm so that the gun was touching the man's cheek just below his eye in a parody.

'Tell your banker to give me what I'm owed. I don't want a penny more, just what I won.' There was silence until she shoved the gun harder into his flesh, the tip of the Velo-dog making an indentation in his skin which would leave a bruise to remember her by.

'Do it then,' he complained. The banker pushed the money across the table and Sofia pushed the whip away before gathering her winnings.

'Clear the way behind me,' she ordered and the men moved without argument.

'I see your face here again and I'll have your cunny stuffed and mounted on my mantlepiece!' he shouted.

Sofia sighed. Arguing wouldn't make her day any better. She would have enjoyed shooting him but even that was too easy so she put the gun to the temple of the man with the terrible teeth and motioned for him to take her out. At the end of the corridor he unlocked the door and let her pass.

'Good for you, lovey,' he whispered. She laughed, taken utterly by surprise, then took a note from her pocket and thrust it into his hand.

'Thank you,' she said, making sure no one at the end of the corridor could hear or see. His eyes widened in disbelief at his good fortune and Sofia disappeared around the corner as he closed the door.

That morning Sofia achieved only one end and that was to ensure she wouldn't need to worry about money for a long time. William had been right, they were high stake tables for a pub cellar. During the journey home she didn't think once about the game or the risks she'd taken. Her only thoughts were of how the gun had seemed to melt into the man's saggy flesh, how strong her arm had felt holding it, how much she would have given to obliterate his nasty smile and leave him a black-edged hole in place of his ruddy cheek.

They were hours spent confirming a truth she had already known but been either unwilling or unable to confront. The thrill she had felt with cards in her hand and money on the table had shifted with effortless and fluid grace to another obsession, one which brought with it far greater risk and more compulsive gratification. She was able to ponder quite dispassionately her father's part in bridging gambling and murder. Had Bergen's death by her rock-wielding hands been the start of it all or was she born to this? Either way, her captivation with cards had been rendered a skeleton of the past. She could not reclaim it or resurrect its magic nor did she desire to. The stilling of beating hearts was all that enthralled her now, God help her. And where, as a child, she'd dreamed of cards, coins and winning, her nights now were filled with the coppery magic of blood and oblivion.

The experience had left her with a desire to do something wild and reckless that she couldn't put into words. She'd hoped the game would allay her frustrations but it had made them worse, like drinking salt water to quench a thirst. Sofia knew she should wait until the children got home. She wanted to be there for them, but nothing was a match for the sickness that was creeping around her heart, squeezing until she couldn't breathe. She ran to Nora's door.

'Could you watch the children after school?' she asked. 'I have to see someone about work.'

'In that state?' Nora asked, looking at her dishevelled clothes. 'You stink worse than a breweryman. What have you been up to?'

Sofia knew she should slow down, at least be respectful, but there was a heat building inside her and if she didn't get away she would explode.

'Will you do it or not?' she asked and Nora raised her eyebrows.

'You know I will, but those children are missing their mother. You're not doing right by them, Sofia. I wasn't going to say anything.'

'Then don't,' Sofia replied sharply, thrusting a key into her neighbour's hand and leaving her gasping in the doorway.

At the end of Brewhouse Yard she flew head first into Charlie who caught her in his arms with a huge smile.

'Hello, beautiful. Nice of you to come and meet me! I've just finished...' but she cut him off.

'I'm going out,' she panted. 'Got to see someone.'

Charlie frowned as he studied her and she didn't like his look at all. 'What about the children? They'll be home in an hour.'

'Would you just leave me alone!' she screeched, pushing against his chest and baring her teeth. 'My children are none of your bloody business. Stay away from me.' She turned away before he could react and began to run.

She had no idea where she was going, only that she hadn't felt this bad even when Tom had died. Her first day at the farm had been terrifying but there was none of this hopelessness. She was filled with the destructive certainty that there was nothing left worth living for. She didn't even want to be around the children any more. Charlie was suffocating her with his cheeriness and attention, she was a failure as a mother and as a partner. Worse, her only stimulation came from the blood and guts of dying men.

'What am I?' she asked aloud as she reached the Thames and finally stopped for breath. Sofia had been unaware of the stares from the men and women she'd barged from her path as she'd sprinted through the streets like a thief, tripping on her skirt and grazing her hands on brickwork as she turned corners.

'What am I?' she repeated, watching the water flow beneath her.

'You quite all right, Miss?' a deep voice said from behind. She saw the uniform before anything else.

'Oh Charlie, I'm sorry, thank God,' she cried, taking a step towards the constable.

'Do you need help? I can walk you home if you like or take you to the hospital.'

Confusion took her.

'You're not Charlie' she said.

'I think you'd better come with me,' the policeman said more firmly.

'I won't do it again,' she said. 'I'm not what you think I am.' As he reached out to restrain her she bolted over Blackfriars Bridge to the south bank, losing herself in Southwark's backstreets until she felt safe enough to rest. She found a pub and drank vinegary red wine until she was sick, unable to eat, longing to sleep. It was dark by the time she wandered east along the river, captivated by the view of Tower Bridge, majestic above the Thames. Sofia longed to stand in its high walkways and feel the wind cleanse her.

Soon she was climbing the south tower, pushing past prostitutes waiting for men coming home from work and pickpockets eyeing easy targets. The towers had become unhappy places of late but the view was worth the climb. Sofia made her way to the middle. She could have been flying, with the river streaming beneath and the wind in her hair, the city lights like stars below as if the whole of London had become a reflection of the clear sky. Sofia longed for the freedom she'd had as a child. She wanted to shed her responsibilities and take impossible risks. The cold air sobered her. Suddenly she felt ridiculous, standing on her own and murmuring to herself. She moved north, taking the other tower down to street level, when a man blocked her way. He was probably only nineteen, with two younger, pimply faced mates behind him. There was only the dimmest of lighting and when she asked him to move, he leered at her.

'I said, would you move out of my way, please?' Sofia repeated, in no mood for tomfoolery.

'Be my guest, sweetheart,' said the youth but as Sofia passed him he pressed his body into hers against the wall. She could feel the erection through his trousers, pathetically small and over excited. He would be dangerous if she didn't respond immediately.

'Get off me right now or I'll hurt you,' she said, loud enough that he knew she meant business. The problem was that he couldn't risk losing face in front of the other boys.

'You'll hurt me will you? Like to see you try.' He thrust against her, grinding his crotch.

Sofia drove her right fist, as hard as his proximity would allow, into his Adam's apple. He staggered backwards choking and spluttering, and as he moved she kicked him in the testicles as if he were no more than a rabid dog. He collapsed on the stairs, crying out in pain, too scared of the lunatic attacking him to retaliate. She could have left it there, his companions were already running away, but her blood was up. Sofia slapped a flat palm against his ear to make the drum ring and burn. She knew how bad it would feel. Mac had done it to her once at the farm and she'd never forgotten how excruciating it was. As he lay in a sobbing ball, she aimed one last kick into his kidneys then took the last few steps very slowly, her own body sore not from his attack on her but from hers on him.

At the exit she should have made her way inland but turned back to the river and wandered to the centre of the lower walkway. Sofia didn't recognise herself. She was feral. How badly would it scar her children to see her behave like this? She'd always thought that fear was bad, that being afraid was shameful and childish. Now she understood that fear kept you human. When she'd let go of it, conquered it, she'd become diabolical. Isaac and Sadie were better off without her. Someone would look after them: Nora or Charlie, perhaps even Mary would make a preferable mother. At least they'd never have to witness her being carted off by the police and tried for murder. As much as it pained her, she knew she was no longer good enough for them.

Sofia stared into the inky depths, so calm from a distance but a cauldron up close. The bridge wasn't high but the river was cold and fast with unique and treacherous tides. She wasn't much of a swimmer. No doubt the water would take her before she could change her mind. She climbed onto the side, sitting on the thin ledge at first, contemplating how much easier it would be to die than to live. She would fall asleep, that's all, rest forever released from the petty concerns of daily life, from the prospect of her past coming back to haunt her and free of the taint of blood. She hadn't asked to be this way. A murderous trait had been thrust upon her and she was fixated by it, completely at its mercy.

At least Vinsant had given her a purpose, albeit for his own ends, but it had kept her sane. He wasn't to know she would become so entranced by her crimes that she'd be no good for anything else. She wondered that men like Thorne ever came back from war to lead normal lives. How could they go from wielding the power to take or spare a life, to working as greengrocers, farm hands or bank clerks? There was no going back for her. It was as if the act of killing had stripped away every other aspect of her. Everything else was just excess.

She looked into the deep water, hypnotised by its constant movement and swung her legs over the side. This was the way. She could be with Tom again, she thought, although Tom had betrayed her. She remembered Saul instead but his face held pain, not peace. Her mother? She could fall into the water, not fight it, just drift with the current until cold and fatigue immersed her in its everlasting depths. But her mother's voice was neither soft nor sweet. It told her to buck up, to remember who she was and where she came from, that no one of Romani blood would take such a feeble way out.

Sofia hung her head. It wasn't right. However much she wanted to escape the pain of what she'd become and the agony of denying it, she knew that suicide was impossible. She was pitiful, couldn't even take her own life. The irony was almost laughable. Sofia put one shaking leg back over the railings and prepared to climb down as the wind buffeted her and she grabbed tight. It seemed she still had the will to live, even if she didn't know why. She hobbled home in freezing rain that cleared her thoughts. If she couldn't change what she was, then shouldn't she embrace it? She'd been brought up tough and independent. Had years of marriage softened her so that she was unable to cope? She would have to eat some humble pie, be prepared to take a beating if necessary. The next few months would be difficult but she had looked death in the face and it had found her wanting. It was time to pay penance. Tonight, all she wanted was sleep. Tomorrow, she would find a way of proving to Emmett Vinsant that she was both loyal and invaluable.

The next day, Sofia considered Vinsant's enemies and what value their deaths would have to him. She knew most of the big gamblers from the St. James' club but had no way of knowing which ones were paying off their debts. His political opponents were high profile, difficult to get close to and, after Joseph Carlisle, that might be too risky. His real bugbear had always been the unions. Vinsant had regularly cursed the new Trade Disputes Act which exempted unions from being sued for the damage caused to employers during union action. They were becoming increasingly troublesome at his factories, pushing up wages and pressuring him to reduce hours. Under the Liberal Government they had become even more powerful. She'd heard enough talk about it at the club to be familiar with the key players. The individual who'd been most active in stirring up trouble at Vinsant's railway components factories was Alasdair Craig.

All Sofia knew was that Craig was Scottish, unmarried and living in Brighton. Craig was a popular union leader so she'd have no trouble getting hold of a photograph. He was the perfect target, likely living alone as it was against his political beliefs to have staff, even if he could afford them. She needed only to ensure that she could claim credit for his death and to do that she needed to contact Vinsant once more. The last thing she wanted was to enrage him again, not now she needed him so desperately, so she couldn't turn up at Doughty Street or leave another message with Mrs Hasselbrook.

Sofia went to see Lefevre, taking food as an excuse but knowing he had ways of contacting Vinsant. When she arrived, the lady from the hat shop below was visiting. He looked papery thin. Sofia made small talk until the woman left, then asked how to get in touch with Vinsant without causing a fuss. Monsieur Lefevre might have been physically wasted but his brain was unaffected.

'Why Sofia? I thought you'd left all that behind you and good riddance,' he said, breathing heavily between words.

'I need work,' she told him. 'Can you help?'

'I can, but I don't want to. It didn't end well, Sofia. The little I know about it made me sorry you ever came to work at the club. He's ruthless about debts.' He took her hand, his fingers so boney Sofia couldn't bear to look at them.

'I know what to expect now,' she said.

'No, you don't,' he replied. 'I'll give you a number to call at one of the factories. You can say I gave it to you, he won't bother with me now. But you have to promise me you'll think about this before going ahead. Try to find another way forward that doesn't involve Vinsant.'

'All right,' Sofia replied but Lefevre wasn't going to be put off.

'Give me your word, Sofia.'

'I promise,' she said and Lefevre wrote the number down with the last of his energy. She left him slipping into an exhausted sleep.

She'd meant to keep her word. It had been a promise honestly made but even as she walked away from his front door, she knew that it was a falsehood. She mustn't lose her nerve, she told herself. She just had to focus on making it to the telephone booth and calling Vinsant. It wasn't far. Just a few minutes and it would be done. By the time the line was ringing, she'd persuaded herself that Lefevre understood nothing and that Vinsant was the only answer. A woman answered and she was told to wait. Soon she was speaking to Thorne, Emmett Vinsant's voice loud in conversation in the background.

'It's Sofia,' she said. 'I'm going for a short break in Brighton.'

Thorne was silent, obviously bemused. 'And you're notifying me because?'

'Tell Mr. Vinsant, would you?' Sofia asked.

'He doesn't like people wasting his time, Mrs Logan. Be grateful you've been left alone after what you did.'

'Just tell him, Captain Thorne. By way of an apology from me.' She put the phone down. It was time to go home. She had plenty more to do today and none of it was pleasant. Sofia steeled herself as she walked, facing the inevitable losses to come and hardening her heart. There was no point pretending any longer that she could live like other people. Pandora's box wasn't just open, she'd walked into it and pulled the doors shut behind her. If she were to carry on functioning, it could only be without trying to play two different roles. There were sacrifices to be made and, she told herself, she was ready for them.

Charlie opened the door before she'd even knocked and Sofia realised he'd been waiting for her to go past. He motioned with his head for her to enter and she noticed how exhausted he looked. She didn't sit down and he didn't try to touch her.

'I was concerned about you,' he said simply.

'Thank you,' Sofia answered. 'I'm sorry for the way I've been Charlie but things have changed.'

He leaned against the wall, arms crossed, frowning.

'Explain it to me then,' he replied. 'What is it exactly that's changed? It isn't me. Are you gambling again?'

'That would be easy. I could blame it on gambling, Charlie, but it isn't. We're not right together and you know it.'

'Don't do that,' he said, and for the first time she heard anger in his voice.

'Don't do what?' she asked, stepping up to the argument, wanting it.

'Make the mistake of thinking you can pass this off as some sort of compatibility issue. If you don't want me any more then say so. I think I'm entitled to some honesty.'

'All right,' Sofia answered. 'If that's what you need. I don't want you any more.' She pulled the beautiful ruby ring from her pocket and laid it on his table. 'It just wasn't meant to be.'

'That's not true,' he said, picking the ring up. 'We make our own destinies. You just haven't figured that out yet.'

'You have no idea what you're talking about,' she snapped, annoyed at losing her temper when he seemed so detached.

'Just be careful how you treat the children, Sofia. You're all they have left. Whatever it is you're going through, they still need you.' His voice was softer now. She knew he cared about Isaac and Sadie and on this subject he was right. They did need more than she was able to give. Sofia changed the subject rather than answer.

'Good luck with your detective interview. I hope you get what you want.'

Charlie laughed. 'The interview was a few days ago. I got the job. Doesn't mean I've got what I want.' He held the door for her.

'Goodbye, Charlie,' she said.

At home, she paid Nora a few pennies and her friend left without a word. Sofia preferred it that way, easier not to have to answer questions at all than to lie and apparently Nora had finally taken the point. The children were settling down for bedtime.

'Where were you, Mummy?' Isaac asked.

'Just out,' she replied, taking a pen and paper from the drawer. 'Go to bed, Isaac.'

'Sadie wanted you,' he continued. 'She fell over and cut her knee. Nora put a rag over it but she cried for ages.'

'It'll heal,' Sofia said. 'And I can't always look after you. It's better to learn that now. Go to bed Isaac, I have a lot to do.' The boy stared at her so Sofia turned her face away, focussing on the paper and writing a letter that seemed to be both the best and worst thing she could do for her children. She felt nothing and that, she knew, was all the proof she needed that she was doing what was right.

Chapter Twenty-four

November 1906

Hour after hour she spent on the London to Brighton train. The south coast station became such familiar ground that she had memorised the precise time of each return train marked on the board that hung below the Platform Three sign and the face of every vendor who touted their wares to visiting Londoners. It wasn't a bad journey but this was entirely her own folly and the expenses were being met from her own purse. Nora was babysitting every day and that all added to the cost of the venture although Sofia found it easier to see as little as possible of the children in the circumstances. Nora had never asked why Charlie stopped coming. Likewise, there was no discussion about where Sofia went on her long days out, nor question about the hour of her return. Theirs had become a business relationship only and so it would have to remain.

Brighton was always cold compared to London, a harsh wind blowing in off the sea that had few lulls. The Lanes were full of pretty, wasteful things and the seafront would have been fun with the children but she was hunting, not playing. Sofia lingered in pubs for hours on end, never bold enough to ask after Alasdair Craig but getting the lie of the land, figuring out where such a man might spend his time. It wasn't until she spotted a poster for a union rally that she realised she'd been wasting her time wondering what he did after work. He was a man absolutely consumed by campaigning.

The rally was held outside the Grand Hotel on King's Road to effect maximum disruption and gather press attention. The hotel was an icon of wealth and class and, as such, the ideal spot to protest as an underclass. There were so many people crowded between its stately facade and the incoming tide that she needn't have been concerned about being noticed. She was further away from the hastily erected dais of wooden boxes than she wanted so when the pale skinned, stick thin Craig climbed up, she felt a surge of familiarity but couldn't immediately place him. Sofia sidled through the melee of shouting men, here and there supported by a wife or girlfriend, until she was close enough to get a better view. She'd had a photograph from a newspaper for some time but it was the voice that prompted a memory from the St. James' club during her first visit. She still remembered the shame when Thorne had caught her spying on the men and prostitutes in a private room. He'd been the ringleader then and she could see why. Craig was an audacious speaker, neither charming nor good looking, but undeniably arresting. The Scottish accent was well suited to his passionate preaching about the evils of capitalism and his bright red hair made him stand out from his peers as if he were alight. He was a man possessed. Sofia studied the faces around her and saw they were enthralled, but she had witnessed another side to him, surely at Vinsant's invitation, on the basis of keeping his enemies close. Craig was obviously not averse to being treated when he wasn't paying for it. He'd probably relished the irony of eating, drinking and whoring at Emmett Vinsant's expense. It hadn't done Vinsant any good though, Alasdair Craig was not to be bought. After the rally disbanded, Sofia followed him to one pub then another then home. She was exhausted but she had an address and that was where she went every day for the next week as she made it her business to understand his routine and habits.

Fit and limber, Craig would make no easy victim. Each day, irrespective of weather, he walked for miles around the city but his favourite haunt was the seafront. He thrived in the freezing winds where Sofia, in contrast, felt that the rushing air seemed literally to bite. Her eyes would stream and her nose run after just minutes. Perhaps the Scots really were made of sterner stuff. There was no obvious means of getting him alone and going into his house would be too dangerous. He attended a variety of meetings, some public, some covert, had lunch out but in a different place almost every day and ended up on the pier smoking hand-rolled cigarettes. She had little chance to watch him late at night given that trailing a man in dark, unfamiliar streets was a likely recipe for disaster. All she could do was follow and wait, becoming more irritated with each passing day. Sofia counselled herself towards patience. Rushing would make her reckless and recklessness would end in a noose, but the days were pushing past.

It was a Friday evening when she arrived home to find Nora standing outside her front door, wringing her hands and biting her bottom lip.

'What is it, Nora?' Sofia asked, anxious to be inside to warm her aching bones.

'Your sister-in-law's here,' Nora said. 'She told me I was to leave the children with her and go home but I said you wouldn't be happy about it.'

'Mary,' replied Sofia.

Nora nodded. 'I thought you wanted her kept away from the children. The nerve of her coming down unannounced.'

'It's all right, Nora,' said Sofia, a tight smile on her lips. 'This time I invited her. You go on home now. I shan't be needing any help tomorrow.' With that Sofia went in, composed and unperturbed. 'Mary, how lovely to see you again,' she said. Her sister-in-law greeted her with a dry kiss to the cheek but eyed her suspiciously.

'We were most surprised to receive your letter,' she said. 'Mr Flathers thought it odd so soon after you'd made it clear the children were to have nothing to do with us. What changed your mind?'

'Go to your bedroom and get your clothes from their drawers, please, children,' Sofia told Isaac and Sadie.

'I don't understand, Mummy. What will we do with them?' Isaac asked.

'You're to pack them,' his mother responded simply. 'I shall fetch you a case in a moment. Now off you go. Your aunt and I need to talk privately.'

Isaac stood his ground. 'We're not going with her,' he said vehemently, pointing a finger at Mary. Sadie slipped one hand into her brother's and Sofia could see she was trying not to cry.

'Don't make a scene. Remember your manners and do what you're told. Now off you go and take your sister with you.' The boy wavered a few seconds longer then gave in. 'You'll see that they write to me every week?' Sofia asked. 'I'll visit when I can. Shall I pack their toys?'

'No,' Mary responded. 'We've bought new ones. It's best they have as few reminders of this place as possible.'

Sofia couldn't answer, itching to slap her sister-in-law's face. She made balls of her hands instead and shoved the fists hard into her pockets. A soft sobbing came from the bedroom. Sofia started to go to Sadie but Mary reached out a hand and stopped her.

'I'll go,' she said. 'They have to get used to me.' The logic was unarguable.

It was another half-hour before they left. Sadie didn't stop crying in spite of Mary's cajoling, sternness and finally threats. Sofia couldn't and didn't interfere.

'Goodbye, Isaac,' Sofia said, bending to kiss his cheek.

'I hate you!' he shouted, stepping away. 'Daddy wouldn't have done this to us. I'm not going to write to you and I never want to see you again.'

'This is for your own good,' she said reaching for him, but it was too little too late.

'I wish you were dead!' he yelled. 'Why couldn't you have died instead of Daddy?' Before she knew what she was doing she had slapped his face. She stared in wonder at her smarting palm which had left bright finger marks on her son's cheek.

'Oh God, Isaac, forgive me please. I'm so sorry.' But the boy had moved to Mary's side, taking his sister with him beyond Sofia's reach.

'We're ready to go now,' Isaac told his aunt.

Sofia went to hug her daughter goodbye but Mary intervened. 'I think you've done enough, don't you?'

Mary carried their little cases and neither Isaac nor Sadie looked back. Brewhouse Yard had never seemed such a dreadful place. It was some time after they'd disappeared from sight that she found herself still standing there, looking at the end of the road as if time had stood still. Nora was watching from a window, but pulled the curtains across when their eyes met and her old friend made no attempt to comfort her. Sofia realised she hadn't given her the chance to say goodbye to the children she'd cared for so long but as much as she wished it differently, she hadn't the words to apologise.

Indoors, Sofia turned the locked and made sure no chink of daylight could find her. She set about clearing the ashes from the fireplace to keep busy and managed to hold her emotions in check until she went into the bedroom. On the bed was a photo of her and Tom that the children had always kept on a chest of drawers, except now it was ripped in half with her face left in a crumpled mess on Isaac's pillow and Tom's portion missing. The children had taken it with them to keep their father close. Of her, naturally, they wanted no reminder.

The tears that welled up were as unwelcome as lice. Sofia threw a punch at the wall and screeched as a bone snapped in her hand but it wasn't enough so she pounded the brickwork until the pain was all consuming. She couldn't care for her children and had chosen to do what her own mother had done to her, to keep them safe. That was how she'd justified it to begin with but it was so much more than that. It was having a single purpose in her head and her heart that the children only distracted her from and sometimes, God help her, sometimes she wanted to pour liquor into their drinks so that they would sleep and leave her alone with her gun and her knife and her memories. There were whole days now, they came more often because it had been so long since she'd killed, days when her hands would shake with the need to extinguish the last living breath from someone. It was beyond her control. If she couldn't be alone to gratify her need to kill, then she would explode with it. She had let the children go for her own selfish reasons, of course. But she wasn't a good enough parent for them, enslaved as she was. It was all for the best and it was still the end of the world. The circle was complete.

The next morning, Sofia bound up her throbbing hand and took the early train to a grey and rainy Brighton. She kept her thoughts on the task at hand and refused to look at the children on the street, squeezing the broken bone in her hand to bring her back to the present when her mind tried to recreate the scene from the night before. The pain was sharp and therapeutic.

Outside Alasdair Craig's house she stood partly hidden by a lamppost, glancing up at his small windows, hungry and impatient, wondering where he was.

'You lookin' for me, girl?' a voice rasped in her ear. Sofia held her breath, the accent enough to tell her that Craig had found her first. What she didn't know was how he'd figured out she was watching him. She turned round slowly, sliding one hand into her pocket to grip the handle of the knife secreted there.

'Ye Gods, you're a pretty wee thing,' he whistled. 'Now what would you be doin' outside ma house? Did you no' think I'd notice you or was that what you wanted?' Sofia said nothing, waiting to see what Craig would do. She was ready to defend herself if necessary but averse to drawing attention in such a residential area.

Up close, she saw that the Scot was older than she'd guessed, his vigor belying his true age. Crow's feet spread from each eye and his skin was ruddy and rough from exposure to the elements and, quite probably, the too regular consumption of whisky. He was no fool though, wary and suspicious. A man who knew he had enemies was rarely at rest. He reminded Sofia of her father, as hard as rock and unpredictable as a pack dog.

'Is it the police who've put you here?' he asked, so close she could smell the meat he'd eaten for breakfast. She had to say something then. He wasn't just suspicious, he was paranoid and a paranoid man was a risk.

223

'I was told...' she stuttered, cutting off the sentence halfway through deliberately, making him force it out of her. He didn't disappoint.

'Spit it out. I've only so much patience and a girl with a bandaged fist is rarely shy, I've found.'

Sofia blanched. The man missed nothing. She wondered how long he'd been aware of her, if he'd seen her before today and been waiting for her to make a move.

'I was told that you were my...my father,' she stammered, casting her eyes towards the pavement as she said it, hoping she'd judged his age right. He must surely be in his late forties and old enough to have got a young woman into trouble twenty-seven years ago.

'Is that right?' he asked, tipping her head back so he could look into her eyes. 'You hardly resemble me now, do you? I wouldn't have said you had highland blood in your veins. You look more like a damned foreigner to me.'

'It's true,' Sofia replied. 'My mother was Romani and she travelled with her family. She never said exactly where she met you, only that she was young and it was just one night.'

'And how many other men did she sleep with the same week, did you ask her that? I'm no more likely to be your father than the butcher, the baker or the bloody candlestick-maker if she was that easy to bed. What is it you want with me anyway? If it's money, you came to the wrong man.'

'No, I just hoped you might remember her. She died when I was young and I always wanted to find you then I saw you at the rally outside the Grand Hotel. Her name was Isabel.' She smiled with something like hope, genuinely enough for him to believe her.

'Girl, I bedded enough women in my youth to populate the new world and I've no doubt that somewhere I have offspring I've nae met but I don't remember your mother, nor do I have any wish for a family or to be spied on. There's no reason for me to believe you're my daughter but more importantly I couldn't care either way. If I see you here again, I'll be less understanding about it. Now get yourself gone.' He spat on the ground between them, his statement of disgust at being approached as clear as he could make it. Sofia waited until he reached his front door then walked away.

She made her way to the seafront, the wind gathering pace as she walked and foamy spray firing at her face as she stared out to sea. It was over. She couldn't go near him again. Without the element of surprise she'd be no match for him physically and there was little prospect of getting him somewhere alone and quiet to use the gun. Her upset over sending the children with Mary had made her careless. Little wonder he'd noticed her. She had virtually no memory of getting to Brighton that morning, let alone how long she'd stood watching his house.

Her train didn't leave for another hour. With heavy feet she wandered to the Brighton Marine and Palace Pier which a salt damaged plaque announced had opened to the public in May 1899. It was busy with visitors almost every day come rain or shine, advertisers' boards on every surface and posters for the latest shows hastily erected and just as soon replaced by a rival's. Today it was bustling as usual, but most of the footfall was towards town rather than sea as the sky became darker by the minute and on the horizon black clouds rolled in against a backdrop of eerie yellow light. Sofia was halfway along the pier when she saw the first crackling line of lightning. She smiled bitterly. It was the perfect day for a storm. She continued to stroll, undeterred by the freezing rain, the driving saline stinging her eyes and lips. People were running now and traders were folding up carts and heading for cover. The boards of the pier were already slippery with surface water but Sofia enjoyed the feeling of danger, the sense that control was an illusion and nature could sweep her away as it chose.

Day trippers began racing for the horse buses and the trams that followed the mesh of overhead lines along the front. Down on the beach, the few wheeled bathing huts being used by those stoic or lunatic enough to brave the icy waters were being hastily dragged beyond reach of the sea. The flags atop the pier whipped uncontrollably back and forth as if trying to work their way free. Waves had begun to batter the high stilts supporting the boards beneath Sofia's feet and spray burst from every direction. Still she kept her back to the shore and continued, hypnotised, towards the squall. Through the rattling windows of the impressive domed structure situated half way along the pier, she could see a few stragglers huddling together in a tea room as if even from inside they could be blown out to sea. Twice, men stopped her and shouted against the racket of the wind that she should turn back. Each time she grinned and shook her head, ignoring the gusts that took her hat, flapping hair about her face and wrapping the long skirt around her legs so that every pace was a battle. Towards the end of the pier a bill board proclaiming that tourists should not miss the spectacular sights of the Royal Pavilion and the Aquarium flew off a post and cartwheeled towards her, scratching her arm and narrowly missing her face. Sofia grabbed the railings to steady herself, common sense demanding that she retreat, willfulness refusing to be conquered. Onwards she heaved herself, eyes fixed upon the terrifying and awe inspiring light show in the black depths of the sky. The thunder dominated, drowning out even the pounding of the rain and waves. By then visibility was reduced to just a few feet and she realised that with one false move, one strong gust with less than iron grip on the railings and all her troubles would be gone. Then she saw him.

The sight of Alasdair Craig, who cared so little if he had sired one or one hundred children, made her sigh as if kissed by a lover. It was a gift, the first she had received from her vengeful god and surely a sign that her life wasn't meant to be wasted. His routine brought him here every day but still, what madman did not turn back in such foul and ferocious weather? One like her, of course. They were just a few feet apart. His back was towards her but she could see it was him by his red hair and sinewy body. For a second, the sight of him silhouetted in the white-gold lightning was the most unspeakably beautiful thing.

He turned round as she staggered closer, his face a question mark, as though he couldn't place her, but then recognition dawned. He must have thought she'd followed him to plead again, because he stared at her, this young woman he believed was so desperate to find her father that she would follow him through the worst storm imaginable, and he laughed. He laughed and carried on laughing as he returned his gaze to the attacking waves and the descent of darkness as it reached them.

Sofia took off one boot. She lost her footing briefly as she did it but Craig was still there. He was a man who couldn't stand to be beaten. Unheard, unseen or perhaps deliberately ignored she was able to move closer until she was directly behind him then she grasped the boot by the length of leather that ran half way up her calf and swung the wooden heel as hard as a man bringing an axe to a tree. She didn't hear the contact but the thud reverberated from his skull to her hands as she dropped the makeshift weapon and dropped to her knees. As Craig's hands reached for the wound on his head, she grabbed his ankles, pulled his legs backwards and shoved her body weight forwards, hoisting him up and over the railings in his disorientation. Down he went into the waiting water and, although Sofia couldn't see his body as it met the waves, she could imagine it. She could feel his terror as the cruel smile was dashed from his face, never knowing quite what had happened. Sofia played the image in her mind of him tumbling beneath the waves, consumed alive by the airless machine of the sea as he fought to reach the surface. No one had seen, no one had heard, only her.

She began the walk to the station. Her hand didn't hurt any more and the memory of her children leaving was less raw. The dreadful hunger inside her was sated and Sofia felt something close to euphoria as she let the storm batter her because for now the one raging inside had grown quiet.

She slept on the train, exhausted and blissful. The only nagging remnant of the day was a missing coin but perhaps even that was the way it should be. Wasn't Alasdair Craig supposed to be her payment to Vinsant to be allowed to return to his service? Perhaps that was why she couldn't profit from it herself. In place of a physical memento, she fixed the copper of his hair in her memory, and would take that out to polish occasionally instead. By the time she arrived in London it was late afternoon and the gas lamps were being lit in the streets. London was quieter in the harsh weather. Even the beggars had quit their corners and sought refuge from the November wet and cold. Sofia felt a glow of invincibility around her as she thought of a broken body and an unforgiving tide, and left the station delighted that she need no longer walk the Brighton streets like a dog following the scent of raw meat. In the glory of the kill, she failed to see the figures waiting either side of the street near her door until the first stepped forward. When he reached for her arm she could only stare at his uniform in confusion.

'Mrs Logan?' he enquired politely but firmly.

'Yes,' said Sofia as the world began to spin.

'You need to come with us, Ma'am.'

Chapter Twenty-five

Childhood 1894

For Sofia, the farm had always been a grim place in the winter. It wasn't so much the cold that bothered her, more that the outside conditions forced her into Mac's company for more hours than were tolerable and, although she was with Saul, they were rarely alone together. Mac was a constant lurking presence, delighting in teasing them, often roughly, and the Marneys couldn't have done less to stop it. Mac was worth twice her and Saul put together, strong as an ox and easily pacified with food. Winter had begun in November and showed no sign of abating by the start of February. Christmas had come and gone, barely noted, and supplies had run so low after a poor summer that food was rationed starting with Sofia and Saul on the smallest portions, then the farmer's wife, and Mac next. Bill Marney never went hungry unless Letty wanted a black eye to go with her single rasher of salted bacon at breakfast.

The nights were the worst. By the time she was fourteen, Mac had started to take an interest in Sofia that sickened her. He never actually touched her, he was cruel but not stupid, so he'd look and let everyone around know he was looking. To her it felt like the leeches that stuck to your legs when you stepped in the mudbanks. Saul had got angry with him about it once but Sofia had intervened, knowing it would do no good and that the only result would be a fist fight Saul couldn't possibly win.

She'd heard Mac making nasty noises when Saul passed by plenty of times before, but it hadn't been until New Year's Eve that things got really bad. During the night, Mac had crept into Saul's room, stolen all his clothes and left only a dress. In the morning poor Saul had had no choice but to come down to breakfast wearing the dress to ask where his clothes had gone. Bill and Letty had roared with laughter, and Mac had taken it as a sign that Saul was fair game. It was only then that Sofia began to fully comprehend why Saul hadn't returned her attentions. It didn't bother her that Saul didn't like girls, but she felt sad in a way she didn't entirely understand and uneasy whenever Saul was left alone with Mac.

In February she'd caught Mac in the stables with the farmhands from a neighbouring plot. They were gathered around Saul, pinned on his back in the dirt, and plastering him with Letty's lipstick. After screaming at them to leave, she'd found his face painted like a ghastly man-doll. Sofia got a bucket and rag, gently washing the rouge away. Mac earned a proper beating for that one from Bill, but not because of his cruelty to Saul: he had ruined Letty's only, precious cosmetic. Not that she ever wore it on the farm. It was something she kept and treasured. Sofia suspected it was a token of the life Letty would never have.

After that things got worse. Saul ended up with a cracked rib a few days later when Bill and Letty had gone to the market giving Mac an opportunity to take his revenge for the beating from Bill. Sofia could have kicked herself that she didn't see it coming. She was incensed and stupidly made matters worse by filling Mac's bed with nettles, covering him in a burning rash from head to toe that nothing could soothe. It was the first of only two occasions when Sofia saw him cry. Their war might have ended then if she'd been able to control her appetite for vengeance, but in her youth and outrage she did the worst thing she could. She laughed at his tears, mocking, calling him a baby. It was the beginning of the end.

A few days later Bill celebrated his fiftieth birthday. Letty had been putting food by and they'd bought ale and cider at market from selling a cow. They invited the neighbouring farmers, Sofia served food, Saul poured drinks and a massive bonfire was built in the yard to keep everyone warm. The evening went well enough with Bill and Letty staggering drunk by ten o'clock and supplies already dwindling. The few people left standing took refuge from the wind in the farmhouse kitchen which was when Sofia realised she hadn't seen Saul for some time. It was only when she couldn't find Mac or his thuggish friends either that she became first suspicious then worried.

She took a lamp and set out among the farm buildings to find them, her anxiousness making her clumsy and noisy. Even then, she still didn't believe they would do anything truly terrible to Saul. A few punches perhaps but Saul was gentle and wouldn't fight back. Even Mac couldn't punish him too much if he didn't retaliate. Shouts from the cattle barn made Sofia run, caution forgotten. It wasn't until she was grabbed from behind that she knew they'd been waiting for her all along. Whoever it was lifted her with ease, laughing at her pathetic kicks as he walked into the barn.

'Here you go, Mac. This the one you wanted?'

'Hold her over there,' Mac grunted, motioning to a hay bale. 'She can watch this little girl getting what she wants.' Through Mac's legs Sofia could see a figure rolled into a ball on the ground, shaking with fright, covering his face with his hands. She had no idea how long they'd had Saul here, only that there was no one outside sober enough to hear or help.

'Let him go, Mac,' she said. 'If you hurt him, I'll tell. Not just Bill, I'll go to the police.'

'I'm not gonna hurt her,' Mac persisted with the crass joke as his friends guffawed along. 'I'm gonna give her some country medicine.'

Sofia was terrified. Mac's audience meant he would never back down. She tried to calm herself, to think of a way to get Saul out of it, more scared than she could remember ever having been in her life. Except it wasn't just fear she was feeling, it was guilt. She shouldn't have made things worse by trying to get even with Mac and now it was out of hand.

'Mac, the nettles were my idea, Saul wasn't involved. I'm really sorry. I'll make it up to you. You can have my food, my bedding, whatever you want but please don't hurt him.' For the first time Saul showed his face, the streaks of his tears visible where they'd run streams through the dirt that covered the rest of him.

'Get out of here, Sofia. This is nothing to do with you,' Saul spluttered until one of Mac's goons pushed his face back down into the mud.

'You'll stay and watch,' Mac growled into Sofia's face. 'Teach you to be such a bitch. Maybe you'll like seeing a real man in action instead of this nancy. Keep her quiet!" he yelled at the lad holding her and a huge, stinking hand covered Sofia's mouth so that all she could do was drag short, panicky breaths in through her nose.

One of the boys grabbed Saul's legs and another his arms. When Mac took his gutting knife from a pocket Saul began to scream. As much as Sofia wanted to close her eyes, she couldn't. It felt too much like leaving Saul alone not to witness what was happening. Mac slit Saul's trousers so that he could pull them off in two pieces. Saul's eyes bulged wide as Mac lowered the knife again but he simply cut off the pants underneath, leaving him in just a shirt, shivering and flinching as Mac ran the point of his knife over his legs and buttocks.

'Go on Mac, cut his balls off,' one of the lads yelled, squealing in excitement.

'Yeah, he doesn't need 'em anyway,' replied the oaf holding Sofia.

'Nah,' said Mac. 'I'm not gonna leave any marks. I'm not bloody stupid whatever she thinks,' he said, casting a look of pure loathing at Sofia. 'I've got something here that little Saul's been wanting for ages.' Mac picked up a pitchfork, turning it upside-down and pointing the splintered wooden handle at his friends. 'Now keep him still.'

Then Sofia did close her eyes. Saul's screams as they used the handle on him were all the picture she needed. His cries were so awful, so pitiful that she reached a point where to her own disgust she wished he would just pass out. The hand that had been silencing her fell away in the heat of the moment but she didn't cry out. There was no point. Her only friend, the first boy she had loved, was beyond help. When she opened her eyes again he was no longer fighting. His face crushed into the dirt as he moaned, the broom handle and floor bloody, his legs thrashing with each violation.

Finally they'd had enough. Mac threw the broom into a pile of cow dung and stood up, wiping his hands on his trousers. He bent down into Sofia's face before leaving the barn.

'Not laughing at me now, are you?' he said and spat across her eyes and forehead. Sofia looked at the floor. They swaggered out into the night to find whatever left over dregs of ale they could as Sofia crawled over to Saul.

She grabbed his scraps of clothing, covering him as best she could, then reached out to hold his face.

'Get away from me!' he screamed.

'Saul, they've gone. It's just us now.'

'Leave me alone,' he screeched, clawing his way towards the darkest corner of the barn, his legs almost useless.

'I'll get a doctor, some blankets, anything.' Sofia was sobbing hard now, the shock sinking in, her uselessness nauseating.

'Just get out, Sofia. I don't want you or anybody else seeing me like this!' He was doubled over, writhing from whatever damage they'd done to his insides, crying and rocking as he hid in the shadows.

'Saul, I'm your friend. Let me help you?' It was a desperate plea. Sofia couldn't stand to see him so broken and do nothing, not when her taunting of Mac had been the catalyst for the assault.

'My parents were right. I'm unnatural. I'm everything Mac thinks I am and worse. They said I was covered in sin and now I'm being punished for it. If you love me, Sofia, leave me alone.'

She wanted to say something that would help but no words were enough. She fetched him a bucket of water, lay her coat over him and stole away to the farmhouse.

It was the longest night of her life, listening to Bill and Letty's drunken snores and the raucous laughter of men still in the yard, all the while waiting to hear the creak of the back stairs that meant Saul had

233

finally come in. Every second was torture and she had no clock to measure it by. She wasn't sure if she slept of not. Eventually Sofia saw the glow of dawn and ran to Saul's bedroom but there was no sign of him. No one else was awake and she guessed they wouldn't be for many hours so she dressed and ran to the barn where she'd left him, taking bread and blankets. It was still in half darkness but there was no figure on the ground and Saul had used the bucket of water to wash away the telltale blood. Sofia found her coat folded carefully on a bale to keep it dry and her heart jumped at Saul's thoughtfulness even in his desperation. All was quiet except for the noise of the rafters creaking. She called out his name but there was no reply. Perhaps he'd run away, although he'd not been to his room to take any spare clothes. Mac had been snoring at the kitchen table and it was unlikely he'd done any more harm. She looked out of the small window to the fields beyond but saw no movement except the flicker of shadows as the sun rose east of the barn.

She was in the yard looking for signs of Saul's presence when the wrongness of the scene hit her. The rhythmic creaks from above her head. The wavering light.

'Saul!' she screamed. She tried to run but her legs were melting, the ground tipping her left and right, no breath in her lungs, every pace sluggishly slow. It felt like forever, that twenty yard journey back to the barn, and yet when she arrived she wished she hadn't made it.

From the top rafter he swung, to and fro, ever so gently in the breeze, his spine in pieces, face a bloated disfiguration of the beautiful, sweet boy he'd been in life. She couldn't reach him from below and even when she got the ladder to the rafter she couldn't get hold of him. Sofia tried to shout for help but no sound left her except a low moaning.

'How could you leave me?' she shouted, sobbing onto the rafter from which he'd thrown himself with only a noose to catch him. 'You're all I had.'

As the ladder began to slip she didn't try to grab the beam. She waited for the ground to rise up and smash the pain from her heart. After that, she knew nothing at all until a cold glass rim hit her nose, followed by a smell like mothballs in acid.

Chapter Twenty-six

November 1906

The smelling salts the surgeon used to bring her round at Bow Street Police Station were offensive and harsh, bringing water to her eyes as she jerked away from the bottle. It was a while longer before she was fully conscious but the surgeon left only when satisfied that she was quite well. In the room with her was the police constable who had asked her name outside the house. She was sitting at a small wooden table, upon which was a cup of tea. There was one high window and a solid door with a hefty lock. So this is how it ends, she thought. It couldn't have been Brighton, they'd never have identified her so quickly and she was positive no one had witnessed it. Whatever had led them to her related to an older murder, perhaps the conductor from the Peterborough train or the door lady from the whorehouse. It didn't really matter any more, she mused, picking up the tea and sniffing it suspiciously. In some ways it was a relief to have been caught.

Charlie appeared. He didn't greet her or smile and Sofia found she had nothing to say. How must he feel poor thing, knowing what the woman he'd once loved had turned out to be? He placed a formal looking paper and pencil on the desk in front of him and cleared his throat.

'The surgeon says you're well enough to answer some questions. Do you feel able to do that now?' Sofia nodded. 'You took quite a blow to the head when you passed out. Is there any injury?'

'Nothing serious,' Sofia said. 'Do what you brought me here to do.'

'Very well. You've been brought in as part of our investigation into the death of Jonathan Fitzpatrick. He died in March of this year and the papers said it was a heart attack but the post mortem concluded he was poisoned.' Sofia tried to swallow and found her throat wouldn't obey the order. He was the first one so of course she had made mistakes. It had been chaotic and ill-planned. 'We've found a link,' Charlie continued 'between him and another man, namely Desmond Banks, who was suffocated at his home, in June. Did you know either of them?'

'I don't think so,' said Sofia, hating the fact that Charlie was playing games with her, stringing the accusations out.

'What we know is that both men, at the time of their deaths, owed substantial amounts of money.' Sofia looked up and met Charlie's eyes. He might want to play games but she'd had enough. 'Specifically to Mr Emmett Vinsant of Doughty Street, your late husband's employer. A man you certainly do know.'

'Oh stop it, Charlie,' Sofia snapped. 'If you have something to say to me, just say it.'

Charlie gazed at her. If he was surprised by her outburst he hid it well. 'All right. I would like to know if you can confirm any other link between these two men. Have you ever seen them at card games together or in Emmett Vinsant's presence? Has Vinsant ever spoken to you about either of them?'

Sofia remained silent. The other man in the room tutted and Charlie directed his attention towards him instead.

'Constable Jones, would you leave us for a few minutes, please?' He did as he'd been told. 'Sofia, I need you to answer these questions for me. There are two murders that cannot be ignored and you may have important information, even if you don't realise it.'

She hesitated. She'd been so sure they'd suspected her when the police had appeared at her door. Her pulse quickened with a burst of hope.

'I don't see how I can help you,' she told Charlie quietly. 'And I don't like being arrested and brought to a police station.'

'No one arrested you,' he replied. 'You were asked to come and answer some questions and when you fainted the officers brought you here to see the police surgeon. This is an official investigation and I have to carry out my enquiries here. Besides, I didn't think you'd want me calling at your house. Not after the way things ended.'

Sofia picked up the empty mug for something to do with her hands. They were shaking badly albeit relief rather than fear. It was all she could do not to let out a nervous laugh.

'I didn't know them and I hardly ever saw Mr Vinsant. Is that all, Charlie? I've had a long day and I'd like to get home.'

'There's one more thing,' he said. 'The other reason I wanted you to come here. Take this seriously, Sofia. Nora told me you've let the children go to your sister-in-law. It can only be because you're gambling again and you must be losing or there's no way you'd have done such a thing. If I'm right about the connection between the two dead men, then Emmett Vinsant might be very dangerous indeed. If you're in debt to him you need to be careful and if you're scared, whatever happened between us, I'd rather you came to me for help. Don't think that just because you're a woman he won't expect you to pay what you owe.'

'Thank you, but I'll be fine,' Sofia spoke gently. 'Am I free to go?' He nodded. 'I can tell you this much. If those men were regular gamblers with debts worth killing over, they'll have had more loans than you'll ever be able to trace. People like that go from one game to the next, taking credit wherever they can get it. You'll need to cast your net pretty wide to find everyone they owed. Emmett Vinsant won't have been the only one chasing them.'

Sofia closed the door behind her and left the police station with as much dignity as she could muster. The walk home seemed to go on forever and with every step she thought her legs might fail. It seemed that she must have pushed her heart to its very limits that day. She collapsed onto her bed and slept for fourteen hours.

As much as Sofia wanted to contact Vinsant, she knew she needed proof of her actions in Brighton. For the next week she read every newspaper she could find and wandered the streets desperate to hear gossip about the missing unionist. Eventually his absence would be noted but the police might well think he'd just taken himself off to visit family in Scotland. By the sixth day she was beginning to give up hope when the paper bore the news she'd been praying for. The day after the storm, a badly battered body had been washed up on Brighton beach. The post mortem confirmed death by drowning although there was also a serious head injury. It was a further two days until Craig was reported as missing. When a close friend identified the body, Craig's daily walk along the Palace Pier were remarked upon, leading to speculation that the head wound had occurred when he'd fallen from the pier in the storm. Sofia kept the paper to show Vinsant, hoping it would be enough.

Sofia called the telephone number Lefevre had given her and three hours later she was on her way to a building site in London's East End where a new factory was being built. She had no weapon, no plan, and if they decided to kill her, she knew they would. Even that didn't matter any more. The man who had brought her to her knees was now her last hope.

The early afternoon sun made the site orange with flying dust. Emmett was enjoying his industrial empire, she thought, as she watched him from the street, inspecting every square yard, looking at scrolls of paper, interrogating the man she presumed was an architect as he fumbled nervously. Sofia wondered what sort of money it took to buy land in the city and build such huge creations from the ground up, but the railways were growing at an incredible rate and Vinsant had been at the forefront of that gold mine a long time. The clubs were a sideline really, a way to make friends and influence people, to access the right ears and line useful wallets. He looked at his watch seconds before a local church bell chimed the hour which was her signal to go to the back entrance, knock and wait to be let in. She'd been careful to make sure she wasn't being followed, with a scarf over her head, ragged clothes and taking a circuitous route. Sofia was wary after her brush with Charlie in his official capacity yesterday although she was fairly sure he didn't suspect her of anything more than gross naivety.

Captain Thorne was nowhere to be seen. Instead, Sofia was escorted down steep steps into a basement where there was a single chair on which she was told to sit. One of the men checked her for weapons, caring nothing for the sensitivities of her gender, running his hands across her chest and up each leg. She'd known this was the way it would be. It was the reason she hadn't even considered arming herself. If they'd found anything, the meeting with Vinsant would never have happened. They were thorough and Sofia knew their jobs would have been lost, or worse, if they weren't. Afterwards she was left alone in the half-dark long enough to make her nervous until heavy footsteps came down the stairs. She waited for Emmett Vinsant to speak. He puffed on a cigar and the look in his eyes was that of a dog deciding whether or not to bite. Fair enough, she thought, after the last time.

'Make it good,' was all he said. She had laid the newspaper on the floor before the men searched her.

'You need to read that paper, where I've folded it open,' she said, kicking it towards him. Vinsant stayed where he was.

'I don't need to do anything. Tell me why you're here or this meeting is over and you might not enjoy my method of saying goodbye.'

'Brighton,' said Sofia. 'I phoned Thorne, you were in the room, I told him I was going there. I was looking for Alasdair Craig.' Vinsant looked unimpressed but curious as he glanced at the paper without picking it up.

'Looking for a dead man, were you?' he mocked.

'He was alive when I found him, although he didn't remain that way for long. The paper reports he suffered an injury. That was from a blow I dealt him just before I tipped him off the end of the pier. It was luck, really and I'll admit it wasn't how I planned it but everyone thinks his death was accidental. I came here to tell you that it wasn't.'

Vinsant took his time reading the report, giving nothing away and Sofia wondered if she'd over-estimated how important an opponent Craig was.

'Suppose I accept that this was your doing. What of it? As I recall you made it clear you no longer wanted to work for me. No, let me rephrase that, you actually threatened to expose me if I didn't release you from my service.' He was unimpressed by Craig's assassination. Sofia hadn't expected it to be that easy but she'd hoped it would soften him towards her.

'That was a mistake,' she said, making Emmett Vinsant roar unexpectedly with laughter.

'A mistake? You think that was a mistake? If you hadn't had the forethought to write to your solicitor, your body would be ashes by now.' He screwed up the paper and threw it full force into her face. She didn't raise her hands to stop it.

'I was wrong,' she said. 'And I understand that you saw what I am more clearly than I ever saw myself. It's not just Craig. I've ended my relationship with Charlie Danes.'

'Too late,' said Vinsant, his patience wearing thin.

'I gave up my children!' Sofia shouted. 'I sent them away to live with their aunt in Yorkshire. I have no idea when or even if I'll see them again. I know I shouldn't have threatened you but I was trying to pretend I could lead a normal life, that I was normal, but I know now that I'm not. I need some sort of structure, a reason to carry on. It's all I can think of. Please! I'll be careful and follow orders but I need things to be the way they were.'

She was crying, spitting out every word, her desperation filling the air in a way that had Vinsant transfixed.

'Is that everything?' he said.

Yes,' said Sofia then shook her head. 'Actually, no. The police investigation has progressed. They've made a connection between Jonathan Fitzpatrick and Desmond Banks, that both men owed you large amounts of money. I thought you should know. You might be able to leave a trail to other people who'd loaned them both money, or make sure you have paperwork proving that their debts had been cleared before their deaths.'

Now Vinsant was interested. It had been a risky admission but she knew that she had to tell him everything if she wanted him to trust her again.

'Leave that to me,' he said. 'Say nothing at all to your police constable friend. I don't want you so much as wishing him a pleasant morning, understand?' She nodded keenly. 'And the letter with your solicitor?'

This was the problem, Sofia knew. It was the point where she'd find out if she were more useful to Vinsant dead or alive. She crossed her fingers for luck and hoped that the sacrifices she'd made were evidence enough of her change of heart.

'Destroyed,' she said, bracing herself for his response.

'So I could kill you now, end this once and for all and hear no more about it?' Sofia tried to assess his mood but he was reptilian in his emotions. Nothing would show on his face until he was about to strike. Too late, she thought. It was all or nothing.

'You can kill me now,' she answered. 'Nothing will lead them to you.' She closed her eyes and her imagination played out his hand reaching for a gun, knife or wire. Her body could disappear under a ton of building rubble and never be discovered.

'I won't kill you yet,' he whispered. 'There's something I want first. Do it without arousing suspicion, without error and exactly the way I want and you can rejoin my service. I'll look after you and give you what you need. Fail, take a step out of line and you're a walking corpse. How do you like my terms, Mrs Logan?'

'Sounds fair,' she said. 'What is it you want me to do?'

'I want your word that you'll speak to no one, whisper no secrets in your sleep, not discuss this with even my most trusted employees.'

'Of course. Why would I? A trail would lead to me before you.'

He leaned down so his lips were touching her ear and she could feel his venom as he hissed at her.

'What I want, Sofia, is for you to kill my wife.'

Chapter Twenty-seven

December 1906

The nights were at their longest and darkest as the prospect of Christmas put smiles on the faces of the children Sofia pretended not to notice, and money in the pockets of the traders she ignored when they tried to entice her into their shops. She'd received two letters from Mary in the five weeks since the children had left and the latest detailed their Christmas plans which, Sofia noted gratefully, did not include a trip to London. There would be parties, gifts bought with the Flathers' new found wealth and enough food to sustain a navy. She wasn't sure if Mary meant to make her jealous or reassure her but, either way, Isaac and Sadie were safe and being cared for. That wasn't what was causing her so many sleepless nights. Beatrice Vinsant was.

It had never occurred to Sofia that she might take a woman's life. As hard as she thought about it, there wasn't any tangible reason why it should be different from a killing a man, but it was. She knew why Vinsant wanted his wife dead. He had married her for social positioning which was long since established, whilst she had allied herself with what many saw as a revolutionary group and in the process had become an embarrassment to her husband. His tolerance in all things was time limited. Now, unbeknownst to Beatrice, her husband had had enough.

Although Sofia had no particular fondness for Mrs Vinsant, separated as they were by money, class and education, Sofia couldn't justify the woman's death. It wasn't something she'd really considered before. Every life she'd taken had already been mired in life's muck, thieves, deviants or in debt beyond saving, but Beatrice did not belong in the same category. She was aware, though, that in judging Vinsant's wife too good to be killed, she was giving herself the status of a god, having already agreed that so many others should die. If she had no right to decide one then surely she had no right to decide the others. Wasn't that precisely why she had crawled back to Emmett Vinsant, so that he made the decisions, gave the orders, and exempted her from the process of determination, freeing her from the burden of conscience?

It was too great a riddle to solve so she'd given up thinking and dedicated herself to acting instead, beginning the process of following Beatrice a week ago. It was more difficult this time, knowing recognition was inevitable if she got too close, and because the activists attracted attention wherever they went. The Women's Social and Political Union had taken against the Prime Minister and Government, many of whom had pledged to support their cause before being elected and who had just as soon forgotten their promises when they took their seats. The Houses of Parliament were now a central focus of their campaigning and for two days Sofia had huddled in Parliament Square, wishing her clothes were warmer and wondering at the fortitude of the protesting women who seemed so unaffected by the environment. The whole area buzzed constantly with police constables, business men, traders, beggars and pickpockets. More motorcars came and went from here than Sofia had ever seen before, the new status symbol of those so rich they already owned every other modern convenience. A few other factions set up stall around the square, unionist, religious and migrant, but the WSPU was the best organised. There was always a small group of them making their presence felt, waving banners, handing out leaflets and singing. Sofia began to recognise the regular faces. The much admired Christabel Pankhurst arrived on December 16th. Sofia knew her from the papers. Her arrival caused a stir and the usual activity stopped for a day whilst a discreet series of meetings were held under cover of a multitude of umbrellas. Sofia wanted to move forward and see if she could hear anything that would help, but Beatrice would surely have noticed her.

Their plans were vital to Sofia because Emmett Vinsant had been clear in his instructions about his wife's demise. As she had so many times since leaving the factory basement, Sofia recalled his last words before leaving him alone to stew in his hatred.

'And I want you to do it in the middle of one her damned rallies or protests or whatever those self-righteous bitches call them. I want her to know why.' His face had been purple with rage. When he spoke of Beatrice he was a man possessed. Sofia knew she'd been lucky to escape with her life and now that she'd given up so much, she had no choice but to do as he commanded, especially without the threat of the letter to protect her.

The urgency of the suffragettes' meetings made Sofia believe that whatever they were planning was imminent. The group disbanded at five that evening and Beatrice drifted away, whispering excitedly to a companion as she went. She was an oddity, taller than the others, always straight-backed, head held high. Years of marriage hadn't broken her pride and perhaps all Emmett had done was to strengthen her resolve that women should be treated as men's equals. She must have known some of what her husband was capable of. How could she live with a man and not suspect what went on in his heart? Her estate, if she had any wealth of her own, would pass to Vinsant on her death and he would be free to take a more obedient wife, probably some years younger, and have the sympathy of his peers for his dreadful loss. It was a no-lose situation for him but for Sofia it was an almost impossible task: killing in public and escaping. It could only be done in a crowd, in confusion or in the dark. She had to be ready to strike at any time, not knowing when the next opportunity might arise.

The next morning was a Monday and London began its day in the dark, the markets opening up irrespective of the cold, barrow boys heckling one another and horses splashing mud in every direction as they trotted through the streets. It was a day to be sat in front of the fire, not outside in the drizzle, gloves all but useless, coat not warm enough, with a pair of Tom's socks on over her stockings. Sofia was in Parliament

Square by eight, hoping the man who sold hot chestnuts to the throngs of Christmas shoppers would arrive early. They were the best way she'd found to keep her hands warm. She loved the sweet nutty smell of them and they'd always been Isaac's favourite. She stopped herself there. Such thoughts were a forbidden pleasure. This was her world now.

The knife was in her pocket, hidden but accessible. It was the only way to kill in public but it would have to go in just once, accurately aimed, as she'd learned to slaughter animals at the farm. No fuss, no noise, no second chance and she needed to be behind Beatrice to slip the blade into her back so that it pierced a lung and she could move away. If she was fast enough she could be gone before the woman even hit the ground. The gloves she wore kept her fingerprints off the blade in case she dropped it. She'd worn heavy make-up, too, hoping Beatrice wouldn't recognise her and that any reports of her likeness would be incompatible with her natural appearance.

The women were gathered before the sun came up, smartly dressed, most in long black skirts and good winter hats. If it weren't for the banners, passers-by would take them for a church group. They were understated and respectful, quiet and demure until 11 o'clock when a woman Sofia hadn't seen before marched to the public entrance of the Houses of Parliament and tried to go inside. A constable blocked the woman's way and Sofia saw the confrontation, noting both the intransigence on the man's face and the determination on hers. Lowering her hat, Sofia moved in.

Another woman went to her leader's side, pleading their right to enter and questioning the authority to prevent them. The constable made it clear he had orders and that they were not to be admitted, putting one hand up to block the women's passage and that was it. Banners were hoisted, voices raised and as one, the group moved towards the entrance with the rising chant "Deeds, not words".

A crowd was forming, always delighted to witness a disturbance. Soon more police were running to the scene and additional women arrived to swell the WSPU ranks. Sofia positioned herself at the back of

246

the group, keeping a close eye on Beatrice, when the mass lurched forward with several of the women bursting into the lobby. She was thrust forward with the rest, tumbling to the ground and rolling to avoid the crush of bodies coming after. Now she couldn't see Beatrice at all. Shouts of "votes for women" and "the Liberal Government has betrayed us" echoed through the halls met by the police yelling instructions in an attempt to restore order.

Sofia scrabbled to her feet in time to see Beatrice being manhandled by a constable and dropping herself heavily to her knees to avoid being removed from the building. One of her fellow protestors put their arms around Beatrice's waist to add to the weight but more police were piling in by the minute and Beatrice was soon dragged bodily out on to the street. When Sofia was approached by an angry looking constable she put her hands in the air in a gesture of surrender, walking quickly to the exit of her own accord. Outside, eleven women were restrained but continued to shout slogans in spite of commands to be silent. One by one they were bundled into the back of a Black Maria to be transported to a police station. In spite of her bitter disappointment at having missed such an opportunity, she admired the women. They had been entirely unafraid, wholly focussed on achieving one end which was to draw attention to their campaign. Their well-tailored clothes and expensive shoes belied the fervour of their intent. This was an army, Sofia thought. A small, well structured, resolute army and if the Government thought it could go on ignoring them, then it was going to look very foolish indeed. The thought made her smile until she felt a blade pressing into the small of her back.

'Walk with me,' Thorne said. 'We need to talk.' He kept one hand around her waist as they went, looking to the rest of the world like sweethearts as his hand concealed the knife Sofia had no wish to become any more familiar with. They walked for several minutes and every time Sofia tried to speak he shushed her until he found a tiny alleyway and shoved her roughly against the wall.

'What the hell do you think you're doing?' he spat.

'I'm sorry,' said Sofia, shocked by his ferocity. 'I tried but things moved too fast. I won't fail next time.'

'What the hell are you talking about?' he demanded. 'Why are you following Beatrice?'

Sofia bit her tongue before it could reap any more damage as it sank in that Thorne had no idea what she had been tasked to do. So Emmett Vinsant didn't trust even his closest man with this.

'What were you doing there?' Sofia countered and at once Thorne looked defensive. He paused before answering.

'I'd been sent to pick up Mrs Vinsant,' he replied. 'We couldn't get into Parliament Square with the disturbance so I walked the last part of the way. But you haven't answered my question.' Sofia wasn't about to take any chances. Vinsant had told her to discuss her purpose with no one and she wouldn't. This could easily be another test of loyalty.

'I've been interested in the suffragettes since I saw Mrs Vinsant at the hall in Kensington. I heard they were planning a rally today and came down to see what it was all about.' Thorne didn't try to hide his disbelief.

'The speaker in Kensington ended up dead not long after,' he said.

'If you want to discuss such things you should speak to the man who gives the orders,' Sofia answered. Thorne straightened his jacket, gathering his composure and Sofia watched him curiously. It was odd that Vinsant had kept him in the dark about his plans. Still, the fewer people who knew, the less likely was the prospect of discovery.

'Just get on with what you're supposed to be doing and stay away from Mrs Vinsant,' Thorne said. 'She's in enough trouble without you poking around.' As he walked away Sofia realised that he'd initially referred to Mrs Vinsant as Beatrice. It was an odd mistake, she mused, unless you were used to using someone's first name. Sofia considered and reconsidered their conversation and wondered just how much more there was that she didn't know.

The next day the newspapers reported that, in spite of the police not pursuing a charge of disorderly conduct, the Magistrate had taken a more strict view. The women had been offered the choice of paying a small fine or spending the following two weeks in Holloway prison whereupon each one had proudly chosen the latter. They would have a markedly new experience of Christmas, Sofia thought, trying to imagine what their meal would comprise on December 25. Unlike male political prisoners, Sofia had read that the suffragettes were treated like common criminals in prison, extended no courtesies or privileges. It would be a frightening and freezing end to the year for them. She felt sorry for Beatrice, a confusing sensation given what she'd set out to do yesterday but there it was, whether she liked it or not. Whatever she'd thought previously, the suffragettes were not privileged ladies filling their endless spare time with tea, high talk and philosophising. They were real women trying to change the way things worked, not that it meant anything for Sofia. She had her orders and knew all too well the consequences of failing to carry them out. It was best not dwelt upon, so she didn't.

She knew she would achieve nothing for the next two weeks. Beatrice wasn't due for release until New Year's Eve and without the children Christmas was going to seem interminably long. Sofia had to keep herself occupied. Having not seen Lefevre for some time, the guilt had been plaguing her so that was what she'd do. She could see that he ate more, keep him warm and fill every minute caring for him. It was exactly what her conscience needed so she collected him in a cab that afternoon, ignoring his arguments, packing his bags and taking him back to Brewhouse Yard where she'd already made up a bed in front of the fire. For the fourteen days that followed, Sofia was as good a nurse and friend as any could have been but no amount of food or medicine would halt the onward march of the illness as it consumed Lefevre's body from the inside out. Every day, it seemed a greater miracle that he opened his eyes at all.

By late afternoon on the last day of the year, Sofia knew her friend had hours rather than days left to live. He had repeatedly told her how selfless she was over Christmas, never leaving him unless it was to fetch food or fuel, holding his hand and soothing his pain. The truth was that Lefevre had saved her when the loneliness and long nights would have proved too much. Her memories came alive at night, the fire casting shadows like demons on the walls as if she were surrounded by the dead. With Lefevre here she had been able to exhaust herself and he had been the perfect patient: compliant, grateful, uncomplaining. She mourned the thought of the loss of him before he had even gone and yet she longed, genuinely, for an end to his suffering. Such a sweet man deserved an easier death. He'd eaten practically nothing for days, a few sips of soup was all. Sofia was relieved that he slept because awake he was in such pain that it brought tears to her eyes.

'I can't see,' he said, in a voice that was faint from dehydration and muscle wastage. Sofia perched next to him and bent her head to hear.

'You don't need to see,' Sofia whispered. 'I'm right here and I shan't leave you.'

'I shall be the one leaving you, my dear,' he said, a faint smile lighting his face.

'Don't talk like that...' she began, interrupted by a coughing fit that made him sound entirely hollow inside.

'There's something I must tell you,' he said when he was still again.

Sofia shook her head. 'There's nothing you need to do but rest.' She held his hand tightly and for a second he returned her grip.

'I shall have no rest until this is said,' he replied. Water filled the deep pits of his eyes and Sofia picked up a handkerchief to dab at the tears.

'You're upsetting yourself. Please don't.'

'You don't understand,' he replied. 'I know Vinsant made you do terrible things and I don't want you to tell me what they were, but he gave you no choice.'

'No one's to blame except me for the things I've done. You never talked about it before. Why now?'

'Because I helped him, God forgive me,' Lefevre whispered, a stray tear wetting his gaunt cheek.

'Don't do this,' said Sofia.

'Yes,' Lefevre insisted. 'I'm out of time. Vinsant wanted you in his debt so he told me to deal in the games with the bonnets and ordered me to fix the cards,' he whispered.

Sofia closed her eyes briefly but when she opened them again her face was serene.

'You know, with or without you, I would have gambled on and on until I was out of my depth. I saw the signs. You're not responsible for the mess I made.'

'That's not true,' Lefevre gasped, his breath catching in the back of his throat as he wheezed his words out at her. 'There's one more thing. It was at the very start, before I knew you properly. I hoped you would never find out but you need to know,' the coughing began again.

'Lefevre, you must stop. Drink a sip of water. You can't breathe,' she held a cup to his lips but he turned his head away.

'For God's sake Sofia, you have to understand what Vinsant really is. You have to break free of him. He will stop at nothing.'

'I know that already,' she whispered.

'No, you don't. At Isaac's school, the visitor from Quebec who was there the day he was accused of taking the purse. It was me. Vinsant arranged my visit there, told me to take the money and put it in your son's bag. He wanted you brought so low you had no choice but to turn to him for help. It was only your friend's intervention that kept Isaac out of prison and moved to the workhouse. Vinsant didn't save Isaac as you thought. He set the whole thing up. And I made it happen.'

There was silence save for Lefevre's whistling breaths. Sofia sat with her hands in her lap, head bowed, unblinking. When finally she spoke her voice was as faint as her patient's.

'I don't understand. Why would you do that to me?' she asked.

'He had evidence of my love affair with a high born gentleman. Vinsant threatened to expose him if I didn't do as instructed. We would both have been imprisoned and his family would have disowned him. I'm so sorry. I saved my lover and betrayed you.'

'And I betrayed my son. I refused to believe him. He told me he was innocent. And he was taken into that filthy hole, he was beaten,' she doubled over, hands pressed into her stomach, panting for air.

'Sofia, I don't want to die without making this right. Please.' His breathing had become increasingly shallow and his lips were grey.

Sofia slowly reached out one shaking hand across to take his. 'You're too weak for this,' Sofia said.

'Forgive me,' he rasped.

'It wasn't you. It was Vinsant. There's nothing to forgive.'

'Please say it.' Sofia looked in his eyes and saw his desperation. She fought the horror rising inside her and made herself kiss his forehead.

'I forgive you,' she said, 'I do.' He closed his eyes and Sofia stroked his head as he slipped into sleep. He did not wake again.

It was a dark night, more so inside her own head that outside her door. There was a constant jumble of images - her first trip to the club, Vinsant playing benefactor, Charlie at her door telling her Isaac had been arrested, and worse, the worst by far was her screaming at her son to stop lying, that he could never make it better unless he admitted what he'd done. She meant what she'd told Lefevre. He wasn't to blame. Look at all she'd done on Vinsant's orders, ever justified by the thought of what she had to lose if she refused. Everyone made choices. What right had she to judge Lefevre's?

But it was the thought of Vinsant that enraged her. She had gone back to him like a dog with its tail between its legs, begging for scraps and a kind hand. And now here she was, whiling her time away waiting to do more of his dirty work. But she'd given up so much to get here. Even the children were gone, not that she had any doubt it was the best thing for them and given what she knew about how badly she'd failed Isaac, she was only amazed he hadn't been more keen to get away from her. Little wonder he had refused to write. She sat for hours, considering

Vinsant's part in it, each time concluding that she had brought disaster on her own head. She had known from the start that she shouldn't work at the club, should have tried harder to get other work, not been so proud about the washing work she was offered in the laundry. Even then, all it would have taken was to be stronger, refuse to gamble, to have known when enough was enough. But she had to win, to have more, pretending it was for the children when all the time the sickness was burning within her. She just couldn't admit it. At every turn she could have done more to stop it. Vinsant hadn't asked her to go back to him. That she had done all by herself. Alasdair Craig had been the grease that set the wheels in motion once more. If she allowed herself to blame Vinsant for it all now, to be swept away by the tide of misery that was welling inside her, it would all have been for nothing.

She hid the fury she refused to acknowledge with layer upon layer of bad wine and cheap whisky, knowing that once she began to hold Vinsant accountable there would be no returning from it. And that meant the unthinkable. It meant feeling the way she did on the bridge when only killing others or killing herself seemed to be the options, both fates damnation.

'What's done is done,' she whispered each time her thoughts turned to Vinsant's manipulations. 'Too many sacrifices.'

Sofia arranged Lefevre's funeral, taking the money from her savings. She wouldn't let him be treated as a pauper, he had too much dignity in life to be so disrespected in death. Having notified the club, a handful of staff members attended the funeral later that week. At the end of the short service, Sofia laid roses on the grave and said a silent prayer. It was a black afternoon. She returned home and tried to keep busy but there was nothing left to do. She would have gone to Nora's but her old friend was keeping her distance, not offish but almost afraid, making Sofia wonder if Nora could finally see her for what she really was. She tried to replace missing buttons but couldn't focus on the thread and scrubbed the floor instead. At six o'clock she took to her bed, gun under one pillow and knife under the other. Reliving each kill, moment by moment, she captured the sounds, smells and textures of them until ecstasy conquered her despondency.

Beatrice seemed to have disappeared entirely since her release from prison and it was only by orchestrating a meeting with Mrs Hasselbrook where she regularly shopped for fresh fruit and vegetables that Sofia learned the mistress had retreated to her family's home to recover. There didn't seem to be any particular date set for her return. Sofia was frustrated, needing it to be over and finding contemplating it almost as unsettling as the act itself would be. In the meantime, she did all she could to prepare. She returned to her old position in Parliament Square, able to get closer without fear of recognition, so that she could listen in on some of the conversations. An event was being organised from the Manchester headquarters but she couldn't catch any specifics other than that it would take place in London in February.

It was another ten days before Sofia saw the posters that had been nailed to fences throughout the city overnight. The National Union of Women's Suffrage Societies was holding a march between Hyde Park and Exeter Hall in the Strand and calling every woman, and any man who supported their cause, to join them. Without a doubt, Beatrice would be in attendance. No suffragist willing to go to prison for their cause would miss it. Sofia had only to wait until 9 February.

Chapter Twenty-eight

February 1907

On Saturday 9 February Sofia put her affairs in order. She left an envelope on the mantelpiece addressed for the attention of Ambrose Friendly inside which were photos of Tom, Sofia and the children, all the money she had left and a letter for Isaac and Sadie. It was marked to be opened in the event of her death or incapacitation. She made no mention of the things she'd done but left one sheet of paper for each child telling them simply how much they were loved, how much she wished she could have been part of their lives as they grew up and how proud she was when she imagined the adults they would become. She asked only for their forgiveness and told them their father was watching from Heaven and that they would never truly be alone. With it were instructions for the lawyer to see that the money reached the children save for a few shillings set aside for Nora with thanks for all her kindness. Sofia had wanted to leave a note for her as well but each time she tried to start it she wrote a lie, and the time for untruths was past.

She had prepared thoroughly for the march, making a banner exactly like those she'd seen suffragettes waving at the House of Commons and buying a WSPU pin for her lapel. The meeting place was the band stand at Hyde Park Corner at two in the afternoon.

Sofia was at her front door, hand gripping handle, when it occurred to her to run. To pack what few belongings she had left, pluck a name from the air, and just go. She smiled thinking of it. She could be anyone she liked, widowed, single, perhaps a lady fallen on hard times. She could go anywhere, start again. Vinsant would never find her out of the city, if he even bothered to try. It meant she wouldn't have to kill Beatrice Vinsant. Picturing herself in the little cottage of her childhood dreams, sea stretching for miles to the hazy horizon, she wondered how she had come so very far only to find herself back at the start again. Her whole life had been one vicious circle. She had tried to escape, to be the person she wanted to believe she was, but as hard as she prayed and fought there seemed to be no relief. As for killing Beatrice Vinsant, she was damned if she did and damned if she didn't. She'd sent her children away because of this insane need to kill, an unstoppable hunger that had become the pivotal point of her world. Emmett Vinsant had created her as his toy and she moved her hands and feet to his bidding. Was it the monster inside him that had so easily identified the monster within her? There was no point pretending Vinsant was the enemy. The truth was that he was more her soulmate than Tom had ever been. If he was evil and despicable, then he was exactly what she deserved. She buttoned her coat and raised the collar against the downpour outside and set off for Hyde Park.

The rain had been falling for hours. Gutters were blocked already, the streets a mess of slush, spattering every pedestrian and colouring the pavements brown. Sofia hadn't expected so many people heading towards the rally. It was one o'clock, still an hour to go and already there was an excited buzz in the crowds. Women, as if practising, were holding banners high as they made their way to the rendezvous point. If anyone thought it was going to be a wash out courtesy of the weather then they would be proved wrong. By the time the band stand was in sight, there was a mass of bodies in a shifting collage of white, purple and green, chattering, laughing, organising, serious and triumphant. The women broke into different groups, each under their own banner. Sofia could see The Central Society for Women's Suffrage, the Women's Textile Workers' Committee, the Women's Trades' Council and the Women's Liberation Federation just in the small area around her. What she couldn't see was a banner proclaiming the presence of the Women's Social and Political Union and that was what she needed. She knew that the WSPU was frowned upon by some other groups as too militant, unlike the other more peaceful suffragists, but she'd expected Beatrice to attend anyway. There were thousands of women here. Finding one amongst such a horde was a hopeless task. She decided to leave the crowds and moved to a better vantage point at the top of Piccadilly. Already the streets were lined with spectators, members of the press and photographers trying desperately to keep their cameras dry. Men, women and children had turned out to view the procession, as if they expected royalty.

Sofia stood where she could watch the marchers filing through and slip in easily if she spotted Beatrice. It was another thirty minutes before they were ready to go but at two o'clock, as if some divine presence were looking down and giving their blessing, the rain stopped and a band struck up.

The musicians came first, heralding the arrival of the leaders of the group. There was Millicent Garrett Fawcett, leader of the NUWSS next to the leader of the new Labour Party, Keir Hardie. They walked proudly, slowly, speaking to one another but not engaging with the crowd. A hush descended when they went past, as if the onlookers had found an unexpected respect for the protestors. Then the different groups began to go past, often just three abreast, for the spectators had taken up so much of the route. There were a few jokers in the crowds, some asking the women where their husbands were or why they weren't at home where they should be, but in truth remarkably few dared jeer.

The drizzle picked up again after an hour and it was then that Sofia recognised the young woman who had questioned Joseph Carlisle at the Kensington hall. She was a member of Beatrice's group and likely not far from the rest of her companions. Sofia moved through the crowd, slipped under the barrier, careful to keep away from the photographers and unfurled her banner, holding it up on its short stick to cover her face as she marched. She overtook one line here and another line there until she was just a few bodies behind Beatrice's colleague then, with a mixture of relief and resignation, she spotted her target some way ahead but moving against the flow of marchers towards her. Sofia held her breath until Beatrice stopped. For a moment Sofia had thought she would just keeping moving back through the protestors until she ended up right next to her. Perhaps Sofia had wanted to be seen, to sabotage her own mission. It would have brought an early end to the day, one way or another, but it was not to be. Sofia continued marching, settling into a rhythm and chanting along with the women either side of her, all the time never losing sight of Beatrice. It had been hard enough to find her. She couldn't lose her now.

The roads were muddy rivers. It was an uncomfortable walk with wet skirts clinging to calves and constant drizzle from above but there was a remarkable camaraderie in evidence. In the preceding days, the newspapers had published wildly differing views of the appropriateness of the procession but there was no doubt now that the marchers were a force to be reckoned with. Beatrice looked in her element, arms linked through her friends' on either side, face shining with pride and determination. She was utterly involved, thought Sofia, completely captivated by the moment which was precisely the state Sofia needed her to be in.

A small boy darted from the spectators into the centre of the marchers where a woman picked him up. A man in the crowd shook his head and laughed at the woman, sharing a secret look that said everything: I couldn't stop him, he wanted his mother, we're so proud of you. The longing to feel Isaac and Sadie's hands in hers was overwhelming. Sofia frowned: not now. She'd done so well not to think about them. Beatrice looked backwards towards the woman with the boy in her arms and instinctively reached out a hand to him. She would never know the feel of her own child clinging for comfort which may have been why Vinsant found it so easy to get rid of her. If she'd borne children, whatever her politics, Sofia was sure she would have secured her future. Vinsant cared nothing for other people's children, of course, when they could be used to help him achieve his goals. Sofia knew she should be exploring her fury and indignation but she was deliberately silencing the internal debate. She just wanted to get through the day.

Part of Sofia was tempted to run. She wasn't enjoying being part of this mass of righteous, commendable women parading themselves on the streets for what they believed, not when she was here for a purpose so at odds with theirs. She didn't want to kill Beatrice but if she failed then Vinsant wouldn't take her back and she'd soon find herself on another bridge, staring into the abyss, devoid of purpose, life draining away. If she couldn't kill, couldn't feel the extraordinary sense of release, then she would die and Sofia didn't want to die. She very much did not want to die. She had given up everything for this chance to prove herself to Vinsant and she wasn't going to fall short, not after all the pain and sacrifice and grief.

The procession headed along Pall Mall East towards Trafalgar Square. Sofia could hear one band ahead of her and another behind, the music discordant, cacophonous amidst the shouting and clapping from the crowd. This was the moment. The street narrowed as they rounded a corner and people were pushing into one another's backs, jostling to stay upright on the slippery ground. Sofia drew her knife, shielding it with her palm and shoved forward. She made it through two rows, got stuck, then went on again. Beatrice's hat was still in view, only a few bodies ahead. She gritted her teeth and forced onwards again, standing on tiptoes to peer over the shoulder of a man in front. That was when Beatrice turned. She looked at Sofia, face on, eye-to-eye and she smiled. It wasn't a greeting and there was no surprise in her expression. It was resigned, understanding and it sent a shudder through Sofia that put her off guard. She lost her footing in the rain-loosened gravel and fell.

In seconds she was back up, jumping to locate Beatrice again, already doubting her impression of that smile, or at least doubting that it was meant for her. She scrambled to the pavement to escape the constant onward movement, balancing one knee on a low window ledge and hoisting herself up. Behind her was the end of the procession, the last few women on foot followed by a stream of horse-drawn carriages and a handful of motorcars. At the front, Trafalgar Square was just visible but Beatrice couldn't have got that far. Then Sofia saw her, hat visible thanks to her height, breaking off from the main procession and leaving up a side road heading north. Sofia barged her way up the road to see where Beatrice was going. She was with a small group of friends and Sofia had no idea why they weren't heading for Exeter Hall as planned. Sofia followed as the group wandered through side roads until they could only be heading for Doughty Street, and she fought a rising tide of panic and anger. If she didn't finish this now Vinsant would lose faith and withdraw his offer to take her back. Beatrice's friends said their farewells at her house, waving as they left.

For a moment it seemed odd that there wasn't a member of staff available to open the front door but as Beatrice let herself in, Sofia realised she would have given them the afternoon off to watch the march. If she didn't finish this today, she would lose her nerve forever. With the front door firmly shut, Sofia ran up the alley to the kitchen door. She had no plan and no excuse ready if she should meet Mrs Hasselbrook. Never had she felt so unprepared for a kill. It was terrifying, thrilling and compulsive all at once. At the back door something felt wrong. There was no noise from inside the house and the kitchen door was ajar, although what she could see of the room beyond was empty. She considered going home but there was no one to go home to, so Sofia stepped inside.

Chapter Twenty-nine

Sofia went through the house on tiptoe, checking each room, knife concealed between palm and sleeve. There was no one on the lower floor and she eyed the staircase with distrust. It would creak, announcing her presence, but she could remove her shoes to minimise the noise. Step by step she went, at the very edge where the boards were likely to be most stable. Half way up it occurred to her that perhaps she wasn't the sole assassin Vinsant had set upon his wife. Was that why the back door was open or had Beatrice seen her from the window and fled into the back garden, calling the police as Sofia trapped herself on the upper floors? It was too late to go back, she was in the middle of a scene which had to be played out. She took a deep breath outside Beatrice's bedroom and entered, looking behind the door first then around the room. It was empty.

Footsteps at her rear made her jump. She shot round, holding out the knife instinctively, ready to stab, but saw the pistol pointed towards her chest in time to stop. There stood the unlikely figure of Beatrice, armed and unafraid. Her hand was not shaking like Sofia's and there was nothing about her but attentive calm. Sofia wished she'd had the foresight to bring a gun as well, but then she hadn't envisaged approaching Beatrice anywhere other than in the crowd. Still, she had something that Beatrice didn't, a proven ability to kill and a desire to match it. Pointing a gun was not the same thing as pulling the trigger. Sofia bided her time.

'Sit down, Sofia,' Beatrice said motioning towards a red velvet armchair. It felt ridiculous to be sinking into such luxurious furniture with a knife in her hand. 'Please lower your weapon. I promise not to use mine if you don't use yours.' Beatrice gave a smile Sofia couldn't return. This had spiralled out of control and surely the police were on their way.

'You were expecting me,' Sofia said.

'Yes, I was warned but I'm glad you followed me here, Sofia. This has to end now.' Beatrice sat down at the far side of the room, her gun lowered but resting on her lap and aimed in Sofia's direction. 'You were sent to kill me.'

Denial seemed pointless and Sofia was too tired for games so she simply nodded.

'By my husband, if I'm not mistaken?' She was remarkably at ease with it, Sofia thought, for a woman who had discovered that her partner wanted her dead.

'Yes,' Sofia replied. 'Have you called the police?'

'Not yet,' Beatrice said and faint hope reappeared. 'But the staff won't be long. They need to return in time to prepare dinner and Mrs Hasselbrook is never late with a meal. We have a few minutes, though, and I wanted a chance to talk.'

'How did you find out?' blurted Sofia. 'How did you know it would be today?'

'Captain Thorne told me he'd seen you at the House of Commons before my time away, at least that's how I've taken to thinking of it. There was no reason for you to be there other than to follow me and I've known for a long time how much Emmett would like me disposed of. It didn't take much to figure out what was happening. I haven't called the police yet Sofia because I hate to think of anyone, even someone who could kill me for money, inside the living hell that is Holloway Prison. The two weeks I spent there was experience enough to last a lifetime so I can only imagine the horror of a life sentence.'

Kindness was the chink in Beatrice's armour. If she was to stand a chance of leaving Doughty Street any other way than inside a Black Maria, then pleading was her best bet.

'Please let me go. If you call the police who'll look after my children?'

'Your sister-in-law Mary, presumably,' Beatrice replied sharply. 'Don't let's do this. I know more than you realise and I am not a fool.'

Sofia's face burned red. She'd come here to commit murder and felt like a schoolgirl embarrassed by lies. Her anger surfaced.

'And I am not a servant.'

'I know that,' Beatrice said.

'No, you don't,' shouted Sofia. 'You have no idea who I am or what I can do.'

Beatrice sat forward, gun up, face deadly serious. 'You are a killer. You have killed men on my husband's orders, at least one of whom I saw speak in a church hall in Kensington.' Sofia's face gave away more than she intended. 'Yes, John told me he saw you there too. I know who you are, Sofia and how you reached this point.'

'You know nothing,' Sofia muttered but she had backed into the chair.

'I know that my husband tricked you, that he put you in his debt. I know that you fought him once, bravely, and tried to stop. The inclination you have for taking lives has brought you to your knees and I can't stand to think what you've suffered along the way.'

'Captain Thorne was working for you all along,' murmured Sofia. 'So why didn't he stop me killing those men?'

'That wasn't his task,' Beatrice replied thoughtfully. 'If he had intervened, he'd have lost my husband's trust. Captain Thorne applied for this position at my father's suggestion. He saw how unhappy I was and the man Emmett was becoming as word of his ruthlessness and ambition spread. When I began to support the suffrage cause, Emmett distanced himself from me completely but he wouldn't divorce me. After all, he married me for social standing and didn't want to ruin it with a scandal. My father decided to position someone here to protect me and I knew the idea of having a distinguished soldier at Emmett's side would play to his vanity. John had only to prove himself, some rough-housing, blackmailing, nothing compared to what you've done, and my husband was convinced he owned him.' Noise on the street made Sofia jump and Beatrice checked the view from the window. 'Just next door's chimney sweep,' she said. 'We have a little time yet.'

'I understand why your father would want to protect you but not why Captain Thorne would go to such lengths.'

'We grew up together,' Beatrice said. 'My parents were land owners with a large estate who understood the value of me mixing with all the local children, not just those from the higher classes. John and I played together every day for ten years until I was sent to boarding school at fourteen. It's one of the reasons I fight so hard for equality now, not just for women but for everyone.'

'So why marry someone like Mr Vinsant at all?' Sofia demanded, curious in spite of her perilous situation, still waiting for Beatrice to drop her guard.

'He seemed charming and I was regarded as a spinster, well above the age at which I should have married. My parents hoped for me to bear children, join London society, do all the things I'd never done and Emmett covered his ambition better then. Once we were married he was able to drop the pretence.' She was lost in the memory and her fingers slipped from the pistol's trigger. Sofia was up in an instant, leaping across the room with the knife outstretched, thrusting the blade towards Beatrice's throat before the older woman could move. She threw the gun away leaving Beatrice unarmed and exposed.

'If you know so much about me then you know why I have to do this,' she said. 'It's not about you. I need your husband, however corrupt he might be.'

'You don't need him,' Beatrice said, making no effort to avoid the knife. 'That's why I brought you here. I can offer you a better life and give you a purpose.'

'I've tried living a normal life,' cried Sofia. 'I've looked for work and been a mother but it's too late to go back. You don't know what it's like to lie in bed at night dreaming of blood and destruction and wanting nothing more than to crush the life from someone. I'm a monster. He made me a monster and I can't stop. If I don't kill the people he wants me to then God only knows what I'll do, look for victims on the streets, take my chance wherever I find it. I'm a murderer and I'm past pretending that I can be anything else. I don't know how to live without the release it gives me. You can't change me or help me and I'm sorry, I'm truly sorry, but your death was the price he demanded and he won't be satisfied with anything less.'

Sofia felt her face wet with tears but couldn't remember starting to cry. She willed herself to stick the blade into Beatrice's throat but her arm wouldn't comply. Meanwhile Beatrice had reached up a hand, not to the blade, but to Sofia's face, cupping her cheek as Sofia would have done with Sadie.

'I understand that this is what you are now but it is not all that you are. I know how much you want your children back and my lawyers can deal with the Flathers. John told me how you cared for Lefevre in his last weeks. There is still good in you, Sofia, even if you can no longer see it. Let me help you.'

'I don't want you to talk any more,' Sofia choked, steeling herself to end the conversation. 'Nothing you say can change what I have to do.'

'My work with the suffragettes concerns other things than the right to vote. That's why we broke away from the suffragist movement and the reason you didn't see our banners flying at the march today. We're known as the militant arm of suffrage but people see only the protests and arrests. There's much more to what we do than that. We help women and girls, much like yourself, who have no family to care for them when they arrive in London. We also run shelters, secret places where we can provide care for women and children who have been beaten and raped by husbands, fathers or brothers and who have nowhere else to go. The police won't listen because the law says that a man cannot rape his wife so we intervene where society will not. The vast majority of women have no money to rehouse or feed themselves and without us they would end up on the streets. We can use you, Sofia. There are vile men out there who believe they can visit whatever despicable acts they choose upon their wives and remain unaccountable. We're fighting for change and in need of soldiers.'

'I still don't understand what it is you think I can do,' Sofia said, captivated by the hope shining in Beatrice's eyes.

'These women need to feel protected. The men they leave are angry and the humiliation they experience when their wife disappears is a dangerous drug. You can make sure no one comes near our charges and perhaps even teach them to defend themselves. You have a better understanding than many of our volunteers what these women have been through and it seems to me that your advice and experience would be invaluable. We can pay you. Wealthy benefactors donate enough money to make our shelters comfortable, if not exactly luxurious. Work with me, Sofia, not for me but alongside me. I believe you can control whatever violent urges you have, not easily perhaps and not without hardship but you were made a killer, not born one. Let me help you. You have to believe you have a choice.'

'No, she doesn't,' a deep voice said from the doorway. 'Stand up.'

'Emmett, listen,' Beatrice said and Sofia saw fear in her eyes that hadn't been there even when she'd pressed the knife into her throat. He cut off whatever his wife had been about to say by grabbing her blouse and hoisting her to her feet. Sofia jerked the knife away before Beatrice could be impaled.

'Shut your mouth. There's been enough talk here,' he growled.

'Mr Vinsant,' Sofia began. 'I'm sorry, I was just about to...'

'Do it,' he said. 'I'll hold her and you do it. I gave you an order and you failed me. Now just finish this and get out before the staff get back.'

That was when Beatrice began to scream. With no hesitation at all, Vinsant swung one massive arm and back-handed her across the face so hard that she flew through the air to the fireplace, cracking her head against the hearth and landing in a twisted heap, silent and unmoving.

'Now,' he said. 'I've done most of the work for you. So finish her, as we agreed.' Sofia took a tentative step towards her motionless body, then paused.

'What will you say to the police? How do I know I'll be safe?'

Vinsant sighed. 'I'll say I came back and found her dead. I won't give them your name, you're more valuable to me where I can use you than rotting in a cell or hanging from a rope. Now do it. At least this way I can watch her die.' He pushed Sofia across the room and she knelt down with the knife.

Her hand trembled. She imagined the blood flowing from Beatrice's neck onto the polished wooden floor, how far it would spread with nowhere to sink in. She thought of how she would regain consciousness for a few seconds with the pain, panicking, looking for help and finding none. She got back on her feet.

'I can't kill her,' she said. 'If you want her dead, do it yourself.'

'You'll do what I tell you or I'll gut you both.'

'I don't think you'll murder your wife,' said Sofia. 'It takes a strength you don't have.'

In the pause that followed she almost believed he would walk away, go back down the stairs and out of the house, leaving her to tend his wife. Then he bared his teeth, muscles straining through his jacket, feral. Sofia raised the knife as he came for her. He knocked it from her hand as if it were a twig and raised his arms to grab her throat. She used what advantage she had and ducked, as quick as he was strong, and ran across the landing into his study where she locked the door before he could barge his way in behind her. She was defenceless. The telephone was in the downstairs hallway and what could she possibly say to the police anyway? She had far more to lose by their presence than Vinsant.

He hammered on the door as she shoved a chair under the handle. It wouldn't keep him out for long and she couldn't move any of the other pieces of furniture. She was trying to drag his desk across to buy herself enough time before the staff arrived when the door flew open. She turned round, backed up against the desk, as he approached.

'You made it easy for me,' he said. 'It's a bit disappointing really, I'd expected better of you. All I have to do now is say I came in to find my wife on the floor with you standing over her body so I acted to defend her. Two dead women, me left to my own devices. I should really be thanking you rather than punishing you, Sofia, and I'm very grateful to Tom. He did me a real service sending you to beg money for that doctor.' He put one huge hand around her throat, tight enough to make breathing difficult but not enough for her to lose consciousness yet.

Sofia drew what breath she could. 'Don't speak my husband's name. He was worth more than you'll ever be.' The room was spinning. Vinsant had her feet off the floor.

'Your husband,' he roared, 'betrayed you with his pride. How beautiful you were, what fine children you'd produced and then, when he had nothing left to boast about, he told me how you'd killed a man when you were no more than a girl. How does that feel? Knowing that you lost everything because your husband was too boastful to keep your secrets?'

Sofia was repulsed by his proximity, by the sound of his voice and the hatred that spewed from him. She spat into his face and he reacted by lifting her higher and crushing her windpipe.

'You dare to spit at me?' he shouted. 'I am your God, you soulless devil. The only way you can function, your only chance for life was through me, you proved that when you came crawling to me to get your thief of a boy out of the workhouse!' Sofia moved her lips but no sound came out. Vinsant released her throat just enough to allow air through to her vocal cords, grinning as if it was all the most wonderful joke. 'Something you wanted to say?' he smirked. Sofia nodded.

'I can kill for one other reason,' she whispered, reaching her free hand behind her and running it across the surface of his desk, searching for something, anything.

'And what would that be?' Vinsant asked, his hand tightening again, so that breathing in was no longer an option.

With feet lifted clean off the floor Sofia was able push her knees into his thighs and create space between their bodies. She jabbed the sharp metal tool from Vinsant's desk upwards through the top of his abdomen, bursting his diaphragm like a balloon. She thrust on and up under his ribs towards his heart, ignoring the inhuman sucking, bubbling sounds that echoed through his chest.

Chapter Thirty

Childhood 1894

Saul's body was transported back to his parents and so Sofia was deprived of the chance to see him buried. The day his body was wheeled away in the undertaker's carriage she refused to rise from her bed. It was the first time she had failed in her duties at the farm and Letty Marney, by some miracle, was understanding. Mac disappeared for several hours and Bill made him work late into the night for the time he'd missed.

No one spoke of Saul's death. The Marneys weren't religious people nor were they given to soul searching, but a suicide on their property was bound to attract gossip and speculation meaning it would be harder, for a while, to attract new farm hands. Sofia could have told what she witnessed, could have named names and insisted that the police be informed but it would serve no purpose except to make malicious tongues whisper foul words about her friend. Besides, she wanted Mac left alone. Saul's few possessions were cleaned out of his room and it was emptied in readiness for the next poor idiot who was dumped there.

For the next three months she spent her half-hour lunch time trekking into the woods, retracing her steps over and over, committing to memory each boulder, every log, the way the ditches ran, what the light showed or hid at different times of the day. For the first two months she spoke not one word to Mac. Then gradually, day by day, she allowed herself the briefest of exchanges, a nod as she passed him in the yard or a thank you if he handed her a bucket. She sometimes caught him staring at her. He must always have wondered why she hadn't reported the assault to the police. Occasionally his look was tinged with fear, other times it was simple confusion then later, as the days stretched into lighter nights and constant warmth when she worked in the lightest of shirts, her body blooming into womanhood, she would catch him with the ugly spark of lust in his gaze.

Three weeks more she had to bide her time and work on Mac. Each day she was a little more friendly, subtly, exercising the caution he would have expected, but her approach was conciliatory. One morning, busy mucking out the pigs together, Mac took a fall that provided the opportunity she'd been waiting for. Sofia saw his humiliation and before it could turn to anger she threw a bucket of clean water over him, laughing good-naturedly then offering him a hand up. He splashed her with the drips that remained in the bottom of the bucket and she ran, giggling, into the farmhouse. After that, he said please when he asked her for something and thank you when she obliged, less sullen and more awkwardly pleasant with her. His eyes told a less wholesome story though. She knew he desired her and Sofia, in return, desired his attentions.

On June 21, the summer solstice, the local village held a party in the best pagan country traditions. They would drink cider or ale, the women each baked a pie, savoury or sweet, and the local folk would eat a meal together on the highest hill, watching the longest sundown of the season. Sofia had ticked off the days until that sundown with a passion bordering on obsessive. She had stayed awake each night until midnight then carved a tiny scratch in her wall, one day closer, one less to wait.

She baked the pies for the Marneys and the rest of the farm hands that year, two beef, one mutton and an apple and blackberry that she had left cooling on a windowsill until the last minute. She packed the savoury pies into a basket and locked the door behind Letty. They were the best part of a mile from the house when she feigned remembering the apple and blackberry. No one wanted to miss out on pudding so when she offered to go back for it, there was no dissent. She flashed sparkling eyes at Mac as she walked close by him in the opposite direction, giving the tiniest wink and brushing the back of her hand against his.

'Want me to walk with you?' he asked. 'I could carry the pie. It's a long way on your own.'

271

'Thank you, I'd like that,' she said.

They walked back to the farm happily enough, discussing the evening, who would be there, who would get the most drunk and which couples would disappear off together. The solstice was a time for merry-making and most indiscretions were forgiven on the hot June night.

'So, have you got your eye on anyone?' asked Sofia.

'No, not me,' said Mac. 'What about you?' They were near the farm and their pace slowed as they reached the gates. Sofia hitched one foot onto the lowest bar and neatly vaulted over the top, lifting her skirt high as she jumped and ensuring Mac caught a good glimpse of her legs, bare, smooth and golden. When she whirled round he was red with embarrassment and she leaned on the top bar of the gate before he could climb over.

'I suppose I thought that you and I...' she let her voice trail off, teasing, stepping back. Mac scaled the gate, landing with an ungraceful thud.

'What?' he asked, almost panting. 'You and I what?' He was an oaf, Sofia thought. A big lug with no manners or intelligence at all. How could such a beast have taken Saul from her?

'You know what,' she said, head coyly to one side, walking towards the house. He ran behind her.

'I thought you liked Saul,' he replied, and she hated him saying the name out loud but forced herself to look at him as she answered.

'Saul was never interested in me,' she said. 'You know that better than anyone. And it's midsummer. A girl should be with a real man for midsummer's night. You wait here while I go in and get the pie.' She went down the narrow pathway, unlocked the house and left Mac to his colourful imaginings. She had more important things to do. Sofia fastened her boots so that they wouldn't slip as she ran, then took the pie from the windowsill, smelling of honey and berries. Carefully she carried it out of the house making sure Mac was still a good distance away at the end of the path, watching her lock the door and waiting for her to join him. Instead, she put the pie down on the table outside the door and paused to let her hair loose. It fell to her shoulders, dark and long, and she met Mac's eyes as he stared. Then slowly, calmly, she took off her outer shirt to leave only her delicate white cotton camisole, flashed a look of abandon at Mac that even he couldn't fail to understand and ran. Off she sprinted around the side of the house, laughing girlishly, leaving Mac calling after her. By the time he'd followed she was in the meadow behind, running through the crops with ease as she had every day since she'd decided her plan.

'Come on,' she shouted gaily.

'Stop, wait for me,' yelled Mac but she was gone, occasionally checking his progress and ensuring she hadn't left him too far behind. If she had to go back for him, it wouldn't work.

Sofia ran into the woods, her feet so familiar with the route that she didn't even need to look down. In the shade of the trees she had to reduce her pace so that he could keep up. She kept shouting, calling him to her, shrieking excitedly as she went. It wasn't until she reached a small grassy hollow that she stopped, pretending to be out of breath, leaning with hands on knees, letting her camisole slip off one arm so that he could see the treat that awaited him.

'Going to keep me waiting all day?' she asked, her voice low and inviting. Mac had paused to recover until he saw her like that, beautiful in her semi-nakedness and youth, and then he ran. He raced through the undergrowth, a straight line from him to her through the trees, just fifty feet more and she would be his for the taking. He roared good-naturedly as he tore through the leaves and twigs in his path, his face the picture of joy and longing. He may be feeling, Sofia thought, the very best he has ever felt in his whole, pointless, destructive, stupid life. She was ecstatic. That was when he fell.

It wasn't exactly falling though. It was more being grabbed from beneath. The grinding metallic snap of the foothold trap could be heard only for a fraction of a second before the more impressive noise began. As Mac's mind finally registered the pain of his broken leg, the sound he emitted was like a fox being ripped apart by hounds, high pitched and ear-splittingly loud. Sofia had to put her hands over her ears, as much as she wanted to listen to every bit of his agony, to drink it in, to bathe in it. She went to him and at first couldn't decipher a word he said.

'Calm down,' she said. 'What is it you want?'

'Get it off me,' he yelped. 'Help me, please help me.' He was dribbling, crying and thrashing but she had no concerns that he would move. It had taken Sofia weeks to get the massive iron badger trap here, hauling it a little further each day until she'd found the right spot. It was terribly heavy, although he'd have been able to lift it if he weren't so badly injured. Its vicious jaws, now clamped inches above Mac's right knee were filled with jagged, rusty teeth that had cut into the flesh causing deep gashes and partly crushing the bone when they'd snapped together. The farmer didn't use the traps any more. They'd long since been abandoned in a heap of broken machinery and rusting parts in a corner of the hay barn, too much trouble to mend or move. It had been a painful task restoring the trap to working order, oiling its hinges, scraping fingers on its blades and trapping skin in its rusty spring. She'd paid a high price for her scheme in blood blisters. Sofia suspected that years ago the traps were left out to deter poachers as much as the wildlife and vermin that took the lambs or ruined the crops. Surely there were some forgotten in these sprawling woods, unfound for years until an unsuspecting man or boy walked in the wrong place at the wrong time. Unlucky for Mac.

'Go back to the farm,' he spluttered. 'If you don't get help, I'll die.'

'There's nobody at the farm, Mac. They're miles away on the hill at the other side of the village. By the time I get there you'll be dead already. And I'll never get that trap off you, I'm just a girl after all. I'll sit here with you though and wait. Happily.'

'No,' he said, shaking his head so hard it seemed like he'd gone quite mad. 'No, you can't wait. I'll bleed to death like a bloody pig.'

Sofia smiled. 'Yes, you will,' she replied. 'You're going to die and I'm going to watch you. I didn't see Saul die because he was too ashamed after what you did to ever let anybody see him again. And I couldn't watch what you did to him because it was so awful.'

Nothing she said was sinking in. He kept clawing at his leg and the trap, trying at first to open the jaws, then pulling at his leg as if he could get it out. It wasn't such a ridiculous notion. Sofia knew that animals sometimes gnawed off their own limbs to get free of traps. If Mac were willing to do that then maybe he deserved a second chance.

'You killed Saul and now you're getting what you deserve,' she said, making it plain enough that even he could understand. 'The more you thrash around, the faster you'll die. You've already lost a lot of blood.' That seemed to wake him up. He was silent, studying the ground beneath him, now a sticky red carpet crawling with the flies and beetles that had been attracted to the scent. 'Don't worry, I'll tell Bill and Letty how brave you were. I won't say you screamed and cried. That'll be our little secret.'

He focussed his eyes on Sofia as if seeing her for the first time. 'You bitch!' he shouted. 'Why couldn't you just leave me alone? I never hurt you.' The screams changed to sobs and then to pleading. Sofia felt nothing. 'Please,' he moaned. 'I won't tell anyone what you did. Just let me out and I'll say nothing. Let me get to the village. Please. Sofia, please.' He reached one glistening red hand towards her and she moved back. She didn't want him making marks on her clothes, the blood would never come out. Shaking her head, she sat down at the base of a tree further up the path. That was when the shouting began.

Mac called for help for perhaps twenty minutes. It was impressive, his battle to live, given how much pain he was in. It made her understand how much pain Saul had experienced, for death to seem so welcoming.

'There, Saul,' Sofia said softly into the forest as Mac bellowed for a rescuer. 'I promised I would make him pay and I have. He'll never hurt anyone ever again. You can sleep peacefully now.' She could see Saul's gentle face as it had been on their many walks through the woods, whole again, free of distortion from the rope that had strangled him. In her mind, he was finally at peace. Mac, too, was quiet now, not dead yet, but passed out with the effort of yelling and blood loss.

He woke again then passed out several times more before pleading with her in a constant stream of groans and whispers. Sofia didn't bother to respond. She wasn't cruel enough to pretend that she might help. That would demean Saul's memory when all she was doing was imposing a sentence. Saul wouldn't have wanted her to be cruel about it.

Mac took a long time to die. If the jaws had clamped higher up the leg it would have been faster but she'd underestimated his height. By the time his eyes closed forever he had called her every name under the sun and offered her the moon if she saved him. Neither moved her. Sofia thought she might have to spend time searching through his belongings at the farmhouse, but when she went through his pockets she found what she was looking for as if it had been waiting for her. One penny. Only one, sticky and grubby, but rubbed clean in her skirt it began to shine for her. She left his exsanguinated corpse where it lay and made her way back to the farmhouse. She'd have to walk to the hill, running at the last as if she'd sprinted the whole way. Once there she would tell them he'd run off into the woods as she was collecting the pie and that she'd gone after him when she'd heard his screams. She fastened her clothes, put her over-shirt back on and tied up her hair just as it had been. Two hours later chaos descended on the Marneys' farmstead and Sofia was largely unnoticed in the middle of it all. She'd told her story and no one had disbelieved her.

Letty and Bill would find a new farm hand although perhaps not as strong and compliant as Mac, certainly not as cruel, and Sofia decided it was time to leave. She could find her own way in the world, not returning to her family, she didn't want to live that life anymore either. Sofia could look after herself, find work, earn enough to live on and was beyond fear or intimidation. Packing what little was hers and concealing Mac's last penny in the stocking untouched since the night with Bergen, she disappeared before the solstice was done.

Chapter Thirty-one

February 1907

'Revenge,' Sofia told Vinsant.

She twisted the weapon as far and hard as she could to widen the wound. The faster he bled out, the better. The blood pumping from his chest was not just warm but hot like bath water, as if she'd cut through to the very essence of him. With each breath in, his pain increased until he was clinging to her, terrified and desperate. His breathing became increasingly laboured and he slid to his knees, Sofia unable to support him if even she'd been inclined to do so. He tried to get up again but his heart had ceased to drive blood around his body, his legs robbed of their strength. It was only then that Sofia noticed the weapon with which she'd stabbed him. It was his silver letter opener, the one he'd been using when she'd pleaded for a doctor to save Tom's life.

'You don't know about the other man I killed,' she whispered to him. 'No one told me to. I did it because he deserved it. Like you. This is for the beating my boy took in the workhouse after you'd had him falsely accused and then played guardian angel. You can spill a pint of blood for every blow he endured on your orders and one more,' she reached down and twisted the letter opener another ninety degrees, 'For the pain you caused Lefevre.' She bent down so that he could see her face clearly in his dying seconds. 'I may be a monster but I'm not your monster, not any more.'

Vinsant's strength finally depleted, he fell face down on the floor, the letter opener disappearing completely into his chest. Death found him fast and his last moments were unremarkable. Sofia took nothing from it: no satisfaction, no thrill, no sensation of any kind and she was pleased about that. Even in death, she didn't want to give him the satisfaction of affecting her.

Beatrice let out a horrified shriek from the doorway as she stumbled across the landing, a blue-black lump on the side of her head, nose bleeding and eyes already blackened. It was a wonder Vinsant hadn't killed her. Beatrice wasn't looking at her husband though. She held a hand up to Sofia's purple, swollen throat with tears in her eyes.

'Are you all right?' she asked. 'Do you need a doctor?'

'No,' Sofia managed although talking was hard and would be for many days. It felt as if she'd swallowed a large nut without bothering to shell it first. She stared at Beatrice. 'You do, though.'

The front door burst open and John Thorne's voice reached them before he did.

'Beatrice? Beatrice!' He stopped momentarily at the study door before rushing forward to pull her into his arms. 'My God, what happened here?'

Sofia saw the tenderness between them, the way his eyes had filled with tears at the sight of her injuries and how gently he ran his hands over her bruised face. They'd been more than just childhood friends, Sofia realised. No wonder Thorne had been willing to do anything for Vinsant if it meant staying close to his sweetheart. Looking at him now he seemed a completely different man, softer, entranced by Beatrice. The Captain's presence seemed to give the new widow the fortitude to pull herself together and she assessed the situation.

'John, please go downstairs and call the police. Say there has been an attack on a woman and a man is dead. We mustn't lose any more time.' Obviously loath to leave her side, Thorne retreated unwillingly to the hallway where he could be heard talking to the operator.

With a surprising amount of force, Beatrice ripped open Sofia's blouse and tore the strap of the camisole beneath. Then she pulled half of Sofia's hair from its pins and yanked the button from the fastening on her skirt.

'Help me,' she said, motioning to the desk where she began to throw papers to the floor. Sofia followed suit, smashing a lamp from a side-table and scattering cushions off chairs. That was when the kitchen door opened and the house filled with excited voices. It wasn't until Mrs Hasselbrook came upstairs that hysteria set in.

There followed ten minutes of wailing, fetching cold flannels for bruises, and keeping the staff out of the study. Sofia knelt at Vinsant's side as if feeling for a pulse, the hand she slipped into his pocket invisible to all but her, no one witnessing her theft from the corpse, not that Emmett Vinsant was going to miss the coin his killer secreted in her shoe. Soon enough the police arrived, four of them at first but they soon called for others to join them, including the police surgeon. Sofia and Beatrice were ushered into the bedroom while they secured the study and asked what had happened.

'I was in the suffrage procession,' Beatrice said. 'Just before we reached Trafalgar Square I felt I'd walked enough so a couple of my friends walked me home and I came in, obviously surprising my husband. I'd heard Mrs Logan's shouts from the front door so I came up to the study and saw him pushing her against his desk, trying to tear off her clothes like an animal. She was fighting but he was too strong.' She began to sob more convincingly than Sofia thought she would manage herself. 'When I ran to the bedroom to fetch my pistol he followed and threw me against the fireplace. By the time I came to, he was back in the study strangling poor Mrs Logan which is when I saw her grab the letter opener. She had no choice.'

Sofia studied the newly widowed Mrs Vinsant. She was extraordinarily self-possessed. Sofia waited to be interrogated but all that came were some delicate enquiries as to how far Vinsant's attack had gone and if she would like to be transported to a hospital. She told them that she had stopped the assault before it had gone too far and they seemed satisfied, leaving her to sip sweet tea. They allowed Thorne back in the room while the surgeon inspected Vinsant's body.

'I should have been here to protect you,' Thorne told Beatrice. 'Emmett had been nervy all morning then he asked his driver to bring him back here and sent me off on a wild goose chase. It took longer than it should've for me to realise something was wrong. Are you sure you don't need a physician?' Beatrice shook her head and allowed her lover to wrap his arms around her as she lay her head on his shoulder. Sofia surrendered the room to give them some privacy.

From the landing, Sofia saw the front door open and two detectives walked in. It shouldn't have been a shock to see Charlie there, knowing he was investigating Emmett Vinsant already, but she felt as if he would take one look at her and see through all the lies and subterfuge. Sofia was dizzy, the shock of all that she'd seen and done taking its toll. It was Charlie who ran up the stairs to catch her as she tilted forwards.

'Come on,' he said. 'You need to rest.' He sat her down in the bedroom as Beatrice retold her story. When she'd finished, Charlie asked Thorne and Beatrice if they would vacate the room a while. 'Is that the way he wanted you to repay your debts, Sofia?' he asked and she was relieved when he took her silence as a positive. 'Why didn't you tell me? I would have helped.' Charlie's voice was quiet but she could hear the underlying distress.

'I'm still in one piece, Charlie,' Sofia told him. 'You were right, I didn't understand quite how dangerous a man he was but I'm safe now and my injuries will heal. I'm glad you're here.'

'I have to go and view the body with the surgeon. Stay here until I can get a constable to take your statement then I'll call a carriage to take you home.' He walked to the door. 'Is there anything I'm missing, Sofia?' he asked. She responded with a confused look. 'It just doesn't seem like you to come to a man's house alone, knowing what he was capable of. Why put yourself in so much danger?'

Sofia thought about it for a moment. Simplicity seemed to be the only convincing option. 'I came because he told me to. He gave the orders. I know it doesn't make sense but everything had stopped making sense to me. I just did whatever he told me. Until now.'

He stared at her a few moments longer then wandered over to the table in front of the window. Without a word he bent down and picked up the knife that had landed there when Vinsant knocked it from Sofia's hand. Sofia's eyes widened as he held it up but said nothing, holding her breath. Charlie rolled it in the lower part of his jacket where he rubbed it until every smear was gone from the metal.

'Dangerous to leave a knife like this lying around,' he said. 'Tell Mrs Vinsant it's in here if anyone's missing it.' He dropped the knife into a drawer and left the room. Sofia was interviewed and escorted from the building.

Two hours later she was home. The first thing she did was throw the letters into the fire and return the photographs to their proper places, then she went to visit a friend too long neglected. The door opened straight away. Sofia opened her mouth to speak but all that came was a moan and tears. Nora, tiny, frail Nora, pulled Sofia into her arms and into her house like a mother taking in an injured child.

'Don't you say a word, my love,' she said. 'Come and sit down while I fetch some tea. We'll see about those bruises and you can get some rest.'

'I'm sorry, Nora,' was all Sofia managed. 'Forgive me.'

Nora knelt before her, putting a hot mug into her hands and a soothing cloth around the marks on her neck. 'Forgive yourself,' she replied. 'I'm nothing but glad you're alive.'

Chapter Thirty-two

June 1907

It took Sofia a month to recover from the injuries to her neck. During that time she wrote every other day to Isaac and Sadie, spent time with Nora, and had the photographs of Tom and the children framed to sit on the mantlepiece. Beatrice took some time to recover from her own injuries but sent a food hamper wishing Sofia well and inviting her to visit when she felt well enough.

Sofia had thought it might be difficult to return to Doughty Street but when she did in March, there was remarkably little emotion involved. She and Beatrice had spoken only of the suffragettes who were causing some new scandal almost weekly, disrupting Parliament and protesting outside 10 Downing Street where a friend of Beatrice's managed to barge her way in, although the Prime Minister proved elusive. It certainly seemed that the campaign was gaining ground and Beatrice was delighted that Keir Hardie had put a motion before Parliament to prevent gender from being a reason to refuse voting rights. It had been talked out, of course, an old and much abused tactic to make a motion run out of time for approval, but still progress.

Captain Thorne was rarely far from Beatrice and sometimes when they looked at one another or touched hands, it seemed to Sofia that his face lit up, scar forgotten, envisaging a new life with the woman he had loved for decades. It was a chance that Sofia had delivered. In return Beatrice had been true to her word about helping with Isaac and Sadie, and polite letters had already been sent to the Flathers from her solicitor. Sofia didn't allow herself to get her hopes up for their return. It was her, after all, who had sent them away.

A nervous but enthusiastic Mrs Logan began to work for the Women's Social and Political Union in April at a well-hidden and much in demand refuge, with regular hours and a decent wage. It suited her, being around other women who had a strong sense of self-worth and who believed in their cause. If, at the start, she felt like an interloper, she didn't by May. The days were long and bright, and the women most in need of their help had begun to find them and pass word to others.

By day, Sofia listened to the troubles of brave but broken women, offered gentle, realistic advice, treated their injuries and reported the worst and most worrying cases to Beatrice. On only one occasion had she strayed from the strict regime of passivity. An eighteen year old girl had been brought in by a local nurse who had recognised that returning her patient home would be a death sentence. The girl's fifty year old husband had beaten her so badly when she'd lost a few pennies down a street drain that she would never again walk without the aid of a stick. Sofia was late home that night, following a detour to wait outside the man's home with some lead piping and teach him how it felt to have his leg smashed to smithereens. There were many regulars at the shelter. Women who couldn't break away from the men who battered and abused them, for whom life on the streets was an even more terrifying prospect than they faced at home. Sofia found that hardest of all - patching up the same bruised bodies month after month. One of the most frequent visitors to the shelter was Tess Eliot, who came in every four weeks like clockwork, and occasionally more often if her husband found a good enough excuse. Tess was sweet, forgiving and never spoke a bad word about her husband, always blaming herself for inciting his violence with such dreadful sins as burning the porridge or allowing the children to become too loud. Sofia tried not to lecture, tried only to listen and not get involved but Tess was fading with each visit. If her body still had the strength to mend, her soul, Sofia thought, did not. She begged Tess to leave, to pack up the children and run but there was just the same resigned smile, a night's stay until her wounds were dressed and the bleeding stopped.

It was trying work, often maddening, always rewarding and that was enough, for now, anyway. Sofia was ever aware that at some point the beast slumbering within would awake and demand satisfaction but she wouldn't worry until it happened. There was enough injustice and brutality on her doorstep to provide a vent for her simmering needs.

The first day of June was a Saturday and Sofia wasn't working as Beatrice had given her the day off to prepare a lunch she'd been dreaming of for weeks. She'd toiled all the previous evening and that morning to cook every type of favourite food she could remember and by the time 12 noon came, she was a wreck of nerves and bursting with anticipation.

When she met Isaac and Sadie from the train station, she was terrified that they would either refuse to speak or not stop telling her how much they'd loved their time in Yorkshire but they did neither. The afternoon passed without a glitch. There was only a joyful reunion and a sense of completeness around the table as every morsel of food was consumed and jokes were told and retold, and the retelling became a joke in itself as was the way with children.

That evening, as Sofia was finally ready to fall into bed, she picked up the small picture that Charlie had sketched over lunch. In it, Sofia was smiling across the table at Nora who was regaling them with tales of her childhood, whilst Sadie snoozed on her mother's lap and a grinning Isaac leaned against her, his head on her shoulder. It was, she prayed, a picture that captured not just one moment in time, but that celebrated the starting point for a better future waiting to be lived. And if, every now and then, she pulled out a girl's stocking and polished nine coins until they gleamed and she felt calm descend, no harm would be done. Just so long as she could stay her desire to add to their number.

Murder Victim Identified

Daily Telegraph 12 February 1908

A man's body found floating in the Thames on 10 February has, the police say, been identified as John Eliot of Basing Road, Southwark. On Friday 7 February Mr Eliot had been acquitted of the charge of wilful murder of his wife Tess Eliot at the direction of the judge, Mr Justice Brownsedge, who had found insufficient evidence for the case to be left to the jury.

John Eliot's body was discovered late at night when a fisherman rowing past heard a disturbance and saw the corpse floating in the water. The head, he said, was all but severed from the body. An axe was located nearby and police report that they are studying the weapon for evidence. A person seen fleeing the area was described as slender, dressed in dark trousers and a jacket, their face covered by a scarf. No suspect has yet been detained. The police physician has stated that that death was caused by a single blow to the back of the neck with the axe, crushing the vertebrae and damaging the windpipe. Eliot was believed to have been on his way home from celebrating his acquittal at a local public house when the attack occurred.

The deceased was thirty-five years old, worked as a butcher and is survived by three children aged six, four and one year. Any person with knowledge that might assist the police in their investigation of this murder is asked to contact Bow Street Police Station as a matter of urgency.

About the Author

An international and Amazon #1 best-selling author, Helen Fields is a former criminal and family law barrister. Every book in the Scottish set Callanach series has claimed an Amazon #1 bestseller flag. Helen also writes as HS Chandler, and last year released legal thriller 'Degrees of Guilt'. Her previous audio book 'Perfect Crime' knocked Michelle Obama off the #1 spot. Translated into 15 languages, and also selling in the USA, Canada & Australasia, Helen's books have gained global recognition. 'These Lost & Broken Things' is her first historical thriller. She currently commutes between Hampshire, Scotland and the USA, where she lives with her husband and three children. Helen can be found on Twitter @Helen_Fields.

For a chance to download a FREE Ebook and for all the latest news, sign up to the newsletter at
HELENFIELDS.COM

Made in United States
Orlando, FL
01 February 2023

29347951R00176